Phoebe uttered one terrible scream and looked around, but there was no one in sight. The man's strong grasp held her fast, and her screams brought no help. Desperately, Phoebe caught hold of the horse's reins and pulled back with all her might, while her heart lifted in a swift prayer of help. The horse reared back and plunged wildly in the air.

With an oath of rage, Hiram pushed Phoebe from him and reached for the reins. He lashed at the horse, which brought his forefeet to the ground and caused him to start down the road at a terrific gallop. It was in that instant that Phoebe gave a wild spring and jumped from the chaise. But her dress caught, and for one instant she poised over the ditch—then the fabric gave way and she fell heavily, striking her head against the fence, and laying huddled in the muddy depths. . . .

Tyndale House books by
Grace Livingston Hill
Check with your area bookstore
for these bestsellers.

Grace Livingston Hill

PHOEBE DEANE

LIVING BOOKS®
Tyndale House Publishers, Inc.
Wheaton, Illinois

This Tyndale House book
by Grace Livingston Hill
contains the complete text
of the original hard-cover edition.
NOT ONE WORD
HAS BEEN OMITTED.

Printing History
Grosset & Dunlap edition published 1909
Tyndale House edition/1990

Living Books is a registered trademark of
Tyndale House Publishers, Inc.

Library of Congress Catalog Card Number 89-50879
ISBN 0-8423-5033-0
Copyright © 1909 by J.B. Lippincott Company
Cover illustration © 1990 by Corbert Gauthier
All rights reserved
Printed in the United States of America

95 94 93 92
6   5   4   3

I

THE night was hot and dark, for the moon rose late. The perfume of the petunia bed hung heavy in the air, and the katydids and crickets kept up a continual symphony in the orchard close to the house. Its music floated in at the open window, and called to the girl alluringly, as she sat in the darkened upper room patiently rocking Emmeline's baby to sleep in the little wooden cradle.

She had washed the supper dishes. The tea towels hung smoothly on the little line in the woodshed, the milk pans stood in a shining row ready for the early milking, and the kitchen, swept and garnished and dark, had settled into its nightly repose. The day had been long and full of hard work, but now as soon as the baby slept Phoebe would be free for a while before bedtime.

Unconsciously her foot tapped faster on the rocker in her impatience to be out, and the baby stirred and opened his round eyes at her, murmuring sleepily:

"Pee-bee, up-e-knee! Pee-bee, up-e-knee!" which being interpreted was a demand to be taken up on Phoebe's knee. But Phoebe, knowing from experience that she would be tied for the evening if she acceded to this request, toned her rocking into a sleepy motion, and the long lashes suddenly dropped again upon the fat little cheeks. At last the baby was asleep.

With careful touch Phoebe slowed the rocking until the motion was scarcely perceptible, waiting a minute in hushed attention to hear the soft regular breathing after the cradle had stopped. Then she rose noiselessly from her chair, and poised on tiptoe over the cradle to listen once more and be sure, before she stole softly from the room.

As she reached the door the baby heaved a long, deep sigh, doubtless of satisfaction with its toys in dreamland, and Phoebe paused, her heart standing still for an instant lest, after all, that naughty baby would waken and demand to be taken up. How many times had she just reached the door, on other hot summer nights, and been greeted by a loud cry which served to bring Emmeline to the foot of the stairs, with: "I declare, Phoebe Deane! I should think if you would half try you could keep that poor child from crying all night!" and Phoebe would be in for an hour or two of singing, and rocking and amusing the fretful baby.

But the baby slept on, and Phoebe stepped cautiously over the creaking boards in the floor, and down the stairs lightly, scarcely daring yet to breathe. Like a fairy she slipped past the sitting-room door, scarcely daring to glance in lest she would be seen, yet carrying with her the perfect mental picture of the room and its occupants as she glided out into the night.

Albert, her half-brother, was in the sitting-room. She could see his outline through the window: Albert, with his long, thin, kindly-careless face bent over the village paper he had brought home just before supper. Emmeline sat over by the table close to the candle, with her sharp features intent upon the hole in Johnny's stocking. She had been threading her needle as Phoebe passed the door, and the fretful lines between her eyes were intensified by the effort to get the thread into the eye of the needle.

Hiram Green was in the sitting-room also. He was the neighbor whose farm adjoined Albert Deane's on the side next the village. He was sitting opposite the hall door, his lank form in a splint-bottomed chair tilted back against the wall. His slouch hat was drawn down over his eyes and his hands were in his pockets. He often sat so with Albert in the evening. Sometimes Emmeline called Phoebe in and gave her some darning or mending, and then Phoebe had to listen to Hiram Green's dull talk, to escape which she had fallen into the habit of slipping out into the orchard after her work was done. But it was not always that she could elude the vigilance of Emmeline, who seemed to be determined that Phoebe should not have a moment to herself, day or night.

Phoebe wore a thin white frock—that was one of Emmeline's grievances, those thin white frocks that Phoebe would insist on wearing afternoons, so uneconomical and foolish; besides they would wear out some time. Emmeline felt that Phoebe should keep her mother's frocks till she married, and so save Albert having to spend so much on her setting out. Emmeline had a very poor opinion of Phoebe's dead mother; her frocks had been too fine and too daintily trimmed to belong to a sensible woman, Emmeline thought.

Phoebe flashed across the path of light that fell from the door and into the orchard like some winged creature. She loved the night with its sounds and its scents and its darkness—darkness like velvet, with depths for hiding and a glimpse of the vaulted sky set with far-away stars. Soon the summer would be gone, the branches would be bare against the stark whiteness of the snow, and all her solitude and dreaming would be over until the spring again. She cherished every moment of the summer as if it were worth rich gold. She loved to sit on the fence that separated the orchard from the meadow, and wonder what the rusty-throated crickets were saying as they chirped or moaned. She liked to listen to the argument about Katy, and wonder over and over again what it was that Katy-did and why she did it, and whether she really did it at all as the little green creatures in the branches declared, for all the world the way people were picked to pieces at the sewing bees. That was just the way they used to talk about that young Mrs. Spafford. Nobody was safe from gossip—for they said Mrs. Spafford belonged to the old Schuyler family. When she came a bride to the town, how cruel tongues were, and how babbling and irresponsible, like the katydids!

The girl seated herself in her usual place, leaning against the high crotch of the two upright rails which supported that section of fence. It was cool and delicious here, with the orchard for screening and the wide pasture meadow for scenery. The sky was powdered with stars, the fragrant breath of the pasture fanned her cheek, the tree-toads joined in the nightly concert, with a deep frog-bass keeping time. A stray night-owl with a piccolo note, the far-away bleat of a sheep, and the deep sweet moo-oo of a cow thrilled along her sensitive soul as some great orchestra might have done. Then, suddenly, there came a discordant crackle of the apple branches and Hiram Green stepped heavily out from the shadows and stood beside her.

Phoebe had never liked Hiram Green since the day she had seen him shove his wife out of his way and say to her roughly, "Aw, shut up, can't you? Women are forever talking about what they don't understand!" She had watched the faint color flicker into the white-cheeked wife's face and then flicker out whitely again as she tried to laugh his roughness off before Phoebe, but the girl had never forgotten it. She had been but a little girl, then, very shy and quiet, almost a stranger in the town, for her mother had just died and she had come to live with the half-brother who had been married so long that he was almost a stranger to her. Hiram Green had not noticed the young girl then, and had treated his wife as if no one were present. But Phoebe had remembered. She had grown to know and love the sad wife, to watch her gentle, patient ways with her boisterous boys, and her blowsy little girl who looked like Hiram and had none of her mother's delicacy; and her heart used to fill with indignation over the rude ways of the coarse man with his wife.

Hiram Green's wife had been dead a year. Phoebe had been with her for a week before she died, and watched the stolid husband with never a shadow of anxiety in his eyes while he told the neighbors that "Annie would be all right in a few days. It was her own fault, anyway, that she got down sick. She *would* drive over to see her mother when she wasn't able." He neglected to state that she had been making preserves and jelly for his special benefit, and had prepared dinner for twelve men who were harvesting for a week. He did not state that she only went to see her mother once in six months, and it was her only holiday.

Phoebe had listened, and inwardly fumed over the blindness and hardness of his nature. When Annie died he blamed her as he had always done, and hinted that he guessed now she was sorry she hadn't listened to him and been content at home. As if any kind of heaven wouldn't be better than Hiram Green's house to his poor disappointed wife.

But Phoebe had stood beside the dying woman as her life flickered out and heard her say: "I ain't sorry to go, Phoebe, for I'm tired. I'm that tired that I'd rather rest through eternity than do anything else. I don't think Hiram'll miss me much, and the children ain't like me. They never took after me, only the baby that died. They didn't care when I went away to mother's. I don't think anybody in the world'll miss me, unless it's mother, and she has the other girls, and never saw me much anyway now. Maybe the baby that died'll want me."

And so the weary eyes had closed, and Phoebe had been glad to fold the thin, work-worn hands across her breast and feel that she was at rest. The only expression of regret that Hiram gave was, "It's going to be mighty unhandy, her dying just now. Harvesting ain't over yet, and the meadow lot ought to be cut before it rains or the hull thing'll be lost." Then Phoebe felt a fierce delight in the fact that everything had to stop for Annie. Whether Hiram would or no, for very decency's sake, the work must stop and the forms of respect must be gone through with even though his heart was not in it. The rain came, too, to do Annie honor, and before the meadow lot was cut.

The funeral over, the farm work had gone on with doubled vigor, and Phoebe overheard Hiram tell Albert that "burying Annie had been mighty expensive 'count o' that thunder-storm coming so soon, it spoiled the whole south meadow; and it was just like Annie to upset everything. If she had only been a little more careful and not gone off to her mother's on pleasure, she might have kept up a little longer till harvest was over."

Phoebe had been coming into the sitting-room with her sewing when Hiram said that—it was a fall evening, not six weeks after Annie had been laid to rest—and she looked indignantly at her brother to see if he would not give Hiram a rebuke; but he only leaned back against the wall and said, "Such things were to be expected in the natural course of life," he supposed. Phoebe turned her chair so that she would not have to look at Hiram. She despised him. She wished she knew how to show him what a despicable creature he was, but as she was only a young girl she could do nothing but turn her back. Perhaps Phoebe never realized how effective that method might be. At least she never knew that all that evening Hiram Green watched the back of her shining head, its waves of bright hair bound about with a ribbon, and conforming to the beautiful shape of her head with exquisite grace. He studied the shapely shoulders and graceful movements of the indignant girl as she patiently mended Johnny's stockings, let down the hem of Alma's linsey-woolsey, and set a patch on the seat of Bertie's trousers, with her slender capable fingers. He remembered that Annie had been "pretty" when he married her, and it gratified him to feel that he had given her this tribute in his thoughts. He felt himself to be a truly sorrowful widower. At the same time he could see the good points in the girl Phoebe, even though she sat with her indignant shoulders toward him. In fact, the very sauciness of those shoulders, as the winter went by, attracted him more and more. Annie had never dared be saucy nor indifferent. Annie had loved him from the first and had unfortunately let him know it too soon and too often. It was a new experience to have some one indifferent to him. He rather liked it, knowing as he did that he had always had his own way when he got ready for it.

As the winter went by Hiram had more and more spent his evenings with the Deanes and Phoebe had more and more spent her evenings with Johnny, or the cradle, or in her own room—anything as an excuse to get away from the constant unwelcome companionship. Then Emmeline had objected to the extravagance of an extra candle; and moreover, Phoebe's room was cold. It was not that there was not plenty of wood stored in the Deane wood-house, or that there was need for rigid economy, but Emmeline was "thrifty," and could see no sense in a girl wasting a candle when one light would do for all, so the days went by for Phoebe full of hard work, and constant companionship, and the evenings also with no leisure, and no seclusion. Phoebe had longed and longed for the spring to come, when she might get out into the night alone, and take long deep breaths that were all her own, for it seemed as if even her breathing were ordered and supervised.

But through it all, strange to say, it had never once entered Phoebe's head that Hiram was turning his thoughts toward her, and so, when he came and stood there beside her in the darkness he startled her merely because he was something she disliked, and she shrank from him as one would shrink from a snake in the grass.

Then Hiram came closer to her and her heart gave one warning thud of alarm as she shrank away from him.

"Phoebe," he said, boldly, putting out his hand to where he supposed her hands would be in the darkness—though he did not find hers, "ain't it about time you and I was comin' to an understandin'?"

Phoebe slid off the fence and backed away in the darkness. She knew the location of every apple-tree and could have led him a chase through their labyrinths if she had chosen. Her heart froze within her for fear of what might be coming, and she felt she must not run away, but stay and face it whatever it was.

"What do you mean?" asked Phoebe, her voice full of antagonism.

"Mean?" said Hiram, sidling after her. "I mean it's time we set up a partnership. I've waited long enough. I need somebody to look after the children. You suit me pretty well, and I guess you'd be well enough fixed with me."

Hiram's air of assurance made Phoebe's heart chill with fear. For a moment she was speechless with horror and indignation.

Taking her silence as a favorable indication Hiram drew near her and once more tried to find her hands in the darkness.

"I've always liked you, Phoebe," he said, insinuatingly. "Don't you like me?"

"No, No, No!" almost screamed Phoebe, snatching her hands away. "Don't ever dare to think of such a thing again!"

Then she turned and vanished in the dark like a wraith of mist, leaving the crestfallen Hiram alone, feeling very foolish, and not a little astonished. He had not expected his suit to be met quite in this way.

"Phoebe, is that you?" called Emmeline's metallic voice, as she lifted her sharp eyes to peer into the darkness of the entry. "Albert, I wonder if Hiram went the wrong way and missed her?"

But Phoebe, keen of instinct, light of foot, drifted like a breath past the door, and was up in her room before

Emmeline decided whether she had heard anything or not, and Albert went on reading his paper.

Phoebe sat alone in her little kitchen chamber, with the button on the door fastened, and faced the situation, looking out into the night. She kept very still that Emmeline might not know she was there. She almost held her breath for a time, for it seemed as if Hiram had so much assurance that he almost had the power to draw her from her room against her will. Her indignation and fear were beyond all possible need of the occasion. Yet every time she thought of the hateful sound of his voice as he made his cold-blooded proposition, the fierce anger boiled within her, so that she wished over and over again that she might have another opportunity to answer him and make her refusal more emphatic. Yet, when she thought of it, what could she say more than "No"? Great waves of hate surged through her soul for the man who had treated one woman so that she was glad to die, and now wanted to take her life and crush it out. With the intensity of a very young girl she took up the cause of the dead Annie, and felt like fighting for her memory.

By and by she heard Albert and Emmeline shutting up the house for the night. Hiram did not come back as she feared he might.

He half started to come, then thought better of it, and felt his way through the orchard to the other fence and climbed lumberingly over it into the road. His self-love had been wounded and he did not care to appear before his neighbors to-night. Moreover, he felt a little dazed and wanted to think things over and adjust himself to Phoebe's point of view. He felt a half resentment toward the Deanes for Phoebe's action, as if the rebuff she had given him had been their fault somehow. They should have prepared her better. They understood the situation fully. There had often been an interchange of remarks between them on the subject and Albert had responded by a nod and wink. It was tacitly understood that it would be a good thing to have the farms join, and

13

keep them "all in the family." Emmeline, too, had often given some practical hints about Phoebe's capabilities as a housewife and mother to his wild little children. It was Emmeline who had given the hint to-night as to Phoebe's hiding-place. He began to feel as if Emmeline had somehow tricked him. He resolved to stay away from the Deanes for a long time—perhaps a week, or at any rate two or three days—certainly one day, at least. Then he began to wonder if perhaps after all Phoebe was not just flirting with him. Surely she could not refuse him in earnest. His farm was as pretty as any in the county, and every one knew he had money in the bank. Surely, Phoebe was only being coy for a time. After all, perhaps, it was natural for a girl to be a little shy. It was a way they had, and if it pleased them to hold off a little, why it showed they would be all the more sensible afterward. Now Annie had always been a great one for sweet speeches. "Soft-soap" he had designated it after their marriage. Perhaps he ought to have made a little more palaver about it to Phoebe, and not have frightened her. But pooh! It was a good sign. A bad beginning made a good ending generally. Maybe it was a good thing that Phoebe wasn't just ready to fall into his arms, the minute he asked her, then she wouldn't be always bothering around, clinging to him and sobbing in that maddening way that Annie had.

By the time he had reached home he had reasoned himself into complaisance again, and was pretty well satisfied with himself. As he closed the kitchen door he reflected that perhaps he might fix things up a bit about the house in view of a new mistress. That would probably please Phoebe, and he certainly did need a wife. Then Hiram went to bed and slept soundly.

Emmeline came to Phoebe's door before she went to bed, calling softly, "Phoebe, are you in there?" and tapping on the door two or three times. When no answer came from the breathless girl in the dark behind the buttoned door, Emmeline lifted the latch and tried to open the door, but when she found it resisted her, she turned away and said to Albert in a fretful tone:

"I s'pose she's sound asleep, but I don't see what call she has to fasten her door every night. It looks so unsociable, as if she was afraid we weren't to be trusted. I wonder you don't speak to her about it."

But Albert only yawned good-naturedly, and said: "I don't see how it hurts you any."

"It hurts my self-respect," said Emmeline in an injured tone, as she shut her own door with a click.

Far into the night sat Phoebe, looking out of the window on the world which she loved, but could not enjoy any more. The storm of rage and shame and hatred passed, and left her weak and miserable and lonely. At last she put her head down on the window-sill and cried out softly: "Oh, mother, mother, mother! If you were only here to-night! You would take me away where I would never see his hateful face again."

The symphony of the night wailed on about her, as if echoing her cry in sobbing, throbbing chords, growing fainter as the moon arose, with now and then a hint of a theme of comfort, until there came a sudden hush. Then softly, tenderly, the music changed into the night's lullaby. All the world slept, and Phoebe slept, too.

2

PHOEBE was late coming down stairs the next morning.
Emmeline was already in the kitchen rattling the pots and pans
significantly. Emmeline always did that when Phoebe was late,
as her room was directly over the kitchen, and the degree of
her displeasure could be plainly heard.

She looked up sharply as Phoebe entered, and eyed the girl
keenly. There were dark circles under Phoebe's eyes, but otherwise her spirits had arisen with the morning light, and she almost
wondered at the fear that had possessed her the night before.
She felt only scorn now for Hiram Green, and was ready to protect herself. She went straight at her work without a word.
Emmeline had long ago expressed herself with regard to the
"Good-morning" with which the child Phoebe used to greet her
when she came down in the morning. Emmeline said it was "a
foolish waste of time, and only stuck-up folks used it. It was all
of a piece with dressing up at home with no one to see you, and
curling your hair"—this with a meaning look at Phoebe's bright
waves. Emmeline's light, fady hair was straight as a die.

They worked in silence. The bacon was spluttering to the
eggs, and Phoebe was taking up the mush when Emmeline
asked:

"Didn't Hiram find you last night?" She cast one of her sideways searching looks at the girl as if she would look her through and through.

Phoebe started and dropped the spoon back into the mush where it sank with a sigh and a mutter. There was something enlightening in Emmeline's tone. Phoebe saw it at once. The family had been aware of Hiram's intention! Her eyes flashed one spark of anger, then she turned abruptly back to the kettle and went on with her work.

"Yes," she answered, inscrutably. Emmeline was always irritated at the difficulty with which she found out anything from Phoebe.

"Well, I didn't hear you come in," she complained, "you must have been out a long time."

Wary Emmeline. She had touched the spring that opened the secret.

"I wasn't out five minutes in all."

"You don't say!" said Emmeline, in surprise. "Why, I thought you said Hiram found you."

Phoebe put the cover on the dish of mush and set it on the table before she deigned any reply. Then she came over and stood beside Emmeline calmly and spoke in a cool, clear voice:

"Emmeline, did Hiram Green tell you what he was coming out to the orchard for last night?"

"For mercy's sake, Phoebe, don't put on heroics! I'm not blind, I hope. One couldn't very well help seeing what Hiram Green wants. Did you think you were the only member of the family with eyes?"

When Emmeline looked up from cutting the bread at the conclusion of these remarks she was startled to see Phoebe's face. It was white as marble even to the lips, and her great beautiful eyes shone like two luminous stars.

"Emmeline, did you and Albert know what Hiram Green wanted of me, and did you let him come out there to find me after you knew that?"

Her voice was very calm and low. It reminded one of some coolly flowing river, with unknown depths in its shadowed bosom. Emmeline was awed by it for a moment. She laid down the bread-knife and stood and stared. Phoebe was small and dainty, with features cut like a cameo, and a singularly sweet, childlike expression when her face was in repose. That she was rarely beautiful her family had never noticed, though sometimes Albert liked to watch her as she sat sewing. She seemed to him a pleasant thing to have around, like a bright posy-bed. Emmeline thought her too frail-looking and pale. But for the moment the delicate girl was transformed. Her face shone with a light of righteous anger, and her eyes blazed dark with feeling. Two spots of lovely rose-color glowed upon her cheeks. The morning sun had just reached the south window by the table where Emmeline had been cutting bread, and it laid its golden fingers over the bright waves of brown hair in a halo round her head, as if the sun would sanction her righteous wrath. She looked like some beautiful, injured saint, and before the intensity of the maiden's emotion her sister-in-law fairly quailed.

"Fer the land! Phoebe! Now don't!" said Emmeline, in a tone conciliatory. "What if I did know? Was that any sin? You must remember your brother and I are looking to your best interests, and Hiram is considered a real fine ketch."

Slowly Phoebe's righteous wrath sank again into her heart. The fire went out of her eyes, and in its place came ice that seemed to pierce Emmeline till she felt like shrinking away.

"You're the queerest girl I ever saw," said Emmeline, fretfully restive under Phoebe's gaze. "What's the matter with you? Didn't you ever expect to have any beaux?"

Phoebe shivered as if a north blast had struck her at that last word.

"Did you mean, then," she said, coldly, in a voice that sounded as if it came from very far away, "that you thought that I would ever be willing to marry Hiram Green? Did you and Albert talk it over and think that?"

Emmeline found it hard to answer the question, put in a tone which seemed to imply a great offence. Phoebe lived on a plane far too high for Emmeline to even try to understand without a great effort. The effort wearied her.

"Well, I should like to know why you shouldn't marry him!" declared Emmeline, impatiently. "There's plenty of girls would be glad to get him." Emmeline glanced hurriedly out of the window and saw Albert and the hired man coming to breakfast. It was time the children were down. Alma came lagging into the kitchen, asking to have her frock buttoned, and Johnny and Bertie were heard scuffling in the rooms overhead. There was no time for further conversation. Emmeline was about to dismiss the subject, but Phoebe stepped between her and the little girl and laid her small supple hands on Emmeline's stout rounding shoulders, looking her square in the eyes.

"Emmeline, how can you possibly be so unkind as to think such a thing for me when you know how Annie suffered?"

"Oh, fiddlesticks!" said Emmeline, shoving the girl away roughly. "Annie was a milk-and-water baby who wanted to be coddled. The right woman could wind Hiram Green around her little finger. You're a little fool if you think about that. Annie's dead and gone and you've no need to trouble with her. Come, put the things on the table while I button Alma. I'm sure there never was as silly a girl as you are in this world. Anybody'd think you was a princess in disguise instead of a poor orphan dependent on her brother, and he only a *half* at that!"

With which parting shot Emmeline slammed the kitchen door and called to the two little boys in a loud, harsh tone.

The crimson rose in Phoebe's cheeks till it covered her face and neck in a sweet, shamed tide and threatened to bring the tears into her eyes. Her very soul seemed wrenched from its moorings at the cruel reminder of her dependence upon the bounty of this coarse woman and her husband. Phoebe felt as if she must leave the house at once never to return, only there was no place—no place in this wide world for her to go.

Then Albert appeared in the kitchen door with the hired man behind him, and the sense of her duty made her turn to work, that old, blessed refuge for those who are turned out of their bits of Edens for a time. She hurried to take up the breakfast, while the two men washed their faces at the pump and dried them on the long roller-towel that hung from the inside of the door.

"Hello, Phoebe," called Albert, as he turned to surrender his place at the comb and the looking-glass. "I say, Phoebe, you're looking like a rose this morning. What makes your cheeks so red? Anybody been kissing you this early?"

This pleasantry was intended as a joke. Albert had never said anything of the sort to her before. She felt instinctively that Emmeline had been putting ideas about her and Hiram into his head. It almost brought the tears to have Albert speak in this way. He was so uniformly kind to her and treated her as if she were still almost a child. She hated jokes of this sort, and it was all the worse because of the presence of Alma and the hired man. Alma grinned knowingly, and went over where she could look into Phoebe's face. Henry Williams, with the freedom born of his own social equality—he being the son of a neighboring farmer who had hired himself out for the season as there were more brothers at home than were needed—turned and stared admiringly at Phoebe.

"Say, Phoebe," put in Henry, "you do look real pretty this morning, now if I do say it. I never noticed before how handsome your eyes were. What's that you said about kissing, Albert? I wouldn't mind taking the job, if it's going. How about it, Phoebe?"

Pleasantry of this sort was common in the neighborhood, but Phoebe had never joined in it, and she had always looked upon it as unrefined, and a form of amusement that her mother would not have liked. Now when it was directed toward her, and she realized that it trifled with the most sacred and personal relations of her life, it filled her with horror.

"Please don't, Albert!" she said, with trembling lips in a low voice. "Don't! I don't like it." And Alma saw with wonder, and gloated over the fact, that there were tears in Aunt Phoebe's eyes. That would be something to remember and tell. Aunt Phoebe usually kept her emotions to herself with the door shut too tight for Alma to peep in.

"No?" said Albert, perplexed. "Well, of course I won't if you don't like it. I was only telling you how bright and pretty you looked and making you know how nice it was to have you around. Sit down, child, and let's have breakfast. Where's your mother, Alma?"

Emmeline entered with a flushed face, and a couple of cowed and dejected small boys held firmly by the shoulders.

Somewhat comforted by Albert's assurance, Phoebe was able to finish her work and sit down at the table; but although she busied herself industriously in putting on the baby's bib, spreading Johnny's bread, handing Alma the syrup-jug, and preventing her from emptying its entire contents over her personal breakfast, inside and out, she ate nothing herself: for every time she raised her eyes she found a battalion of other eyes staring at her.

Emmeline was looking her through, in puzzled annoyance and chagrin, taking in the fact that her well-planned match-making was not running as smoothly as had been expected. Albert was studying her in the astonishing discovery that the thin, sad little half-sister he had brought into his home, who had seemed so lifeless and colorless and unlike the bouncing pretty girls of the neighborhood, had suddenly become beautiful, and was almost a woman. Several times he opened his mouth to say this in the bosom of his family, and then the dignified poise of the lovely head, or a something in the stately set of the small shoulders, or a pleading look in the large soft eyes raised to him, held him quiet; and his own eyes tried to tell her again that he would not say it if she did not like it.

Alma was staring at her between mouthfuls of mush, and thinking how she would tell about those tears, and how perhaps she would taunt Aunt Phoebe with them sometime when she tried to "boss," when ma was out to a sewing-bee. "Ehh! I saw you cry once, Aunt Phoebe! Ehh! Right before folks. *EHH-HH!* Cry baby! You had great big tears in your eyes, when my pa teased you. I saw um. Eh-hh-hh!" How would that sound? Alma felt the roll of the taunt now, and wished it were time to try it. She knew she could make Aunt Phoebe writhe sometime, and that was what she had always wanted to do, for Aunt Phoebe was always discovering her best laid plans and revealing them to Emmeline, and Alma longed sorely for revenge.

But the worst pair of eyes of all were those of Henry Williams, bold, and intimate, who sat directly opposite her. He seemed to feel that the way had been opened to him by Albert Deane's words, and was only waiting his opportunity to enter in. He had been admiring Phoebe ever since he came there, early in the spring, and wondering that no one seemed to think her of much account, but somehow her quiet dignity had always kept him at a distance. But now he felt he was justified in making more free with her.

"Did you hear that singing-school was going to open early this fall, Phoebe?" he asked, after many clearings of his throat.

"No," said Phoebe, without looking up. That was rather disappointing to him, for it had taken him a long time to think up that subject, and it was too much to have it disposed of so quickly, without even a glimpse of her eyes.

"Do you usually 'tend?" he asked again, after a pause filled in by Alma and the little boys in a squabble for the last scrap of mush and molasses.

"No!" said Phoebe again, her eyes still down.

"Phoebe didn't go because there wasn't anyone for her to

come home with, before, Hank, but I guess there'll be plenty now," said Emmeline, with a meaningful laugh.

"Yes," said Phoebe, now looking up calmly without a flicker of the anger she was feeling. "Hester McVane and Polly said they were going this winter. If I decide to go I'm going with them. Emmeline, if you're trying to dry those apples to-day I'd better begin them. Excuse me, please."

"You haven't eaten any breakfast, Aunt Phoebe! Ma, Aunt Phoebe never touched a bite!" announced Alma, gleefully.

"I'm not hungry this morning," said Phoebe truthfully, and went in triumph from the room, having baffled the gaze of the man and the child, and wrested the dart from her sister-in-law's arrow. It was hard on the man, for he had decided to ask Phoebe if she would go to singing-school with him. He had been a long time making up his mind as to whether he wouldn't rather ask Harriet Woodgate, but now he had decided on Phoebe he did not like to be balked in the asking. He sought her out in the wood-shed where she sat, and gave his invitation, but she only made her white fingers fly the faster round the apple she was peeling as she answered: "Thank you, it won't be necessary for you to go with me if I decide to go." Then as she perceived by his prolonged "H'm-m-m!" that he was about to urge his case she arose hastily, exclaiming: "Emmeline, did you call me? I'm coming," and vanished into the kitchen. The hired man looked after her wistfully and wondered if he had not better ask Harriet Woodgate after all.

Phoebe was not a weeping girl. Ever since her mother died she had lived a life of self-repression, hiding her inmost feelings from the world, for her world since then had not proved to be a sympathetic one. When annoyances came she buried them in her heart and grieved over them in silence, for she quickly perceived that there was no one in this new atmosphere who would understand her sensitive nature.

Refinements and culture had been hers that these new relatives did not know nor understand. What to her had been necessities were to them foolish nonsense. She looked at Albert wistfully sometimes, for she felt if it were not for Emmeline she might perhaps in time make him understand and change a little in some ways. But Emmeline resented any suggestions she made to Albert, especially when he good-naturedly tried to please her. Emmeline resented almost everything about Phoebe. She had resented her coming in the first place. Albert was grown up and living away from home when his father married Phoebe's mother, a delicate, refined woman, far different from himself. Emmeline felt that Albert had no call to take the child in at all for her to bring up when she was not a "real relation." Besides, Emmeline had an older sister of her own who would have been glad to come and live with them and help with the work, but of course there was no room nor excuse for her with Phoebe there, and they could not afford to have them both, though Albert was ready to take in any stray chick or child that came along. It was only Emmeline's forbidding attitude that kept him from adopting all the lonely creatures, be they animal or human, that appealed to his sympathy. There were a great many nice points about Albert, and Phoebe recognized them gratefully, the more as she grew older, though he *would* come to the table in his shirt-sleeves and eat his pie with his knife.

But in spite of her nature this morning Phoebe had much ado to keep from crying. The annoyances increased as the day grew, and if it had not been for her work she would have felt desperate. As it was she kept steadily at it, conquering everything that came in her way. The apples fairly flew out of their coats into the pan, and Emmeline, glancing into the back shed, noting the set of the forbidding young shoulders, and the undaunted tilt of the head, also the fast diminishing pile of apples on the floor and the multiplying quarters in the pans, forbore to disturb her. Emmeline was far-seeing, and she was anxious to have those apples off her mind. With Phoebe in that mood she knew it would be done before she could possibly get around to help. There was time enough for remarks later; meantime perhaps it was just as well to let my lady alone until she came to her senses a little.

The old stone sun-dial by the side door shadowed the hour of eleven, and the apples were almost gone from the pile on the floor, when Emmeline came into the back shed with a knife and sat down to help. She looked at Phoebe sharply as she seated herself with a show of finishing things up in a hurry, but she intended, and Phoebe knew she did, to have it out with the girl before her.

Phoebe did not help her to begin. Her fingers flew faster than ever, though they ached with the motion, and the juicy knife against her sensitive skin made every nerve cry out to be released. With set lips she went on with her work, though she longed to fling the apple away and run out to the fields for a long, deep breath.

Emmeline had pared two whole apples before she began, in a conciliatory tone. She had eyed Phoebe furtively several times, but the girl might have been a sphinx, or some lovely mountain wrapped about with mist, for all she could read of her mood. This was what Emmeline could not stand, this distant, proud silence that would not mix with other folk. She longed to break through it by force, and reduce the pride to the dust. It would do her heart good to see Phoebe humbled for once, she often told herself.

"Phoebe, I don't see what you find to dislike so in Hiram Green," she began. "He's a good man. He always attends church on Sundays."

"I would respect him more if he was a good man in his home on week-days. Anybody can be good once a week before people. A man needs to be good at home in his family."

"Well, now, he provides well for his family. Look at his comfortable home, and his farm. There isn't a finer in this county. He has his name up all round the region for the fine stock he raises. You can't find a barn like his anywhere. It's the biggest and most expensive in this town."

"He certainly has a fine barn," said Phoebe, "but I don't suppose he expects his family to live in it. He takes better care of his stock than he does of his family. Look at the house—"

Phoebe's eyes waxed scornful, and Emmeline marvelled. She was brought up to think a barn a most important feature of one's possessions.

"His house is away back from the road out of sight," went on Phoebe. "Annie used to hunger for a sight of people going by on the road when she sat down to sew in the afternoon, but there was that great barn right out on the road, and straight in front of the house. He ought to have put the barn back of the house. And the house is a miserable affair. Low, and ugly, and with two steps between the kitchen and the shed, enough to kill one who does the work. He ought to have built Annie a pleasant home up on that lovely little knoll of maples, where she could have seen out and down the road, and have had a little company now and then. She might have been alive to-day if she had one-half the care and attention that Hiram gave the stock!" Phoebe's words were bitter and vehement.

"It sounds dreadful silly for a girl of your age to be talking like that. You don't know anything about Annie, and if I was you I wouldn't think about her. As for the barn, I should think a wife would be proud to have her husband's barn the nicest one in the country. Of course the barn had to have the best place. That's his business. I declare you do have the queerest notions!"

Nevertheless she set it down in her mind that she would give Hiram a hint about the house.

Phoebe did not reply. She was peeling the last apple, and as soon as it lay meekly in quarters with the rest she shoved back her chair and left the room. Emmeline felt that she had failed again to make any impression on her sister-in-law. It maddened her almost to distraction to have a girl like that around her, a girl who thought everything beneath her and who criticised the customs of the entire neighborhood. She was an annoyance and a reproach. Emmeline felt she would like to get rid of her if it could be done in a legitimate way.

At dinner Henry Williams looked at Phoebe meaningfully and asked if she made the pie. Phoebe had to own that she did.

"It tastes like you, nice and sweet," he declared, gallantly. Whereat Albert laughed, and Alma leaned forward to look into her aunt's flaming face, impudently.

"Betsy Green says she thinks her pa is going to get her a new ma," she remarked, knowingly, when the laugh had subsided. "And Betsy says she bet she knows who 'tis, too!"

"You shut up!" remarked Emmeline to her offspring, in a low tone, giving Alma a dig under the table. But Phoebe hastily drew back her chair and fled from the table.

There was a moment of uncomfortable silence after Phoebe left the room. Emmeline felt that things had gone too far. Albert asked what was the matter with Phoebe, but instead of answering him Emmeline yanked Alma from the table and out into the wood-shed, where a whispered scolding was administered as a sort of obligato solo to the accompaniment of some stinging cuts from a little switch that hung conveniently on the wall.

Alma returned to the table chastened outwardly, but inwardly vowing vengeance on her aunt, her anger in no wise softened by the disappearance of her piece of pie with Bertie. Her mother told her she deserved to lose her pie, and she determined to get even with Aunt Phoebe even if another switching happened.

Phoebe did not come down stairs again that afternoon. Emmeline hesitated about sending for her, and finally decided to wait until she came. The unwilling Alma was pressed into service to dry the dishes, and the long, yellow, sunny afternoon dragged drowsily on, while Phoebe lay upon her bed up in her kitchen chamber, and pressed her aching eye balls hard with her cold fingers, wondering why so many tortures were coming to her all at once.

3

HIRAM Green kept his word to himself and did not go to see Phoebe for two evenings. By that time Emmeline had begun to wonder what in the world Phoebe had said to him to keep him away when he seemed so anxious to get her; and Phoebe, with the hopefulness of youth, had decided that her trouble in that direction was over. But the third evening he arrived promptly, attired with unusual care, and asked Emmeline if he might see Phoebe alone.

It happened that Phoebe had finished her work in the kitchen and gone up to rock the baby to sleep. Emmeline swept the younger children out of the sitting-room with alacrity, and called Albert sharply to help her with something in the kitchen, sending Alma up at once with a carefully worded message to Phoebe. Emmeline was relieved to see Hiram again. She knew by his face that he meant business this time, and she hoped to see Phoebe conquered at once.

"Ma says you please"—the word sounded strangely on Alma's unloving lips—"come down to the settin'-room now—*to once,*" she added.

The baby was just dropping asleep and roused of course at Alma's boisterous tone. Phoebe nodded, and shoved the child from the room, keeping the cradle going all the time. The naughty little girl delighted to have authority behind her evil doing, and called loudly:

"Well, ma wants you RIGHT OFF, *so,* and I don't care!" as she thumped down stairs with her copper-toed shoes.

The baby gave a crow of glee and arose to the occasion in his cradle, but Phoebe resolutely disregarded the call below, and went on rocking until the little restless head was still on its pillow again. Then she stole softly down to the sitting-room, her eyes blinded by the darkness where she had been sitting, and explained quietly as she entered the room, "I couldn't come sooner. Alma woke the baby again."

Hiram, quite mollified by the gentle tone of explanation, arose, blandly answering: "Oh, that's all right. I'm glad to see you now you're here," and went forward with the evident intention of taking both her hands in his.

Phoebe rubbed her blinded eyes and looked up in horror! Knowing Alma stood behind the crack of the door and watched it all with wicked joy.

"I beg your pardon, Mr. Green, I thought Emmeline was in here. She sent for me. Excuse me, I must find her."

"Oh, that's all right!" said Hiram, easily, putting out his hand and shutting the door sharply in Alma's impudent face, thereby almost pinching her inquisitive nose in the crack. "She don't expect you, Emmeline don't. She sent for you to see me. I asked her could I see you alone. She understands all about us, Emmeline does. She won't come in here for a while. She knows I want to talk to you."

Cold chills crept down Phoebe's nerves and froze her heart and finger-tips. Had the horror returned upon her with redoubled vigor, and with her family behind it? Where was Albert? Would he not help her? Then she realized that she must help herself and at once, for it was evident that Hiram Green meant to press his suit energetically. He was coming towards her with his hateful, confident smile. He stood between her and the door of retreat. Besides, what good would it do to run away? She had tried that once and it did not work. She must speak to him decidedly and end the matter. She summoned all her dignity and courage and backed over to the other side of the room, where a single chair stood.

"Won't you sit down, Mr. Green?" she said, trying to get the tremble out of her voice.

"Why, yes, I will; let's sit right here together," he said, sitting down at one end of the couch and making room for her. "Come, you sit here beside me, Phoebe, and then we can talk better. It's more sociable."

Phoebe sat down on the chair opposite him.

"I would rather sit here, Mr. Green," she said.

"Well, of course, if you'd rather," he said, reluctantly, "but it seems to be kind of unsociable. And say, Phoebe, I wish you wouldn't 'mister' me any more. Can't you call me Hiram?"

"I would rather not."

"Say, Phoebe, that sounds real unfriendly," blamed Hiram, in a tone which suggested he would not be trifled with much longer.

"Did you wish to speak to me, Mr. Green?" said Phoebe, her clear eyes looking at him steadily over the candle-light, with the bearing of a queen.

"Well, yes," he said, straightening up, and hitching a chair around to the side nearer to her. "I thought we better talk that matter over a little that I was mentioning to you several nights ago."

"I don't think that is necessary, Mr. Green," answered Phoebe quickly; "I thought I made you understand that that was impossible."

"Oh, I didn't take account of what you said that night," said Hiram. "I saw you was sort of upset, not expecting me out there in the dark, so I thought I better come round again after you had plenty chance to think over what I said."

"I couldn't say anything different if I thought over it a thousand years," declared Phoebe, with characteristic emphasis. Hiram Green was not thin-skinned, and did not need saving. It was just as well to tell the truth and be done with it.

But the fellow was in no wise daunted. He rather admired Phoebe the more for her vehemence, for here was a prize that promised to be worth his winning. For the first time as he looked at her he felt his blood stir with a sense of pleasure such as one feels in a well matched race, where one is yet sure of winning.

"Aw, git out!" scouted Hiram, pleasantly. "That ain't the way to talk. Course you're young yet, and ain't had much experience, but you certainly had time enough to consider the matter all this year I been comin' to see you."

Phoebe arose with two red spots burning on her cheeks.

"Coming to see me!" she gasped. "You didn't come to see me!"

"Aw, git out now, Phoebe. You needn't pertend you didn't know I was comin to see you. Who did you s'pose I was comin to see, then?"

"I supposed of course you were coming to see Albert," said Phoebe, her voice settling into that deep calm that betokened she was overwhelmed.

"Albert! You s'posed I was comin' to see Albert every night! Aw, yes, you did a whole lot! Phoebe, you're a sly one. You must of thought I was gettin' fond of Albert!"

"I did not think anything about it," said Phoebe, haughtily, "and you may be sure, Mr. Green, if I had dreamed of such a thing I would have told you it was useless."

There was something in her tone and manner that ruffled the self-assurance of Hiram Green. Up to this minute he had persuaded himself that Phoebe was but acting the part of a coy and modest maiden who wished to pretend that she never dreamed that he was courting her. Now a suspicion began to glimmer in his consciousness that perhaps, after all, she was honest, and had not suspected his attentions. Could it be possible that she did not care for them, and really wished to dismiss him? Hiram could not credit such a thought. Yet as he looked at the firm set of her lips he was bewildered.

"What on earth makes you keep sayin' that?" he asked, in an irritated tone. "What's your reason for not wantin' to marry me?"

"There are so many reasons that I wouldn't know where to begin," answered the girl shortly.

Hiram gave his shoulders a little shake, as if to rouse himself. Had he heard her words aright?

"What reasons?" he growled, frowning. He began to feel that Phoebe was trifling with him. He would make her understand that he would not endure much of that.

Phoebe looked troubled. She wished he would not insist on further talk, but she was too honest and too angry not to tell the exact truth.

"The first and greatest reason of all is that I do not love you, and never could," she said, vehemently, looking him straight in the eyes.

"Shucks!" said Hiram, laughing. "I don't mind that a mite. In fact, I think it's an advantage. Folks mostly get over it when they do feel that sentimental kind of way. It don't last but a few weeks, anyway, and it's better to begin on a practical basis I think. That was the trouble with Annie, she was so blamed sentimental she hadn't time to get dinner. I think you an' I'd get along much better. You're practical and a good worker. We could make things real prosperous over to the farm—"

Phoebe arose quickly and interrupted him.

"Mr. Green, you must please stop talking this way. It is horrible! I don't want to listen to any more of it."

"You set down, Phoebe," commanded Hiram. "I've got some things to tell you. It ain't worth while fer you to act foolish. I mean business. I want to get married. It's high time there was somebody to see to things at home, but I can wait a little while if you're wantin' to get ready more, only don't be long about it. As I said, I don't mind about the love part. That'll come all right. And you remember, Phoebe, if I do say so as shouldn't, there's plenty of girls around here would be glad to marry me if they got the chance."

"Then by all means let them marry you!" said Phoebe, grandly, steadying her trembling limbs for flight. "I shall never, never marry you! Good-night, Mr. Green."

She swept him a ceremonious bit of courtesy at the door, like a flutter of wings as a bird takes affright, and was gone before he fully took it in. He reached out detaining hands towards her in protest, but it was too late. The latch clicked behind her, and he could hear the soft stir of her garments on the stairs. She had fled to her room. He heard the button on her door creak and turn. He unfolded his lank limbs from their comfortable pose around the legs of his chair, and went after her as far as the door, but the stairway was quiet and dark. He could hear Albert and Emmeline in the kitchen. He stood a moment in puzzled chagrin, going over his inter-view and trying to make it all out. What mistake had he made? He had failed, that was certain. It was a new experi-ence and one that angered him, but somehow the anger was numbed by the remembrance of the look of the girl's eyes, the dainty movements of her hands, the set of her shapely head. He did not know that he was fascinated by her beauty; he only knew that a dogged determination to have her for his own in spite of everything was settling down upon him.

Albert and Emmeline were conversing in low tones in the kitchen when the door was flung open and Hiram Green stepped in, his brow dark, his eyes sullen. He felt that Emmeline owed him some explanation of Phoebe's behavior. He had come for it.

"I can't make her out!" he muttered, as he flung himself into a kitchen chair, "she's just for all the world like a wild colt. When you think you have her she gives you the slip and is off further away than when you begun. I think mebbe ef I had her where she couldn't get away I'd be able to find out the difficulty."

"Better take her out riding," suggested Albert, slyly, "and

drive fast. She couldn't get out very well then."

"I ain't so sure," growled Hiram. "The way she looked she might jump over a precipice. What's the matter with her anyway?" turning to Emmeline, as though she were responsible for the whole of womankind. "Is there anybody else? She ain't got in with Hank Williams, has she?"

"She won't look at him," declared Emmeline, positively. "He tried to get her to go to singin'-school with her just to-day and she shut him off short. What reason did she give you?"

"She spoke about not havin' proper affection," he answered, diffidently, "but if I was dead sure that was the hull trouble I think I could fix her up. I'd like to get things settled 'fore winter comes on. I can't afford to waste time like this."

"I think I know what's the matter of her," said Emmeline, mysteriously. "She isn't such a fool as to give up a good chance in life for reasons of affection, though it is mighty high-soundin' to say so. But there's somethin' back of it all. I shouldn't wonder, Hiram, if she's tryin' you to see if you want her enough to fix things handy the way she'd like em."

"What do you mean?" asked Hiram, gruffly, showing sudden interest. "Has she spoke of anything to you?"

"Well, she did let on that your house was too far back from the street to be pleasant, and she seemed to think the barn had the best situation. She spoke about the knoll being a good place fer a house."

Hiram brightened. If Phoebe had taken interest in his affairs to say all this surely she was not so indifferent after all.

"You don't say!" said Hiram, meditatively. "When did she say that?"

"Just to-day," Emmeline answered.

"Well, if that's the hitch why didn't she say so? She didn't seem shy."

"Mebbe she was waitin' fer you to ask her what she wanted."

"Well, she didn't wait long. She lit out before I had a chance to half talk things over."

"She's young yet, you know," said Emmeline, in a sooth-ing tone. "Young folks take queer notions. I shouldn't won-der but she hates to go to that house and live way back from the road that way. She ain't much more than a child, any-way, in some things—though she's first class to work."

"Well," said Hiram, reluctantly, "I been thinkin' the house needed fixin' up some. I don't know as I should object to buildin' all new. The old house would come in handy fer the men. Bill would like to have his ma come and keep house right well. It would help me out in one way, fer Bill is gettin' uneasy, and I'd rather spare any man I've got than Bill, he works so steady and good. Say, you might mention to Phoebe, if you like, that I'm thinkin' of buildin' a new house. Say I'd thought of the knoll for a location. Think that would ease her up a little?"

"All right, I'll see what can be done," said Emmeline, im-portantly.

The atmosphere of the kitchen brightened cheerfully as if extra candles had been brought in. Hiram, with the air of having settled to his satisfaction a troublesome bit of busi-ness, lighted his pipe and tilted his chair back in his accus-tomed fashion, entering into a brisk discussion of politics while Emmeline set the sponge for bread.

Emmeline was going over the line of argument with which she intended to ply Phoebe the next day. She felt tri-umphant over her. Not every woman and match-maker would have had the grit to tell Hiram just what was wanted. Emmeline felt that she had been entrusted with a commis-sion worthy of her best efforts, and surely Phoebe would lis-ten now.

Up in her kitchen chamber the hum of their conversation came to Phoebe, as she sat with burning cheeks looking widely into the darkness. She did not hear the nightly sym-phony as it sang on all about the house. She was thinking of what she had been through, and wondering if she had finally freed herself from the hateful attentions of Hiram Green.

Would he take her answer as final, or not? She thought not, judging from his nature. He was one of those men who never give up what they have set themselves to get, be it sunny pasture lot, young heifer, or pretty wife. She shuddered at the thought of many more encounters such as she had passed through to-night. It was all dreadful to her. It touched a side of life that jarred her inexpressibly. It made the world seem an intolerable place to her.

She fell to wondering what her life would have been if her mother had lived—a quiet little home, of course, plain and sweet and cosy, with plenty of hard work, but always some one to sympathize. Her frail little mother had not been able to stand the rough world and the hard work, but she had left behind her a memory of gentleness and refinement that could never be wholly crushed out of her young daughter's heart, no matter how much she came in contact with the coarse, rude world. Often the girl in her silent meditations would take her mother into her thoughts and tell her all that had passed in her life that day. But to-night she felt that were her mother here, and helpless to help her, she could not bear to tell her of this torturing experience through which she was passing. She knew instinctively that a living mother such as hers had been would shrink with horror from the thought of seeing her child united to a man like Hiram Green—would rather see her dead than married to him.

Somehow she could not get the comfort from thinking of her mother to-night that she usually could. She wanted some close, tangible help, some one all-wise and powerful; some one that could tell what life meant, and what God meant her particular life to be, and make her sure she was right in her fierce recoil from what life now seemed to be offering. She felt sure she was right, yet she wanted another to say so also, to take her part against the world that was troubling her. There were perhaps people who could do that for her if she only dared to go to them, but what would they think!

Her young pride arose and bore her up. She must tell nobody but God. And so thinking, she knelt timidly down and tried to pour out her proud, hurt spirit in a prayer. She had always prayed, but had never felt that it meant anything to her until to-night; and when she arose, not knowing what she had asked, or if indeed she had asked anything for herself, she yet felt stronger to face her life, which somehow stretched out ahead in one blank of monotonous tortures.

Meantime the man who desired to have her, and the woman who desired to have him have her, were forming their plans for a regular campaign against her.

4

IT was the first day of October, and it was Phoebe's birthday. The sun shone clear and high, the sky overhead was a dazzling blue, and the air was good to breathe. Off in the distance a blue haze lay softly over the horizon, mingling the crimsons and golds of the autumn foliage with the fading greens. It was a perfect day, and Phoebe was out in it.

She walked rapidly and with a purpose, as though it did her good to push the road back under her impatient feet. She was not walking towards the village, but out into the open country, past the farm, where presently the road turned and skirted a maple grove. But she did not pause here, though she dearly loved the crimson maple leaves that carpeted the ground alluringly. On she went, as though her only object was to get away, as though she would like to run if there were not danger she might be seen.

A farm wagon was coming. She strained her eyes ahead to see who was driving. If it should happen to be Hank, and he should stop to talk! Oh! She put her hand on her heart and hurried forward, for she would not go back. She wished she had worn her sunbonnet, for then she might hide in its depths, but her coming away had been too sudden for that.

She had merely untied her large apron, and flung it from her as she started. Even now she knew not whether it hung upon the chair where she had been sitting shelling dried beans, or whether it adorned the rosebush by the kitchen door. She had not looked back to see, and did not care.

No one knew it was her birthday, or, if they knew, they had not remembered. Perhaps that made it harder to stay and shell beans and bear Emmeline's talk.

Matters had been going on in much the way they had gone all summer—that is, outwardly; Hiram Green had spent the evenings regularly talking with Albert, while Emmeline darned stockings, and Phoebe escaped upstairs when she could, and sewed with her back turned to the guest when she could not. Phoebe had taken diligent care that Hiram should have no more tête-à-têtes with her, even at the expense of having to spend many evenings in her dark room when all outdoors was calling her with the tender lovely sounds of the dying summer. Grimly and silently she went through the days of work.

Emmeline, since the morning she attempted to discuss Hiram's proposed new house and found Phoebe utterly unresponsive, had held her peace. Not that she was by any means vanquished, but as she made so little headway in talking to the girl she concluded that it would be well to let her alone awhile. In fact Albert had advised that line of action in his easy, kindly way, and Emmeline, partly because she did not know how else to move her sister-in-law, shut her lips and went around with an air of offended dignity. She spoke disagreeably whenever it was necessary to speak at all to Phoebe, and whenever the girl came downstairs in other than her working garments she looked her disapproval in unspeakable volumes.

Phoebe went about her daily routine without noticing, much as a bird might whose plumage was being criticised. She could not help putting herself in dainty array, even though the materials at hand might be only a hair brush and a bit of ribbon. Her hair was always waving about her lovely face, softly, and smoothly, and a tiny rim of white collar outlined the throat, even in her homespun morning gown, which sat upon her like a young queen's garment.

It was all hateful to Emmeline—"impudent," she styled it, in speaking to herself. She had tried the phrase once in a confidence to Albert—for Phoebe was only a half sister; why should Albert care?—but somehow Albert had not understood. He had almost resented it. He said he thought Phoebe always looked "real neat and pretty" and he "liked to see her 'round." This had fired Emmeline's jealousy, although she would not have owned it. Albert made so many remarks of this sort that Emmeline felt they would spoil his sister and make her unbearable to live with. Albert used to talk like that to her when they were first married, but she told him it was silly for married people to say such things, and he never gave her any more compliments. She had not missed them herself, but it was another thing to find him speaking that way about his sister—so foolish for a grown-up man to care about looks.

But Emmeline continued to meditate upon Phoebe's "impudent" attire, until this afternoon of her birthday the thoughts had culminated in words.

Phoebe had gone upstairs after the dinner work was done, and had come down arrayed in a gown that Emmeline had never seen. It was of soft buff merino, trimmed with narrow lines of brown velvet ribbon, and a bit of the same velvet around the white throat held a small plain gold locket that nestled in the white hollow of Phoebe's neck as if it loved to be there. The brown hair was dressed in its usual way except for a knot of brown velvet. It was a simple girlish costume, and Phoebe wore it with the same easy grace she wore her homespun, which made it doubly annoying to Emmeline, who felt that Phoebe had no right to act as if she was doing nothing unusual.

Years ago when the child Phoebe had come to live with

them she had brought with her some boxes and trunks, and a
few pieces of furniture for her own room. They were things
of her mother's which she wished to keep. Emmeline had
gone carefully over the collection with ruthless hand and
critical tongue, casting out what she considered useless, laying aside what she considered unfit for present use, and freely commenting upon all she saw. Phoebe, fresh from her
mother's grave, and the memory of that mother's living
words, had stood by in stony silence, holding back by main
force the angry tears that tried to get their way, and letting
none of the storm of passion that surged through her heart
be seen. But when Emmeline had reached the large hair-
covered trunk and demanded the key, Phoebe had quietly
dropped the string that held it round her neck inside her
dress, where it lay cold against her little sorrowful heart, and
answered decidedly:

"You needn't open that, Emmeline; it holds my mother's
dresses that she has put away for me when I grow up."

"Nonsense!" Emmeline had answered, sharply. "I think
I'm the best judge of whether it needs to opened or not.
Give me the key at once. I guess I'm not going to have
things in my house that I don't know anything about. I've
got to see that they are packed away from moth."

Phoebe's lips had trembled, but she continued to talk
steadily:

"It is not necessary, Emmeline. My mother packed them
all away carefully in lavender and rosemary for me. She did
not wish them opened till I got ready to open them myself. I
do not want them opened."

Emmeline had been very angry at that, and told the little
girl she would not have any such talk around her, and demanded the key at once, but Phoebe said:

"I have told you it is not necessary. These are my things
and I will not have any more of them opened, and I will not
give you the key."

That was open rebellion and Emmeline carried her in

high dudgeon to Albert. Albert had looked at the pitiful little face with its pleading eyes under which dark circles sat mournfully, and—sided with Phoebe. He said that Phoebe was right, the things were hers, and he did not see for his part why Emmeline wanted to open them. From that hour Emmeline had hard work to tolerate her little half-sister-in-law, and the enmity between them had never grown less. Little did Phoebe know, whenever she wore one of the frocks from that unopened trunk, how she roused her sister-in-law's wrath.

The trunk had been stored in the deep closet in Phoebe's room, and the key had never left its resting-place against her heart, night or day. Sometimes Phoebe had unlocked it in the still hours of the early summer mornings when no one else was stirring, and had looked long and lovingly at the garments folded within. It was there she kept the daguerreotype of the mother who was the idol of her child heart. Her father she could not remember, as he died when she was but a year old. In the depths of that trunk were laid several large packages, labeled. The mother had told her about them before she died, and with her own hand had placed the boxes in the bottom of the trunk. The upper one was labeled, "For my dear daughter Phoebe Deane on her eighteenth birthday."

For several days before her birthday Phoebe had felt an undertone of excitement. It was almost time to open the box which had been laid there over eight years ago by that beloved hand. Phoebe did not know what was in that box, but she knew it was something her mother put there for her. It contained her mother's thought for her grown-up daughter. It was like a voice from the grave. It thrilled her to think of it.

On her birthday morning she had awakened with the light, and slipping out of bed had applied the little black key to the keyhole. Her fingers trembled as she turned the lock, and opened the lid, softly lest she should wake some one. She wanted this holy gift all to herself now, this moment when her soul would touch again the soul of the lost mother.

Carefully she lifted out the treasures in the trunk until she reached the box, then drew it forth, and placing the other things back closed the trunk and locked it. Then she took the box to her bed and untied it. Her heart was beating so fast she felt almost as if she had been running. She lifted the cover. There lay the buff merino in all its beauty, complete even to the brown knot for the hair, and the locket which had been her mother's at eighteen. And there on the top lay a letter in her mother's handwriting. Ah! This was what she had hoped for—a real word from her mother which should be a guide to her in this grown-up life that was so lonely and different from the life she had lived with her mother. She hugged the letter to her heart and cried over it and kissed it. She felt that she was nestling her head in her dear mother's lap as she cried, and it gave her aching, longing heart a rest just to think so.

But there were sounds of stirring in the house, and Phoebe knew that she would be expected in the kitchen before long, so she dried her tears and read her letter.

Before it was half done the clatter in the kitchen had begun, and Emmeline's strident voice was calling up the stairway: "Phoebe! Phoebe! Are you going to stay up there all day?"

Phoebe had cast a wistful look at the rest of her letter, patted the soft folds of her merino tenderly, swept it out of sight into her closet, and answered Emmeline pleasantly, "Yes, I'm coming!" Not even the interruption could quite dim her pleasure on this day of days. She sprang up conscience stricken. She had not meant to be so late.

It did not take long to dress, and with the letter tucked in with the key against her heart she hurried down, only to meet Emmeline's frowning words, and be ordered around like a little child. Emmeline had been very disagreeable ever since Hiram Green had proposed to Phoebe.

The morning had been crowded full of work and the letter

had had no chance, except to crackle lovingly against the blue homespun.

The thought of the buff merino upstairs made her thrill with pleasure, and the morning passed away happily in spite of Emmeline and hard work. Words from her mother's hastily read letter came floating to her, and calling. She longed to pull it out and read once more to be sure just how they had been phrased. But there was no time.

After dinner, however, as soon as she had finished the dishes, and while Emmeline was looking after something in the wood-shed, she slipped away upstairs, without, as usual, asking if there was anything else to be done. She had decided that she would put on her new frock, for it had been her mother's wish in the letter, and go down to the village and call on that sweet-faced Mrs. Spafford. It was two years since Mrs. Spafford had invited her to spend the afternoon, and she had never plucked up the courage to go, for Emmeline always had something ready for her to do. But she felt that she had a right to a little time to herself on her birthday, and she meant to slip away without Emmeline seeing, if she could. She took her letter out, intending to read it quietly first before she dressed, but a sudden thought of Emmeline and her ability to break in upon her quietness made her decide instead to dress and start, stopping in a maple grove on the way to the village to read her letter undisturbed; so with all haste she smoothed her hair, fastened in the velvet knot, and put on the pretty frock. For just a moment she paused in front of the glass and looked at herself, thrilling with the thought that this dress was planned by her dear mother, and that the loved hand had set every perfect stitch in its place. And this girl in the glass was the daughter her mother had wished her to be, at least in outward appearance. Was she also in heart life? She looked earnestly at the face in the glass, longing to ask herself many questions, and unable to answer. Then with the letter safely hidden she hurried down.

But her conscience would not let her go out the front

door unobserved as she had planned. It seemed a mean, sneaking thing to do on her birthday. She would be open and frank. She would step into the kitchen and tell Emmeline that she was going out for the afternoon. That would be the way her mother would desire her to do. So, though much against her own desire, she went.

And there sat Emmeline with a large basket of dried beans to be shelled and put away for the winter. Phoebe stood aghast, and hesitated.

"Well, really!" said Emmeline, looking up severely at the apparition in buff that stood in the doorway. "Are you going to play the fine lady while I shell beans? It seems to me that's rather taking a high hand for one who's dependent on her relatives for every mouthful she eats, and seems to be likely to be for the rest of her days. That's gratitude, that is. But I take notice you eat the beans—oh, yes! the beans that Albert provides, and I shell, while you gallivant round in party clo'es."

The hateful speech brought the color to Phoebe's cheeks.

"Emmeline," she broke in, "you know I didn't know you wanted those beans shelled to-day. I would have done this morning between times if you had said so."

"You didn't know," sniffed Emmeline. "You knew the beans was to shell, and you knew this was the first chance to do it. Besides, there wasn't any between times this morning. You didn't get up till most noon. Everything was clear put back, and now you wash your white hands and dress up no matter what the folks that keeps you have to do. That wasn't the way *I* was brought up, if I *didn't* have a fine lady mother like yours. *My* mother taught me *gratitude*."

Phoebe reflected on the long hard days of work she had done for Emmeline without a word of praise or thanks, work as hard, and harder than any wage-earner in the house in the same position would have been expected to do. She had earned her board and more, and she knew it. Her clothes she made altogether from the stores her mother had left for her. She had not cost Albert a cent in that way. Never-

theless, her conscience hurt her because of the late hour of
her coming down that morning. With one desperate glance
at the size of the bean basket, and a rapid calculation how
long it would take her to finish them, she seized her clean
apron that hung behind the door, and enveloped herself in it.

"I have wanted to go out for a little while this afternoon.
I have been wanting to go for a long time, but if those beans
have got to be done this afternoon I can do them first."

She said it calmly, and went at the beans with determined
fingers, that fairly made the beans shiver as they hustled out
of their resisting withered pods.

Emmeline sniffed.

"You're a pretty figure shellin' beans in that rig. I s'pose
that's one of your ma's contoguments, but if she had any
sense at all she wouldn't want you to put it on. It ain't fit for
ordinary life. It might do to have your picture took in, or go
to a weddin', but you do look like a fool in it now. Besides,
if it's worth anything, an' it looks like there was good stuff in
it, you'll spoil it shellin' beans."

Phoebe shelled away feverishly and said not a word. Her
eyes looked as though there might be anything behind their
lowered lashes, from tears to fire-flashes. Emmeline surveyed her angrily. Her wrath was on the boiling point and
she felt the time had come to let it boil.

A little bird, perched on the roof of the barn, piped out:
"Phoe-bee! Phoe-bee!" The girl lifted her head toward the
outside door and listened. The bird seemed to be a reminder
that there were other things in the world worth while besides
having one's own way even on one's birthday. The paper in
her bosom crackled, and Emmeline eyed her suspiciously,
but the swift fingers shelled on unremittingly.

"I think the time has come to have an understandin',"
said Emmeline, raising her voice harshly. "If you won't talk
to me, Albert'll have to tend to you, but I'm the proper one
to speak, and I'm goin' to do it. I won't have this sort of
thing goin' on in my house. It's a disgrace. I'd like to know

what you mean, treatin' Hiram Green in this way. He's a re-spectable man, and you've no call to keep him danglin' after you forever. People'll talk about you, and I won't have it!"

There was an angry flash in Emmeline's eyes. She had made up her mind to have her say.

Phoebe raised astonished eyes to her sister-in-law's excited face.

"I don't know what you mean, Emmeline. I have nothing whatever to do with Hiram Green. I can't prevent him coming to my brother's house. I'm sure I wish I could, for it's most unpleasant to have him around continually."

The lofty air and cool words angered Emmeline beyond expression. She almost always lost her temper at once when she began to talk with Phoebe. Her most violent effort seemed at once so futile, and the girl was so provokingly calm that it was out of the question to keep one's temper.

"You don't know what I mean!" mocked Emmeline. "No, of course not. You don't know who he comes here to see. You think, I suppose, that he comes to see Albert and me perhaps. Well, you're not so much of a little fool as you want to pretend. You know well enough Hiram Green is just waitin' round on your whims, and I say it's high time you stopped this nonsense, keepin' a respectable man danglin' after you forever just to show off your power over him, and when all the time he needs a housekeeper, and his children are runnin' wild. You'll get your pay, miss, when you do marry him. Those young ones will be so wild you'll never get 'em tamed. They'll lead you a life of it. It's a strange way for any decent girl to act. If it's a new house you're waitin' on I guess you can have your way at once by just sayin' so. And I think it's time for you to speak, for I tell you plainly it ain't likely another such good chance'll come your way ever, and I don't suppose you want to be a hanger-on all your life on people that can't afford to keep you."

Phoebe's fingers were still shelling beans rapidly, but her eyes were on Emmeline's angry face.

"I thought I had told you," she said, and her voice was steady, "that I would never marry Hiram Green. Nothing and nobody on earth could make me marry him. I despise him. You know perfectly well that the things you are saying are wrong. It is not my fault that he comes here. I do not want him to come and he knows it. I have told him I will never marry him. I do not want him to build a house nor do anything else, for nothing that he could do would make any difference."

"You certainly are a little fool!" screamed Emmeline, "to let such a chance go. If he wasn't entirely daft about you he'd give you up at once. Well, what are you intendin' to do then? Answer me that! Are you layin' out to live on Albert and me the rest of your life? It's best to know what to expect and be prepared. Answer me!" she demanded again, as Phoebe dropped her eyes to hide the sudden tears that threatened to overwhelm her calm.

"I don't know." The girl tried to say it quietly, but the angry woman snatched the words from her lips and tossed them back:

"You don't know! You don't know! Well, you better know! I can tell you right now that there's goin' to be a new order of things. If you stay here any longer you've got to do as *I* say. You're not goin' on your high and mighty way doin' as you please an hour longer. And to begin with you can march up stairs and take off that ridiculous rig of your foolish mother's—"

Phoebe shoved the kitchen chair back with a sharp noise on the bare floor, and stood up, her face white with anger.

"Emmeline," said she, and her voice was low and controlled, but reminded Emmeline somehow of the first low rumbling of a storm, and when she looked at Phoebe's white face she fancied a flash like livid lightning passed over it. "Emmeline, don't you dare to speak my mother's name in that way! I will not listen to you!"

Then in the pause of the clashing voices the little bird

from the weathervane on the barn called out again: "Phoe-bee! Phoe-bee!"

And it was then that Phoebe cast her apron from her and went out through the kitchen door, into the golden glorious October afternoon, away from the pitiless tongue, and the endless beans, and the sorrow of her life.

The little bird on the weathervane left his perch and flew along from tree to tree, calling joyously, "Phoe-bee! Phoe-bee!" as she went down the road. He seemed as glad as though she were a comrade come to roam the woods with him. The sunlight lingered lovingly on the buff merino, as though it were a piece of itself come out to meet it, and she flitted breathlessly down the way, she knew not whither, only to get out and away.

Queer, wintry-looking worms crawled lazily to their homes across the long white road, woolly caterpillars in early fur overcoats. Large leaves floated solemnly down to their long home. Patches of rank grass rose green and pert, passionately pretending that summer was not done, scorning the deadness all about them. All the air was filled with a golden haze and Phoebe in her golden, sunlit garments, seemed a part of it.

5

THE rage and sorrow that seethed in Phoebe's soul were such as in some passionate hearts have led to deeds of desperation. And indeed she did feel desperate as she fled along the road, pursued by the thought of her sister-in-law's angry words.

To have such awful words spoken to her, and on her birthday; to feel so cornered and badgered, and to have no home where one was welcome, save that hateful alternative of going to Hiram Green's house! Oh, why was it that one had to live when life had become a torture?

She had gone a long distance before her mind cleared sufficiently to think where she was going. The sight of a distant red farm-house made her pause in her wild walk. If she went on she would be seen from the well-watched windows of that red house, and the two women who lived there were noted alike for their curiosity and for their ability to impart news.

In sudden panic, Phoebe climbed a fence and struck out across the field toward Chestnut Ridge, a small hill rising to the left of the village. There she might hope to be alone a little while and think it out, and perhaps creep close to her mother once more through the letter which she pressed against her heart. She hurried over the rough stubble of the field, gathering her buff garments with the other hand to hold them from any detaining briars. She seemed like some bright golden leaf blowing across the pasture to frolic with the other leaves on the nut-crowned hillside.

Breathless at last she reached the hill and found a great log where she sat down to read her letter.

"My dear little grown-up girl," it began, and as Phoebe read the precious words again the tears burst from her smarting eyes, welling up from her aching heart, and she buried her face in the letter and stained it with her tears.

It was some time before she could conquer herself and read farther:

> This is your eighteenth birthday, dear child, and I have thought so much about you and how you will be when you are a young woman, that I want to be with you a little while on your birthday and let you know how much, how very much, I love you. I cannot look forward into your life and see how it will be with you. I do not know whether you will have had sad years or bright ones between the time when I said good-by to you and now when you are reading this. I could not plan positively, dear little girl, to have them bright ones, else you surely know I would. I had to leave you in God's care, and I know you will be taken care of, whatever comes. If there have been trials, somehow, Phoebe, little girl, they must have been good for you. Sometime you will learn why, perhaps, and sometime there will be a way out. Never forget that. God has His brightness ready somewhere for you if you are true to Him and brave. Somehow I am afraid that there will have been trials, perhaps very heavy ones, for you were always such a sensitive little soul, and you are going among people who may not understand.

In thinking about your life I have been afraid for you that you would be tempted because of unhappiness to take some rash impulsive step before God is ready to show you His plan for your life. I would like to give you a little warning through the years, and tell you to be careful.

You have entered young womanhood, and will perhaps be asked to give your life into the keeping of some man. If I were going to live I would try to train you through the years for this great crisis of your life. But when it comes, remember that I have thought about you and longed for you that you may find another soul who will love you better than himself, and whom you can love better than you love anything else in the world, and who will be grand and noble in every way. Dear child, hear your mother's voice, and don't take anything less. It will not matter so much if he is poor, if only he loves you better than himself and is worthy of your love. Never marry anyone for a home, or a chance to have your own way, or freedom from good honest work. There will be no happiness in it. Trust your mother, for she knows. Do not marry anyone to whom you cannot look up and give honor next to God. Unless you can marry such a man it is better not to marry at all, believe your mother, child. I say it lovingly, for I have seen much sorrow and would protect you.

And now, my sweet child, with a face like the dawn of the morning, and eyes so untroubled, if when you read this anything has come into your life to make you unhappy, just try to lay it all down for a little while and feel your mother's love about you. See, I have made this bright sunny dress for you, every stitch set with love, and I want you to wear it on your birthday to remind you of me. It is yellow, because that is the glory color, the color of the sunshine I have always loved so much. I want you to think of me in a bright, sunny, happy way, and as in a glory of happiness, waiting for you; not as dead, and lying in the grave. Think of my love for you as a joy, and not a lost one either, for I am sure that where I am going I shall love you just the same, and more.

I am very tired and must not write any more, for there are other letters yet to write and much to do before I can feel ready to go and leave you, but as I am writing this birthday letter for you I am praying God that He will bring some brightness into your life, the beginning of some great joy, on this your eighteenth birthday, that shall be His blessing, and my birthday gift to my child. I put a kiss here where I write my name and give you with it more love than you can ever understand.

Your Mother

The tears rained down upon her hands as she held the letter, and when it was finished she put her head down on her lap and cried as she had not cried since her mother died. It seemed as if her head were once more upon that dear mother's lap and she could feel the smooth, gentle touch of her mother's hand passing over her hair and her hot temples as when she was a little child.

The sunlight sifted softly down between the yellowed chestnut leaves, sprinkling gold upon the golden hem of her gown, and glinting on her shining hair. The brown nuts dropped now and then about her, reverently, as if they would not disturb her if they could help it, and the fat gray squirrels silently regarded her, pausing in their work of gathering in the winter's store, then whisked noiselessly away. It was all quite still in the woods except for the occasional falling of a nut, or the stir of a leaf, or the skitter of a squirrel, for Phoebe did not sob aloud. Her grief was deeper than that. Her soul was crying out to one who was far away and yet who seemed so near to her that nothing else mattered for the time.

She was thinking over all her sad little life, telling it to her mother in imagination, trying to draw comfort from the letter, and to reconcile the realities with what her mother had said. Would her mother have been just as sure that it would all come out right if she had known the real facts? Would she have given the same advice? Carefully she thought it over, washing the anger away in her tears. Yes, she felt sure if her mother had known all she could not have written more truly than she had done. She would have had her say "No" to Hiram, just as she had done, and would have exhorted to patience with Emmeline, and to trust that brightness would sometime come.

She thought of her mother's prayer for her, and almost smiled through her tears to think how impossible that could be. Yet—the day was not done—perhaps there might be some little pleasant thing yet, that she might consider as a blessing and her mother's gift. She would look and wait for it and perhaps it would come. It might be Albert would be kind—he was, sometimes—or if it were not too late she might go down to the village and make her call on Mrs. Spafford. That might be a beautiful thing and the beginning of a joy—but no, that was too far away and her eyes were red with weeping. She must just take this quiet hour in the woods as her blessing and be glad over it because her mother and God had sent it to her to help her bear the rest of the days. She lifted her tear-wet face to look around on the golden autumn world, and the sun caught the tears on her lashes and turned them into flashing jewels, till the sweet, sad face looked like a tired flower with the dew upon it.

Then quite suddenly she knew she was not alone.

A young man stood in the shadow of the tallest chestnut-tree, regarding her with troubled gaze. His hat was in his hand and his head slightly bowed in deference, as if in the presence of something holy.

He was tall, well-formed, and his face fine and handsome. His eyes were deep and brown, with lights in them like those on the shadowed depths of a quiet woodland stream. His heavy dark hair was tossed back from a white forehead that had not been exposed to the summer sun of the hayfield, one could see at a glance, and the hand that held the hat was white and smooth also. There was a grace about his attitude that reminded Phoebe of David Spafford, who had seemed to her the ideal of a gentleman. He was dressed in dark brown and his black silk stock set off a finely cut, clean-shaven chin of unusual strength and firmness. If it had not been for the lights in his eyes, and the hint of a smile behind the almost tender strength of the lips, Phoebe would have been afraid of him as she lifted shy, ashamed eyes to the intruder's face.

"I beg your pardon, I did not mean to intrude," he said, apologetically, "but a party of young people are coming up the hill. They will be here in a moment, and I thought perhaps you would not care to meet them. You seem to be in trouble."

"Oh, thank you!" said Phoebe, arising in sudden panic and dropping her mother's letter at her feet. She stooped to pick it up, but the young man had reached it first and their fingers met for one brief instant over the letter of the dead. In her confusion Phoebe did not know what to say but "Thank you," and then felt like a parrot repeating the same phrase.

Voices were distinctly audible now and the girl turned to flee, but ahead and around there seemed nowhere to go for hiding except a dense growth of mountain laurel that still stood green and shining amid the autumn brown. She looked for a way around it, but the young man caught her thought, and reaching forward with a quick motion of his arms he parted the strong branches and made a way for her.

"Here, jump right in there! Nobody will see you. Hurry, they are almost here!" he whispered, kindly.

The girl sprang quickly on the log, paused just an instant to gather her golden draperies about her, and then fluttered into the green hiding-place and settled down like a drift of yellow leaves.

The laurel swung back into place, nodding quite as if it understood the secret. The young man stooped and she saw him deliberately take from his pocket a letter and put it down behind the log that lay across her hiding-place.

The letter settled softly into place and looked at her knowingly as if it, too, were in the secret and were there to help her. For even a letter has an expression if one has but eyes to see and understand.

Up the hill-side came a troop of young people. Phoebe could not see them, for the growth of laurel was very dense, but she could hear their voices.

"Oh, Janet Bristol, how fast you go! I'm all out of breath. Why do you hurry so? The nuts will keep till we get there, and we have all the afternoon before us."

"Go slow as you like, Caroline," said a sweet, imperious voice; "when I start anywhere I like to get there. I wonder where Nathaniel can be. It is fully five minutes since he went out of sight, and he promised to hail us at once and tell us the best way to go."

"Oh, Nathaniel isn't lost," said another girl's voice crossly; "he'll take care of himself likely. Don't hurry so, Janet. Maria is all out of breath."

"Hullo! Nathaniel! Nathaniel Graham, where are you!" called a chorus of male voices.

Then from a few paces in front of the laurel hiding-place came the voice that Phoebe had heard but a moment before:

"Aye, aye, sir! That way!" it called. "There are plenty of nuts up there!" He stood with his back toward her hiding-place, and pointed farther up the hill. Then, laughing, scrambling over slippery leaves and protruding logs the gay company frolicked past, and Phoebe was left, undiscovered, alone with the letter that smiled back at her in a friendly way.

She stooped a little to look at it and read the address, "Nathaniel Graham, Esq.," written in a fine commanding hand, a chirography that gave the impression of honoring the name it wrote.

The girl studied the beautiful name, till every turn of the pen was graven on her mind, the fine, even clearness of the small letters, the bold downward stroke in the capitals. It was unusual writing of an unusual name and the girl felt that it belonged to an unusual man.

Then all of a sudden, while she waited and listened to the happy jingle of voices, like bells of different tones, exclaiming over rich finds in nuts, the barren loneliness of her own life came over her and brought a rush of tears. Why was she here in hiding from those girls and boys that should have been her companions? Why did she shrink from meeting Janet Bristol, the sweetly haughty beauty of the village? Why was she never invited to their pleasant tea-drinkings, and their berry and nut gatherings? She saw them in church, and that was all. They never seemed to see her. True, she had not been brought up from childhood among them, but she had lived there long enough to have known them intimately if her life had not always been so full of care. Janet Bristol had gone away to school for several years, and was only at home in summer when Phoebe's life was full of farm work—cooking for the hands, and for the harvesters. But Maria Finch and Caroline Penfield had gone to school with Phoebe. She felt a bitterness that they were in these good times and she was not. They were not to blame, perhaps, for she had always avoided them, keeping much to herself and her studies in school, and hurrying home at Emmeline's strict command. They had never attracted her as had the tall, fair Janet, in the few summer glimpses she had had of her. Yet she would never likely know Janet Bristol or come any nearer to her than she was now, hidden behind God's screen of laurel on the hill-side, while the gay company gathered nuts a few rods away. The young man with the beautiful face and the kind ways would forget her and leave her to scramble out of her hiding place as best she could while he helped Janet Bristol over the stile and carried her basket of nuts home for her. He would not cross her path again. Nevertheless she was glad he had met her this once, and she could know there was in the world one so kind and noble; it was a beautiful thing to have come into her life. She would stay here till they were all out of hearing, and then creep out and steal away as she had come. Her sad life and its annoyances, forgotten for the moment, settled down upon her, but with this change. They now seemed possible to bear. She could go back to Albert's house, to Emmeline where she was unwelcome, and work her way twice over. She could doff the golden garments, and take up her daily toil, even patiently perhaps, and bear Emmeline's hateful insinuations, Alma's impudence, the disagreeable attentions of Hank and the hateful presence of Hiram Green, but never again would she be troubled with the horrible thought that perhaps after all she was wrong and ought to accept the home that Hiram Green was offering her. *Never,* for now she had seen a man, who had looked at her as she felt sure God meant a man to look at a woman, with honor, and respect, and gentle helpfulness and deference.

All at once she knew that her mother's prayer had been answered and that something beautiful had come into her life. It would not stay and grow as her mother had hoped. This stranger could be nothing to her, but the memory of his helpfulness and the smile of sympathy that had lighted his eyes would remain with her, a beautiful joy, always. It was something that had come to save her at the moment of her utter despair.

Meantime, under the chestnut-trees but a few rods away the baskets were being filled rapidly, for the nuts were many and the squirrels had been idle, thinking they owned them all. Nathaniel Graham helped each girl impartially, and seemed to be especially successful in finding the largest and shiniest nuts. The laughing and joking went on, but Nathaniel said little. Phoebe from her covert could watch them, and felt that the young man would soon pilot them farther away. She could hear bits of their talk.

"What's the matter with Nathaniel?" said Caroline Penfield. "He's hardly said a word since we started. What deep subject is your massive mind engaged upon, young man?"

"Oh, Nate is thinking about Texas," said Daniel Westgate flippantly. "He has no thoughts or words for anything but setting Texas free. We'll hear of him joining the volunteers to help them fight Mexico the next thing. I wouldn't be one bit surprised."

"Don't Daniel," said Janet Bristol, sharply. "Nathaniel has far more sense than that."

"I should hope so!" echoed Maria Finch. "Nathaniel isn't a hot-headed fanatic."

"Don't you be too sure!" said the irrepressible Daniel. "If you'd heard the fine heroics he was getting off to David Spafford yesterday you wouldn't be surprised at anything. Speak up, Nate, and tell them whether you are going or not."

"Perhaps," said Nathaniel, lifting pleasant eyes of amusement towards the company.

"Nonsense!" said Janet, sharply. "As if he would think of such a thing! Daniel, you ought to be ashamed to spoil the lovely afternoon with talk of politics. Come, let us move on to that next clump of trees. See, it is just loaded, and the nuts are falling with every breath of wind."

"Just look at that squirrel, leaning against his tail as if it were the back of an easy chair. He is mincing away at that nut as daintily as any lady," called Caroline.

The merry company picked up baskets and began to move out of sight, but the young man Nathaniel stood still thoughtfully and felt in his pockets, until Phoebe, from her hiding-place, could see none of the others. Then she heard him call in a pleasant voice, "Janet, I have dropped a letter. It cannot be far away. Go on without me for a moment. I will be with you right away."

Then came Janet's sweet, vexed tones:

"Oh, Nathaniel! How tiresome! Can't you let it go? Was it of any consequence? Shall we come and help you find it?"

"No, Janet, thank you. I know just where I dropped it, and I will be with you again before you have missed me. Keep right on."

Then he turned, swiftly, and came back to the laurel, before the startled Phoebe, who had intended running away at once, could realize that he was coming.

She sprang up with the instinct of fleeing from him, but as if the laurel were loath to part with her, it reached out detaining fingers and caught her by the strands of her fine brown hair; and down came the soft, shining waves of hair, in shameless, lovely disorder about the flushed face, and rippling far below the waist of the buff frock. The sun caught it and kissed it into a thousand lights and shadows of brown and red and purple and gold. A strand here and there clung to the laurel as if the charm were mutual, and made a fine veil of spun gold before her face. Thus she stood abashed, with her hair unbound before the stranger, her face in a beautiful confusion.

Now this young man had gazed upon many a maiden's hair with entire indifference. In the days of his boyhood he had even dared to attach a paper kite to the yellow braids of a girl who sat in front of him in school, and laughed with the rest at recess, as after carefully following her with hidden kite and wound-up cord they had succeeded in launching the paper thing in the breeze till it lifted the astonished victim's yellow plaits high in the air and she cried out angrily upon them. He had even pulled many a girl's hair. He had watched his cousin Janet brush and plait and curl her abundant locks into the various changing fashions, and criticised the effect freely. He had once untied a hard knot in a bonnet-string among a mass of golden curls without a thrill. Why therefore did he feel such awe as he approached a deep embarrassment to offer his assistance! Why did his fingers tremble as he laid them reverently upon a strand of hair that had tangled itself in the laurel? Why did it bring a fine ecstasy into his being as the wind blew it across his face? Did all hair have that delicate, indescribable perfume about it?

When he had set her free from the entangling bushes, he marvelled at the dexterity with which she reduced the flying hair to order and imprisoned it meekly. It seemed like magic.

Then before she had time to spring out of her covert, he took her hands, firmly, reverently, without undue familiarity, and helped her to the top of the log and thence to the ground. She liked him for the way he did it, so different from the way the other men she knew would have done it. She shuddered to think if it had been Hank, or Hiram Green.

"Come this way, it is nearer to the road," he said, quietly, parting the branches at his right to let her pass, and when she had gone a few steps, behold, not two rods below lay the cross road, which met the highway by which she had come, a quarter of a mile farther on.

"But you have forgotten your letter," she turned to say, as they came out of the woods and began to descend the hill; "and I can get out quite well now. You have been very kind—"

"I will get the letter presently," he said with a smile. "Just let me help you over the fence. I want to ask your pardon for my intrusion. I did not see you at first, the woods were so quiet, and you looked so much like the yellow leaves that lay all about—" and his eyes cast an admiring glance at the buff merino.

"Oh, it was not an intrusion," she exclaimed, her cheeks rosy with the remembrance, "and I am so grateful to you for telling me they were coming. I would not have liked to be found there—so." She looked shyly up. "I thank you very much!"

He saw that her eyes were beautiful, with ripples of laughter and shadows of sorrow in their glance. He experienced a deep and unnecessary satisfaction that his first impression of her face was verified, and he stood looking down upon her as if she were something he was proud of having discovered and rescued from an unpleasant fate.

Phoebe felt a warm glow like sunshine breaking over her in the kindness of his look.

"Don't thank me," he said. "I felt like a criminal, intruding so upon your trouble."

"But you must not feel so. It was only that I had been reading a letter from my mother, and it made me feel so lonely that I cried."

"That is trouble enough," he said, with quick sympathy. "Is your mother away from home, or are you?"

"My mother is dead. She has been gone a good many years," she said, with quivering lips. "She wrote this letter long ago for me to read to-day, and I came away here by myself to read it. Now, you will understand."

He had helped her over the rail fence that separated the field from the road, and they were standing, she on the road side, he on the field side of the fence as they talked. Neither of them saw a farm wagon coming down the road over the brow of the hill, a mere speck against the autumn sky when they came out of the woods. The young man's face kindled as he answered:

"Thank you for telling me. Yes, now I will understand. My mother has been gone a long time, too. I wish she had written me a letter to read to-day."

Then, as if he knew he must not stay longer, he lifted his hat, smiled, and walked quickly up the hill, while Phoebe sped swiftly down the road, not noticing the glories of the day, nor thinking so much of her own troubles, but marvelling at what had happened and living it all over once more in imagination. She knew without thinking that a wagon was rumbling nearer and nearer, but she gave it no heed.

Nathaniel Graham, when he reached the edge of the wood, turned and looked back down the road; saw the girl in her yellow draperies moving in the autumn sunshine, and watched her intently. The driver of the farm wagon, now almost opposite to him, watched glumly from behind his bags of wheat, high piled, sneered under his breath at the fine attire, half guessed who he was; then wondered who the girl was who kept tryst so far from any houses, and with a last glance at the man just vanishing into the woods he whipped up his team, resolved to find out.

6

NATHANIEL Graham went to pick up the letter he had left
behind the log, but as he did so his eye caught something
brown, lying on the ground among the laurel near the letter.
He reached out and took it. It was a bit of a bow of brown
velvet, and seemed strangely a part of the girl who had been
there but a few moments before. What part had this bit of
velvet played in her make-up? Had it been worn at her
throat, or in her wonderful hair? He never doubted that it
was hers. As he raised it wonderingly in his hand to look at it
more closely he fancied he caught the same subtle fragrance
that had been in her hair. His fingers closed pleasantly about
the soft little thing. For a moment he pondered whether he
ought to go after her and give it to her. Then farther up the
hill he heard the voices calling him, and with a pleasant
smile he tucked it into his inner pocket beside the letter that
had played so important a part in the little affair. He rather
liked to think he had that bit of velvet himself, and perhaps
it was not of much value to the owner. It might at least make
another opportunity of seeing her. And so he passed on up
the hill with something besides the freedom of Texas to
think upon.

Meantime, the load of wheat went down the road after Phoebe at a lively pace, and its driver, in no pleasant mood because he had been all the way to Albany with his wheat and had been unable to sell it, studied the graceful sunlit figure ahead of him, and wondered what there was about it so strangely familiar.

Phoebe had just reached the highroad and paused to think which way she would go, when the wagon overtook her, and turning with her face bright with pleasure, and momentary forgetfulness, she faced the lowering astonishment of Hiram Green! Her face grew deadly white with the revulsion, and she caught at the fence to steady herself. She felt as if the earth were reeling under her unprotected feet. One hand flew to her heart and her frightened eyes, with a wild thought of her late protector, sought the way by which she had come; but the hill-side lay unresponsive in the late sunshine, and not a soul was to be seen. Nathaniel Graham had just picked up his cousin Janet's basket.

"Well, I swow!" said Hiram Green, pulling his horses up sharply. "It ain't *you* tricked out that way, away off here!" Then slowly his little pig eyes traveled to the lonely hill-side, gathered up an idea, came back to the girl's guilty face, and narrowed to a hateful slit through which shone a gleam of something that might be likely to illumine outer darkness. He brought his thin, cruel lips together with satisfaction. He felt that at last he had a hold upon the girl, but he could wait and use it to its best advantage.

She, poor child, never dreamed that he had seen the young man with her, and was only frightened for the moment with instinctive dread of being alone in an unfrequented spot with him. In an instant her courage came to her aid, and she steadied her voice to reply naturally:

"Oh, is that you, Mr. Green? You almost frightened me. I was taking a walk and did not expect to see anyone I knew. This is the Albany road isn't it? Have you been to Albany?"

Her unusually friendly tones threw the man off his guard

for a moment. He could not resist the charm of having her speak so pleasantly to him.

"Yes, been to Albany on business," he responded. "Won't you get up and ride? 'Tain't a very pretty seat, but I guess it's clean and comfortable. Sorry I ain't got the carryall. You're a long piece from home."

"Oh, thank you, Mr. Green," she said, cordially. "I'm sure the seat would be very comfortable, and just as nice as the carryall, but I'm out taking a walk this beautiful afternoon, and I'm enjoying every minute of it. I would much rather walk. Besides, I am not going directly home. I may stop at Granny McVane's and perhaps another place before I get home. Thank you for the invitation."

Then without waiting for a reply she flew lightly in front of the horses and sped up the main highway toward the old red farm-house. It was not the direction she would have chosen, but there was no time to do anything else, and her frightened heart gave wings to her feet. She dared not look behind lest she was being pursued.

Hiram Green, thus left alone after his attempt at gallantry, looked after the flying maiden with venom in his little eyes. His mouth hardened once more into its cruel lines and he took up the reins again and said to his horses in no pleasant tones: "G'long there!" pointing his remark with a stinging cut of the whip, which made the weary beasts leap forward at a lively gait.

He did not watch Phoebe any longer, but once he turned his head and looked threateningly at the barren hill-side, and shook the fist that held his whip in a menacing way.

When Phoebe neared the old red house, where lived the two women who always saw and enlarged and told everything, she noted with relief that the shades were drawn down and there was a general air of not-at-home-ness about the place that betokened the inhabitants were away for the afternoon. With joy she went on by the house and turned down another cross road which would lead to a second road going into the village. On this road, just on the border of the town, lived Granny McVane all alone save for her silent old husband. She was a sweet old lady whom care and disappointment had not hardened, but only made more humble and patient. Phoebe had been there on occasional errands, and her kindness had won the girl's heart. From Granny McVane's it would be but a short run home across the fields, and she would thus escape meeting any more prying eyes. She was not accustomed to making calls on the neighbors without an errand, but the fancy came to her now that she would just stop and ask how Granny's rheumatism was, and wish her good-day. Perhaps, if she seemed glad to see her, she might tell her it was her birthday and this was the frock her mother had made. The girl had a longing to confide in some one.

As she walked along the country road, she began to think of home and the inevitable black looks that would be hers from Emmeline. But the day was good yet, though a chill was creeping into the air that made her cheeks tingle. The sun was dropping low now, and the rays were glowing deeper. The stubble in the cornfields that she passed was bathed in its light. The buff merino was touched with a ruddy glow and the girl, as she sped along, seemed like a living topaz in the golden setting of the day.

She reached the little double door of Granny McVane's cottage, and knocked. The old lady, in her white ruffled cap with its black band, and soft kerchief folded across her bosom, opened the upper half of the door, and on seeing Phoebe opened the lower door, too, and brought her in most cordially. She made her sit down, and looked her over with delight, her old eyes glowing with pleasure at the sweet picture the girl made sitting in the flowered calico rocking-chair. She seemed to catch the long sunbeams that slanted low across the kitchen floor, and reflect them with her gown and face till all the little room was filled with sunny brightness.

She made Phoebe tell about the frock, her birthday, her

mother's letter, and her walk; and then she told her she must stay to tea with her, for the 'Squire was off to Albany on business and would not be back that night.

The old cat was winking cordially before the hearth, the pot of mush was sputtering sleepily on its crane over the fire, the kettle was singing cheerily beside it, and the old lady's face was so wistful that Phoebe put by her thought of home, and the supper that she ought to be getting this minute, and decided to stay just for once, as it was her birthday. The stiff white curtains shut the little room in cosily from the outside world, and a scarlet geranium bloomed happily on the broad window-seat. Phoebe looked around at the polished old mahogany, and the shining pewter dishes that adorned the shelf, touched the drowsy cat with gentle fingers that brought forth a purr, glanced up at the great old clock with its measured, unhurried tick-tock, tick-tock, and felt like a person who has turned her back upon life and all its duties and abandoned herself to pleasure pure and simple. Yes, for one short hour more she would have what her day offered her of joy, without a thought of trouble, and then she would go back to her duty and cherish the memory of her pleasure. Thus did Phoebe give herself over to the wild excitement of a birthday tea at Granny McVane's cottage.

Precisely at five o'clock the little round table was drawn out from the wall, and its leaves put up. A snow-white homespun cloth was laid upon it and lovely blue dishes of quaint designs in blue set upon it; a bowl, a plate, cup and saucer for each; steel knives; a great pitcher of creamy milk; a pat of Granny's delicious butter; a pitcher of "sugar-house" molasses, looking like distilled drops of amber, and delectable to the taste; a plate of shining brown rusks; a loaf of soft gingerbread, rich and dark like brown velvet. Then the tea was made in the little brown earthenware teapot, the great bowl of yellow mush taken up, and no modern debutante's dinner-party, with its hand-painted dinner cards, its beribboned favors, its flowers, and its carefully-planned menu could have a lovelier color scheme, or one that better fitted the gown of the guest of honor, than was set forth for Phoebe Deane's birthday tea, all yellows and beautiful browns, with the last rays of the setting sun over all. The lazy cat got up, stretched, and yawned, and came over by the table as they sat down. The cat, by the way, was yellow too.

It was a delicious meal, and Phoebe ate it with the appetite gained in her long walk. After it was over she bade Granny McVane good-evening, kissed her for the beautiful ending to her birthday, and hurried guiltily across the fields to the farm-house she called home, not allowing herself to think of what was before her until she reached the very door, for she would not have one moment of her precious day spoiled.

The family had just sat down to supper when Phoebe opened the door and came in. She had hoped this ceremony would be over, for the usual hour for supper was half past five, but Emmeline had waited longer than usual, thinking Phoebe would surely come back to help, and having it all to do herself had not been able to get it ready as soon as usual. Moreover, an undertone of apprehension as to what Albert might say if Phoebe should be headstrong enough to remain away after dark, kept her going to the window to look up the road for the possible sight of a girlish figure in a curious yellow frock. Emmeline had been angry, astonished, and bewildered all the afternoon. She had not been able to decide what she would do about the way her young sister-in-law had acted. She had been a little anxious, too, lest she had gone too far, and would be blamed if the truth should be known. She would have been glad, many times during the afternoon, to have seen Phoebe meekly returning, but now that she had come, after staying away till the work was done and Albert had come home and found out her absence, Emmeline's wrath was kindled anew. She stood at the hearth taking up the second pan of johnnycake when the girl came in, and when she saw Phoebe apparently as cheerful as if she had stayed at home and done her duty all the afternoon, Emmeline set her lips in cold and haughty disapproval.

Alma, with her mouth full of fried potatoes, stopped her fork midway with another supply and stared. The little boys chorused in unison: "Hullo, Aunt Phoebe! Where'd'ye get the clo'es?" Hank, who was just helping himself to a slice of bread with his fork, turned full around and after the first glimpse of the girl in her unfamiliar garments he sat in awed embarrassment. Only Albert sat in pleased surprise, his knife and fork akimbo on his plate, his chair tipped back, and a look of real welcome in his face.

"Well, now, Phoebe, I'm real glad you've got back. I was getting uneasy about you, off so long. It isn't like you to stay away from your meals. My, but you do look pretty in that rig! What took you, anyway? Where've you been?"

Not to the others would she have told for the world, but somehow Albert's pleasant tones and kindly eyes unsealed her lips, and without a thought she spoke:

"I've just been for a walk in the woods this afternoon, and I stopped a few minutes to see Granny McVane. She made me stay to tea with her. I did not mean to stay so late."

"That sounds very sweet, I'm sure," broke in Emmeline's sharp voice, "but she forgets that she left me with all her work to do on top of my own."

Phoebe's cheeks flushed.

"I am sorry I did not get back in time to help get supper," she said, looking straight at Albert as if explaining to him alone, "but it was my birthday, and I thought I might take a little time to myself."

"Your birthday! To be sure you can. You don't go out half enough. Emmeline, you wouldn't want her to work all day on her birthday, of course. Sit down, child, and have some more supper. This is real good johnnycake; have a piece? You ought to have told us before that you had a birthday, and then we might have celebrated. Eh, Hank! What do you say?"

"I say, yes," said Hank, chuckling in a vain endeavor to regain his usual composure. He had visions of a certain red ribbon at the village store that he might have bought her, or a green glass breastpin. He watched her furtively and wondered if it was too late yet to improve the occasion.

"Other people have birthdays too, and I don't see much fuss made over 'em either," sniffed Emmeline, flinging the tea towel up to its nail with an impatient movement. She had burned her finger, and her temper burned in sympathy.

"Thank you, Albert," said Phoebe, quietly, "I don't care for any more supper. I will go up and change my frock and be ready to wash the dishes."

She was going toward the door, but Albert detained her.

"Wait, Phoebe! You come here and sit down. I've got something to tell you. I'd clean forgot about the birthday myself, but now I remember all right. Let's see, you're eighteen to-day, aren't you? I thought so."

Hank lifted bold, admiring eyes to her face, and the girl, standing patiently behind her chair at the table waiting for her brother to finish, felt she would like to extinguish him for a little while till the conference was over.

"Well, now, child, I've got a surprise for you. You're eighteen, and of age, so you've got a right to know it."

"Wouldn't it be better for you to tell me by and by when the work is done?" pleaded Phoebe, casting a frightened glance about on the wide-eyed, interested audience.

"No," said Albert, genially, looking about the room. "It isn't a secret, leastways not from any that's here. You needn't look so scared, child. It's only that there's a little money coming to you, about five or six hundred dollars. It's a nice tidy little sum for a girl eighteen with good prospects. You certainly deserve it, for you've been a good girl ever since you came to live with us. Your mother wanted me to keep the money for you till you was eighteen, and then she said you would know how to use it and be more likely to need it."

"Say, Aunt Phoebe," broke in Alma, tilting her turn-up nose to its most inquisitive point, and sticking out her chin in a grown-up manner she had copied after her mother, "does Hiram Green know you got a birthday?"

"Shut up!" said Emmeline, applying the palm of her hand in a stinging slap to her offspring's cheek.

"Sister! Sister!" said Albert, in gentle reproof. "Now, Emmeline, don't be so severe with the child! She doesn't realize how impertinent she is. Sister, you mustn't talk like that to Aunt Phoebe." Then in an aside to Hank, with a wink, "It does beat all how keen children will be sometimes."

Phoebe, with scarlet cheeks, felt as if she could bear no more. "Thank you, Albert," she said, with a voice that *would* tremble despite her best efforts. "Now if you will excuse me I'll change my frock."

"Wait a minute, child; that's a mighty pretty frock you've got on. Look pretty as a peach in it. Let's have a look at you. Where'd you get it? Make it yourself?"

"Mother made it for me to wear to-day," said Phoebe, in a low voice, and then she vanished into the hall, leaving somehow an impression of victory behind her, and a sense of embarrassment among the family.

"There'll be no livin' with her now," snapped Emmeline over the tea-cups. "I'm sure I thought you had better sense. You never told me there was any money left for her, or I'd've advised you about it. It wasn't necessary to tell her anything about it. I'm sure we've spent it for her, and if there's anything left her it belongs to you. Here she's had a good home, and paid not a cent for it, and had everything just the same as us. If she had any spirit of right she wouldn't touch a cent of that money!"

"Now look here, Emmeline," said Albert, in his kind, conciliatory tone. "You don't quite understand this matter. Not having known about it before of course you couldn't judge rightly. And as it was her ma's request that I didn't tell anybody, I couldn't very well tell you. Besides, I don't see why it should affect you any. The money was hers, and we'd nothing to do with it. As for her home here, she's been very welcome, and I'm sure she's earned her way. She's a good worker, Phoebe is."

"That's so, she is," assented Hank, warmly. "I don't know a girl in the county can beat her workin'."

"I don't know as anybody asked your opinion, Hank Williams. I'm able to judge of work a little myself, and if she works well, who taught her? She'd never done a stroke when she came here, and nobody thinks of the hard time I've had breakin' her in, and puttin' up with her mistakes when she was young and her hands lily white, and soft as a baby's."

"Now, Emmeline, don't go and get excited," said Albert, anxiously. "You know we ain't letting go a mite of what you've done. Only it's fair to the girl to say she's earned her way."

"H'm!" said Emmeline, contemptuously, "that depends on who's the judge!"

"Won't Aunt Phoebe do any more work now she's got some money, ma?" broke in Alma in a panic of what might be the possibilities in store for her small selfish self.

"Haven't I told you to keep still, Alma," reproved her mother, angrily. "If you say another word I'll send you to bed without any cake."

At this dire threat Alma retired temporarily from the conversation till the cake should be passed, and a kind of family gloom settled over the room. Hank felt the constraint and made haste to bolt the last of his supper and escape.

Phoebe came down shortly afterward, attired in her everyday garb, and looking meekly sensible. Albert felt somehow a relief to see her so, though he protested weakly.

"Say, Phoebe, it's too bad for you to wash dishes your birthday night. You go back and put on your pretty things, and Alma'll help her ma wash up this time."

"No, she won't, either," broke in Emmeline. "Alma ain't

a bit well, and she's not goin' to be made to work at her age unless she likes. Here, honey, you may have this piece of ma's cake, she don't want it all. It seems to me you're kind of an unnatural father, Albert Deane. I guess it won't hurt Phoebe to wash a few dishes when she's been lyin' around havin' a good time all day, while I've worked my fingers half off doin' her work. We've all had to work on our birthdays, and I guess if Phoebe's goin' to stay here she'll have to put up with what the rest of us gets, unless she's got money to pay for better."

With that Albert looked helplessly about the room and retired to his newspaper in the sitting-room, while Phoebe went swiftly about the usual evening work. Emmeline yanked the boys away from the cake plate, and marched them and Alma out of the kitchen with her head held high and her chin in the air. She did not even do the usual little duties of putting away the cake and bread and pickles and jelly, but left it all for Phoebe. Of this Phoebe was glad.

Before the dishes were quite done, the front door opened and Hiram Green sauntered into the sitting-room. Phoebe heard him, and hurried to hang up her dish towels and flee to her own room.

And thus ended the birthday, though the girl lay awake far into the night thinking over all its wonderful happenings, and not allowing her mind to dwell upon the possibilities of trouble in the future.

7

WHEN little Rose Spafford was born the sweet girl-mother, who had been Marcia Schuyler, found no one so helpful and reliable in the whole town as Miranda Griscom, grand-daughter and household drudge of her next door neighbor, Mrs. Heath. David Spafford "borrowed" her for the first three or four weeks, and Mrs. Heath gave reluctant consent, because the Heaths and the Spaffords had always been inti-mate friends; but Grandma Heath realized during that time just how many steps the eccentric Miranda saved her, and she began to look forward to her return with more eagerness than she cared to show. Miranda, as she revelled in doing as she pleased in the large well-furnished kitchen of the Spafford house, using the best sprigged china to send a pret-ty tray upstairs to Mrs. Spafford, used often to look trium-phantly over toward her grandmother's house, and wonder if she was missed. One little gleam of appreciation would have started a flame of abounding love in the queer, lonely heart of Miranda. But the grim grandmother never appreci-ated anything that this unloved grandchild, the daughter of an undesired son-in-law, tried to do.

As the delightful days sped by in loving service Miranda

began to dread the time when she must go back to her grandmother's house again, and Marcia and David dreaded it also. They set about planning how they might keep her, and presently they had it all arranged.

David suggested it first.

It was while they both hung over the little Rose's cradle, watching her wake up, like the opening of the little bud she was. Miranda had come to the door for a direction, and stood a moment, remarking "I thought I'd find you two a-worshippin'. Just keep right on. My heart's with you. I'll see to supper. Don't you give it a thought." And then a moment later they heard her high, nasal tones voicing something about a "Sweet, sweet rose on a garden wall," and they smiled at the quaint loving soul. Then David spoke.

"Marcia, we must contrive to keep her here. She has blossomed out in the last month. It would be cruel to send her back to that dismal house over there again. They don't need her in the least with Hannah's cousin there all the time. I mean to offer her wages to stay with us. You are not strong enough to care for baby and do the housework, anyway, and I would feel safer about you if Miranda were here. Wouldn't you like her?"

Marcia's sweet laugh rang out. "Oh, David, you will spoil me! I'm sure I'm perfectly able to do the work and look after this wee flower. But of course I'd like to have Miranda here. I think it would be a good thing if she could get away from her surroundings, and she is a comfort to me in a good many ways."

"Then it is settled, dear," said David, with his most loving smile.

"Oh, but David, what will Aunt Amelia say? And Aunt Hortense! Think! They will tell me I am weak—or proud, which would be worse yet."

"What does it matter what my aunts think? We are certainly free to do as we please in our own home, and I'm sure of one thing—Aunt Clarinda will think it is all right. She'll be quite pleased. Besides, I shall explain to Aunt Hortense that I want to have you more to myself and take you with me often, and therefore it is my own selfishness, not yours, that makes me do this. She will listen to that argument, I am sure."

Marcia smiled, half doubtfully.

"And then, there is Mrs. Heath. She never will consent."

"Leave that to me, my little wife, and don't worry about it. Let us first settle it with Miranda."

"Oh, but if Mrs. Heath wouldn't hear to it, Miranda would be so disappointed," suggested Marcia.

Just then Miranda presented herself at the door.

"Your supper's spoilin' on the table. Will you two just walk down and eat it while I have my try at that baby? I haven't seen scarcely a wink of her all this blessed day."

"Miranda," said David, not looking at his wife's warning eyes, "would you be willing to stay with us altogether?"

"H'm!" said Miranda. "Jes' gimme the try and see!" and she stooped over the cradle with such a wistful longing in her gaze that the young mother's heart went out to her with a real love.

"Very well, Miranda, then we'll consider it a bargain. I'll pay you wages so that we shall feel quite comfortable about asking you to do anything, and you shall call this your home from now on."

"What!" gasped the astonished girl, straightening up. "Did you mean what you said? I never knew you to do a mean thing like tease any one, David Spafford, but you can't mean what you say. It couldn't come around so nice as that fer me. Don't go to talk about wages. I'd work from mornin' to night fer one chance at that blessed baby there in the cradle. But I know it can't be."

The supper grew quite cold while they were persuading her that it was all true and that they really wanted her; and while they talked over the possibilities of having trouble with her grandmother; but at last with her sandy eyelashes wet with tears of joy and hope Miranda went down stairs and heated the supper all over again for them, and the two upstairs, beside the little bud of life that had bloomed for them, rejoiced that a heart so faithful and true would be her watchful attendant through babyhood.

Perhaps it was with a feeling that he desired to burn his bridges behind him before his maiden aunts should hear of the new arrangement, that David went over to see old Mrs. Heath that very evening. Perhaps it was to relieve the excitement of poor Miranda, who felt that though heaven had opened before her, it could not really be for her, and was counting on being put out of her Eden at once.

No one but Marcia ever heard what passed between David and old Mrs. Heath, and no one else quite knows what arguments he used to finally bring the determined old woman to terms. Miranda, with her nose flattened against the window pane of the dark kitchen chamber, watching the two blurred figures in the candle light of Grandmother Heath's "settin-room," wondered, and prayed, and hoped, and feared, and prayed again.

It was well that David had gone over to see Mrs. Heath that night and made all arrangements, if he cared to escape criticism from his relatives. It was the very next afternoon that Miss Amelia, on her daily visit to the shrine of her new grandniece, remarked: "Well, Marcia, has Miranda gone home yet? I should think her grandmother would need her, all this time away, poor old lady. And you're perfectly strong and able now to attend to your own work again."

Marcia's fair face flushed delicately, and she gathered her baby closer as if to protect her from the chill that would follow the words that she must speak.

"Why, Aunt Amelia," she said, brightly, "what do you think! Miranda is not going home at all. David has a foolish notion that he wants her to stay with me, and help look after baby. Besides, he wants me to go with him as I have been doing. I told him it was not necessary, but he wanted it, so he has arranged it all, and Mrs. Heath has given her consent."

"Miranda stay here!" The words fell like long slanting icicles that seemed to pierce as they fell. They lingered in the air until their full surprise and displeasure could be distinctly felt, and then followed more.

"I am *surprised* at you, Marcia. I thought you had more self-respect than that! It is a disgrace to a young strong woman to let her husband hire a girl to do her work while she gads about the country and leaves her house and her young child. If your own mother had lived she would have taught you better than that. And then, *Miranda, of all people to select!* The child of a renegade! A waif dependent, utterly thankless, and irresponsible! She is scatter-brained, and untrustworthy. If you needed anyone at any time to sit with the child while you were out for a legitimate cause to pay a call, or make an occasional visit, either Hortense or I would be glad to come and relieve you. Indeed, you must not think of leaving this wild, good-for-nothing Miranda Griscom with my nephew's child. I shall speak to my sister Hortense, and we will make it our business to come down every day, one or the other of us, and do anything that you find your strength is unequal to doing. We are still strong enough, I hope, to do anything for the family honor. I should be ashamed to have it known that David Spafford's wife was such a weakling that she had to have hired help in. The young wives of our family have always been proud of their housekeeping."

Now Miranda Griscom, whatever might be said of her other virtues, had no convictions against eavesdropping; and in the case of this particular caller, she felt it most necessary to serve her mistress in any way she could. She was keen enough to know that Miss Amelia would by no means be in favor of her advent in David Spafford's household, and she felt that her beloved mistress would have to bear some persecution on her account. She therefore resolved that, come what might, she would be on hand to protect her. So, soon after the good aunt was seated in state with Marcia in the large front bedroom where the cradle was established, and which had become the centre of the little household since Rose Spafford's birth, Miranda, soft-stepping, approached the door, and applied her ear to the generous crack. She could feel the subject of herself coming on, and her ready brain had devised a plan by which she thought she could relieve the pressure if it should become unduly heavy upon Marcia at any time.

So, just as Marcia lifted her face, white with control, and tried to take the angry flash out of her eyes and think what to reply to her tormentor, Miranda, without ceremony of approach, burst into the room, exclaiming, "Oh, Miss Amelia, 'scuse me fer interruptin', but *did* your nice old gray cat mebbe foller you down here, and *could* it a' ben her out on our front porch fightin' with Bob Sykes's yellow dog? 'Cause ef 'tis, sumpin' ought to be done right off, 'r he'll make hash out a' her. S'pose you come down an' look. I wouldn't like to make a mistake 'bout it."

Miss Amelia placed her hand upon her heart and looked helplessly at Marcia for an instant. "Oh, my dear, you don't suppose—" she began, in a trembling voice quite unlike her usual tones. Then she gathered up her shawl, which had slipped off her shoulders, and utterly unheeding that her bonnet was awry she hurried down the stairs after the sympathetic Miranda.

"Come right out here, softly," Miranda said, opening the front door cautiously. "Why, they must a' gone around the house!"

The old lady followed the girl out on the porch, and together they looked on both sides of the house, but there was no trace of dog or cat, any more than if, like the gingham dog and the calico cat of later days, they had "eaten each other up." "Where could they a' gone?" inquired Miranda, excitedly. "Mebbe I ought a' jus' called you and stayed here an' watched, but I was afraid to wake baby. You don't suppose that cat would a' run home, an' he after her? Is that them up the street? Don't you see a whirl o' dust in the road? Would you like me to go an' see? Cause I'm most afraid ef she's tried to run home; fer Bob Sykes hes trained thet dog to run races, an' he's a turrible fast runner, an' your cat is gettin' on in years. It might go hard with her." Miranda's sympathetic tone quite excited the old lady, whose old gray cat was very dear to her, being the last descendant of an ancient line of cats traditional in the family.

"No, Miranda, you just stay right here. Mrs. Spafford might need you after all this excitement. Tell her not to worry until I know the worst. I will go right home and see if anything has happened to Matthew. It really would be very distressing to me and my sister. If he has escaped from that dog he will need attention. Just tell Mrs. Spafford I will come down or send Hortense to-morrow as I promised." And the dignified old lady hurried off up the village street, for once unmindful of her dignity.

"Miranda!" called Marcia, when she had waited a reasonable time for the aunt's return and not even the girl presented herself.

Miranda appeared in a minute, with meek yet triumphant mien.

Marcia's eyes were laughing, but she tried to look grave.

"Miranda," she began, trying to suppress the merriment in her voice, "did you really see that cat out there?"

Miranda put on a dogged air and hesitated for a reply.

"Well, I heard a dog bark—" she began.

"Miranda, was that quite honest?" protested Marcia, who felt she ought to try to improve the moral standard of the girl thus under her charge and influence.

"I don't see anythin' wrong with that," asserted Miranda. "I didn't say a word that want true. I'm always careful 'bout that sence I see how much you think of such things. I asked her ef it might a' ben her cat, an' how do I know but 'twas? And it would be easy to a' ben Bob Sykes's dog, ef she *was* round, fer that dog never lets a cat come on this block. Anyway I heard a dog bark, and I thought it sounded like Bob's dog's voice. I'm pretty good on sounds."

"But you shouldn't frighten Aunt Amelia. She's an old lady, and it isn't good for old people to get frightened. You know she thinks a great deal of her cat."

"Well, it ain't good fer you to be badgered, and Mr. David told me to look after you, an' I'm doin' it the best way I know how. If I don't do it right I s'pose you'll send me back to Grandma's an' then who'll take care of that blessed baby!"

When Marcia told it all to David he laughed until the tears came.

"Good for Miranda!" he said. "She'll do, and Aunt Amelia'll never know what happened to poor old Matthew, who was probably sitting quietly by the hearth purring out his afternoon nap. Well, little girl, I'm glad you didn't have to answer Aunt Amelia's questions. Leave her to me. I'll shoulder all the blame and exonerate you. Don't worry."

"But, David," began Marcia, in her troubled tone, "Miranda ought not to tell things that are not exactly true. How can I teach her?"

"Well, Miranda's standards are not exactly right, and we must try little by little to raise them higher, but I'll miss my guess if she doesn't manage some way to protect you, even if she does have to tell the truth."

And thus it was that Miranda Griscom became a fixture in the household of David Spafford, and did about as she pleased with her master and mistress and the baby, because she usually pleased to do pretty well.

The years had gone by and little Rose Spafford had grown into a lovely, laughing, dimpled child with charming ways that reminded one of her mother, and Miranda was her devoted slave.

On the Sunday after Phoebe Deane's birthday, David and Marcia, and Rose, and Miranda were all in church together.

Little Rose, in dainty pantalettes and frock, with her rebellious curls brushed smoothly, her fat hands folded demurely in her lap, sat between her mother and Miranda, and waited for the sugared caraway seeds that she knew would be sure to be dropped occasionally into her nicely starched lap if she were good. David sat at the end of his pew, happy and devout, with Marcia, sweet and worshipful, beside him, and Miranda alert, one eye on her worship, the other on what might happen about her—or was it, quaint soul, but her way of watching for an opportunity to do good in her way?

Across the aisle the sweet face of Phoebe Deane attracted her attention. It was clouded with trouble. Miranda's keen eyes read that at once. Miranda had often noticed that about Phoebe Deane, and wondered, but there were so many other people that Miranda knew better to look after, that Phoebe Deane had heretofore not received her undivided attention.

But this particular morning Phoebe looked so pretty in her buff merino, which after much hesitation she had finally put on for church because her old church dress was so exceedingly shabby, that Miranda was all attention at once. Miranda, who had always been homely and red-haired and freckled, whose clothes had most of them been made over from Hannah Heath's cast-off wardrobe, yet loved beautiful things and beautiful people, and Phoebe, with her brown hair and deep, starry eyes, seemed like a lovely picture to her in the buff merino and with her face framed in its neat straw bonnet. The bonnet Miranda had seen for two or three summers past, but the frock was new, and a thing of beauty; therefore she studied its every detail and rejoiced that her position in the pew gave her a pretty good view of the young girl across the aisle, for something was wrong with the hinge of the door of Albert Deane's pew and it stood open wide.

As her eyes travelled over Phoebe's frock they came finally to the face, so grave and sweet and troubled, as if already life was too filled with perplexities to have much joy left in

it. Her keen gaze detected the droop to the pretty lips and
the dark lines under the eyes; and then she looked at the
sharp lines of Emmeline's sour face with its thin, pursed lips,
and decided that Emmeline was not a pleasant woman to live
with. Alma, preening herself in her Sunday clothes with her
self-conscious smirk, was not a pleasant child, either, and she
wondered if Phoebe could possibly take any pleasure in
putting on her little garments for her, and planning surprises,
and plays, the way she did for Rose. It seemed impossible.
Miranda, the homely, looked down tenderly at the little
Rose, and then gratefully toward David and Marcia at the
end of the pew, and pitied the beautiful Phoebe, wishing for
her the happiness that had come into her own barren life.

The service was about to commence when Judge Bristol,
with his daughter Janet, and her cousin Nathaniel Graham,
walked up the aisle to their pew, just in front of Albert
Deane's.

Now there had been much debate in the heart of Phoebe
Deane about coming to church that morning, for she could
not keep out of her mind the thought of the stranger who
had been so kind to her but a few days before, and it was impossible not to wonder if he would be there, and whether he
would see her, and speak to her. It was in order to crucify
this thought that she had half made up her mind not to wear
the buff merino to church, and then nature triumphed and
she put it on, realizing that her mother had made it for her to
wear, and she had a perfect right to wear it, though
Emmeline should disapprove. And Emmeline had disap-
proved in no uncertain tones. When she came downstairs
ready for church Emmeline lifted her disagreeable eyebrows
and exclaimed: "You're not going to wear that ridiculous rig to
church, I hope? I should think you'd be ashamed to be decked
out like that in the house of God! I'd sooner stay at home!"

And poor Phoebe would gladly have stayed at home if it
had not been that Hank would have been there, and that she
would have had to explain her reasons to Albert.

"I s'pose she wants people to know she's rich," piped in Alma, after a pause. This reference to her poor little pittance had been made almost hourly since Albert had told her of it, and it was growing unbearable to Phoebe. Altogether it was not with a very happy heart that she rode to church that morning, and she was half ashamed of herself for that undeniable wish to see the stranger once more. When she got out of the carryall at the church she would not look around nor even lift her eyes to see who was standing by the door. She had resolved not to think about him. If he came up the aisle, she would not know it, and her eyes should be otherwise occupied. No one should dare to say she was watching for him.

Nevertheless, as Janet and her cousin came up the aisle, Phoebe knew by the wild little beating of her heart that he was coming, and she commanded her eyes most strenuously that they should not lift from the psalm-book she had opened, albeit upside down. Yet, in spite of all resolves, when the occupants of the Bristol pew had entered it and were about to sit down, and while Nathaniel Graham stood so that his head and shoulders were just above the top of the high-back pew, those truant eyes fluttered up for one instant's glance, and in that instant were caught and held by the eyes of the young man in front in pleased recognition. 'Twas but a flash and Phoebe's eyes were back upon her book, and the young man was seated in the pew with only the top of his fine dark head showing, yet the pretty color flew into the cheek of the girl, and in the eyes of the young man there was a light of satisfaction that lasted all through the service. The glance had been too brief for any actual act of recognition like a bow or a smile, and neither would it have been in place, for the whole audience could have seen them as he was faced about; moreover the service had begun. It had merely been the knowledge that each had of the other's presence in a warm glow like sunshine through the being. Not a soul had witnessed the glance, save the keen-

eyed Miranda, and instantly she recognized a certain something which put her on the watch. She at once pricked up
the ears of her consciousness, and if she had been living to-
day would have said to herself, "There's 'somethin' doing'
there." So Miranda, whether to her shame or her praise, sat
through the whole long service, studied the faces of those
two, and wove a pretty romance for herself out of the gold-
en fabric of a glance.

8

WHEN the service was ended Phoebe took good care of her eyes that they should not look toward the stranger. Nathaniel Graham was kept busy for the first few moments shaking hands with old friends, and talking with the minister, who came down from the pulpit on purpose to greet him, and when he turned, as he did on the first opportunity, the pew behind him was empty, and the eyes that had met his when he came in were nowhere to be seen. He looked anxiously over the receding audience towards the open door, and caught the glimmer of the buff merino. Hastily excusing himself to Janet on the plea that he wished to speak to someone and would join her later, Nathaniel made his way down the aisle, disappointing some good old ladies who had been friends of his mother, and who were lying in wait for him at various pew doors.

Miranda, who had been awaiting the pleasure of David and Marcia, saw it all, and her eager eyes watched to see if he would catch Phoebe. The way being open just then, she pressed out into the aisle, and, for once leaving Rose to follow with her mother, hurried to the door.

Nathaniel did not overtake Phoebe until she had gone

down the church steps, and was on the path in front of the church-yard that led to the shed where many of the conveyances were tied. He stepped up beside her, taking off his hat with a cheery, "Good morning," and Phoebe's pink cheeks and smiling eyes welcomed him happily.

"I wanted to be quite sure you were all right after your adventure the other day," he said, looking down into the lovely face with real pleasure; and then, before she could even answer, Hiram Green stepped up airily as if he belonged, and looked at Nathaniel questioningly as though he were intruding, saying, "Well, here you are, Phoebe; I lost track of you at the church door. We better step along. The carryall is waitin'."

Nathaniel looked up annoyed, then puzzled, recognized Hiram with astonishment, and said, "I beg your pardon, I did not know I was keeping you from your friends," to Phoebe, and, lifting his hat with a courteous "Good morning, Mr. Green," to Hiram, stepped back among the little throng coming out of the church door.

Now Miranda had been close behind, for she was determined to read every chapter of her romance that appeared in sight. She saw the whole maneuver on Hiram Green's part, and the color that flamed angrily into Phoebe's cheek when she recognized Hiram's interference. She also saw the dismay that showed in the girl's face as Nathaniel left her and Hiram Green made as if to walk beside her. Phoebe looked wildly about. There seemed no escape from him as a companion without making a deliberate scene, yet her whole soul revolted at having Nathaniel Graham see her walk off with Hiram.

Quick as a flash Miranda caught the meaning of Phoebe's look, and flew to her assistance.

She called quite clearly, "Phoebe! Phoebe Deane! Wait a minute, I want to tell you something!" She had raised her voice on purpose, for she stood directly behind Nathaniel, and, as she had hoped, he turned to see Phoebe respond. She noted the sudden light in his eyes as he saw that the girl to whom he had just been talking responded to the name, but she did not know that it was a light of satisfaction because he had found out her name without asking anyone. He stood a moment and looked after them. He saw quite plainly that Phoebe dismissed the sulky Hiram with a word and went off with Miranda. He saw that Hiram did not even raise his hat on leaving Phoebe, but slouched off angrily without a word.

"Say, Phoebe Deane," said Miranda, familiarly, "my Mrs. Spafford,"—this was Miranda's common way of speaking of Marcia in the possessive—"she's ben talkin' a long time 'bout you, and wishin' you'd come to see her, an' she's ben layin' out to ask you to tea, but things hes prevented. So, could you come Tuesday? You better come early and stay all the afternoon, so you can play with Rose. She's the sweetest thing!"

"Oh, I'd love to come," said Phoebe, her face aglow with pleasure. "I've always admired Mrs. Spafford so much, and little Rose is beautiful, just like a rose. Yes, tell her I will come."

Just then came the strident voice of Emmeline.

"Phoebe! Phoebe Deane! Was you intendin' to go home with us, or had you calculated to ride with Hiram Green? If you're comin' with us we can't wait all day."

With scarlet cheeks, angry heart, and trembling limbs Phoebe bade Miranda a frightened good-by and climbed into the carriage, not daring to look behind her to see who had heard the hateful words of her sister-in-law. Oh, had the stranger heard them? How dreadful if he had! How contemptible, how unforgivable in Emmeline! How could she endure this persecution any longer? She did not even dare lift her eyes as they drove by the church, but sat with drooping lashes and burning cheeks, so missing the glance of the young man Nathaniel as he stood on the sidewalk with his cousin, waiting for another opportunity to lift his hat. Perhaps it was as well, for she would have been most unmercifully teased and cross-questioned if Emmeline and Alma had seen him speak to her.

Miranda watched the Deanes drive away, and turned with a vindictive look of triumph to stare at Hiram Green getting into his chaise alone. Then she began to reflect upon what she had done.

About four o'clock that afternoon, the dinner dishes being well out of the way, and the Sunday quiet resting upon the house, Miranda presented herself before Marcia with the most guilty look upon her face that Marcia had ever seen her wear.

"Well, I've up an' done it now, Mrs. Marcia, an' no mistake. I expect I'll have to leave you, an' the thought of it jes' breaks my heart."

"Why, Miranda!" said Marcia, sitting up very suddenly from the couch where she had been reading Bible stories to Rose. "You're not—you're surely not going to get married!"

"Not by a jugful I ain't. Do you s'pose I'd hev enny man that would take up with freckles an' a turn-up nose in a wife? I've gone and done sumpin' you'll think is a heap worse'n gittin' married. But I didn't tell no lie. I was keerful enough 'bout that. I only told her you'd been talkin' 'long back 'bout askin' her, an' you hed all right 'nough, only I oughtn't to a ast her, an' set the day an' all 'thout you knowin'. I knowed it at the time well 'nough, but I hed to do it, 'cause the circumstances wuz sech. You see that squint-eyed Hiram Green was makin' it out that she was somewhat great to him, a paradin' down the walk there from the church, an' a driven' off that nice city cousin of Janet Bristol's with his nice, genteel manners, an' his tippin's of his hat, an' her a lookin' like she'd drop from shame, so I called her to wait, an' I runs up an' talks to her, an' course then she tells Hiram Green he needn't to trouble to wait fer her, an' we goes off together in full sight of all. My, I was glad I beat that skin-flint of a Hiram Green, but I was that excited I jes' couldn't think of 'nother thing to do 'cept to invite her."

"Who in the world are you talking about, Miranda? And what terrible thing have you done?"

Marcia's laughing eyes reassured Miranda and she went on with her story.

"Why that pretty little Phoebe Deane," she explained. "I've invited her to tea Tuesday night. I thought that would suit you better than any other time. Monday night things ain't straight from wash-day yet, and I didn't want to put it off too long, an' I can make everything myself. But if you don't like it I'll go an' tell her the hull truth on't, only she did look so mortal pleased I hate to spoil her fun."

By degrees Marcia drew the whole story from Miranda, even to a voluble description of the buff merino, and its owner's drooping expression.

"Well, I don't see why you thought I would be displeased," said Marcia. "It is only right you should invite company once in a while. I am glad you invited her, and as you do most of the work, and know our plans pretty well, you knew it would likely be convenient. I am glad you invited her."

"But I didn't invite her," said Miranda, "leastways she doesn't know I did. She thinks you done it yourself, and she sent you a whole lot of thanks, and said she 'dmired you turrible. And I didn't tell a thing but the truth either," Miranda added, doggedly.

"You blessed old Miranda. You always have a way of wiggling out. But you do manage to make things go your way in spite of truth or anything else. And it was truth after all, for I did want her, and would have asked her myself if I had known. You see you were just my messenger that time, acting in my place." And she gave Miranda one of the smiles that had so endeared her to the heart of the lonely girl. Then Miranda went back to her kitchen comforted.

Thus it came about that the buff merino had the prospect of another tea-party, and the thought of it made Phoebe forget the annoyances of her home all through the dull Sabbath

afternoon, when she could not get away from the family because Emmeline had ordered her to "stay downstairs and
mind the baby, and not prance off to her room like a royal
lady," and through the trials of Monday with its heavy work,
which did not even cease with the washing of the tea things,
but continued in the form of a great basket of mending
which Emmeline announced at the supper table were "all to
be finished and put away that evening." Emmeline seemed
to have made up her mind to be as disagreeable as possible.
Phoebe sat beside the candle and sewed with weary fingers,
and longed to be away from them all where she might think
over quietly the pleasant things that had come into her life of
late. Hiram Green came in, too, and seemed to have come
with a purpose, for he was hardly seated in his usual chair
with its back tilted against the wall, and the fore-legs tipped
up, when he began with:

"Say, Albert, did you see that nincompoop of a nephew
of Judge Bristol in the church? Does beat all how he takes on
airs jest because he's been off to college. Gosh! I ken remember him goin' fishin' in his bare feet, and here he was
bowin' round among the ladies like he'd always been a fine
gentleman and never done a stroke of work in his life. His
hands are ez white and soft ez a woman's. He strikes me very
ladylike, indeed, he does. Smirkin' round and takin' off his
hat ez if he'd nothin' better to do. Fine feathers don't make
fine birds, I say. I don't believe he could cut a swath o' hay
now to save his precious little life. He made me sick with his
airs. Seems like Miss Janet better look after him ef she expects to marry him, er he'll lose his head to every girl he
meets."

Something uncontrollable seemed to have stolen the
blood out of Phoebe's heart for a moment, and all her
strength was slipping away from her. Then a mighty anger
rolled through her being, and surged to her very finger-tips,
yet she held those fingers steadily, as her needle pierced back
and forth through the stocking she was darning with

unnecessary care. She knew perfectly well that these remarks were entirely for her benefit and she resolved not to let Hiram see that she understood or cared.

"Is he going to marry his cousin Janet?" asked Albert, interestedly. "I never heard that."

"You didn't? Well, where've you ben, all these years? It's ben common talk sence they was little tads. Their mothers 'lowed that was the way it was to be, and they was sent away to separate schools on that account; I s'pose they was afraid they'd take a dislike to each other ef they saw each other constant. 'Pon my word I think Janet could look higher, an' ef I was her I wouldn't be held by no promise of no dead mothers. But they do say she worships the very ground he walks on, an' she'll hold him to it all right enough, so it's no sort o' use fer any other girls to go anglin' after him."

"I heard he was real bright," said Albert, genially. "They say he's taken honors, a good many of 'em. He was president of the Philomathean Society in Union College, you know, and that's a great honor."

Albert read a good deal, and knew more about the world's affairs than Hiram.

"Oh, bah! That's child's play!" sneered Hiram. "Who couldn't be president of a literary society? It don't take much spunk to preside. I take it I ran the town meetin' last year 'bout's well 's ef I'd ben a college president. My opinion is Nate Graham would 'v 'mounted to more ef he'd stayed t' home an' learned farmin', er studied law with his uncle an' worked fer his board. A feller thet's all give over to lyin' around makin' nuthin' of himself don't amount to a row o' pins."

"But they say Dr. Nott thinks he's got brains," persisted Albert. "I'm sure I'd like to see him come out on top. I heard he was studying law in New York now. He was always a pleasant-spoken boy when he was here."

"What's pleasant speakin'?" growled Hiram. "It can't sell a load o' wheat." His unsold wheat was bitterly in his thoughts.

"Well, I don't know 'bout that, Hiram." Albert felt pleasantly argumentative. "I don't know but if I was going to buy wheat I'd a little sooner buy off the man that was pleasant spoken than the man that wasn't."

Hiram sat glumly and pondered this saying for a few minutes, and Phoebe took advantage of the pause in conversation to lay down her work-basket, determinedly saying to Emmeline:

"I'll finish these stockings to-morrow, Emmeline. I feel tired and I'm going upstairs."

It was the first time that Phoebe had ever dared to take a stand against Emmeline's orders. Emmeline was too astonished to speak for a minute, but just as Phoebe reached the door she said:

"Well, really! Tired! I was down half an hour before you this mornin', and I'm not tired to speak of, but I suppose ef I was I'd have to keep right on. And who's to do your work to-morrow mornin' while you do this, I'd like to know?"

But Phoebe had escaped out of hearing, and Emmeline relapsed into vexed silence. Hiram, however, narrowed his cruel little eyes, and thought he understood why she had gone.

9

PHOEBE had pondered much on how she should announce her intended absence that afternoon, almost deciding at one time to slip away without saying a word, but her conscientious little heart would not allow that. So while the family were at breakfast she said to Emmeline:

"I wish you'd tell me what work you want done besides the rest of the ironing. I'm invited out to tea this afternoon, and I want to get everything done this morning."

"Where to?" exploded Alma, her curiosity getting the better of her superiority to her aunt for once.

"Indeed!" said Emmeline, disdainfully. "Invited out to tea! What airs we are takin' on with our money! Pretty soon you won't have any time to give at home at all. If I was you I'd go and board somewhere, you have so many social engagements. I'm sure I don't feel like askin' a young lady like you to soil her hands washin' my dishes. I'll wash 'em myself after this. Alma, you go get your apern on and help ma this mornin'. Aunt Phoebe hasn't got time. She'll have to take all the mornin' to curl her hair."

"Now, Emmeline!" said Albert, gently reproachful, "don't tease the child. It's real nice for her to get invited out.

She don't get much chance, that's sure."

"Oh, no, two tea-parties inside of a week's nothin'. I've heard of New York ladies goin' out as often as every other day," said Emmeline, sarcastically.

Albert never could quite understand his wife's sarcasm, so he turned to Phoebe and voiced the question that the rest were just bursting with curiosity to have answered.

"Who invited you, Phoebe?"

"Mrs. Spafford," said Phoebe, trying not to show how near she was to crying over Emmeline's hateful speeches.

"Well, now, that's real nice," said Albert, in genuine earnest. "There isn't a finer man in town than David Spafford. His paper's the best edited in the whole state of New York, and he's got a fine little wife. I don't believe she's many days older than you are, Phoebe, either. She looked real young when he brought her here, and she hasn't grown a day older that I can see."

"Good reason why," sniffed Emmeline; "she's nothin' to do but lie around and be waited on. I'm sure Phoebe's welcome to such friends if they suit her; fer my part I'd ruther go to see good self-respectin' women that did a woman's work in the world, and not let their husbands make babies of them, and go ridin' round in a carriage forever lookin' like a June mornin'. I call it *lazy,* I do. It's nothin' more'n or less— and she keepin' that poor good-fer-nothin' Miranda Griscom slavin' from mornin' to night fer her. Besides, she hasn't got very good manners not to invite your wife, too, Albert Deane, but I suppose you never thought o' that. I shouldn't think Phoebe would care to accept an invitation that was an insult to her relations, even if they wasn't just blood relations—they're all she's got, that's sure."

"Say, look here, Emmeline. Your speech don't hang together. You just said you didn't care to make friends of Mrs. Spafford, and now you're fussing because she didn't invite you, too. It looks like a case of sour grapes. Eh, Phoebe?"

Hank caught the joke and laughed uproariously, though

Phoebe looked grave, knowing how bitter it would be to Emmeline to be laughed at. Two red spots flamed out on the wife's cheeks, and her eyes snapped.

"Seems to me things has gone pretty far, Albert Deane," she said in a high, excited voice, "when you—*YOU*—can insult your wife in public, and then *LAUGH!* I shan't forget this of you, Albert Deane!" and with her head well up she shoved her chair back from the table and left the room, closing the door with loud decision behind her.

Albert's merry laugh came to an abrupt end. He looked after his wife with startled surprise. Never in all their one-sidedly-harmonious wedded life had Emmeline taken offence like that in the presence of others. He looked helplessly, inquiringly, from one to another.

"Well, now!" he began, aimlessly. "You don't suppose she thought I meant that, do you?"

" 'Course!" said Alma, knowingly. "You've made her dreadful mad, Pa. My! But you're goin' to get it!"

"Looks mighty like it," snickered Hank.

Albert continued to look at Phoebe for a reply.

"I'm afraid she thought you were in earnest, Albert. You better go and explain," said Phoebe, commiseratingly.

"You better not go fer a while, Pa," called out Johnny, sympathetically. "Wait till she gets over it a little. Go hide in the barn. That's the way I do!"

But Albert was going heavily up the stairs after his offended wife and did not hear his young hopeful's voice. Albert was tender-hearted and could not bear to hurt any one's feelings. Besides, it never was pleasant to have Emmeline angry. He wished if possible to explain away the offence before it struck in too deep for healing and had to be lived down.

This state of things was rather more helpful to Phoebe than otherwise. Hank took himself off, finding a certain embarrassment in Phoebe's dignified silence. The children slipped away, glad to get rid of any little duties usually required by their mother. Phoebe went at her work unhindered and it vanished before her while her thoughts took happy flight away from the unhappy home to the afternoon that was before her. Upstairs the conference was long and uncertain. Phoebe could hear the low rumbling of Albert's conciliatory tones, and the angry rasp of Emmeline's tearful charges. Albert came downstairs looking sad and tired about an hour before dinner-time, and hurried out to the barn to his neglected duties. He paused in the kitchen to say to Phoebe, apologetically:

"You mustn't mind what Emmeline says, child. Her bark's a great deal worse than her bite always. And after all, she's had it pretty hard with all the children and staying in so much. I'm sure she appreciates what you do. I'm sure she does, but it isn't her way to say much about it. You just go out to tea and have a good time and don't think any more about this. It'll blow over, you know. Most things do."

Phoebe tried to smile, and felt a throb of gratitude toward the brother who was not really her brother at all.

"You're a good girl, Phoebe," he went on, patting her cheek. "You're like your mother. She was little, and pretty, and liked things nice, and had a quiet voice. I sometimes think maybe it isn't as pleasant here for you as it might be. You're made of different kind of stuff, that thinks and feels in a different way. Your mother was so. I've often wondered whether father understood her. Men don't understand women very well, I guess. Now, I don't really always understand Emmeline, and I guess it's pretty hard for her. Father was some rough and blunt, and maybe that was hard for your mother at times. I remember she used to look sad, though I never saw her much, come to think about it. I was off working for myself when they were married, you know. Say, Phoebe, you didn't for a minute think I meant what I said about sour grapes and Emmeline did you? I told her you didn't, but I promised her I'd make sure about it. I knew you didn't. Well, I must go out and see if Hank's done everything."

He went out drawing a long breath as if he had accomplished an unpleasant task, and left Phoebe wondering about her own mother, and trying to get a little glimpse into her possible sorrows and joys through the words that Albert had spoken. Somehow that sentence in her birthday letter came back to her: "Unless you can marry a man to whom you can look up and honor next to God it is better not to marry at all, believe your mother, child. I say it lovingly, for I have seen much sorrow and would protect you."

Had her father been hard to live with? Phoebe put the thought from her and was half glad she could not answer it. Her own life was enough of a problem without going back and sorrowing for her mother's. But it made her heart throb with a sense of a fuller understanding of her mother's life and warnings.

Emmeline did not come downstairs until dinner time, and her manner was freezing. Phoebe was glad that the work was all done carefully, even to the scrubbing of the back steps, and that the dinner was more than usually inviting. But Emmeline seemed not to see anything, and her manner remained as severe as when she first entered the kitchen. She poured the coffee, and drank a cup of it herself, and ate a bit of bread, but would not touch anything else on the table. She waited on the children with ostentatious care, but would not respond to the solicitations of her anxious husband, who urged this and that dainty upon her. Hank even suggested that the hot biscuits were nicer than usual. But that remark had to be lived down by Hank, for Emmeline usually made the biscuits, and Phoebe had made these. She did not condescend to even look at him in response.

Phoebe was glad when the last bit of pumpkin pie and cheese had disappeared and she could rise from her chair and go about the after-dinner work. Glad, too, that Emmeline went away again and left her to herself, for so she could more quickly finish up.

She was just hanging up her wiping towels when

Emmeline came downstairs with the look of a martyr on her face, and the quilting frames in her hand. Over her shoulder was thrown her latest achievement in patchwork, a brilliant combination of reds and yellows and white known as the "rising sun" pattern. It was a large quilt, and would be quite a job to put on the frames. It was a herculean task for one person without an assistant.

Phoebe stopped with an exclamation of dismay.

"You're not going to put that on the frames to-day, Emmeline? I thought you were saving that for next month!"

Emmeline's grim mouth remained shut for several seconds. At last she snapped out: "I don't know that it makes any difference what you thought. This is a free country and I've surely a right to do what I please in my own house."

"But, Emmeline, I can't help you this afternoon!"

"I don't know that I've asked you!"

"But you can't do it alone!"

"Indeed! What makes you think I can't! Go right along to your tea-party and take your ease. I was brought up to work, thank fortune, and a few burdens more or less can't make much difference. I'm not a lady of leisure and means like you."

Phoebe stood a minute watching Emmeline's stubby, determined fingers as they fitted a wooden peg into its socket like a period to the conversation. It seemed dreadful to go away and leave Emmeline to put up that quilt alone, but what was she to do? There seemed to be no law in the universe that would compel her to give up her first invitation out to tea in order that Emmeline might finish the quilt, this particular week. It was plain that she had brought it down on purpose to hold her at home. Indignation boiled within her. If she had slipped stealthily away this would not have happened, but she had done her duty in telling Emmeline, and she felt perfectly justified in going. It wasn't as if she had invited herself. It would not be polite, now she had accepted the invitation, not to go. So, with sudden determination

Phoebe left the kitchen and went up to dress.

With swift fingers she fastened the buff merino, put her hair in order, and tied on her locket, but nowhere was the little brown velvet bow to be found that belonged to her hair. She had not missed it before, for on Sunday she had worn her bonnet, and had dressed in a hurry. In perplexity she looked over her neat boxes of scant finery, but could not find it. She had to hurry away without it. She went out the other door, for she could not bear the sight of Emmeline putting up that sunrise bedquilt all alone. The thought of it seemed to cloud the sun and spoil the anticipation of her precious afternoon.

Once out in the crisp autumn air she drew a long breath of relief. It was so good to get away from the gloomy atmosphere that had been cramping her life for so many years. In a lonely place in the road between farm-houses she uttered a soft little scream under her breath. She felt as if she *must* do something to let out the agony of wrath and longing and hurt and indignity that were trying to burst her soul. Then she walked on to the town with demure dignity, and the people in the passing carryalls and farm wagons never suspected that she was aught but a happy maiden with thoughts busy with the joys of life.

The autumn days were lingering in sunny deep-blue haze, though the reds were changing into brown, and in the fields were gathering huddled groups of cornshocks like old crones, waving skeleton arms in the breeze, and whispering weird gossip. A rusty-throated cricket in the thicket by the way piped out his monotonous dirge to the summer now deceased. A flight of birds sprang into sight across the sky, calling and chattering to one another of a warmer climate. An old red cow stood in her well-grazed meadow, snuffed the short grass, and, looking at Phoebe as she passed, bawled a gentle protest at the decline of fresh vegetables. Everything spoke of autumn and the winter that was to come. But Phoebe, every step she took from home, grew lighter and lighter hearted, and could only think of the happy time she was to have.

It was not that she was thinking of the stranger, for there was no possibility of meeting him. The Bristol place, a fine old Colonial house behind a tall white fence and high privet hedge with a glimpse of a wonderful garden set off with dark borders of box through the imposing gateway, was over near the Presbyterian church. It was not near the Spaffords' house. She felt the freer and happier because there was no question of him to trouble her careful conscience.

Miranda had gone to the window that looked up the road towards the Deanes' at least twenty times since the dinner dishes were washed. She was more nervous over the success of this her first tea-party than over anything she had ever done. She was beginning to be afraid that her guest would not arrive.

Everything was in train for supper. There was to be stewed chicken, with "riz biscuits" and honey, raspberry preserves, spiced peaches, fruitcake and caraway-seed cookies with delectable sugary tops. The tea was to be served in the very thinnest of the blue china cups. It was with difficulty that Marcia had suppressed a multitude of varieties of pickles and jellies and preserves and cakes, for Miranda could not understand why it wasn't "skimpin'" to have so few dishes upon the table.

"Gran'ma was never half satisfied ef you could see the tablecloth much between dishes," she was wont to say, dubiously. But Marcia tried patiently to explain that it was not refined to load the table with too many varieties, and Miranda, half convinced, gave it up, thinking Marcia sweet, but "inexperienced."

Miranda, fidgeting from window to door and back again to the kitchen, came at last to the library where sat Marcia with her work, watching a frolic between Rose and her kitten outside the window.

"Say, Mrs. Marcia," she began, ingratiatingly, "you'll

find out what troubles that poor little thing, and see ef you can't help her, won't you? She's your size an' kind, more'n she is mine, an' you ought to be able to give her some help. You needn't think you've got to tell out to me every thing you find out. I shan't ask. I can find out enough fer my own use when I'm needed, but I think she needs you this time. When there's any use fer me I seem always to kind o' feel it in the air."

"Bless your heart, Miranda, I don't believe you care much for any one unless they need helping!" exclaimed Marcia, laughing. "What makes you so sure Phoebe Deane needs helping?"

"Oh, I know," said Miranda, mysteriously, "an' so will you when you look at her real hard. There she comes now. Don't you go an' tell I said nothing 'bout her. You jes' make her tell you. She's that sweet an' so are you that you two can't help pourin' out your perfume to each other like two flowers."

"But trouble isn't perfume, Miranda."

"H'm! Flowers smells all the sweeter when you crush 'em a little, don't they? There, you set right still where you be. I'll go to the door. Don't you stir. I want her to see you lookin' that way with the sun across the top o' your pretty hair. She'll like it, I know she will."

Marcia sat quite still as she was bidden with the madonna smile upon her lips that David loved so well, smiling over Miranda's strange fancies, yet never thinking of herself as a picture against the window panes. In a moment more Phoebe Deane stood in the doorway, with Miranda beside her, looking from one to another of the two sweet girl-faces in deep admiration, and noting with delight that Phoebe fully appreciated the loveliness of her "Mrs. Marcia."

THE afternoon was one of unalloyed bliss to Phoebe. She laid aside her troubles with her bonnet and mantilla, and basked in the sunlight of Marcia's smile. Here was something she had never known, the friendship of another girl not much older than herself; for Marcia, though she had grown in heart and intellect during her five years of beautiful companionship with David Spafford, had not lost the years she had skipped by her early marriage, but kept their memory fresh in her heart. Perhaps it was the girl in her that had attracted her to Phoebe Deane.

They fell into happy converse at once, Phoebe begging for a seam to sew on the frock of pale blue merino that Marcia was making for Rose, all exquisitely braided with white silk braid in a rosebud pattern.

They talked about their mothers, these two who had known so little of real mothering; and Marcia, because she had felt it herself, understood the wistfulness in Phoebe's tone when she spoke of her loneliness and her longing for her mother. Then Phoebe, with a half-apologetic flush, told of her mother's birthday letter and the buff merino, and Marcia smoothed down the soft folds of the skirt reverently, half wistfully, and told Phoebe it was beautiful, just like a present and a letter from heaven. Then she kissed her gently and made her come out where little Rose was playing. There they frolicked until the child was Phoebe's devoted slave, and then they all went back to the big stately parlor, where Miranda had a great fire of logs blazing, and there in a deep easy chair Phoebe was ensconsed with Rose cuddled in her lap playing with her locket, and having it tied at will about her own dimpled neck.

While this was going on Marcia played exquisite music on her pianoforte, which to the ear of the girl, who had seldom heard any music in her life save the singing in church or singing-school, seemed entrancing. She almost forgot the charming child in her lap, forgot to look about on the beautiful room so full of interesting things, forgot even to think, as she listened, and her very soul responded to the music, which seemed to be calling a great comfort across the immense distances that separated her from things she loved.

Then suddenly the music ceased and Marcia sprang up, saying in a glad voice, "Oh, there is David!" and went to the door to let him in.

Phoebe exclaimed in dismay that it was so late, and the beautiful afternoon was at an end, but she forgot her disappointment in wonder over Marcia's joy at her husband's coming. It brought back to her the subject that had been uppermost in her thoughts ever since the night when Hiram Green had dared to follow her to the orchard. Somehow she had grown up with very little halo about the institution of marriage. It had seemed to her a kind of necessary arrangement, but never anything that gave great joy. The married people whom she knew did not seem greatly to rejoice in one another's presence. Indeed, they often seemed to be a hindrance each to the other. She had never cherished many bright dreams of any such state for herself, as most girls do. Life had been too dully tinted since her little girlhood for her to indulge fancies. Therefore it was a revelation to her to

see how much these two rare souls cared for one another. It
was not that they displayed their affection by any act of en-
dearment, but she saw it in the glance of each, in a sudden
lighting of the eye, the involuntary cadence of the voice, the
evident pleasure of yielding each to the other, aye, rather
preferring one another; the constant presence of joy as a
guest in that house, because of the presence of the other.
One could never feel that way about Hiram Green—no one
could,—it would be impossible! Wait! Had not that been
the very thing possessed by his poor crushed little wife? But
how could she feel it when it was not returned? She began to
think over the married households she knew, but then she
knew so few of them intimately. There was Granny McVane.
Did the old 'Squire feel so about her? And did she spring to
meet him at the door after all these years of life with its
hardness? There was something about the sweet meek face
in its ruffled cap that made Phoebe think it possible. And
there was Albert. Of course Emmeline did not feel so, for
Emmeline was not that kind of a woman, but might not a
different woman have felt that for Albert? He was kind and
gentle to women. Too slow and easy to gain real respect,
yet—yes, she felt that it might be possible for some women
to feel real joy in his presence. There lurked a possibility
that he felt so toward Emmeline, in some degree; but Hiram
Green, with his chair tilted back against the wall, and his hat
drawn down over his narrow eyes, above his cruel mouth!
Never! He was utterly incapable of so beautiful a feeling. If
he only might in some way pass out of her horizon forever it
would be a great relief.

David Spafford when he entered the parlor not only filled
it with pleasure for his wife and little girl, but he brought an
added cheer for the guest as well, and Phoebe found herself
talking with this man of literature and politics and science as
easily as if she had known him well all her life. Afterward
she wondered at herself for it. Somehow he took it for
granted that she knew as much as he did, and made her feel

at her ease at once. He had ready a bright story from the newspaper office that exactly fitted someone's remark, and a joke for his little one. He asked after Albert Deane as though he were an old friend, and seemed to know more about him than Phoebe dreamed. "He has a good head," he added in response to Phoebe's timid answer about the farm and some improvements that Albert had introduced. "I had a long talk with him the other day and enjoyed it." Somehow that little remark made Phoebe more at home. She knew Albert's short-comings keenly herself, and she was not deeply attached to him, yet he was all she had, and he had been kind to her. He stood for relatives to her before the world, and it was nice to not have him at a discount, even though there were some men brighter, and Phoebe knew it.

Miranda had just called to supper, and they had reached the table, and the little preliminary flutter of getting settled in the right places, when the knocker sounded through the hall.

Phoebe looked up, startled! Living as she did in the country a guest who was not intimate enough to walk in without knocking was rare, and an occasion for the knocker to sound was wont to bring forth startled exclamations in the Deane family. But Marcia gave the sign to be seated, and Miranda hastened to the door.

"It's just one of the boys from the office, I think, Marcia," said David Spafford. "I told him to bring up the mail if anything important came. The coach wasn't in when I left."

But a man's voice was heard conversing with Miranda.

"I won't keep him but a minute! I'm sorry to disturb him." A moment more and Miranda appeared with a guileless face.

"A man to see you, Mr. Spafford. I think it's that nevview of Jedge Bristol's. Shall I tell him you're eatin' supper?"

"What! Nathaniel Graham? No indeed, Miranda; just put on another plate and bring him right in. Come in, Nathaniel, and take tea with us while you tell your errand. You're just the one we need to complete our company."

Miranda, innocent and cheerful, hurried away to obey orders, while David helped the willing guest off with his overcoat, and brought him out to the table. She felt there was no need to say anything of a little conversation she had held with Judge Bristol's "nevview" about half past four that afternoon. It was while Marcia was playing the piano-forte in the parlor. Miranda had gone into the garden to pick a bunch of parsley for her chicken gravy, and as was her wont, to keep a good watch upon all outlying teritory. She had sauntered up to the fence for a glance about to see if there was anything of interest happening, and Nathaniel Graham had happened. She had watched him coming, wistfully. Yet she dared not add another guest to her tea-party, though the very one she would have chosen had wandered her way.

He had tipped his hat to her and smiled. Miranda liked to have hats tipped to her even though she was freckled and red-haired. This young man had been in the highest grade of village school when she entered the lowest class, yet he remembered her enough to bow, freckled though she was, and working for her living. Her heart had swelled up with pride in him, and she decided he would do for the part she wished him to play in life.

"Ah, Miss Miranda," he had paused when almost past, and stepped back a pace, "do you happen to know if Mr. Spafford will be at home this evening? I want to see him very much for a few minutes."

Now, though Miranda had dared not invite another guest, she saw no reason why she should not put him in the way of an invitation, so inclining her head thoughtfully on one side and squinting her eyes introspectively, as if she were the keeper of David Spafford's engagements, she had said, thoughtfully: "Let me see! Yes, I *think* he's at home to-night. Thur's one night this week I heerd him say he was goin' out, but I'm *pretty* sure it ain't this night. But I'll tell you what you better do ef you're real anxious to see him, you better jest stop 'long about six o'clock. He's always home then, 'thout fail, 'n' he'll tell you ef he ain't goin' to be in."

The young man's face had lighted gratefully.

"Thank you," he had said, quite as if he were speaking to a lady Miranda thought, "that will suit me very well. I need not keep him long and he can tell me if he will be in later in the evening. I shall be passing here about that time."

Then Miranda had hustled in with satisfaction to see if her biscuits were beginning to brown. If this plan worked well there was nothing further to be desired.

She had spent the remainder of the afternoon in stealthily vibrating between the kitchen and the parlor door, where, unseen, she could inspect the conversation from time to time and keep advised as to any possible developments. She had set out to see if Phoebe Deane needed any help, and she meant to leave no stone unturned to get at the facts.

So it all happened just as Miranda would have planned. Things were happening her way these days, mostly, she told herself with a chuckle and a triumphant glance over at the lights in her grandmother's kitchen, as she went to get another sprigged plate for Nathaniel Graham. And when Marcia was not looking she slid another plate of quivering jelly, amber tinted to match Phoebe's frock, in between Phoebe's and Nathaniel's plates.

Meantime Phoebe's heart was in a great flutter over the introduction to her knight of the forest. The pretty color came into her cheeks, and her eyes shone like stars in the candle light as David said: "Nathaniel, let me make you acquainted with our friend Miss Phoebe Deane. I think she is a newcomer since you left us. Miss Deane, this is our friend Mr. Graham."

And then she found herself murmuring acknowledgment as the young man took her hand and bowed low over it, saying: "Thank you, David, but I am not so far behind the times as you think. I have met Miss Deane before."

That frightened her quite, so that she hardly could manage to seat herself with her chair properly drawn up to the table, and she fell to wondering if they had noticed how her cheeks burned. Ah! If they had they were keeping it to themselves, especially Miranda, who was dishing up the chicken. Wily Miranda! She had called them to supper without dishing it up, making due allowance for the digression of another guest which she had planned.

The meal moved along quite smoothly, the conversation flowing easily around until Phoebe had regained her balance and could take her small shy part in it. She found pleasure in listening to the talk of David and Nathaniel, so different from that of Albert and Hiram.

It was all about the great outside world. Politics, and the possibilities of war; money and banks and failures, and the probabilities of the future; the coming election and the part it would have in the finance of the world; the trouble with the Indians; the rumblings of trouble about slavery; the annexation of Texas; the extension of the steam railway, and its hindrances by the present state of finance.

It was all new and interesting to Phoebe, to whom had come but a stray word now and again of all these wonderful happenings. Who, for instance, was this "Santa Anna" whose name was spoken of so familiarly? Neither a saint nor a woman apparently. And what had he or she to do with affairs so grave?

And who was this brave Indian Chief, Osceola, languishing in prison because he and his people could not bear to give up the home of their fathers? Why had she never heard of it all before? O, life was very hard for everybody. She had never thought of the Indians before as anything but terrible, bloodthirsty savages, and lo! they had feelings and loves and homes like others. Her cheeks glowed and her eyes were alight with feeling, and when young Nathaniel turned to her now and again he thought how wondrously beautiful she was, and marvelled that he had not heard her praises rung from every mouth so soon as he had reached town. He had been very little at home during his college life and years of law study.

Then the conversation came nearer home, and David and Nathaniel talked of their college days. Nathaniel spoke a great deal of Eliphalet Nott, the honored president of his college, and told many a little anecdote of his wisdom and wit.

"This chicken reminds me," he began, laughingly, as he held up a delicate wishbone toward Phoebe, "of a story that is told of Dr. Nott. It seems a number of students had planned a raid upon his chicken-house. Dr. Nott's family consists of himself and wife and his daughter Miss Sally. Well, the rumor of this plot against his chickens reached the good president's ears, and he prepared to circumvent it.

"The students had planned to go to a tree where it was known that several favorite fowls roosted, and one was to climb up while the others stood below and took the booty. They waited until it was late, and the lights in the doctor's study went out, and then they stole silently into the yard and made for the hen-roost. The man who was to catch the chickens climbed carefully, silently, into the tree so as not to disturb the sleeping birds, and the others waited in the dark below.

"The first hen made a good deal of cackling and fuss as she was caught and while this was going on the students below the tree saw some one approaching them from the house. Very silently they scattered into the dark and fled, leaving the poor man in the tree alone. Dr. Nott, well muffled about his face, came quietly up and took his stand below the tree, and in a moment the man in the tree handed down a big white rooster.

" 'This is Daddy Nott,' he said, in a whisper, and the man below received the bird without a word.

"In a moment more a second fowl was handed down. 'This is Mammy Nott,' whispered the irreverent student. Again the bird was received without comment. Then a third hen was handed down with the comment: 'This is Sally Nott.' The Doctor received the third bird and disappeared into the darkness and the student in the tree came down to find his partners fled, with no knowledge of who had taken the fowls. They were much troubled about the circumstance, but hoped that it was only a joke some fellow student had played upon them. They were however extremely anxious the next day when each one concerned in the affair received an invitation to dine with Dr. Nott that evening. Not daring to refuse, nor being able to find any suitable excuse, they presented themselves dubiously at Dr. Nott's house at the appointed hour, and were received courteously as usual. They were beginning to breathe more freely when they were ushered out to dinner, and there, before the Doctor's place, lay three large platters, each containing a fine fowl cooked to a turn. They dared not look at one another, but their embarrassment came to a climax when Dr. Nott looked up pleasantly at the student on his right, who had been the man to climb the tree, and asked, 'Hastings, will you have a piece of Daddy Nott, or Mammy Nott, or Sally Nott?' pointing in order to each platter. I think if it hadn't been for the twinkle in the Doctor's eye those boys would have taken their hats and left without making any adieus, for they say Hastings looked as if you could knock him over with a feather, but that twinkle broke the horror of it, and they all broke down and laughed until they were most heartily ashamed of themselves, and every man there was cured forever of robbing chicken-roosts. But do you know, the Doctor never said another word to those fellows about that, and they were his most loyal students from that time on."

Amid the laughter over this story they rose from the table. Little Rose, who had fallen asleep at the table, was whisked off to bed by the faithful Miranda, and the others went into the parlor where Marcia played exquisite melodies as David and Nathaniel called for them, and Phoebe, entranced, listened, and did not know how her charmed day was spending itself, until suddenly she realized that it was half past eight o'clock and she was some distance from home.

Now, for a maiden to be abroad after nine o'clock in those days was little short of a crime. It would be deemed most highly improper and disreputable by every good person; therefore, as Phoebe noted the time by the great clock she started to her feet in a panic and made her adieus with haste. Marcia went after her bonnet, and tied it lovingly beneath her chin, kissing her and saying she hoped to have her come soon again. David made as if he would take her home, but Nathaniel waved him back and begged for that privilege himself, and so with happy good-nights the young man and the maiden went out into the quiet village street together and hastened along the way, where already many of the lights were out in the houses and the inhabitants gone to sleep.

II

PHOEBE'S heart, as she stepped out into the moonlight with the young man, fluttered so she scarcely could speak without letting her voice shake. It seemed so wonderful that she, of all the girls in the village, should be going home with this bright, handsome, noble man. There was nothing foolish or vain in her thought about it. He was not to be anything more to her for this walk, for his life was set otherwhere, and he belonged to others—notably, in all likelihood, to his cousin Janet. Nevertheless she felt highly honored that he should take the trouble to see her home, and she knew in her heart that the memory of this walk, her first alone with a young man who was not her brother, would remain long a pleasant spot in her life.

He seemed to enjoy her company as much as he had done David's, for he talked on about the things that had interested them in the evening. He told more college stories, and even spoke of his literary society, so that Phoebe, remembering Albert's words, asked if it was true that he had once been president of the Philomatheans, and he modestly acknowledged it, as though the office gave him honor, not he the office. She asked him shyly of the meetings and what they did and he gave her reminiscences of his college days. Their voices rang out now and then in a merry laugh, whereat all the little cornshock ladies huddled in the moonlight seemed to wave sinister arms and shake their heads mournfully to hear mirth at so unseemly an hour. Out in the quiet country road the young man suddenly asked her:

"Tell me, Miss Deane, suppose I knew of some people who were oppressed, suffering, and wanted their freedom; suppose they needed help to set them free, what do you think I ought to do? Think of myself and my career, or go and help set them free?"

Phoebe raised her sweet eyes to his earnest face in the moonlight and tried to understand.

"I am not wise," she said, "and perhaps I would not know what you ought to do, but I think I can tell what you *would* do. I think you would forget all about yourself and go to set those people free."

He looked down into her face, and thought what it meant to a man to have a girl like this one believe in him.

"Thank you!" he said gravely. "I am honored by your opinion of me. You have told me where duty lies. I will remember your words when the time comes."

In the quiet of her chamber a few minutes later Phoebe remembered the words of the young people that day upon the hill-side, and wondered if it were the people of Texas whom he meant needed to be set free.

He had bade her good-night with a pleasant ring in his voice, saying he was glad to know her, and hoped to see her again before he left for New York, which would be in a few days. Then the door closed behind her and he walked briskly down the frosty way. The night was cold even for October, and each startled blade of grass was furred with a tiny frost-spike.

Suddenly, out from behind a cluster of tall elder bushes that bordered the roadside stepped a man, and without warning dealt him a blow between his eyes that made him stagger and almost fall.

"Thet's to teach you to let my girl alone!" snarled Hiram Green like an angry dog, and the moonlight made his face look fairly livid with unholy wrath. "Hev yeh learned yer lesson, er d'yeh need another? 'Cause there's plenty more where that come from!"

Nathaniel's senses had almost deserted him for an instant, but he was master of the art of self-defence, and before the bully had finished his threat with a curse he found himself lying in the ditch with Nathaniel towering over him in righteous wrath.

"Coward," he said, looking down on him contemptuously, "you have made a mistake, of course, and struck the wrong man, but that makes no difference. A brave man does not strike in the dark."

"No, I haven't made no mistake, either," snarled Hiram, as he got up angrily from the ground. "I seen you myself with my own eyes, Nate Graham. I seen you trail down the hill out o' the woods after her, 'n I seen you try to get a kiss from her, an' she run away. I was an eye-witness. *I* seen yeh. Then you tried to get 'longside her after meetin' was out Sunday, tippin' yer hat so polite, as ef that was everythin' a girl wanted; an' I seen yeh takin' her home to-night after decent folks was a-bed, walkin' 'long a country road talkin' so sweet an' low butter wouldn't melt in yer mouth. No, sir! I ain't made no mistake. An' I jest want you to understand after this you're not to meddle with Phoebe Deane, fer *she belongs to me!*"

By this time Nathaniel had recognized Hiram Green, and his astonishment and dismay knew no bounds. Could it be possible that a girl like that had aught to do in any way with this coarse, ignorant man? Indignation filled him. He longed to pound the insolent wretch before him and make him take back all he had said, but he realized that this might be a serious matter for the young girl, and it was necessary to proceed cautiously, therefore he drew himself up haughtily and replied:

"There has never been anything between myself and Miss Deane to which any one, no matter how close their relationship to her might be, could object. I met her in the woods while nutting with a party of friends, and had the good fortune to help her out of a tangle of laurel that had caught in her hair, and to show her the short cut to the road. I merely spoke to her on Sunday as I spoke to my other acquaintances, and this evening I have been escorting her home from the house of a friend where we have both been taking tea."

"You lie!" snarled Hiram.

"What did I understand you to say, Mr. Green?"

"It don't make any matter what you understood me to say. I *said* YOU LIE, an' I'll say it again, too, ef I like. You needn't git off any more o' your fine words, fer they don't go down with me, even ef you have been to college. All I've got to say is *you let my girl alone from now on!* D'yeh understand that? Ef yeh don't I'll take means to make ye!" And Hiram's big fist was raised threateningly again.

But somehow the next instant Hiram was sprawling in the dust, and this time Nathaniel held something gleaming and sinister in his hand as he stood above him.

"I always go armed," said Nathaniel, in a cool voice. "You will oblige me by lying still where you are until I am out of sight down the road. Then it will be quite safe for you to rise to go home and wash your face. If I see you get up before that I shall shoot. Another thing. If I hear another word of this ridiculous nonsense from you I will have you arrested and brought before my uncle on charge of assault, and blackmail, and several other things perhaps. As for speaking to the young lady in question, or showing her any courtesy whatever that is ordinarily shown between young men and women in good society, that shall be as Miss Deane says, and not in any way as you say. You are not fit to speak her name."

Nathaniel stepped back slowly a few paces, and Hiram attempted to rise, pouring forth a volley of oaths and vile language. Nathaniel halted and raised the pistol, flashing in the moonlight.

"You will keep entirely still, Mr. Green. Remember that this is loaded."

Hiram subsided and Nathaniel walked deliberately backward until the man on the ground could see but a dim speck in the gray of the distance, and a night-hawk in the trees by his home mocked him in a clamorous tone.

Now all this happened not a stone's throw from Albert Deane's front gate, and might almost have been discerned from Phoebe's window if her room had not been upon the other side of the house.

After a little Hiram crawled stiffly up from the ground, looked furtively about, shook his fist menacingly at the distance where the flash of Nathaniel's pistol had disappeared, and slunk like a shadow close to the fence till he reached his house. Presently only a bit of white paper ground down with a great heel-mark, and a few footprints in the frosty dust, told where the encounter had been. The moon spread her obliterating white light over all, and Phoebe slept smiling in her dreams and living over her happy afternoon and evening again. But Nathaniel sat up far into the night till his candle burned low and sputtered out, and even the moon grew weary and bent low. He was thinking, and his thoughts were not all of the oppressed Texans. It had occurred to him that there were other people in the world whom it might be harder to set free than the Texans.

If Hiram Green did not sleep it was because his heart was busy with evil plans for revenge. He was by no means meekly done with Nathaniel Graham. He might submit under necessity, but he was a man in whom a sense of injury dwelt long, and smouldered into a great fire that grew far beyond all proportion of the fancied offence. Hatred and revenge were the ruling passions with him.

But Phoebe slept, and dreamed not that more evil was brewing.

The lights had been out, all save a candle in Emmeline's room, when she came home, but the door was left on the latch for her. She knew Emmeline wished to reprove her for the late hour of her return, and was fully prepared for the greeting next morning, spoken frigidly:

"Oh, so you did come home last night, after all! Or was it this morning? I'm surprised. I thought you had gone for good."

At breakfast things were uncomfortable. Albert persisted in asking Phoebe questions about her tea-party, in spite of Emmeline's disagreeable sarcasms. When Emmeline complained that Phoebe had "sneaked" away without giving her a chance to send for anything to the village, and that she needed thread for her quilting that very morning, Phoebe arose from her almost untasted breakfast and offered to go for it at once.

She stepped into the crisp morning with a sigh of relief, and walked briskly down the road feeling exultantly happy that she had escaped her prison for a little hour of the early freshness. Then she stopped suddenly, for there before her lay a letter ground into the dust, and about the writing there was something strangely familiar, as if she had seen it before, yet it was not anyone's she knew. It was not folded so that the address could be seen, as the manner of letters was in those days of no envelopes, but open and rumpled with the communication uppermost, and the words that stood out clearly to her vision as she stooped to pick it up were these: "It is most important that you present this letter or it will do no good to go but *be sure that no one else sees it*, or great harm may come to you!"

She turned the paper over with reverent fingers, for a bit of writing was not so common then as now and was treated with far more importance. And there on the other side lay the name that had gleamed at her pleasantly but a few days before through the laurel bushes as she lay in hiding, "Nathaniel Graham, Esq." Did it look up at her confidingly now as if it would plead to be restored to its owner? Phoebe started at the foolish fancy, and was appalled with her responsibility.

Was this letter but an old one, useless now, and of no value to its owner? Surely it must be, and he had dropped it on his way home with her last night. The wind had blown it open and a passer-by had trodden upon it. That must be the explanation, for surely if it were important he would not have laid it down behind the log so carelessly in keeping of a stranger. Yet there were the words in the letter: "It is most important that you present it when you come." Well, perhaps he had already "come," wherever that was, and the letter had seen its usefulness and passed out of value. But then it further stated that great harm might come to the owner if anyone saw it. She might make sure no one would see it by destroying it, but how was she to know but that she was really destroying an important document? And she might not read further because of that caution, "Be sure that no one else sees it." A less conscientious soul might not have heeded it, but Phoebe would not have read another word for the world. She felt it was a secret communication to which she had no right, and she must respect it.

More and more as this reasoning became clear to her, she saw that there was only one thing to do, and that was to go at once to the owner and give it to him, telling him that she had not read another word than those she saw at first, and making him understand that not a breath of it would ever pass her lips.

Her troubled gaze saw nothing of the morning beauties. Little jewels gemmed the fringes of the grass along the road, and the dull red and brown leaves that still lingered on their native branches were coated over with silver gauze. It would have given her joy at another time, but now it was as if it was not. She passed by Hiram Green's farm just as he was coming down to his barn near the road. He was in full view, and near enough for recognition. He quickened his pace as he saw her coming in her morning tidiness and beauty. She made a trim and dainty picture. But her eyes were straight ahead and she did not turn her head to look at him. He thought she did it to escape speaking, and he had had it in mind to imitate Nathaniel and call a good-morning. It angered him anew to have her pass him by unseeing, as if he were not good enough to treat with ordinary common politeness as between neighbors at least. If he had needed anything more to justify his heart in its evil plot he had it now. With lowering brow and ugly mien he raised his voice and called unpleasantly:

"Where you goin' this early, Phoebe?" but with her face set straight ahead and eyes that were studying perplexing questions she went on her way and never even heard him. Then the devil entered into Hiram Green.

He waited until she had passed beyond the red schoolhouse that marked the boundary line between the village and the country, and then slouched out from the shelter of the barn, and with long dogged steps followed her; keeping his little eyes narrowed and intent upon the blue of her frock in the distance. He would not let her see him, but he meant to know where she was going. She had a letter in her hand as she passed, at least it was a small white article much like a letter. Was she writing his rival a letter already? The thought brought a throb of hate—hate toward the man who was better than he, toward the girl who had scorned him, and toward the whole world, even the little weak caterpillar that crawled in a sickly way across his path which he crushed with an ugly twist of his cruel boot.

Phoebe, all unsuspecting, thinking only of her duty, which was not at all a pleasant one to her, went on her way. She felt she must get the letter out of her hands at once before she did anything else, so she turned down the street past the church to the stately house with its white fence and high hedge, and her heart beat fast and hard against her blue print frock. In the presence of the great house she suddenly felt that she was not dressed for such a call, yet she would not turn back, nor even hesitate, for it was something that must be done at once. She gave herself no time for thought of what would be said, but entered the great gate, which to her relief stood open. She held the letter tight in her cold trembling hand. Hiram had arrived at the church corner just in time to see her disappear within the white gates, and his jaw dropped down in astonishment. He had not dreamed she would go to his house. Yet after a moment's thought his eyes narrowed and gleamed with the satisfaction they always showed when he had thought out some theory, or seen through some possibility. The situation was one that was trying for the girl, and the fact of his being an eye-witness might some day give him power over her. He took his stand behind the trunk of a weeping willow tree in the churchyard to see what might happen.

Meantime Phoebe raised the great brass knocker held in the mouth of a lion. She felt as if all the lions of the earth were come to meet her at this threshold, and her heart was beating in her throat now, so that she could scarcely speak. How hollow the sound of the knocker was as it reverberated through the great hall, not at all the cheerful thing it had been when Nathaniel knocked at Mrs. Spafford's door. A plump black woman in a large yellow turban and white apron opened the door, and was even more formidable than some of the family whom she had expected to meet might have been. She managed to ask if Mr. Graham were in.

"Missis Gra'm! Dere ain't no missis Gra'm," ejaculated the old woman, looking over her carefully and it must be admitted rather scornfully. The young ladies who came to that house to visit did not dress as Phoebe was dressed just then, in working garb. "Dere's only jes' Mis' Brist'l. Mis' Janet, we calls her."

"Mr. Graham. Mr. Nathaniel Graham," corrected Phoebe, in trepidation. She thought she felt a rebuke in the black woman's words that she should call to see a young man. "I have a message for him," she added, bravely. "I will wait here, please. No, I'd rather not come in."

"I'll call Miss Janet," said the servant briefly, and swept away, closing the door with a bang in Phoebe's face.

She waited several minutes before it was opened again, this time by Janet Bristol.

12

"YOU wished to see me?" questioned the tall, handsome girl in the doorway, scrutinizing Phoebe haughtily. There was nothing encouraging in her attitude.

"I wished to see Mr. Graham," said Phoebe, trying to look as if it were quite the natural thing for a young woman to call on a young man of a morning.

"I thought you had a message for him," said Janet, sharply. She was wondering what business this very pretty girl could possibly have with her cousin.

"Yes, I have a message for him, but I must give it to *him*, if you please," she said with gentle emphasis. She lifted her eyes, and Janet could not help noticing the lovely face, and the beauty of the smile.

"Well, that will not be possible, for he is not here." Janet said it stiffly and Phoebe felt the disapproval in her glance.

"Oh!" said Phoebe, growing troubled. "He is not here? What shall I do? He ought to have it at once. When will he come? I might wait for him."

"He will not be home until evening," said Janet, as if she were glad. "You will have to leave your message."

"I am sorry," said Phoebe, in troubled tone, "I cannot

leave it. The one who sends it said it was private."

"That would not mean you could not tell it to his family," said Janet, in a superior tone. She was bristling with curiosity.

"I do not know," said Phoebe, turning to go.

"I can't understand how it is that you, a young girl, should be trusted with a message if it is so private that his own people are not to know." Her tone was vexed.

"I know," said Phoebe, "it is strange, and I am sorry that it happened so. But there is nothing wrong about it, really," and she looked up wistfully with her clear eyes so that Janet scarce could continue to think evil of her. "Perhaps Mr. Graham may be able to explain it to you. I would have no right." She turned and went down the steps. "I will come back this evening," she said, more as if she were making a resolve than as if it were a communication to Janet.

"Wait," said Janet, sharply. "Who are you? I've seen you in church, haven't I?"

"Oh, yes," said Phoebe, glad to have something natural said. "I sit just behind you. I'm only Phoebe Deane."

"And who sends this message to my cousin?"

Phoebe's face clouded over. "I do not know," she said, slowly.

"Well, that is very strange, indeed. If I were you I would not carry messages for strange people. It doesn't look well. Girls can't be too careful what they do." Janet did not mean to be hateful, but she was deeply annoyed and curious.

Phoebe's face was pained.

"I hope Mr. Graham will be able to explain," she said, sorrowfully. "I do not like to have you think ill of me." Then she went away, while Janet stood preplexed and annoyed.

She tucked the letter safely in the bosom of her gown and held her hand over it as she hurried along, not looking up nor noticing any more than when she had come. She passed Miranda on the other side of the street and never saw her, and Miranda wondered where she was going and why she looked so troubled. If she had not been hurrying to the store for something that was needed at once for the day's dinner, she would have followed her to find out, and perhaps have asked her point blank. It would have been a good thing, for when one is tracked by a devil it is well to be followed also by an angel, even if it be only one with a freckled face.

Without a thought for anything but her perplexities Phoebe made her way through the village and out on the country road, and in a very short time arrived in the kitchen of her home, where Emmeline had just finished the breakfast dishes.

"Well," she said grimly, looking up as Phoebe entered, and noticing her empty hands, "where's the thread? Didn't they have any?"

"Oh!" said Phoebe, blankly. Her hands flew to her heart in dismay as she took in her situation. "I forgot it!" She murmured, humbly; "I'll go right back!" and without waiting for a word from the amazed Emmeline she turned and sped down the road again towards the village.

"Of all things!" ejaculated Emmeline, as she went to close the door that had blown open; "she needs a nurse! I didn't suppose going out to tea and a little money in the bank could make a girl lose her head like that! She has turned into a regular scatterbrain. The idea of her forgetting to get that thread when she hadn't another earthly thing to do! I'd like to know who 'twas brung her home last night. I don't know how I could hev missed him till he was way out in the road. It didn't look 'egzactly like David Spafford, an' yet, who could it 'a' ben ef 't wasn't? She must 'a' went to Mis' Spaffords again this mornin' stead o' goin' to the store, er she never would 'a' forgot. I'll have to find out when she gits back. It's my duty!"

Emmeline snapped her lips together over the words as if she anticipated the duty would be a pleasant one.

Phoebe in her hasty flight down the road almost ran into Hiram Green, who was sulkily plodding back from his fruitless errand to his belated chores.

"Gosh!" he said, as she started back with a hasty, "Excuse me, Mr. Green. I'm in such a hurry I didn't see you." She was gone on before her sentence was quite finished, and the breeze wafted it back to him from her flying figure.

"Gosh!" he said again, looking after her, "I wonder what's up now!" Then he turned doggedly and followed her again. If this kept up, detective business was going to be lively work. He was tired already and his morning's work not half done. Two trips to the village on foot in one morning were wearisome. Yet he was determined to know what all this meant.

Phoebe did her errand swiftly this time, and was so quick in returning with her purchase that she met Hiram face to face outside the store before he had had time to conceal himself.

He was thrown off his guard, but he rallied and tried to play the gallant.

"Thought I'd come 'long and see ef I couldn't carry yer bundle fer yeh."

"Oh, thank you, Mr. Green," said Phoebe, in new dismay at this unwonted display of courtesy on his part. "But I can't wait, for Emmeline is in a great hurry for this. I shall have to run most of the way home. Besides it's very light. I couldn't think of troubling you." She had backed off as she spoke, and with the closing words she turned and flew up the street on feet as light as a thistle-down.

"Gosh!" said Hiram, under his breath, almost dazed at the rebuff. "Gosh! but she's a slippery one! But I'll catch her yet where she can't squirm out so easy. See ef I don't!" And with scowling brows he started slowly after her again. He did not intend any move on her part should go unwatched. He hated her for disliking him.

Miranda, from her watch-tower in the Spafford kitchen window, saw Phoebe's flying figure, and wondered. She did not know what it meant, but it meant something she was sure. She felt "stirrings" in her soul that usually called for some action on her part. Her alert soul was ready when the time should arrive and she felt it "arriving" fast, and sniffed the air like a trained war-horse. To be sure she sniffed nothing more dangerous than the fragrance of mince pies just out of the great brick oven, standing in a row on the shelf to cool.

The remainder of the morning was not pleasant for Phoebe. Her mind was too busy with her perplexity about how to get the letter to Nathaniel for her to spend much time in planning how to excuse her forgetfulness. She merely said: "I was thinking of something else, Emmeline, and so came back without going to the store at all." Emmeline scolded, and sniffed, and scoffed to no purpose. Phoebe silently worked on, her brow thoughtful, her eyes far away, her whole manner showing she was paying little heed to what her sister-in-law said. This made Emmeline still more angry, so that she exhausted the vials of her wrath in fruitless words upon the girl. But Phoebe's lips were sealed. She answered questions when it was necessary and quietly worked on. The tasks disappeared from under her hand as if by a sort of magic. When everything else was done she seated herself at the quilt and began to set tiny stitches in a brilliant corner.

"Don't trouble yourself," said Emmeline coldly. "You might ferget to fasten yer thread, er tie a knot in it. I wouldn't be s'prised." But Phoebe worked mechanically on and soon had got a whole block ahead of Emmeline. Her mind was busy with the problem of the evening. How should she get that letter to Nathaniel without being discovered and questioned at home?

At dinner she was unusually silent, excusing herself to go back to the quilt as soon as she had eaten a few mouthfuls. Emmeline looked scrutinizingly at her, and became silent. It seemed to her there was something strange about Phoebe. She would have given a good deal to know all about her afternoon at the Spaffords', but Phoebe's monosyllabic answers brought forth little in the way of information.

Albert looked at her in a troubled way, then glanced at Emmeline's forbidding face, and forbore to say anything.

The afternoon wore away in silence. Several times Emmeline opened her lips to ask a question, and snapped them shut again. She made up her mind that Phoebe must be thinking about Hiram Green, and if that was so she would better keep still and let her think. Nevertheless there was something serene and lofty about Phoebe's look that was hardly in keeping with a thought of Hiram Green, and there was something sphinx-like in her manner that made Emmeline feel it was useless to ask questions, though of course Emmeline had never heard of the sphinx.

Phoebe acted like one who was making up for lost time. The dishes seemed to marshal themselves into cleanly array on the shelves, and before the darkness came on she had caused a number of suns on the sunrise bedquilt to set forever behind a goodly roll of fine stitches set in most intricate patterns.

She arose like one who was wound up at five o'clock and without a word got the supper. Then, eating little or nothing herself, she cleared it rapidly away and went up to her room. Albert took his newspaper, and Emmeline went grimly at her basket of stockings. She was wondering whether the girl intended coming down to help her with them. After all it was rather profitable to have Phoebe work like that, things got done so quickly.

"Is Phoebe sick?" asked Albert, suddenly looking up from his paper.

Emmeline started and pricked her fingers with the needle.

"I should like to know what makes you think that," she snapped, frowning at the prick. "You seem to think she's made of some kind of perishable stuff that needs more'n ordinary care. You never seem to think I'm sick as I've noticed."

"Now, Emmeline!" he began pleasantly, "you know you aren't ever sick, and this is your home, and you like to stay in it, and you've got your own folks and all. But Phoebe's kind of different. She doesn't seem to quite belong, and I wouldn't want her to miss anything out of her life because she's living with us."

"Bosh!" said Emmeline. "Phoebe's made of no better stuff 'n I am. She ken do more work when the fit's on her than a yoke of oxen. The fit's ben on her to-day. She's got her spunk up. That's all the matter. She's tryin' to make up fer losin' yesterday afternoon, jes' to spite me fer what I said about her goin' out. I know her. She's done a hull lot on that there quilt this afternoon. At this rate we'll hev it off the frames before the week's out. She ain't et much 'cause she's mad, but she'll come out of it all right. You make me sick the way you fret about her doldrums."

Albert subsided and the darning-needle had it all its own way clicking in and out. They could hear Phoebe moving about her chamber quietly, though it was not directly over the sitting-room, and presently the sounds ceased altogether, and they thought she had gone to bed. A few minutes more and Hiram with his customary shuffle opened the sitting-room door and walked in.

"Where's Phoebe?" he asked, looking at the silent group around the candle; "she ain't out to another tea-party is she?"

"She's gone to bed," said Emmeline, shortly. "Is it cold out?"

Phoebe upstairs by her open window, arrayed in her plain brown delaine, brown shirred bonnet, and brown cape, with the letter safely pinned inside her cape, waited until the accustomed sounds downstairs told her Hiram had come and was seated. Then she softly, cautiously climbed out of her window to the roof of a shed a few feet below her window, crept out to the back edge of this and dropped like a cat to the ground. She had performed this feat many times as a child, but never since she wore long dresses. She was glad the moon was not up yet, and she hurried around the back of the house and across the side yard to the fence, which she climbed. Her feet had scarcely left the last rail ere she heard the door-latch click, and a broad beam of light was flung out across the path not far from her. To her horror she saw Hiram Green's tall form coming out and then the door slammed shut and she knew he was out in the night with her.

But she was in the road now with nothing to hinder her, and her light feet fairly flew over the ground, treading on the grassy spots at the edge so she would make no sound, and never turning her head to listen even if he were following. Somehow she felt he was coming nearer and nearer every step she took. Her heart beat wildly, and great tears started to her eyes. She tried to pray as she fled along. Added to her fear of Hiram was her dread of what he would think if he found her out there in the dark alone, and a third fear for the secret of the letter she carried, for instinctively she felt that of all people to find out a secret Hiram Green would be among the most dangerous. She put her hand upon the letter and clenched it fast as though it might be spirited away unless she held it. She was glad it was dark, and yet, if he had seen her, and were pursuing, how dreadful it would be to be captured by him in the dark! If she might but reach the village streets where others would be near to help, her heart would not be so frightened.

When she passed the silent, sleeping school-house she turned her head as she hurried along, and felt sure she heard him coming. The sky was growing luminous. The moon would soon be up, and then she could be seen. Then quite distinctly she heard a man's heavy tread running behind her.

Her heart nearly stopped for an instant, and then, bounding up almost to bursting, she leaped ahead, her lips set, her head down, her hands clenched over the letter. A few more rods. She could not hold out to run like this much further. But at last she reached the village pavement, and could see the blessed friendly lights of the houses all about her.

She hurried on, not daring to run so fast here, for people were coming ahead, and she tried to think and to still the wild fluttering of her heart. If Hiram Green were behind and really following her it would not do for her to go to Judge Bristol's at once. She could scarcely hope to reach there and hide from him now, for her strength for running was almost spent and not for anything must he of all people know where she was going.

This thought gave new wings to her feet, and she fled past the houses, scarcely stopping to realize where she was. She could hear the man's steps on the brick pavement now and his heavy boots rang out distinctly on the frosty air. She felt as if she had been running for years with an evil fate pursuing her. Her limbs grew heavy, and her feet seemed to drag behind. She half closed her eyes to stop the surging of the blood. Her ears rang, her cheeks were burning and perspiration was standing on her lips and brow. Her breath came hard and hurt her.

And then, quite naturally, as if it had all been planned, Miranda, with a little shawl around her shoulders and over her head, stepped out from behind the lilacs in the Spafford garden by the gate, and walked along beside her, fitting her large easy gait to Phoebe's weary, flying steps.

"I heard yeh comin' an' thought I'd go a piece with yeh!" she explained, easily, as if this were a common occurrence. "D'ye hev to hurry like this, 'r was yeh doin' it fer exercise?"

"Oh, Miranda!" gasped Phoebe, slowing down her going, and putting a plaintive hand out to reach the strong red friendly one in the dark, "I am so glad you are here!"

"So'm I!" said Miranda, confidently, "but you jest wait till you git your breath. Can't you come in and set a spell 'fore you go on?"

"No, Miranda, I must hurry. I had an errand and must get right back—but I'm almost sure some one is following me. I don't dare look behind, but I heard footsteps and—I'm—so—frightened." Her voice trailed off, trembling into another gasp for breath.

"Well, all right, we'll fix 'em. You jest keep your breath

fer walkin' an' I'll boss this pilgrimage a spell. We'll go down to the village store fer a spool o' cotton Mis' Spafford ast me t' get the fust thing in the mornin' to sew some sprigged calico curtains she's ben gettin' up to the spare bed, an' while we're down to the store we'll jest natcherally lose sight o' that man till he don't know where he's at, an' then we'll meander on our happy way. Don't talk 'r he'll hear you. You jest foller me."

13

PHOEBE, too much exhausted to demur, walked silently beside the self-reliant Miranda, and in a moment more they were safely in the store.

"Say, Mr. Peebles, is Mis' Peebles to home? 'Cause Phoebe Deane wants t' git a drink o' water powerful bad. Ken she jest go right in and get it whilst I get a spool o' cotton?"

"Why certainly, certainly, young ladies, walk right in," said the affable Mr. Peebles, arising from a nail keg.

Miranda had Phoebe into the back room in no time, and was calmly debating over the virtues of different spools of thread when Hiram Green entered puffing and snorting like a porpoise, and gazed about him confidently. Then suddenly a blank look spread over his face. The one he was searching for was not there? Could he have been mistaken?

Miranda, innocently paying for her thread, eyed him furtively, and began her keen putting of two and two together, figuring out her problem with a relish. "Hiram Green, to be sure—Ah! It was Hiram who had tried to walk beside Phoebe on Sunday. Hiram Green"—contemptuously—"of all men! Umph!"

These were something like her thoughts. Then with wide-eyed good nature she paid for her thread, said good-evening to Mr. Peebles, and deliberately went out the door of the store to the street. Hiram had watched her suspiciously, but she held her head high as if she were going straight home, and slipped in the dark around to the side door where she walked in on Mrs. Peebles and the astonished Phoebe without ceremony.

"Did yeh get yer drink, Phoebe? Ev'nin' Mis' Peebles. Thank yeh, no I can't set down. Mis' Spafford needs this thread t' oncet. She jest ast me wouldn't I run down and git it so's she could finish up some piller-slips she's makin'. Come on, Phoebe, ef yer ready. Ken we go right out this door, Mis' Peebles; there's so many men in the store, an' I can't bear 'em to stare at my pretty red hair, you know." And in a moment more she had whisked Phoebe out the side door into the dark yard, where they could slip through the fence to the side street.

"Now, which way?" demanded Miranda, briefly, in a low tone, as they emerged from the shadow of the store to the sidewalk.

"Oh, Miranda, you're so kind," said Phoebe, hardly knowing what to do, for she dared not tell her errand to her. "I think I can go quite well by myself now. I'm not much afraid, and I'll soon be done and go home."

"See here, Phoebe Deane, d'yeh think I'm goin' t' leave a little white-faced thing like you with them two star eyes t' go buffetin' round alone in the dark when there's liable to be lopsided nimshies follerin' round? Yeh can say what yeh like, but I'm goin' to foller yeh till I see yeh safe inside yer own door."

"Oh, you dear, good Miranda!" choked Phoebe, with a teary smile, clasping her arm tight. "If you only knew how glad I was to see you."

"I knowed all right. I cud see you was scared. But come 'long quick er that hound in there'll be trackin' us again. Which way?"

"To Judge Bristol's," breathed Phoebe, in low frightened whisper.

"That's a good place to go," said Miranda, with satisfaction. "I guess you won't need me inside with you. I'm not much on fancy things, an' I'll fit better outside with the fence-posts, but I'll be thar to take yeh home. My! but you'd orter a' seen Hiram Green's blank look when he got in the store an' seen you want there. I'm calculatin' he'll search quite a spell 'fore he makes out which way we disappeared."

Phoebe's heart beat wildly at the thought of her escape. She felt as if an evil fate were dogging her every step.

"Oh, Miranda!" she shivered. "What if you hadn't come along just then!"

"Well, there ain't no use cipherin' on that proposition. I was thar, an' I generally calculate to be thar when I'm needed. Jest you rest easy. There ain't no long-legged, good-fer-nothin' bully like Hiram Green goin' to gather you in, not while I'm able to bob 'round. Here we be. Now I'll wait in the shadder behind this bush while you go in."

Phoebe timidly approached the house, while Miranda, as usual, selected her post of observation with discernment and a view to the lighted window of the front room where the family were assembled.

Janet did not keep Phoebe waiting long this time, but swept down upon her in a frock of ruby red with a little gold locket hung from a bit of black velvet ribbon about her neck. Her dark hair was arranged in clusters of curls each side of her sparkling face, and the glow on her cheek seemed reflected from the color of her garments. Phoebe almost spoke her admiration, so beautiful did this haughty girl seem to her.

"I am afraid my cousin is too busy to see you," she said, in a kindly, condescending tone. "He is very busy preparing to leave on the early stage in the morning. He finds he must go to New York sooner than he expected."

"I will not keep him," said Phoebe, earnestly, rising, "but

I must see him for just a minute. Will you kindly tell him it is Phoebe Deane, and that she says she *must* see him for just a moment?"

"You will find he will desire you to send the message by me," said Janet, quite confidently. "It does not do to say must to my cousin Nathaniel."

But contrary to Janet's expectation Nathaniel came down at once, with welcome in his face. Phoebe was standing with her hand upon the letter over her heart waiting for him breathlessly. The watching Miranda eyed him jealously through the front window-pane to see if his countenance would light up properly when he saw his visitor, and was fully satisfied. He hastened to meet her, and take her hand in greeting, but she, armed for her mission, did but hold out the letter to him.

"I found this, Mr. Graham, spread out in the road, and read the one sentence which showed it was private. I have not read any more, and I shall never breathe even that one of course. After I had read that sentence I did not dare give it into any hands but yours. I may have been wrong, but I have tried to do right. I hope you can explain it to your cousin, for I can see she thinks it very strange."

He tried to detain her, to thank her, to introduce her to his cousin, who had by this time entered and was watching them distantly, but Phoebe was in haste to leave; and Janet was haughtily irresponsive.

He followed her to the door and said in a low tone: "Miss Deane, you have done me a greater service than I can possibly repay. I have been hunting frantically for this leter all day. It is most important. I know I can trust you not to speak of it to a soul. I am deeply grateful. You may not know it, but not only my life and safety but that of others as well has been in your hands to-day with the keeping of that letter."

"Oh, then I am glad I have brought it safely to you. I have been frightened all day lest something would happen that I could not get it to you without its being found out.

And if it has been of service I am more than glad, because then I have repaid your kindness to me in the woods that day."

Now that she was away from Janet's scrutinizing eyes Phoebe could dimple into a smile.

"Oh, what I did that day was a little, little thing beside your service," said he.

"A kindness is never a little thing," answered Phoebe, gently. "Good-night, Mr. Graham. Miranda is waiting for me," and she sped down the path without giving him opportunity for a reply. Miranda had wandered into the shaft of light down by the gate that streamed from the candle Nathaniel held, and Phoebe flew to her as if to a rock of refuge. They turned and looked back as they reached the gate. Nathaniel was still standing on the top step with the tall candle held above his head to give them light, and through the window they could dimly see Janet's slim figure standing by the mantelpiece toying with some ornaments. Phoebe gave a great sigh of relief that the errand was accomplished, and grasping Miranda's arm clung lovingly to her, and so they two walked softly through the village streets and out the country way into the road that was white with the new risen moon; while Hiram Green, perplexed and baffled, searched vainly through the village for a clue to Phoebe's whereabouts, and finally gave it up and dragged his weary limbs home. Excitement of this sort did not agree with his constitution and he was mortally tired.

Nathaniel turned back into the house again, his vision filled with the face of the girl who had just brought his letter back to him. His great relief at finding it was almost lost in his absorption in the thought of Phoebe Deane, and the sudden pang that came to him with his remembrance of Hiram Green. Could it be? Could it possibly be that she was bound in any way to that man?

Janet roused him from this thought by demanding to know what on earth the message was that made that girl so absurdly secretive.

Nathaniel smiled. "It was just a letter of mine she had found. A letter that I have searched everywhere for."

"How did she know it was your letter?" There was something offensive in Janet's tone. Nathaniel felt his color rising like a girl. He wondered what was the matter with Janet that she should be so curious.

"Why, it was addressed to me of course!"

"Then why in the world couldn't she give it to me? She was here in the morning and we had a long argument about it. She said it was a private message and the person who sent it did not wish anyone but you to see it, and yet she professed not to know who the person was who sent it. I told her that was ridiculous; that of course you had no secrets from your family; but she was quite stubborn and went away. Who is she, anyway, and how does she happen to know you?"

Nathaniel could be haughty, too, when he liked, and now he drew himself up to his greatest height.

"Miss Deane is quite a charming girl, Janet, and you would do well to make her acquaintance. She is a friend of Mrs. Spafford, and was visiting her last evening when I happened in on business and they made me stay to tea."

"That's no sign of where she belongs socially," said Janet, disagreeably; "Mrs. Spafford may have had to invite her just because she didn't know enough to go home before supper. Besides, Mrs. Spafford's choice in friends might not be mine at all."

"Janet, Mr. and Mrs. Spafford are unimpeachable socially and every other way. And I happen to know that Miss Deane was there by invitation. I heard her speaking of it as she bade her good-night."

"Oh, indeed!" sneered Janet, quite beside herself with jealousy. "I suppose you were waiting to take her home!"

"Why, certainly," said Nathaniel, looking surprised. "What has come over you, Janet? You do not talk like your usual kind self."

His tone brought angry tears to Janet's eyes.

"I should think it was enough," she said, trying to hide the tears in her little lace handkerchief, "having you go off suddenly like this when we've scarcely had you a week, and you busy and absent-minded all the time; and then to have this upstart of a girl coming here with secrets that you will not tell me about. I want to know who wrote that letter, Nathaniel, and what it is about. I can't stand it to have that girl smirking behind me in church knowing things about my cousin that I am not told. I *must* know."

"Janet!" said Nathaniel, pained and surprised, "you must be ill. I never saw you act this way before. You know very well that I'm just as sorry as can be to have to rush off sooner than I had planned, but it can't be helped. I'm sorry if I have been absent-minded. I have been trying to decide some matters of my future and I suppose that has made me somewhat abstracted. As for the letter, I would gladly tell you about it, but it is another's secret, and I could not honorably do so. You need fear no such feeling on Miss Deane's part, I am sure. Just meet her with your own pleasant, winning way, and say to her that I have explained to you that it was all right. That ought to satisfy both you and her. She asked me to explain it to you."

"Well, you haven't done so, at all. I am sure I can't see what possible harm it could do for you to tell me about it, inasmuch as that other girl knows all about it too. I should think you would want me to watch and be sure that she doesn't tell—unless, indeed, the secret is between you two."

There was a hint in Janet's tone which seemed almost like an insinuation. Nathaniel grew quite stern.

"The secret is not between Miss Deane and myself," he said, "and she does not know it any more than you do. She found it open, and read only one line which told her it was absolutely private. She tells me she did not read another word."

"Very likely!" sneered Janet, coldly. "Do you think any woman would find it possible to read only one line of a secret?

Your absolute faith in this stranger is quite childlike."

"Janet, would you have read further if it had fallen into your hands?"

"Well—I—why—of course that would be different," said Janet, coloring and looking disconcerted, "but you needn't compare me—"

"Janet, you have no right to think she has a lower sense of honor than you have. I feel sure she has not read it."

But Janet, with haughty mien and flashing eyes in which tears were scarcely concealed, swept up the stairs and took refuge in her room, where a perfect storm of tears and mortification followed.

Nathaniel, confounded, dismayed, after vainly tapping at her door and begging her to come out and explain her strange conduct, went sadly to his packing, puzzling much over the strange ways of girls with one another. Here for instance were two well suited to friendship, and yet he could plainly see that they would have nothing to do with one another. He dearly loved his cousin. She had been his playmate and companion from childhood, and he could not understand why suddenly she had grown so disregardful of his wishes. He tried to put it away, deciding that he would say another little word about this charming Miss Deane to Janet in the morning before he left, but Miss Janet forestalled any such attempt by sending down word that she had a headache and would try to sleep a little longer to get rid of it. She would only call a cool little good-bye to her cousin through the closed door, as he, mildly distressed, was hurrying down to the stage waiting for him at the door.

Meantime Miranda and Phoebe had hurried out past the old red school-house into the country road white with frosty moonlight, Phoebe all the time protesting that Miranda must not go with her.

"Why not, in conscience!" said Miranda. "I'll jest enjoy the walk. I was thinkin' of goin' on a lark this very evenin', only I hadn't picked out a companion."

"But you'll have to come all the way back alone, Miranda."

"Well, what's that? You don't s'pose anybody's goin' to chase *ME,* do yeh? If they want to they're welcome. I'd jest turn round an' say: 'Boo! I'm red-haired an' freckled, an' I don't want nothin' of you, nor you of me. Git 'long with yeh!' " Miranda's inimitable manner brought a merry laugh to Phoebe's lips and helped to relieve the tension of the heavy strain she had been under. She felt like laughing and crying all at once. Miranda seemed to understand and enter into her mood, and kept her in ripples of laughter till they neared her home. Then, suddenly sobering, Phoebe attempted to make Miranda go back at once, but Miranda was stubborn. Not until she saw her charge safe inside her own door would the faithful soul budge an inch.

"Well then, Miranda, I'll have to tell you how I got out," said Pheobe, confidentially. "There was a caller—some one I didn't care to see—so I went upstairs and they thought I'd gone to bed. I just slipped out my window to the low shed roof and dropped down. I'll have to be very still, for I wouldn't care to have them know I slipped away like that. It might make them ask me questions. You see I had found a letter that I knew Mr. Graham had dropped, and it ought to go to him at once. If I had asked Albert to take it there would have been a big fuss and Emmeline would have wanted to know all about it, and maybe read it, and I didn't think it would be best—"

"I see," said Miranda, comprehensively, "so you tuk it yourself. O' course. Who wouldn't, I'd like to know? All right, we'll jest slip in through the pasture and round to your shed, an' I'll give yeh a boost up. Two's better 'n one fer a job like that, even ef one *is* a red-head. I take it yer caller ain't present any longer. Reckon he made out to foller yeh a piece but we run him into a hole, an' he didn't make much. Hush, now; don't go to thankin', 'taint worth while till I git through, fer I've jest begun this job, an' I intend to see it through. Here, put yer hand on my shoulder. Now let me hold this foot,

don't you be 'fraid, I'm good an' strong. There yeh go! Now
yer up! Is that your winder up there? Wal, hope to see yeh
again soon. Happy dreams!" and she slid around the corner
to watch Phoebe till she disappeared into the little dark window above. Then Miranda made for the road, looking curiously in at the side window of the Deanes' sitting-room on
the way, to make sure she was right about the caller being
gone, and to watch if they had heard Phoebe, for she
thought it might be necessary for her to invent a diversion of
some sort. But she only saw Albert asleep in his chair and
Emmeline working grimly at her sewing.

About half way to the red school-house Miranda met Hiram Green. He looked up, frowning. He thought it was
Phoebe, and wondered if it were possible that she was going
to the village for a fourth trip yet that night. If she were, she
must be crazy.

"Ev'nin', Hiram," said Miranda, nonchalantly, "seen
anythin' of a little white kitten with one blue eye and one
green one, an' a black tip to her tail, an' a pink nose? I've
been up to see if she follered Phoebe Deane home from our
house las' night, but she's gone to bed with the toothache an'
I wouldn't disturb her fer the world. I thought I'd mebbe
find her round this way. You ain't seen her, have yeh?"

"No," growled Hiram, suspiciously, "I'd a wrung her
neck ef I had."

"Oh, thank you, Mr. Green. You're very kind," said Miranda, sweetly. "I'll remember that, next little kitten I lose.
I'll know jest who t' apply to fer it. Lovely night, ain't it?
Don't trouble yerself 'bout the kitten. I reckon it's safe
somewheres. 'Taint every one 's ez blood-thirsty's you be.
Good-night." And Miranda flung off down the road before
Hiram could decide whether she was poking fun at him or
was extremely dull. At last he roused himself from his weary
pondering, uttered his accustomed ejaculation, "Gosh!"
looked up the road toward the Deanes' and down toward
the vanishing Miranda, brought forth the expression he re-

served for the perplexing crises in his life, "Gosh Ninety!" and went home to bed. He had not been able all day to quite fathom the mystery which he was attempting to control, and this new unknown quantity was more perplexing than all that had gone before. What, for instance, had Miranda Griscom to do with Phoebe Deane? His slow brain remembered that she had been in the store where Phoebe—it must have been Phoebe; for he did not believe he could have been mistaken—had disappeared. Had Miranda spirited her away somewhere? Ah! And it was Miranda who had come up to Phoebe after church and interrupted their walk together! What had Miranda to do with it all? Hang Miranda! He would like to wring her neck, too. With such charming meditations he fell asleep.

14

NATHANIEL sat inside the coach as it rolled through the village streets and out into the country road toward Albany, and tried to think. All remembrance of Janet and her foolish pet had passed from his mind. He had before him a problem to decide. It was the harder because the advice of his nearest and dearest friends was so at variance.

He took out two letters which represented the two sides of the question and began to reread. The first was the letter which Phoebe had brought, torn, disfigured by the dust, but still legible. It bore a Texas postmark and was brief and businesslike.

> Dear Nephew, (it read), if you are keen as you used to be you have been keeping yourself informed about old Texas, and know the whole state of the case better than I can put it. Ever since Austin went to ask the admission of Texas as a separate state into the Mexican Republic and was denied and thrown into prison, our people have been gathering together; and now things are coming to a crisis. Something will be done and that right soon, perhaps in a few days. The troops are gath-

ering near Gonzales. Resistance will be made. But we need help. We want young blood, and strong arms behind which are heads and hearts with a conviction for right and freedom. No one on earth has a right to deprive us of our property, and say we shall not own slaves which we have come honestly by. We will fight and win, as the United States has fought and won its right to govern itself. Now I call upon you, Nathaniel, to rise up and bring honor to your father's name by raising a company of young men to come down here and set Texas free. I know you are busy with your law studies but they will keep and Texas will not. Texas must be set free now or never. When you were a little chap you had strong convictions about what was right, and I feel pretty sure my appeal will not come to deaf ears. Your father loved Texas and came down here to make his fortune. If he had lived he would have been here fighting. He would have been a slave-owner, and have asserted his right as a free man in a free country to protect his property. He would have taught his son to do the same. I call upon you for your father's sake to come down here in the hour of your Texas' need—for it is the place where you were born—and help us. Use your utmost influence to get other young men to come with you.

Your uncle the Judge will perhaps help you financially. He owns a couple of slaves himself I remember, house servants, does he not? Ask him how he would like the government of the United States to order him to set them free. I feel sure he will sympathize with Texas in her need and help you to do this thing which I have asked.

I am a man of few words, but I trust you, Nathaniel, and I feel sure I am not pleading in vain. I shall expect something from you at once. We need the help now or the cause may be lost. If you feel as I think you do

go to the New York address given below. This letter
will be sufficient identification for you as I have written to them of you, but it is most important that you
present this letter or it will do no good to go, but *be
sure that no one else sees it,* or great harm may come to
you! There is grave danger in being found out, but if I
did not know your brave spirit I would not be writing
you. Come as soon as possible!

Your uncle,
Royal Graham

The other letter was kept waiting a long time while the
young man read and reread this one, and then let his eyes
wander through the window of the coach to the brown
fields and dim hills in the distance. He was going over all he
could remember of his boyhood life in that far-away Southern home. He could dimly remember the form of his father,
who had been to him a great hero; who had taken him with
him on horseback wherever he went and never been too
weary or too busy for his little son. There came a blur of
sadness over the picture, the death of this beloved father,
and an interval of emptiness when the gentle mother was too
full of sorrow to know how the baby heart had felt the utter
loneliness, and then one day this Uncle Royal, so like yet not
like his father, had lifted him in his arms and said: "Good-by,
little chap. Some day you'll come back to us and do your
father's work, and take his place." Then he and his mother
had ridden away in an endless succession of postchaises and
coaches, until one day they had come to Judge Bristol's great
white house set among the green hedges, and there
Nathaniel had found a new home. There, first his mother,
and then Janet's mother, had slipped away into that mysterious door of death, and he had grown up in the home of his
mother's brother, with Janet as a sister. From time to time he
had received letters from his shadowy uncle in Texas, and
once, when he was about twelve, there had been a brief visit

from him which cleared the memory and kept him fresh in Nathaniel's mind; and always there had been some hint or sentence of expectation that when Nathaniel was grown and educated he would come back to the country which had been his father's and help to make it great. This had been a hazy undertone always in his life, in spite of the fact that his other uncle, Judge Bristol, was constantly talking of his future career as a lawyer in New York City, with a possibility of a political career also. Nathaniel had gone on with his life, working out the daily plan as it came, with all the time the feeling that these two plans were contending in him for supremacy. Sometimes during leisure moments lately he had wondered if the two could ever be combined, and if not how possibly they were to both work out. Gradually it had dawned upon him that a day was coming, indeed might not be far away, when he would have to choose. And now, since these two letters had reached him, he knew the time had come. And how was he to know how to choose?

His Uncle Royal's letter had reached him the afternoon of the nutting party on the hill. Pompey, his uncle's house servant, had brought it to him on a silver salver just as they were starting. He had glanced at the familiar writing, known it for his uncle's and put it in his pocket for reading at his leisure. He always enjoyed his uncle's letters, yet they were not of deep moment to him. He had been too long separated from him to have keen interests in common with him. Hence he had not read the letter until after his return from the hill-side, which explains how he had carelessly left it behind the log by Phoebe, as an excuse to return and help her out of the laurel.

In the quiet of his own room after Janet and the others were sleeping he had remembered the letter, and, relighting his candle, which had been extinguished, he had read it, feeling a touch of reproach that he could have so lightly put off attending to his good relative's words. How, then, was he startled to discover its contents! The talk of the afternoon

floated back to him, idle talk, about his going down to set
Texas free. Talk that grew out of his own keen interest in all
the questions of the day, and his readiness to argue them out.
But he had never had a very definite idea of going to Texas
to take part in the struggle that was going on until this letter
brought him face to face with a possible duty.

Perhaps he would have had no question about his decision, if, following hard upon this letter, had not come the
other one, the very next day in fact, which put an entirely
new phase upon some sides of the question, and made duty
seem an uncertain creature with more faces than one.

The coach was half way to Albany before Nathaniel finally folded away his uncle's letter and put it in his inner pocket
with great care. Then he took up the other letter with a perplexed sigh, and read:

Dear Chum:

I am sitting on a high point of white sand, where I
can look off at the blue sea. At my right is a great
hairy, prickly cactus with a few gorgeous yellow blos-
soms in a glory of delicate petals and fringed stamens
that look as out of place amid the sand as a diamond
on a plank. Just now a green lizard peered curiously
out from under one of the hairy balls that pass for
leaves with a cactus, and then slid back out of sight.
But the next time I looked he was blue, brilliant, and
palpitating as a peacock's feathers, and sunning himself, not thinking of me at all. Then just as I moved he
became a dull gray-brown, hardly discernible from the
sand. And thus I know he is not a lizard at all, but a
chameleon. The sun is very warm and bright, and everything about seems basking in it.

As I look off to sea the Gulf Stream is distinct to-
day, a brilliant green ribbon in the brilliant blue of the
sea. It winds along so curiously and so independently
in the great ocean, keeping its own individuality in

spite of storm and wind and tide. I went out in a small boat across it the other day, and could look down and see it as distinctly as if there were a glass wall between it and the other water. I cannot but think that God took pleasure in making this old earth—so curious, mysterious, and beautiful.

A great lazy bird is floating high in the air, looking down to the water for prey, doubtless. I think I could almost see the bright, curious fishes of this strange clime darting in the sunny water myself, if I tried, the air is so clear and the days so bright.

There are orange groves back of me, not far away—a few miles. I fancy their perfume is wafted even here. There is a curious sweet apathy that steals over one down here, which soothes, and rests.

I am having a holiday, for my little pupils are gone away on a visit. This is a delightful land to which I have come, and a charming family with whom my lot is cast. I am having an opportunity to study the South in a most ideal manner, and many of my former ideas of it are becoming much modified. For example, there is slavery. I am by no means so sure as I used to be that it was ordained of God. I wish you were here to talk it over with me, and to study it, too. There are possibilities in the institution that make one shudder. Perhaps, after all, Texas is in the wrong. As you have opportunity drop into an Abolition meeting now and then and see what you think. I have been reading the *Liberator* lately. I find much in it that is strong and appeals to my sense of right. You know what a disturbance it has made in the country recently. I hear some mails have even been broken into and burned on account of it. I wonder if this question of slavery will ever be an issue in our country. If it should be I cannot help wondering what the South will do. From what I have seen I feel sure they will never stand it to have their rights interfered with.

Now, I have to confess that much as I rebelled against giving up my work and coming down here I feel that it has already benefited me. I can take long walks without the least weariness, and can even talk and sing like any one else without becoming hoarse. I do not believe my lungs have ever been affected, and I feel I am going to get well and come back to my work. With that hope in my veins I can go joyfully through these sunny days and feel the new life creeping into me with every breath of balmy air. We shall yet work shoulder to shoulder, my friend—I feel it. God bless you and keep you, and show you the right.

Yours, faithfully,
Martin Van Rensselaer

Nathaniel folded the letter, placed it in his pocket with the other, and leaned his head back to think. It was all perplexing.

This man Van Rensselaer had been his room-mate for four years. They had grown into one another's thoughts as two who are much together and love each other will grow until each had come to depend upon the other's decision as if it were nearly his own judgment. Nathaniel could not quite tell why it was that this letter troubled him, yet he felt breathing through the whole epistle the stirring of a new principle that seemed to antagonize his sympathy with Texas.

So, through the long cold journey the question was debated back and forth. His duty to his uncle demanded that he go to the address given and investigate the matter of helping Texas, else his uncle might think him exceedingly neglectful; and when he looked at the question from his uncle's stand-point, and thought of his father, and his own natural heritage, his sympathy was with Texas. On the other hand his love for his friend and his perfect trust in him demanded that he investigate the other side also. He felt intuitively that the two things could not go together.

Martin Van Rensselaer had been preparing for the Christian ministry. His zeal and earnestness were great, too great for his strength, and before he had finished his theological studies he had broken down and been sent South, as it was feared he had serious lung trouble. This separation had been a great trial to both young men. Martin was three years older than Nathaniel, and two years ahead of him in his studies, but in mind and spirit they were as one, so that the words of the letter had great influence.

The day had grown surly as the coach rumbled on. Sullen clouds lowered in the corners of the sky as if meditating mutiny. There was a hint of snow in the biting air that whistled around the cracks of the coach windows. Nature seemed to have suddenly put on a bare, brown look—hopeless, discouraging cold.

Nathaniel shivered and drew his cloak close about him. He wished the journey were over, or that he had some one with whom to advise. Somehow the question troubled him as if it were of immediate necessity that it be decided, and he could not dismiss it, nor put it off. He had once or twice broached the subject with Judge Bristol, but had hesitated to show him either of the letters which had been the cause of his own perplexity. He felt that his uncle's letter might arouse antagonism in Judge Bristol on account of the claim it seemed to put upon himself, as his father's son, to come and give himself.

Judge Bristol was almost jealously fond of his sister's son, and felt that he belonged to the North. Aside from that, his sympathies would probably have been with Texas. Keeping a few slaves himself as house servants, and treating them as kindly as if they had been his own children, he saw no reason to object to slavery, and deemed it a man's right to do as he pleased with his own property.

Martin Van Rensselaer's letter the Judge would have been likely to look upon as the production of a sentimental, hot-headed fanatic, whose judgment was unsound. Nathaniel was morally certain that if the Judge should read those letters he would advise against having anything to do with either cause personally; yet, dearly as he loved and honored the Judge, who had been a second father to him, Nathaniel's conscience would not let him drop the matter thus easily.

So the coach thumped on over rough roads and smooth. The coachman called to his horses, snapped his whip alluringly, and wondered why Nathaniel, who was usually so sociable, and liked to sit on the box and talk, stayed glumly inside with never a word for him. The coachman was the same one who had brought Nathaniel and his mother to the Judge's door that first time when on their last stage route from Texas. He felt aggrieved, for Nathaniel belonged to him. Had he not allowed him to drive in smooth stretches of road, even when he was a little fellow? Could it be possible that New York had spoiled him, and he was growing too proud to companion with his old friend, or was he in love? The coachman sat gloomily mile after mile, and tried to think what girl of his acquaintance was good enough for Nathaniel.

But all oblivious of his old friend's disquietude, Nathaniel sat inside with closed eyes and tried to think, and ever and anon there came a vision of a sweet-faced girl with brown hair and a golden gown sitting among the falling yellow leaves with bowed head; and somehow in his thoughts her trouble became tangled, and it seemed as if there were three instead of two who needed setting free, and he was to choose between them all.

15

THE cold weather had come suddenly and Phoebe felt like a prisoner. Emmeline's tongue became a daily torture, and the little ways in which she contrived to make Phoebe's life a burden were too numerous to count. Her paltry fortune in the bank was a source of continual trouble. Scarcely a morning passed but it was referred to in some unpleasant way. Every request was prefaced with some such phrase as: "If you're not too grand to soil your hands," or "I don't like to ask a rich lady to do such a thing," till Phoebe felt sometimes that she could bear it no longer and longed to take the few dollars and fling them into the lap of her disagreeable sister-in-law, if thereby she might but gain peace. Like the continual dropping that wears the stone, the unpleasant reference had worn upon a single nerve until the pain was acute.

But there was another source of discomfort still more trying to the girl than all that had gone before, and this was Hiram Green's new role. He had taken it upon himself to act the fine gentleman. It was somewhat surprising considering the fact that Hiram was known in the village as "near," and this new departure demanded an entirely new outfit of clothes. In his selection he aimed to emulate Nathaniel Graham. As he had neither Nathaniel's taste nor his New York tailor the effect was far from perfect, except perhaps in the eyes of Hiram, who felt quite set up in his fine raiment.

On the first Sunday of his proud appearance in church thus arrayed he waited boldly at the door until the Deanes came out and then took his place beside Phoebe and walked with her to the carryall as though he belonged there. Phoebe's thoughts were on other things and for a moment she had not noticed, but suddenly becoming conscious of measured footsteps by her own, she looked up and found the reconstructed Hiram strutting by her side as consciously as a peacock. In spite of her great annoyance her first impulse was to laugh, and that laugh probably did more than any other thing to turn the venom of Hiram Green's hate upon her own innocent head. After all the effort he had made to appear well before her, and before the congregation assembled she had laughed. She had dared to laugh aloud, and that hateful Miranda Griscom, who seemed to be always around in the way whenever he tried to walk with Phoebe had laughed back. A slow ugly red rolled into his sun-burned face, and his little eyes narrowed with resolve to pay back all and more than he had received of scorn.

It happened that Miranda was holding Rose by the hand, and could not without greatly attracting attention get much nearer to Phoebe that morning, so the girl could do nothing to get away from her unpleasant suitor except to hasten to the carryall. And there before the open-eyed congregation Hiram Green helped her into the carryall with a rude imitation of Nathaniel Graham's gallantry. She should see that others besides the New York college dandy could play the fine gentleman. He finished the operation with an exaggerated flourish of his hat, and just because laughter is so very near to tears, the tears sprang up in

Phoebe's eyes. She could do nothing but droop her head and try as best she could to hide them. The all-seeing Alma of course discovered them, and just as they were driving by Judge Bristol and his daughter she called out: "Aunt Phoebe's cryin'. What you cryin' 'bout, Aunt Phoebe? Is it 'cause you can't ride with Hiram Green?"

Thereafter Hiram Green was in attendance upon her at every possible public place. She could not go to church without finding him at her elbow the minute the service was over, ready to walk down the very aisle beside her. She could not go to singing-school but he would step out from behind his gate as she passed and join her, or if she evaded him he would sit beside her and manage to sing out of the same book. She could not go to the village on an errand but he would appear in the way and accompany her. He seemed to have developed a strange intuition as to her every movement. He was ever vigilant, and the girl began to feel like a hunted creature. Even if she stayed at home he appeared at the door ten minutes after the family had gone, a triumphant, unpleasant smile upon his face, and sauntered into the kitchen without waiting for her to bid him, and there, tilted back in a chair in his favorite attitude, he would watch her every movement, and drawl out an occasional remark. That happened only once, however; she never dared to stay again, lest it would be repeated. She had been busy preparing something for dinner, and she turned suddenly and caught a look upon his face that reminded her of a beast of prey. It flashed upon her that he was actually enjoying her annoyance. Without waiting to think she stepped into the wood-shed, and from there fairly fled across the back yard, and the meadows between and burst into the bright little room of Granny McVane.

The dear old lady sat there rocking by the fire, with her open Bible on her knee. Phoebe was relieved to find her alone, and in answer to the gentle: "Why, dearie, what can be the matter?" she flung herself on the floor at the old lady's feet and putting her head in her lap burst into tears.

It was only for a moment that she lost her self-control, but even that moment relieved the heavy strain on her nerves, and she was able to sit up and tell the old lady all about it. She had not intended to tell anything, when in her sudden panic she had beaten a hasty retreat from the enemy, but Granny McVane's sweet face showed so much tender sympathy that all at once it seemed good to tell some one her trouble.

She listened, watched her sympathetically, smoothed back the damp tendrils of hair that had blown about her face, and then stooped over and kissed her.

"Don't you ever marry him, Phoebe. Don't you ever do it, if you don't love him, child!" she said, solemnly, like a warning. "And just you run over here, dearie, whenever he bothers you. I'll take care of you."

Phoebe, with her natural reserve, had not drawn her family into the story except to say that they favored the suit of the would-be lover. But it comforted her greatly to have someone on her side, even if it were but this quiet old lady who could not really help her much.

They watched out the back windows until they saw Hiram emerge from the Deane house and saunter off down the road. Even then Phoebe was afraid to go back until she saw the carryall far down the road. Then she flew across the fields and entered the back door before they had turned in at the great gate. When they got out and came into the house she was demurely paring potatoes, and Emmeline eyed her suspiciously.

"Seems to me you're pretty late with your potatoes," she remarked, disagreeably. "I suppose you had a nice easy time all the morning."

But Phoebe did not explain, only she did not stay at home again when the family were all to be away. She never knew whether Emmeline was aware of Hiram's Sunday morning visit or not.

Phoebe's state of mind after this occurrence was one of constant nervous alarm. She began to hate the thought of the man who seemed to haunt her at every turn.

Heretofore one of her greatest pleasures had been to walk to the village after the daily mail, or for an errand to the store. Now such walks became a dread. One afternoon in early November she had hurried away and gone around by Granny McVane's, hoping thus to escape the vigilance of Hiram Green. She managed to get safely to the village, and get her errands done, but just as she emerged from the post-office the long, lank figure of Hiram loomed before her and slouched into his dogged gait beside her. "Did you get a letter?" he asked, looking suspiciously at the one she held in her hand. Then as she did not answer he went on: "You must have a whole lot of folks writin' you quite constant; you seem to go to the post-office so much."

Phoebe said nothing. She felt too indignant to speak. How could she get away from her tormentor unless she deliberately ran away from him? And how could she do that right here in the village where every one was watching? She glanced up furtively. Hiram wore a look of triumph as he talked on, knowing he was annoying her.

"I s'pose you get letters from New York," he said, and there was a disagreeable insinuation in his tone. Phoebe did not know what he meant, but something in his tone made the color come into her cheeks. They were nearing the Spafford house. If only Miranda would come out and speak to her! She looked up at the great bully beside her and saw he was trying to calculate just how near to the mark he had come. She stopped short on the pavement.

"I do not wish to walk with you," she said, struggling to keep her voice from trembling.

"Oh, you don't," he mocked. "How 'r ye goin' to help yourself?"

She looked up into the pitiless cruelty of his eyes and shuddered involuntarily.

"I am going in to see Mrs. Spafford," she said, with sudden inspiration, and her voice took on a girlish dignity. With that she put wings to her feet and flew to the Spafford front door, wondering if anyone would let her in before Hiram reached her.

Now Miranda was alone in the house that afternoon, and not much went on in the neighborhood that she did not keep herself informed concerning; therefore, when Phoebe, breathless, reached the front stoop the door swung open before her, and she stepped into her refuge with a gasp of relief and heard it close behind her as two strong freckled arms enclosed her and two honest lips greeted her with a resounding kiss.

"Ben waitin' quite a spell fer ye," she declared, as if it were the expected thing for Phoebe to fly into her arms unannounced in that way, "ever sence I see ye comin' down the street with that pleasant friend of yourn. Wonder you could tear yourself away. Take off yer bonnet and set a spell. Mis' Spafford's gone up t' th' aunts fer tea an took Rose. I'm all alone. You set down an' we'll have a real nice time an' then I'll take you home by 'n by."

"Oh, Miranda," gasped Phoebe, struggling hysterically between laughter and tears and trying to control the trembling that had taken possession of her body, "I'm such a miserable coward. I'm always running away when I get frightened!"

"H'm! I should hope you would!" said Miranda significantly. "Such a snake in the grass as that! Le's see ef he's gone!" and she crouched before the window and peered behind the curtain cautiously.

Hiram had watched Phoebe's sudden disappearance within the door with something like awe. It was almost uncanny having that door open and swallow her up. Besides, he had not expected that Phoebe would dare to run away from him. He stood a moment gazing after her, and then sauntered on undecidedly, calling himself a fool for having met her so near to the Spafford house. Another time he would choose his meeting-place away from her friends. He had lost this move in the game, but he by no means meant to lose the game, and the hate in his heart grew with his determination to have this tempting young life in his power and crush out its resistance.

It goaded him to madness to have her dare to tell him she did not wish to walk with him. Why did she say that? Had he not always been respected, and thought well of? His farm was as good a spot of land as could be found in the whole of New York state, and his barn was talked of through all the county. He was prosperous, everybody knew. Before he had married Annie any girl in the vicinity would have thought him a great catch, and he knew well, by all the indescribable signs, that many a girl as good as Phoebe would still be glad to accept his attentions. Why did this little nobody, who was after all merely a poor relation of his neighbor, presume to scorn him? He hated her for it, even while his heart was set upon having her. He had wanted her at first because he admired her. Now he wanted her to conquer her and punish her for her scorn of him.

As he walked on alone his slow brain tried to form a new plan for revenge, and little by little an idea crept out of his thoughts and looked at him with its two snaky eyes until the poison of its fang had stolen into his heart. The post-office! Ah! He would watch to see if she had a letter from that fellow, for surely only the knowledge that another man was at her feet could make her scorn his attentions. If that was so he would crush the rival! He ground his teeth at the thought, and his eyes glittered with hate.

Meantime, Hiram Green's children and Alma Deane were playing together behind the big barn that had been one of the disappointments of Annie Green's married life, because it had not been a house instead of a barn. The children had dug houses in a hay-stack, and chased the few venturesome hens that had not learned to be wary when they were around; now, for the moment weary of their games, they mounted the fence to rest.

"There comes your pa," announced Alma from her perch on the top rail. The young Greens retired precipitately from the fence, and Alma was forced to follow them if she wished company. They hurried around the other side of the barn out of sight.

"Say," said Alma, after they had reached a spot of safety and ensconced themselves on the sunny exposure of a board across two logs, "my Aunt Phoebe went to the village a while ago. She'll be 'long pretty soon. Let's make up somethin' an' shout at her when she comes back. It'll make her mad as hops an' I'd just like to pay her back fer the way she acts sometimes."

"Ain't she good to you?" enquired the youngest Green, anxiously.

"Le's make up sumpin' 'bout her 'n your pa. There ain't nothin' 'll make her so mad. She's mad as mad can be when my ma says anythin' bout her gettin' married," went on Alma, ignoring the question.

"All right! What'll we make up?" agreed the three Greens. They were not anxious to have a step-mother who might make life's restrictions more strenuous than they were already. They were prepared to do battle valiantly if they only had a general, and Alma was thoroughly competent in their eyes to fill that position.

"It'll have to be to a song, you know," went on Alma. "Le's sing the Doxol'gy an' see how that goes." So they all stood in an enquiring row and droned out the Doxology, piping shrilly where they knew the words and filling in with home-made syllables where they did not. Alma had practised the art of rhyming before, and was anxious to display the skill she had acquired since their last meeting.

"Now listen!" she said, and lined it out, slowly, with many haltings and corrections, until at last the doggerel was completed, and so they sang:

There-was-a-man-in-ow-wer-town
   His-name-was-Hi-rum-Gre-ee-een
And-he-did-ma-a-air-ree-a-wife
   Her-name-was-Phe-be-Dee-ee-een.

Alma was no lax general. She drilled her little company
again and again until they could shout the words at the top
of their voices, to say nothing of the way they murdered Old
Hundred. The young scapegraces looked at their leader with
wide-eyed admiration, and fairly palpitated for the moment
when their victim should arrive and they might put their
drill into practice. Between rehearsals they mounted the
fence by the barn and kept a watch-out down the road. At
last it was announced that she was coming.

"But there's somebuddy with 'er," said a disappointed little Green. "We won't dast, will we?"

Alma held up her undaunted chin and mounted the post
of observation to see who it was.

"Aw! That's all right," she presently announced.
" 'Tain't nobody but the red-headed girl down to Spaffords'.
She can't do nothin'. Come on, now, le's get ready."

She marshalled her forces behind the wide board fence
next to the pig-sty and there they waited for the signal to begin. Alma thought it prudent to wait until Phoebe and Miranda had almost passed before they sang. Then she raised
her hand and they piped out shrilly, making the words more
than plain. Phoebe started at the first line and hurried her
steps, but Miranda glanced back and said: "H'm! I thought
'es much. Like father, like child!"

Maddened by such indifference the children ran along inside the fence and continued to yell at the top of their lungs,
regardless of time or tune until they reached the more open
fields near the Deane house, where they dared go no further.
Then they retired in triumph to the shelter of the pig-sty and
the hay-stack to plume themselves upon their success, and
recount the numerous faces they had made, and the times

they had stuck their tongues out. They did not anticipate any trouble from the incident as they were too far away from the house for Hiram to hear, and they felt sure Phoebe would never tell on them, as it involved herself too closely.

Suddenly, in the midst of the gratulations, without the slightest warning, a strong hand seized the sturdy Alma from the rear and pinioned her arms so that she could not get away. She set up a yell that could have been heard for a half mile, and began to kick and squirm, but Miranda's hands held her fast, while she took in the surroundings at a glance, moved her captive toward a convenient seat on a log, and taking her calmly over her knee administered in full measure the spanking that the child deserved, Alma, meanwhile yelling like a loon, unable to believe her senses that the despised "red-haired girl from Spaffords' " had displayed so much ability and thoroughness in her methods of redress.

The valiant army of little Greens had retired with haste from the scene of action, and were even then virtuously combing their hair and washing their hands and faces with a view to proving an alibi should the avenger seek further retribution. Alma was left to the mercy of Miranda and though she kicked and yelled right lustily Miranda spanked on until she was tired.

"There!" she said, at last letting her go. "That ain't half you need, but I can't spend any more time on yeh to-day. Ef yeh ever do that er anythin' like it again I'll come in the night when everybody's asleep and give yeh the rest, an' I ken tell you now I won't let yeh off this easy next time. Mind you behave to yer Aunt Phoebe, er I'll hant yeh! D'yeh understand? Wherever yeh go in the dark I'll be there to hant yeh. And when red-haired people hants yeh at night their hair's all on fire in the dark an' it burns yeh, so yeh better watch out!"

She shook her fist decidedly at the child, who, now thoroughly frightened, began to cry in earnest and ran away home as fast as her fat legs could carry her, not daring to look back lest the supernatural creature with the fiery hair and the strong hand should be upon her again. It was the first time in her brief, impertinent life that Alma had ever been thoroughly frightened.

Her first act on reaching the house was to see how the land lay. She found that her mother had gone out to get some eggs and that Phoebe was up in her room with the door buttoned. No one else was about, so Alma stole noiselessly up to Phoebe's door, righteous innocence upon her tear-stained face, her voice smoother than butter with deceit.

"Aunt Phoebe!" she called, lovingly, "I hope you don't think I sung that mean song at you. I was real 'shamed of them Green chil'dern. I run after 'em an' tried to make em' stop, but they jest wouldn't. I think their pa ought to be told, don't you? Say, Aunt Phoebe, you didn't think 'twas me, did you?"

There was no answer from the other side of the door for Phoebe was lying on her bed shaking with suppressed sobs, and could not control her voice to reply even if she had known what to say. Her heart was filled with pain, too, that this child whom she had tended and been kind to should be so hateful.

Alma, rather nonplussed at receiving no answer, tried once or twice and then calling out sweetly: "Well, I just thought I'd let you know 'twasn't me, Aunt Phoebe," stumped off downstairs to reflect upon the way of sinners. Her main fear was that Phoebe would "tell on her" to her father, and then she knew she would receive the other half of her spanking.

But Phoebe, with a face white with suffering, and dark rings under her eyes, said not a word when she came down stairs, but went about her work not even seeming to see the naughty child, until Alma gradually grew more confident and resolved to put the "hanting" out of her mind entirely. This was easier said than done, however, for when night came she dreaded to go to bed, and she made several unsuccessful attempts to help Phoebe with the supper dishes, thereby calling upon herself much undeserved commendation from her gratified mother and father, which helped ease her conscience not a little.

16

HIRAM Green began to put his new plan into practice the very next day. He took care to be on hand when the mail coach arrived, and as soon as the mail was distributed he presented himself at the post-office corner of the store.

"Any mail fer th' Deanes?" he enquired carelessly, after he had been told there was nothing for himself. "I'm goin' up there on business an' I'll save 'em the trouble o' comin' down."

This question he put in varied forms, until it grew to be a habit with the postmaster to hand over the Deanes' mail to Hiram every day. This was rather expensive business, for Albert frequently received letters from people who did not prepay the postage, and it went much against Hiram's grain to hand out eighteen cents or more for another man's letter, even though he were sure he would receive it again. He made prompt collections from Albert, however, and by this means Phoebe became aware of Hiram's daily visits to the post-office. Not that it made any difference to her, for she did not expect a letter from any one. There was no one to write to her.

This went on for about two weeks, and during that time

Hiram had been able to see very little of Phoebe, for she kept herself well out of his way, when one day a letter bearing a New York post-mark, and closed with heavy seals, arrived, addressed to Miss Phoebe Deane.

Hiram grasped it as if it had been a long sought fortune, put it hastily in his pocket, looking furtively around lest any one had seen it, and slouched off toward home. When he reached there he went straight to his own room and fastened the door. Then he took out the letter and read the address again, written in a fine large hand of a man accustomed to handling the pen. He frowned and turned it over. The seals were stamped with a crest on which was a lion, rampant, that seemed to defy him. He held the letter up to the light, but could not make out any words. Then without hesitation he took out his knife and inserted the sharpest blade under the seals one by one, prying them up carefully so that they should not be broken more than could be helped. The letter lay open before him at last and he read with rising fury:

New York, December 20th, 1835

My Dear Miss Deane:

Will you pardon my presumption in daring thus to address you without permission? My pleasant memory of our brief acquaintance has led me to wish a continuance of it, and I am writing to ask you if you are free and willing to correspond with me occasionally. It will be a great source of pleasure to me if you can accede to my request, and I am sure I shall be profited by it also.

Night before last our city was visited by a great calamity in the shape of a terrible fire which is still burning, although they hope they now have it under control. Its course has been along Wall Street, the line of the East River, and returning to William and Wall Streets. There must be nearly thirteen acres devastated, and I have heard it estimated that there will be a loss of at least eighteen millions of dollars. I am afraid it will be the cause of much suffering and distress. I was out last evening watching the conflagration for a time, and helping to fight the fire. It was a terrible and beautiful sight.

I have just had the honor and privilege of meeting a noble and brave gentleman. His name is William Lloyd Garrison. I feel sure you would like to know about him and the work he is doing. If I am to have the pleasure of writing you again I shall be glad to tell you more of him, as I hope to meet him again, and to know him better.

Hoping that you are quite well, and that I shall soon have a favorable reply from you, I am,

Yours with esteem,
Nathaniel Graham

Hiram Green was not a rapid reader, and in spite of Nathaniel's clear chirography it took him some time to take in all that the letter contained. The first thought that took form in his mind was that this rival of his was not out of his way yet. He had dared to write to her and ask if she was free. Ah! That showed he had taken note of what Hiram had said about her belonging to him, and he was going to find out for himself. Well, he would never find out by that letter, for Phoebe would never see it. That was easy enough. Of course it was against the law to open another person's mail, and was a state's prison offense, but who was to know that he had opened it? A letter could tell no tales when it was in ashes, and the ashes well buried. How else could they prove it? They could not. He was perfectly safe, and more and more was he getting power over these two whom he was coming to hate and to wish to crush. He congratulated himself on having been keen enough to have watched the mails. He had outwitted them, and he was pleased with himself beyond expression.

"H'm!" he ejaculated under his breath. "He's a goin' to get up a correspondence with her, is he? Like to see him! I rather think by the time she answers this letter he'll 'uv give it up. When he gets around again to give her another try—supposin' he ain't stumped at not hearin' from her this time—I reckon she'll be nicely established in my kitchen doin' my work. Yes, she's worth fightin' for, I guess, fer she ken turn off the work faster'n anybody I've seen. Wal, I guess there ain't any cause to worry 'bout this."

Then he read it over again, and yet again, noting down on an old bit of paper the date, and a few items about the fire in New York, also William Lloyd Garrison's name. After that he sent the old woman who was keeping house for him to the attic in search of a coat he knew was not there, while he carefully burned the letter on the hearth, gathering every scrap of its ashes and pulverizing them, to make sure not a trace remained to tell the tale.

As he walked away towards his barn he felt himself a man of consequence. His self-satisfaction fairly radiated from his lanky figure. For had he not outwitted a college man? And no thought of the crime he had just committed troubled his dull conscience for an instant.

That evening he took his eager way to Albert Deane's house and prepared to enjoy himself. The sunrise bedquilt was long since finished and rolled away in the chest of drawers in the spare bedroom. The spinning-wheel had taken the place of the quilting frames. And it happened that on this particular night Emmeline had demanded that Phoebe stay downstairs and spin, declaring that the yarn ought to have been ready long ago for more winter stockings.

Hiram noted this fact with satisfaction, and tilted his chair in pleasurable anticipation.

"Heard anythin' about the big fire in New York?" he began, watching Phoebe's back narrowly to see if she would start. But Phoebe worked steadily on. She paid little heed to anything Hiram said, but as they talked of the fire she wondered whether Nathaniel Graham had been near it, and hoped in a maidenly way that he had been kept safe from harm.

"Why, no," said Albert, sitting up with interest, "I haven't looked at the paper yet—" unfolding it with zest. "How'd you come to know, Hiram? You say you never read the papers."

"Oh, I have better ways o' knowin' than readin' it in the papers," boasted Hiram, airily. "I had a letter from New York straight, an' the fire's goin' on yet, an' mebbe by this time it's all burnt up."

Phoebe stood so that he could see her face distinctly as he spoke about receiving a letter, but there was not a movement of a muscle to show she had heard. Hiram was disappointed. He had expected to catch some flitting expression that would show him she had interests in letters from New York. But Phoebe had no expectations of any letter from New York, so why should she start or look troubled?

"Yes," said Albert, bending over his paper, "an area of thirteen acres—six hundred and ninety-three houses burned!"

"Valued at eighteen millions!" remarked Hiram, dryly. He was enjoying the unique position of knowing more than Albert about something.

"Nonsense!" said Emmeline, sharply. "Thirteen acres! Why, that's not much bigger'n Hiram's ten-acre lot down by the old chestnut-tree. Think of gettin' that many houses on that lot! It couldn't be done. That ain't possible. It's ridiculous! They must think we're all fools to put that in the paper."

"Oh, yes, it could, Emmeline," said Albert, looking up earnestly to convince her. "Why, even so long ago as when I stayed in New York for a month they built the houses real close without much door-yard. They could easy get that many into thirteen acres built close."

"I don't believe it!" said Emmeline, flipping her spinning-wheel around skilfully, "and anyway, if 'twas so I think it was real shiftless to let 'em all burn up. Why didn't they put it out? Those New York folks were born lazy."

"Why, Emmeline, the paper says it was so cold the water froze in the hose-pipes and they couldn't put it out."

"Serves 'em right then fer dependin' on such new-fangled things as hose-pipes. It's jest some more of their laziness. Why didn't they form a line and hand buckets? A good fire line with the women an' all in it would beat all the new lazy ways invented to save folks from liftin' their fingers to even put out a fire. I'm surprised some of 'em didn't jest sit still and expect some kind of a new machine to be made in time to wheel 'em away to safety 'stead of usin' their legs and runnin' out o' harm's way. Haven't they got a river in New York?"

" 'Course" said Hiram, as if he knew it all. "The fire burned the whole line of the East River." He was glad to be reminded of the rest of his newly-acquired information.

"There, that just shows it!" exclaimed Emmeline. "That's just what I said. Shiftless lot, they are. Let their houses burn up right in front of a river! Well, I'm thankful to say I don't live in New York!"

The talk hummed on about her, but Phoebe heard no more. Somehow she kept her busy wheel whirring, but her thoughts had wandered off in a sunlit wood, and she was holding sweet converse with a golden day, and a stranger hovering on the pleasant horizon. It was not until near the close of the evening that her thoughts came back to listen to what was going on. Hiram had brought the front legs of his chair down to the floor with a thud. Phoebe thought he was going home, and she was glad they would soon be rid of his hated presence.

"Oh, by the way!" said Hiram, with a swag of conceit, "Albert, have you ever heard of a man named Garrison?

William Lloyd Garrison, I believe it is."

He rolled the name out fluently, having practised in the barn during the evening milking.

"Oh, yes," said Albert, interestedly. "You know who he is, Hiram. He's a smart fellow, though I'd hate to be in his boots!"

"Why?" Hiram's voice was sharp and his eyes narrowed as they always did when he was reaching out for a clue.

"Why don't you know about Garrison? He's had a price on his head for some time back. He gets mobbed every time he turns around, too, but I guess he's pretty plucky, for he keeps right on."

"What doing?"

"Why, he's the great Abolitionist. He publishes that paper, the *Liberator*, don't you know? You remember two years ago those anti-slavery meetings that were broken up and all the trouble they had? Well, he was the man that started it all. I don't know whether he's very wise or not, but he certainly has got a lot of courage."

Hiram's eyes were narrowing to a slit now with knowledge and satisfaction.

"Oh, yes, I place him now," he drawled out. "He wouldn't be a very comf'table 'quaintance fer a man t' have, would he?"

"Well," considered Albert, thoughtfully, "I wouldn't like to have any of my relations in his place. I'd be afraid of what might happen. I think likely 'twould take a bit of courage to be friend to a man like that. But they say he has friends, a few of them."

"H'm!" said Hiram, and he rolled a thought like a sweet morsel under his tongue. "I guess I better be goin'. Night." And he shuffled away at last, casting a curious smile at Phoebe as he left.

The next morning while they were going about their work in the kitchen Emmeline remarked to Phoebe that Albert thought Hiram Green was changing for the better, he seemed to be growing real intellectual. Had Phoebe noticed how well he talked about that New York fire?

Phoebe had not noticed.

"What a queer girl you are!" exclaimed Emmeline, much vexed; "I should think you'd see he's takin' all this interest in things jest fer you. It ain't like him to care fer such things. He just thinks it will please you, and you are hard as nails not to 'preciate it."

"You are quite mistaken, Emmeline. Hiram Green never did anything to please any one but himself, I am sure," answered Phoebe, and taking her apron off went up to her room.

Phoebe was spending much more time in her room in these days than pleased Emmeline. Not that her work suffered, for Phoebe's swift fingers performed all the tasks required of her in the most approved manner, but so soon as they were done she was off. The fact that the room was cold seemed to affect her in no wise. Emmeline was in a state of chronic rage for this isolation from the rest of the family, though perhaps the only reason she liked to have her around was that she might make sarcastic remarks about her. Then, too, it seemed like an assumption of superiority on Phoebe's part. Emmeline could not bear superiority.

Phoebe's reason for hurrying to the seclusion of her own room on every possible occasion was that a new source of comfort and pleasure had been open to her through the kindness of Marcia Spafford. Miranda had reported promptly Phoebe's two escapes from Hiram Green and not only Marcia but David was greatly interested in the sweet-faced young girl. Shortly after the occasion of Alma's unexpected punishment Miranda was sent up to the Deanes to request that Phoebe come down for the afternoon a little while, as "Mis' Spafford has a new book she thinks you'll enjoy readin' with her awhile." Much to Emmeline's disgust, for she had planned a far different occupation for Phoebe, the girl accepted with alacrity, and was soon seated in the pleasant library poring over one of Whittier's poems which opened up a new world to her. The poem was one which David had just secured to publish in his paper, and they discussed its beauties for a few minutes, and then Marcia opened a delightful new book by Cooper.

Phoebe had naturally a bright mind, and during her days of school she had studied all that came in her way. Always she had stood at the head of her classes, sometimes getting up at the first peep of dawn to study a lesson or work over a problem, and sticking to her books until the very last minute. This had been a great source of trouble, because Emmeline objected most seriously to "taking her education so hard," as she expressed it. "Some children have measles and whooping-cough and chicken-pox and mumps real hard," she was wont to say, "but they most of 'em take learnin' easy. But Phoebe's got learnin' hard. She acts like there wasn't any use fer anything else in the world but them books. Land! What good'll they do her? They won't make her spin a smoother thread, 'er quilt a straighter row, 'er sew a finer seam. She'll jest ferget everything she learnt when she's married. I'm sure I did." And no one ever disputed this convincing fact.

Nevertheless Phoebe had studied on, trying it is true to please Emmeline by doing all the work required of her, but still insisting on getting her lessons even if it deprived her of her rest, or her noon luncheon. She had acquired the habit of devouring every bit of information that came in her way, so that in spite of her environments she had a measure of true mind culture. It may have been this which so mystified and annoyed Emmeline.

So the afternoon was one of unalloyed delight to Phoebe. When she insisted that she must go home to help get supper, Miranda was sent with her, and the precious book went along to be read in odd moments. Since then Phoebe felt she had something to help her through the trying days.

These afternoons of reading with Marcia Spafford had become quite the settled thing every week or two, and always there was a book to carry home, or a new poem or article to think about.

Emmeline had grown wrathful about this constant going out, and had asked questions until she had in a measure discovered what was going on. She held her temper in for a while, for when she spoke to Albert he did not seem to sympathize with her irritation at Phoebe, but only asked the girl to let him see the book she had been reading, and became so delighted with it himself that he forgot to bring in the armful of wood Emmeline asked for until she called him the second time. After that Albert shared in the literary treasures that Phoebe brought to the house, and it became his habit to say when he came in to supper: "Been down to the village this afternoon, Phoebe? Didn't get anything new to read, did you?" This made Emmeline fairly furious, and she decided to express her mind once more freely to the girl.

She chose a morning when Phoebe was tied by a task which she could not well leave, and began:

"Now look here, Phoebe Deane, I must say you are goin' beyond all bounds. I think it's about time you stopped. I want you to understand that I think the way you're actin' is a downright sin. It isn't enough that you should scorn a good honest man that's eatin' his heart out fer yeh, an' you payin' no more 'tention to him 'n if he was the very dust o' your feet, an' him able to keep you well, too; an' you willin' to set round an' live on relations that ain't real relations at all; an' you with money in th' bank a-plenty, an' never even offerin' to give so much as a little present to your little nephews and nieces that are all you've got in the world. It ain't enough that you should do all that, an' be a drug on our hands, but here you must go an' get up a 'quaintance with a woman I don't like ner respect at all, an' let her send that poor, hard-workin', good-fer-nothin', red-headed girl after you every few days a' takin' you away from your home, an' your good honest work that you ought to be willin' to do twice over fer all you've had. Phoebe Deane, d' you realize that we let you go to school clear up to the top grade when other girls hed to stop an' go to work? It was all *his* doin's, I'd never hev allowed it. I think it jest spoils a girl to get so much knowledge. It's jest as I said 'twould be, too. Look at you! Spoiled. You want lily-white hands an' nothin' to do. You want to go to everlastin' tea-parties an' bring home books to read the rest o' the time. Now I stopped school when I was in the fourth reader 'n look at me. There ain't a woman round is better fixed 'n what I am. What do I need of more books? Answer that, Phoebe Deane! Answer me! Would it make me darn the children's stockin's, er cook his meals, er spin, er weave better, er would it make me any better anyway? Answer me?"

Emmeline had two bright red spots on her cheeks and she was very angry. When she was angry she always screamed her sentences at her opponent in a high key. Phoebe had the impulse to throw the wet dish-cloth at her sister-in-law, and it was hard indeed to restrain her indignation at this speech. There was the lovely Mrs. Spafford lending her books and helping her and encouraging her in every way to improve her mind by reading and study, and even Mr. Spafford seemed anxious she should have all the books to read that she desired; and here was this woman talking this way! It was beyond speech. There was nothing to say.

Emmeline stepped up close to the girl, grasped her white arm and shook it fiercely until the dish-cloth came near doing a rash deed of its own accord.

"Answer me!" she hissed in the girl's face.

"It might—" The exasperated girl hesitated. What good would it do to say it?

"Well, go on," said the woman, gripping the arm painfully. "You've got some wicked word to say, just speak it out to the one that hes been more than mother to ye, an' then I s'pose you'll feel better."

"I was only going to say, Emmeline, that more study might have made you understand others better."

"Understand! Understand!" screamed Emmeline, now thoroughly roused. "I should like to know who I don't understand! Don't I understand my husband an' my childern, and my neighbors? I s'pose you mean understand *you,* you good-fer-nothin' hussy! Well, that ain't necessary! You're so different from everybody else on earth that an angel from heaven er a perfesser from college couldn't understand you, an' learnin' won't make you any different, no matter how much time you waste on it."

"Emmeline, listen!" said Phoebe, trying to stop this outburst; "I consider that I've worked for my board since I came here—"

"Consider! Consider! You consider! Well, really! Worked for your board, when you was scarcely more use 'n a baby when you come, an' think o' all the trouble o' raisin' ye! And you consider that you've earned all you've got here! Well, I don't consider any such a thing, I ken tell you."

"Please let me finish, Emmeline. I was going to say that I have tried to make Albert take the money I have in the bank as payment for any expense and trouble I have been to him, but he says he promised my mother he wouldn't touch a cent of it, and he will not take it."

"Oh, yes, Albert is soft-hearted. Well, I didn't promise yer ma, by a long sight, an' I ain't bound to no such fool notions."

"Emmeline, I don't feel that the money belongs to you. It was not you who brought me here, nor paid for whatever I have had. It was Albert. I cannot see why I should give you the money. You have done nothing for me but what you have had to do, and I am sure I have worked for you enough to pay for that, but I would much rather give the money to you than to have you talk in this way—"

"Oh, I wasn't askin' fer yer money. I wouldn't take it es a gift. I was only showin' yeh up to yourself, what a selfish good-fer-nothin' you are, settin' up airs to read books when there's good honest work goin' on."

It happened that Albert came in just then and the discussion dropped, but Phoebe with determined mien went on with her visits to Mrs. Spafford whenever Miranda came for her—never alone, lest she encounter Hiram Green—and so the winter dragged slowly on its way.

17

MEANWHILE Hiram Green still kept up his attention to the post-office, watching the Deanes so vigilantly that it was impossible for them to receive mail without his knowing it. This never annoyed Albert, as he was too good-natured to suspect any one of an ill turn, and he thought it exceedingly kind of Hiram to bring his mail up. As for Phoebe, it simply cut out all opportunity for her to go out, except when Miranda came for her.

"Why can't that Mirandy girl stay home an' mind her business an' let you come when you get ready?" asked Emmeline, in a loud tone, one day when Miranda was waiting in the sitting-room for Phoebe to get ready to go with her. "She ac's 's if she was your nurse."

But Miranda continued her vigilance, and that without Phoebe's asking, and somehow Marcia always planned it that if Phoebe could stay to tea she and David would walk home with her. It was all delightful for Phoebe, but everything that was done merely offended Emmeline the more.

Miranda, in these days, was enjoying herself. She lost no opportunity to observe the detestable Hiram and rejoice that she had foiled his attempts to bother Phoebe. One day, however, she happened to be in the post-office when the mail was distributed. She was buying sugar, and she loitered a moment after the package was handed her, watching Hiram Green, who had slouched over to the counter and asked for his mail.

"Nothin' fer the Deanes?" she heard him ask in a low tone. "Nothin' fer Phoebe? She was 'spectin' somethin' I'm sure."

Miranda cast a sharp glance at him as she passed him. She was glad somehow that he received nothing. She wondered if Phoebe knew he was enquiring for her mail. Miranda laid it by in her mind as something that might be of use in future, and went on her way.

That very day the old woman who kept house for Hiram, in sweeping out his room, came across a bit of red sealing-wax stamped with part of a crest which bore a lion's head with the jaws apart. It was lying on a dark stripe in the rag carpet and had not been noticed before. She saw at once it was of no value and tossed it toward the open window, where it lodged upon the sill close up to the frame, and by and by when the window was closed it was shut in tight between sash and sill, the lion's head, erect and fierce, caught in the crack, a tiny thing and hidden, but reminding one of "truth crushed to earth."

The next day Nathaniel Graham made a flying visit to his home to have a serious conference with his uncle the Judge. His investigations concerning the two questions which had troubled him on his journey back to New York had involved him in matters that had now come to a crisis, and he found that some decision must be reached at once. He had received several more letters from his uncle in Texas, urging him persistently to come down at once and help their cause. More and more it was becoming a dangerous thing to do, as Congress had not sanctioned any such help, and in fact it might involve any one who attempted it in serious difficulties. Yet it was being done every day. People who lived near to Texas were gathering money and arms, and sending men to help, and even so far as New York there were many quietly at work. Public sentiment was strongly with Texas, save only among those who were opposed to slavery, and as yet that question was but in its infancy. Nathaniel had been put to it at last to decide definitely about Texas. He had been offered command of a company of men who were to sail soon, and he must say yes or no at once. The pressure was very strong, and sometimes he almost thought he ought to go. The time had come to speak to Judge Bristol. Nothing could be decided without his final word, for Nathaniel felt too much honor and love for the one who had been his second father to do anything without his sanction.

As was to be expected the Judge was seriously troubled at the thought of Nathaniel's going South to join in the conflict, and he argued long and seriously against any such project, telling his nephew that he had no right to even consider such questions until he had made a place for himself in the world. When Nathaniel admitted that he had been attending Abolition meetings, and was becoming intimate with some of the leaders, the Judge was roused into excited hostility.

"Nathaniel, how could you?" he exclaimed, in deep distress. "I thought your judgment was sound, but to be carried away by these wild, fanatical people is anything but evidence of sound judgment. Can you not see that this is a question that you have no business with? If your uncle in Texas chooses to keep slaves, you have no more right to meddle with his choice than if he chose to keep horses or sheep. And as for this bosh about slavery being such a terrible evil, look at Pompey and Caesar and Dianthe and the rest. Do you fancy they want to be free? Why, what would the poor things do if I didn't care for them as if they were my own children? It is all nonsense.

"Of course, there are a few bad masters, and probably will be as long as sin is in the world; but to condemn the whole system of slavery because a few men who happen to own slaves mistreat them would be like condemning marriage because a few men abused their wives. It is utmost nonsense for a few hot-headed fanatics to try to run the rest of the country into the moulds they have made and call it righteousness. Let other men alone, and they will let you go in peace, is a better motto. Let every man look out to cast the beam from his own eyes before he attempts to find a mote in his brother's."

When his uncle quoted Scripture in this way Nathaniel was at a loss how to answer him.

"I wish you could hear Mr. Garrison talk, Uncle."

"I wouldn't listen to him for a moment," he answered, hotly. "He is a dangerous man! Keep away from all such gatherings, for they only breed discontent and uprisings. You will see that nothing but a lot of mobs will arise from this agitation. Slavery is a thing that cannot be overthrown, and all these meetings are mere talk to let a few men get into prominence. No man in his senses would do the things that that Garrison has done unless he wanted to get notoriety. That's what makes him so foolhardy. Keep away from him, my boy. There's a price on his head, and you'll do yourself and your prospects no good if you have anything to do with him."

They talked far into the night, Nathaniel trying to defend the man whom he had met but once or twice, but whom he had been compelled to admire. Janet pouted through the evening because Nathaniel did not come out to talk with her, and finally went to bed in a fit of the blues.

When at last Nathaniel pressed his uncle's hand at parting they both knew that he would not go to Texas. Indeed, as the young man had reflected during the night, he felt that his purpose of going there had been shaken before he came home to ask Judge Bristol's advice. However, he was not altogether sure that his uncle had considered the matter from the correct view-point either, but the talk had somehow helped to crystallize his own views. So now he felt free, nay bound, to return and complete his law course. As for the other matter, that must be left to develop in its time. He was by no means sure he was done with it yet, for his heart had been too deeply touched, and his reason stirred.

As Nathaniel climbed into the coach at the big white gate he felt that he had only put off all these questions for a time, but there was a certain relief in feeling that a decision had been reached at least for the present.

He was half a mind to ride on top with the driver, though it was a bitterly cold morning, but quite unexpectedly the driver suggested that he better sit inside this time, as the weather was so cold. Without giving it a passing thought he went inside, waving his hand and smiling at Janet, who stood at the front door with a fur-trimmed scarlet cloak about her shapely shoulders. Then the door closed and he sat down.

There was one other passenger, a girl, who sat far back in the shadows of the coach, but her eyes shone out from the heavy wrappings of cloak and bonnet and gave him welcome.

"Oh!" she said, catching her breath.

"And is it you?" he asked eagerly, reaching out to grasp her hand. Then each remembered, the girl that she was alone in the coach with this man, the man that this girl might belong to another. But in spite of it they were glad to see one another.

The coach rolled out into the main street again and as it lurched over the crossing Hiram Green, who was hurrying to his daily vigilance at the post-office, caught a good view of Nathaniel's back through the coach window. The back gave the impression of an animated conversation being carried on in which the owner of the back was deeply interested.

Hiram almost paused in his walk over the crunching snow. "Gosh Ninety!" he ejaculated in consternation, "who knowed he was here!"

Then the reflection that at least Nathaniel was about to depart calmed his perturbation and he hurried on to the office.

Hiram did not know that Phoebe was in the coach. She had managed it very carefully with a view to concealing it from him, for she felt sure that if he knew she was going that morning he would have found it possible to have accompanied her, and she would have found it impossible to get rid of his company. So when the day before Emmeline had suggested that somebody ought to go out to Miss Ann Jane Bloodgood's and get some dried saffron flowers she had promised them last fall, to dye the carpet-rags, Phoebe said nothing until after Hiram had left that night. Then as she was going upstairs with her candle she turned to Emmeline and said:

"I've been thinking, Emmeline, I could go over to Bloodgood's by the morning coach if Albert could drive me down when he takes his corn to the mill. Then perhaps some of them would be coming over to the village, or I could catch a ride back, or if not I could come back by the evening coach."

Emmeline assented grimly. She wanted the dye and she did not relish the long cold ride in the coach. Ann Jane Bloodgood was too condescending to please her, anyway. So, as Albert was going to mill early, Phoebe made her simple preparations that night, and was ready bright and early. Moreover, she coaxed Albert to drive around by Granny McVane's that she might leave a bit of poetry for her which she had told her about. The poem could have waited, but Albert did not tell her that, and Pheobe did not explain to Albert that if they went around by Granny's Hiram would not know she was gone away and therefore would not try to follow her. It was a pity that Phoebe had not confided a little now and then in Albert, though he, poor soul, could do little against such odds as Emmeline and Hiram.

The ten-mile coach ride to Bloodgood's wide farm-house spun itself away into nothing in such company, and before Phoebe could believe it was half over she saw the distant road, low-browed with overhanging snow, and the red barns glimmering warmly a little beyond. Nathaniel saw them, too, for she had told him at once where she was going that he might not think she had planned to go with him. He felt that the moments were precious.

"Do you remember what we talked of that night we walked to your home?" he asked.

"Oh, yes," she breathed, softly. "You were talking of some one who needed setting free. I have been reading some wonderful poems lately that made me think a great deal of what you said."

He looked at her keenly. How could a girl who read poems and talked so well belong to Hiram Green?

"I have been thinking much about it lately," he went on, with just the breath of sigh. "I may have to decide what I will do at no distant day now. I wonder if I may ask you to pray for me?"

He watched her, this girl with the drooping eyes and rosy-hued cheeks, the girl who had by her silence refused to answer his letter, and wondered if perhaps by his request he had offended her. The coach lurched up to the wide piazza and stopped, and the driver jumped heavily into the snowy road. They could hear his steps plowing through the drift by the back wheel. His hand was on the coach door. Then quickly, as if she might be too late, her eyes were lifted to his, and he saw her heart would be in those prayers, as she answered:

"Oh, I will."

Something like a flash of light went through them as they looked for that instant into one another's eyes, and lifted them above the mere petty things of earth. It was intangible. Nathaniel could not explain it to himself as he sat back alone in the empty coach and went over the facts of the case, why his heart felt light, and the day seemed brighter, just because a girl whom he knew ever so little had promised in that tone of voice to pray for him. It thrilled him anew as he thought it over, and his heart went soaring up into heavens of happiness, until he called himself a fool, and told himself nothing was changed, and that Phoebe had not even replied to his letter, and politely declined the correspondence, as she would certainly have been justified in doing even if she were the promised wife of Hiram Green. Yet his heart refused to be anything but buoyant. He began to berate himself that he had not frankly spoken of his letter, and heard what she had to say about the matter. Perhaps in some way it had never reached her, and yet after all that was scarcely possible. Letters clearly addressed were seldom lost. It might only have embarrassed her if he had spoken.

At the next stop he accepted the coach driver's invitation to "come up top a spell, there's a fine sun comin' up now," and he let old Michael babble on about the gossip of the town, until at last the sly old man asked him innocently enough: "And what did ye think av the other passenger, Mr. 'Than'el? An' ain't she a bonnie lassie?" And then he was treated to a list of Phoebe's virtues sounded forth by one who in reality knew very little of her save that as a child on the way home from school one day she had shyly handed him a bunch of wayside posies as he drove by her on the road. That childish act had won his loyalty, and old Michael was not troubled with the truth. He was thoroughly capable of filling in virtues where he knew none. He went on the principle that what ought to be was. And so it was that when Nathaniel arrived in New York his heart was strangely light, and he wondered often if Phoebe Deane would remember to pray for him. It seemed as if the momentous question were now in better hands than his own.

Meantime Hiram Green, having found in the post-office a circular letter for Albert concerning a new kind of plow that was being put upon the market, plodded up to the Deanes. He knew that Albert was gone to mill that morning and would not be home yet, but he thought the letter would be an excuse to see Phoebe. He wanted to judge whether Phoebe knew of this visit of Nathaniel's. He thought he could tell by her face whether she had had a secret meeting with him or not. Yet it puzzled him to know when it could have been, for Phoebe had been quietly sewing carpet rags all the evening before, and he was sure she had not gone by with Miranda in the afternoon to the Spaffords. Had she gone to the woods again in the winter, or did she not know he was here? Perhaps his own skilful manipulating of the mail had nipped this miniature courtship in the bud, as it were, and there would be no further need of his vigilance.

But when Hiram reached the Deanes and looked about for Phoebe she was not there.

"Where's Phoebe?" he demanded, frowning.

"She's gone up to Ann Jane Bloodgood's t' get some saffron flowers," said Emmeline. "Won't you come in, Hiram? She'll be mighty sorry to know she missed you." Emmeline thought it was as well to keep up appearances for Phoebe.

"Yes, I'm sure," drawled Hiram. "How'd she go?" he asked her after an ominous silence in which Emmeline was meditating on what it would be best to say.

"She went in the coach, an' I reckon she'll come back that way by night ef there don't no one come over from Bloodgood's this way. You might meet the coach ef you was goin' in to the village again. I don't know's Albert'll feel he hes time after losin' so much o' the day t' mill."

Hiram said nothing, but Emmeline saw he was angry.

"I'd a sent you word she was goin' an' given you the chance to go 'long with her, only she didn't say a word till after you was gone home last night—" she began apologetically, but Hiram did not seem to heed her. He got up after a minute, his brows still lowering. He was thinking that Phoebe had planned to go with Nathaniel Graham.

"I'll be over t' th' village," he said, as he went out. "Albert needn't go." Emmeline looked after him meditatively.

"I shouldn't be a bit s'prised ef he give her up, the way she goes on. It's wonderful how he holds on to her. She's a fool, that's what she is, an' I've no pity for her. I wish to goodness she was well married an' out o' the way. She does try me beyond all, with her books, an' her visitin's, an' her locked doors, an' notions."

Meantime, Phoebe, all unconscious of the plot that was thickening round her, accepted an invitation to remain over night and the next day with Ann Jane Bloodgood, and drive in to town in the afternoon when she went to missionary meeting. Ann Jane was interested in Christian missions and fascinated Phoebe with her tales of Eliot, Brainerd, Carey, Whitman, and Robert Moffat. Phoebe, as she looked over Ann Jane's pile of missionary papers, began to wonder how many people of one sort and another there were in the world who needed setting free from something. It all seemed to be a part of the one great thing for which she was praying, the thing that Nathaniel Graham was trying to decide, and he was another just like those wonderful men who were giving their lives to save others. Phoebe was glad she had come, though perhaps she might not have been if she could have seen the thought that was working in Hiram Green's heart.

After some reflection Hiram harnessed his horses and took the long ride over to Bloodgood's that afternoon, arriving at the house just after Phoebe and Ann Jane were safely established in Ann Jane's second cousin's best room, a mile away, for a visit. Ann Jane's second cousin was an invalid and liked company, so Phoebe's bright face cheered what would otherwise have been a lonely afternoon, and she escaped the unpleasant encounter with Hiram.

Hiram, his suspicions confirmed, met the evening coach, but no Phoebe appeared. He stepped up to Albert Deane's in the evening long enough to make sure that she had not returned by any private conveyance, and the next day he drove over again, but again found the low farm-house closed and deserted, for Ann Jane had driven with Phoebe by another road to the village missionary meeting.

His temper not much improved with his two fruitless

rides, Hiram returned, watched every passenger from the evening coach alight, and then betook himself to the Deanes again, where he was really surprised to find Phoebe had returned.

That evening when the saffron flowers were being discussed he remarked that there were mighty nice saffron flowers for sale in Albany, and he watched Phoebe narrowly, but the round cheek did not flush nor the long lashes flutter in any suspicious way. Nevertheless, Hiram's mind never let go an evil thought that once lodged there. He felt he had a new power over Phoebe that he might use if occasion demanded. He could bide his time.

18

SPRING was coming on at last, and Hiram Green, who had been biding his time and letting his wrath smoulder, began to think it was time to do something. All winter Phoebe had been able to keep comparatively free from him, save for his company with the family in the evening. Hiram took every opportunity possible to make it apparent that he was "keeping company" with Phoebe, through the medium of this nightly visit, and Phoebe made it plain upon every occasion that she did not consider his visit was for her. She got out of the way when she could, but Emmeline contrived to keep her unusually busy every evening, and her own room was so cold that escape was impossible.

Hiram had made several unsuccessful efforts to establish himself beside Phoebe in public, and he was getting desperate. Every Sunday when he tried to walk down the aisle with her he would find Miranda and Rose one on either side of her, Mrs. Spafford herself, sometimes all three, and all serenely unconscious of his presence. They attended her down to the carryall. She never went to the village any more that he could discover, unless Miranda came for her, or Albert took her back and forth, though once he had seen her flying across the fields from Granny McVane's house with a bundle that looked as if it came from the store. He complained to Emmeline at last and she agreed to help him. Albert was not taken into the scheme. For some reason it was deemed best not to tell Albert about it at all. He was apt to ask kindly, searching questions, and he always took it for granted that one did everything with the best of motives. Besides, he was not quick at evasion and might let the cat out of the bag.

There was to be a barn raising about ten miles the other side of the village, and the whole country round about were invited. It happened that the Woodburys, whose barn was to be raised, were distant relatives of Emmeline, and of course the Deanes were going.

Emmeline had shown plainly that she would be offended if Phoebe did not go, though the girl would have much preferred remaining at home with the new book Mrs. Spafford had sent up the day before. It was a matter of selfishness with Emmeline. She wanted Phoebe to help with the big dinner and relieve her so that she could visit with the other women.

It was a part of the scheme that Albert should go in the chaise with Alma, and should start while Phoebe was still dressing. Emmeline had managed Albert very adroitly, telling him that Hiram wanted a chance to "set in the front seat with Phoebe" in the carryall. Albert, always willing to do a good turn, acceded readily, though Alma was a somewhat reluctant passenger.

When Phoebe came downstairs she found Emmeline already seated in the back seat of the carryall with the other children. She gladly got into the front seat, as it was much pleasanter to be there than beside Emmeline, and she seldom had the opportunity of riding beside her brother, who was more congenial than the others. But in a moment Hiram Green appeared from around the corner of the house. He got quickly into the vacant seat beside Phoebe and whipped up the horses.

"Why, where is Albert?" asked Phoebe in dismay, wishing she could get out.

"He had to go on," exclaimed Emmeline, blandly. "Drive fast, Hiram, we'll be late." This last because she fancied she saw a frightened sideways glance from Phoebe, as if she might be going to get out.

Phoebe turned her head to the road-side and tried to watch for the chance wild flowers, and forget the talk of crops and gossip that was kept up between Emmeline and Hiram, but the whole pleasant day was clouded for her, and her annoyance was double when they passed through the village and Janet Bristol in dainty pink dimity stared at them with haughty sweetness from under her white shirred bonnet and pink-laced sunshade. Janet was not going to the barn-raising evidently. She had many interests outside of the village where she was born, and did not mingle freely with her fellow-townsmen. There were only a favored few who were her friends and had the privileges of the beautiful old house.

Her passing called forth unfavorable comment from Emmeline and Hiram, and Phoebe writhed at her sister-in-law's tone, loud enough for Janet to hear easily, if she had a mind.

"The idea of wearing such fancy things of a mornin'!" she exclaimed. "I didn't think the Judge was such a fool as to let his daughter come up like that, fixed up fit fer a party this early, an' a sunshade, too! What's she think it's for, I wonder! Her complexion's so dark a little more of this weak sunshine couldn't make much difference. Mebbe she thinks she looks fine, but she's much mistaken. A lazy girl all decked out never looks pretty to me."

"That's 'bout right," declared Hiram, as if he knew all about it. "Give me a good worker ev'ry time, I sez, in preference to one with ringlets an' a nosegay on her frock. But you couldn't expec' much of that one. She's goin' to marry that highfolutin' Nate Graham, an' they'll have money 'nough betwixt 'em to keep her in prettys all the rest of her life. Say, did you hear Nate Graham'd turned Abolitionist? Well, it's so; I heard it from a r'liable source. Hev a friend in

Noo York writes me once in a while an' I know what I'm talkin' bout. Hed it from headquarters like, you know. Ef it's so he may git into trouble enny time now. There's prices on them Abolitionists' heads!"

Hiram turned to look straight into Phoebe's startled face, with an ugly leer of a laugh. The girl's cheeks grew pink, and she turned quickly away; Hiram felt he had scored one against her. It made him good-natured all day. But Phoebe found herself trembling with a single thought. Did it mean life or death, this that Nathaniel had asked her to pray about; and had perhaps her prayers helped to put him in the way of danger? Ah! But if it were true, how grand in him to be willing to brave danger for what he thought was right. Phoebe knew very little about the real question at issue, though she had read a number of Whittier's poems which had stirred her heart deeply. The great thought in her mind was that a man should be brave enough and good enough to stand against the whole world, if need be, to help a weak brother.

The day was one of noise and bustle and, for Phoebe, hard work. By instinct the women put tasks upon her young shoulders which they wished to shirk, knowing they would be well done. It was written large on Phoebe's face that she could be trusted. So they trusted her, and the fun and frolic and feasting went on, while she toiled in the kitchen, gladly taking extra burdens upon herself, only so it kept her out of any possibility of being troubled by Hiram.

She was washing dishes and meditating on how she could manage not to sit next to Hiram on the return trip when a little Woodbury entered the kitchen.

"Say, Phoebe Deane," she called out, "your brother says you're to go in the chaise with him this time, an' when you get ready you come out to the barn an' get in. He says you needn't hurry, fer he's busy yet a while."

The child was gone back to her play before Phoebe could thank her, and with lightened heart she went on washing the dishes. Perhaps Albert had surmised her dislike to riding with Hiram and had planned this for her sake. She made up her mind to confide in Albert during this ride and see if he could not help her to get rid of her obnoxious lover once and for all. Albert was usually slow and undecided, but when once in a great while he put his foot down about something things usually went as he said.

She wiped the last dish, washed her hands, and ran upstairs for her bonnet and mantilla. Everybody else was gone. The long, slant rays of the setting sun were streaming in at the window and touching the great four-poster bed where lay her wraps alone. She put them on quickly, glad that every one else was out of the way and she would not have to wait for a lot of good-bys. The day had been a weariness to her, and she was thankful to have it over.

Mr. and Mrs. Woodbury stood together by the great stepping-stone in front of the house. They had said good-by to Albert and Emmeline an hour before, and had just been seeing off the last wagon-load of guests. They turned eagerly to thank Phoebe for her assistance. Indeed, the girl had many warm friends among older people who knew her kindly heart and willing hands.

"What! Your folks all gone and left you, Phoebe!" exclaimed Mrs. Woodbury in dismay. "Why, they must a' forgot you."

"No, they're not all gone, Mrs. Woodbury. Our chaise is out in the barn waiting for me. Albert sent word to me by your Martha that I needn't hurry, so I stopped to finish the dishes."

"Oh! Now that's so good of you, Phoebe Deane," said the tired farmer's wife, who expected she would have plenty of cleaning to do after the departure of her large company of guests. "You shouldn't ov done that. I could a' cleaned up. I'm 'fraid you're real tired. Wouldn't you like to stay over night and get rested?"

But Phoebe shook hands happily with them and hurried down to the chaise. Now the Woodbury barn was out near the road, and the chaise stood facing the road, the horse not tied, but waiting with turned head as if his master was not far away. Phoebe jumped in with a spring, calling, "Come on, Albert. I'm here at last. Did I keep you waiting long?"

Then before she had time to look around or know what was happening Hiram Green stepped out from the barn door, sprang into the seat beside her, and with unwonted swiftness caught up the whip and gave the horse such a cut that it started off at a brisk trot down the road. It was he who had sent the message by little Martha Woodbury, just as it had been given. Emmeline had managed the rest.

"Oh!" gasped Phoebe. "Why, Mr. Green, Albert is here waiting for me somewhere. Please stop the horse and let me find him. He sent word he would wait for me."

"That's all right," said Hiram, nonchalantly. "Albert decided to go in the carryall. Your sister-in-law was in a great stew to get back fer milkin' time an' made him come, so I offered to bring ye back home."

Phoebe's heart froze within her. She looked wildly about her and knew not what to do. The horse was going very fast, and to jump would be dangerous. She had no idea that Hiram would stop and let her out if she should ask him. His talk the last time they had an encounter had shown her that she must not let him see he had her in his power. Besides, what excuse could she give for stopping save that she did not wish to go with him? And how otherwise could she get home that night? How she wished now that she had accepted Mrs. Woodbury's kind invitation. Could she not, perhaps, manage it yet?

"That's very kind of you," she faltered, with white lips, as she tried to marshal her wits and contrive some way out of this predicament. Then she made a feint of looking about her in the seat.

"I wonder if I remembered to bring my apron," she said, faintly. "Would you mind, Mr. Green, just driving back to see?"

"Oh, I reckon you'll find it," Hiram said, easily. "Ef you

don't you got a few more, ain't you? Here, ain't this it?" and he fished out a damp roll from under the seat.

Phoebe had hoped for one wild little moment that she had really dropped it when she got into the chaise, for it did not seem to be about anywhere, but the sight of the damp blue roll dashed all her confidence. There was nothing for it but to accept the situation as bravely as possible and make the best of it. Her impulse was to turn angrily and tell Hiram Green that he had deceived her, but she knew that would do no good, and the safest thing was to act as if it were all right and try to keep the conversation upon every-day topics. If he would only keep on driving at this pace the journey would not be so intolerably long, after all, and they might hope to reach home a trifle before dark perhaps. She summoned all her courage and tried to talk pleasantly, although the countenance of the man beside her as she stole a swift glance at his profile, frightened her. There was both triumph and revenge upon it. "They had a pleasant day for the raising, Mr. Green," she began.

And then to her horror he slowed the horse to a walk and sat back close to her as if he intended to enjoy the tête-à-tête to its full.

It was an awful strain. Phoebe's cheeks blazed out in two red spots, and her eyes were bright with excitement. They dragged their slow way through a woods where the lights and shadows played in all the sweetness of spring odors. Phoebe sat up very straight, very much to her side of the chaise, and laughed and talked as if she were wound up.

Hiram did not say much. He sat watching her, almost devouring the changefulness of her face, fully understanding her horror of him and this ride, yet determined to make her suffer every minute of the time. It made his anger all the greater as he saw her bravely try to keep up a semblance of respect toward him and knew she did not feel it. Why could she not give it freely, and not against her will? What was there about him she disliked? Never mind, she should pay for her dislike. She should see that she would have to treat him as she would treat those she liked, whether she wished or no.

She suggested that they better drive faster, as it was getting late and would soon be dark. He said that did not matter, that Emmeline had said they were not to hurry. She told him she would be needed, but he told her it was right she should have a little rest once in a while, and he smiled grimly as he said it, knowing the present ride was anything but a rest to the poor tried soul beside him. He seemed to delight in torturing her. The farther she edged away from him the nearer he came to her, until when they emerged from the woods and met a carryall with some people they both knew, he was sitting quite over on her side, and she was almost out of her seat, her face a piteous picture of rage and helplessness.

Emboldened by the expression on the faces of their acquaintance, Hiram threw his arm across the back of the chaise, until it quite encircled Phoebe's back, or would have if she had not sat upon the extreme front edge of the seat.

They had reached a settlement of three houses, where a toll-gate, spreading its white pole out across the way, and a little store and school-house, went by the name of The Crossroads. Hiram flung a bit of money out to the toll-man and drove on without stopping. Phoebe's heart was beating wildly. She could not sit thus on the edge of her seat another instant. Something must be done.

"Mr. Green, would you mind moving over just a little, I haven't quite enough room," she gasped.

"Oh, that's all right," said Hiram, as heartily as if he really did not understand the situation. "Just sit clos'ter. Don't be shy." His circling arm came round her waist and by brute strength drew her up to him, so that it looked from behind as if they were a pair of lovers. The top of the chaise was thrown back so that they could easily be seen.

They had just passed the last house. It was the home of old Mrs. Duzenberry and her elderly daughter Suzanna. Living so far from the village they made it a point not to miss anything that went by their door, and at this hour in the afternoon, when their simple tea was brewing, they both sat by the front window, ready to bob to the door the minute there was anything of interest. It is needless to say that they both bobbed on this occasion, the daughter with folded arms and alert beak like some old bird of prey, the mother just behind with quizzical exclamatory interrogations written in every curve of her cap-strings.

Phoebe, glancing back wildly, as she felt herself drawn beyond her power to stop it, saw them gaping at her in amaze, and her cheeks grew crimson with shame.

"Stop!" she cried, putting out her hands and pushing against him.

She might as well have tried to push off a mountain that was in her path. Hiram only laughed and drew her closer, till his ugly, grizzled face was near to her own. She could feel his breath upon her cheek, and the horse was going faster now. She did not know just how it happened, whether Hiram had touched him with the whip, or spoken a low word. They were down the road out of sight of the Duzenberrys before she could wrench herself away from the scoundrel. Even then it was but that he might settle himself a little closer and more comfortably that he let go of her for a moment and then the strong, cruel arm came back as if it had a right around her waist, and Hiram's face came cheek to cheek with her own.

She uttered one terrible scream, and looked around, but there was no one in sight. The sun, which had been slowly sinking like a ball of burning opal, suddenly dropped behind a hill and left the world dull and leaden with a heavy sky of gray. Dark blue clouds seemed all around, which until now had not been noticed, and a quick uncertain wind was springing up; a low rumble behind them seemed to wrap them in a new dread. But the strong man's grasp held her fast, and her screams brought no help.

In the horror of the moment a thought of her mother came, and she wondered if that mother were where she could see her child, and whether it did not give her deep anguish even in the bliss of heaven to know she was in such straits. Then as the sharp stubble of Hiram's upper lip brushed the softness of her cheek fear gave her strength, and with a sudden mighty effort she broke from his grasp.

Reaching out to the only member of the party who seemed at all likely to render any aid, Phoebe caught the reins and pulled back upon them with all her might, while her heart was lifted in a swift prayer for help. Then quick, as if in instant answer, while the grey plow-horse reared back upon his haunches, and plunged wildly in the air, came a brilliant flash of jagged lightning, as if the sky was cloven in wrath, and the light of heaven let through; and this was followed on the instant by a terrible crash of thunder.

With an oath of mingled rage and awe, Hiram pushed Phoebe from him and reached for the reins to try and soothe the frightened horse, who was plunging and snorting and trembling in fear.

The chaise was on the edge of a deep ditch half filled with muddy water. One wheel was almost over the edge. Hiram saw the danger, and reached for his whip. He cut the horse a frantic lash which brought his fore-feet to the ground again and caused him to start off down the road on a terrific gallop. But in that instant, while the chaise poised on the edge of the ditch, Phoebe's resolve had crystallized into action. She gave a wild spring, just as the cut from the whip sent the horse tearing headlong down the road. Her dress caught in the arm of the chaise, and for one instant she poised over the ditch. Then the fabric gave way and she fell heavily, striking her head against the fence, and lay huddled in the muddy depths. Down the hard road echoed the heavy hoof-beats of the horse in frenzied gallop with no abatement, and over all the majestic thunder rolled.

19

HER senses swam off into the relief of unconsciousness for a moment, but the cold water creeping up through her clothing chilled her back to life again, and in a moment more, she had opened her eyes in wonder that she was lying there alone, free from her tormentor. She fancied she could hear the echo of the horse's feet yet, or was it the thunder? Then came the awful thought what would happen if he returned and found her lying here? He would be terribly angry at her for having frightened the horse and jumped out of the chaise. He would visit it upon her in some way she felt sure, and she would be utterly defenceless against him.

There was not a soul in sight and it was growing suddenly dark. She must be at least six or seven miles away from home. She did not come that way often enough to be sure of distances. With new fear she sat up, and crept out of the water. The mud was deep and it was difficult to step, but she managed to get away from the oozy soil, and into the road again. Then in a panic she sprang across the ditch and crept under the fence. She must fly from here. When Hiram succeeded in stopping the horse he would undoubtedly come back for her, and she must get away before he found her.

Which way should she go? She looked back upon the road, but feared to go that way, lest he would go to those houses and search for her. There was no telling what he would say. She had no faith in him. He might say she had given him the right to put his arm around her. She must get away from here at once where he could not find her. Out to the right, across the road, it was all open country. There was nowhere she could take refuge near by. But across this field and another there was a growth of trees and bushes. Perhaps she could reach there and hide and so make her way home after he had gone.

She fled across the spring-sodden field as fast as her soaked shoes and her trembling limbs could carry her; slipping now and then and almost falling, but catching at the fence and going on, wildly, blindly, till she reached the fence. Once she thought she heard the distant bellowing of a bull, but she crept to the other side of the fence and kept on her way, breathless. And now the storm broke into wild splashes of rain, pelting on her face and hair, for her bonnet had fallen back and was hanging around her neck by its ribbons. The net had come off from her hair, and the long locks blew about her face and lashed her in the eyes as she ran. It was dark as night and Phoebe could see but dimly where she was going. Yet this was a comfort to her rather than a source of fear. She felt it would the better cover her hiding. Her worst dread was to come under the power of Hiram Green again.

So she worked her way through the fields, groping for the fences, and at last she reached an open road, and stood almost afraid to try it, lest somewhere she should see Hiram lurking. The lightning blazed and shivered all about her, trailing across the heavens in awful and wonderful display; the thunder shuddered above her until the earth itself seemed to answer, and she felt herself in a rocking abyss of horror; and yet the most awful thing in it all was the fact of Hiram Green.

She had heard all her life that the most dangerous place in a thunderstorm was under tall trees, yet so little did she think of it that she made straight for the shelter of the wood; and though the shocks crashed about her, and seemed to be cleaving the giants of the forest, there she stayed until the storm had abated, and the genuine darkness had succeeded.

She was wet to the skin, and trembling like a leaf. Her strongest impulse was to sink to the earth and weep herself into nothingness, but her common-sense would not let her even sit down to rest. She knew she must start at once if she would hope to reach home. Yet by this time she had very little idea of where she was and how to get home. With another prayer for guidance she started out, keeping sharp lookout along the road with ears and eyes, that there might be no possibility of Hiram's coming upon her unaware. Twice she heard vehicles in the distance, and crept into the shelter of some trees until they passed. She heard pleasant voices talking of the storm and longed to cry out to them for help, yet dared not. What would they think of her, a young girl out alone at that time of night, and in such a condition? Besides, they were all strangers. She dared not speak. And neither to friends would she have spoken, for they would have been all the more astonished to find her so. She thought longingly of Mrs. Spafford, and Miranda, yet dreaded lest even Mrs. Spafford might think she had done wrong to allow herself to ride even a couple of miles with such a man as Hiram Green after all the experience she had had with him. Yet as she plodded along she wondered how she could have done differently, unless indeed she had dared to pull up the horse and jump out at once; yet very likely she would not have been able to make her escape from her tormentor as easily earlier in the afternoon as at the time when she had taken her unpremediated leap into the ditch.

As she looked back upon the experience it seemed as though the storm had been sent by Providence to provide her a shield and a way of escape. If it had not been for the storm the horse would not have been easily frightened into running, and Hiram would soon have found her and compelled her to get into the chaise again. What could she have done against his strength! She shuddered, partly with cold and partly with horror.

A slender thread of a pale moon had come up, but it gave a sickly light, and soon slipped out of sight again, leaving only the kindly stars whose lights looked brilliant but so far away to-night. Everywhere was a soft dripping sound, and the seething of the earth drinking in a good draught.

Once when it seemed as if she had been going for hours she sat down on the wet bank to rest, and a horse and rider galloped out of the blackness past her. She hid her white face in her lap and he may have thought her but a stump beside the fence. She was thankful he did not stop to see, but as yet nothing had given her a clue to her whereabouts, and she was cold, so terribly cold.

At last she passed a house she did not know, and then another, and another. Finally she made out that she was in a little settlement, about three miles from the Deanes' farm. She could not tell how she had wandered, nor how she came to be yet so far away when she must have walked at least twenty miles. But the knowledge of where she was brought her new courage.

There was a road leading from this settlement straight to Granny McVane's, and she would not need to go back by the road where Hiram would search for her, if indeed he had not already given up the search and gone home. The lights were out everywhere in this village, save in one small house at the farthest end, and she stole past that as if she had been a wraith. Then she breathed more freely as she came into the open country road again, and knew there were but two or three houses now between herself and home.

It occurred to her to wonder in a dull way if the horse had thrown Hiram out and maybe he was hurt, and whether she might not after all have to send a search party after him. She wondered what he would do when he could not find her, supposing he was not hurt. Perhaps he had been too angry to go back for her and her dread of him had been unnecessary. But she thought she knew him well enough to know he would not easily give her up.

She wondered if he would tell Albert, and whether Albert would be worried—she was sure he would be, good, kind Albert—and what would Emmeline say? Emmeline, who had been at the bottom of all this she was sure—and then her thoughts would trail on ahead of her in the wet, and her feet would lag behind and she would feel that she could not catch up. If only a kindly coach would appear! Yet she kept on, holding up her heavy head, and gripping her wet mantle close with her cold, cold hands, shivering as she went.

Once she caught herself murmuring: "Oh, mother, mother!" and then wondered what it meant. So stumbling on, slower and more slowly, she came at last to the little house of Granny McVane, all dark and quiet, but so kindly-looking in the night. She longed to crawl to the doorstep and lie down to die, but duty kept her on. No one must know of this if she could help it. That seemed to be the main thought she could grasp with her weary brain.

The fields behind Granny McVane's were very miry. Three times she fell, and the last time almost lay still, but some stirring of brain and conscience helped her up and on again, across the last hillock, over the last fence, through the garden and up to the back door of her home.

There was a light inside, but she was too far gone to think about it now. She tried to open the door but the latch was heavy and would not lift. She fumbled and almost gave it up, but then it was opened sharply by Emmeline with her hair in a hard knot, and old lines under her eyes. She wore a wrapper over her night robe, and a blanket around her shoulders. Her feet were thrust into an old pair of Albert's carpet slippers. She held a candle high above her head, and looked out shrewdly into the night. It was plain she was just awake and fretted at the unusual disturbance.

"Fer pity's sake, Phoebe! Is that you? Where on earth hev you ben? You've hed us all upside down huntin' fer yeh, an' Albert ain't got home yet. I tol' him 'twas no use, you'd mos' likely gone in somewheres out o' the storm, an' you'd be home all right in the mornin', but it's just like your crazy ways to come home in the middle o' th' night. Fer goodness sake, what a sight yeh are! You ain't comin' in the house like that! Why, there'll be mud to clean fer a week. Stop there till I get some water an' a broom."

But Phoebe, with deathly white face, and eyes that saw not, stumbled past her without a word, the water and mud oozing out of her shoes at every step, and dripping from her garments; her sodden bonnet dejectedly upon her shoulders, her hair one long drenched mantle of darkness. Emmeline, half awed by the sight, stood still in the doorway and watched her go up stairs, realizing that the girl did not know what she was doing. Then she shut the door sharply as she had opened it, and followed Phoebe upstairs.

Phoebe held out until she reached her own door, and opened it. Then she sank without a sound upon the floor and lay there as if dead. All breath and consciousness had fluttered out, it seemed, with that last effort.

Emmeline set the candle down with a sudden, startled exclamation and went to her. She felt her hands so cold, like ice, and her face like wet marble, and hard as she was she was frightened. Her conscience, so long enjoying a vacation, leaped into new life and became active. What part had she borne in this that seemed as if it might yet be a tragedy?

She unlaced the clodded shoes, untied the soaked bonnet, pulled off the wet garments one by one and wrapped the girl in thick warm blankets, dragging her light weight to the bed; but still no sign of consciousness had come. She felt her heart and listened for a breath, but she could not tell yet if she were alive or not. Then she went downstairs with hurried steps, flapping over the kitchen floor in the large carpet slippers, and stirred up the fire that had been banked down, putting the kettle over it to heat. In a little while she had plenty of hot water, and various remedies applied, but life seemed scarcely yet to have crept back to her, only a flutter of the eyelids now and then or a fleeting breath like a sigh. The dawn was coming on and Albert's voice in low strained tones could be heard outside:

"No, I'm not going to stop for anything to eat, Hiram, you may if you like, but I shall not stop till I find her. It's been a real bad night, an' to think of that little girl out in it, I can't bear it!" There seemed to be something like a sob in Albert's last words.

"Well, suit yerself," answered Hiram, gruffly. "I'm pretty well played out. I'll go home an' get a bite, an' then I'll come on an' meet yeh. You'll likely find her back at Woodbury's I reckon. She wanted to go back, I mind now. We'd ought to 'a' gone there in the first place."

The voices were under her window. Phoebe slowly opened her eyes and shuddering grasped Emmeline's hands so tightly that it hurt her.

"Oh, don't let him come; don't let him come!" she pleaded, and sank away into unconsciousness again.

It was a long time before they could rouse her, and when she finally opened her eyes she did not know them. A fierce and terrible fever had flamed up in her veins, till her face was brilliant with color, and her long dark hair was scorched dry again in its fires.

Granny McVane came quietly over the next day and offered to nurse her. Then the long blank days of fever stretched themselves out for the unconscious girl, and a fight between life and death began.

Now, it happened that on that very afternoon of the barn-raising, Mistress Janet Bristol, in all the bravery of her pink and white frills and furbelows, with a bunch of pink moss-roses at her breast, and her haughtiest air, drove over to the Deanes to call upon Phoebe, in long-delayed response to her cousin Nathaniel's most cousinly letter requesting her to do so. She had parleyed long with herself whether she would go or not, but at last curiosity to see what there was in this country girl to attract her handsome, brilliant cousin, led her to go.

One can scarcely conjecture what Emmeline would have said and thought if she had seen the grand carriage drive up before her door, with its colored coachman and footman in livery. But no one was at home to tell the tale save the white lilacs on the great bush near the front gate, who waved a welcome rich with fragrance. Perhaps they sent the essence of the welcome Phoebe would have gladly given to this favored girl whom she admired.

So half petulant at this reception when she had condescended to come, she scanned the house for some trace of the life of this unknown girl, and drove away with the memory of lilac fragrance floating about a dull and commonplace house. She drove away half determined she would tell her cousin she had done her best, and would not go again. There was no sign left behind to tell this other girl of the lost call. It is doubtful, if Janet had been able to carry out her purpose that afternoon and make her call upon Phoebe, whether either of the two would have been able to find and understand the other at that time.

Janet drove back to her own world again, and the door between the two closed. That very evening's mail brought a brief letter from Nathaniel, saying his dear friend and chum, Martin Van Rensselaer, would be coming North now in a few days, and he desired Janet to invite him to spend a little time in the old home. He would try and arrange to get away from his work and run up for a few days, and they would all have a good time together. So while this other girl, whose unsheltered life had been so full of sorrow, was plodding her way through the darkness and rain alone in the night with fear, Janet Bristol sat in her stately parlor, where a bright hearth-fire cast rosy lights over her white frock, and planned pretty wiles for the beguiling of the young theologue.

20

MIRANDA was out in the flower-bed by the side gate. She had gathered her hands full of spicy grey-green Southern wood and was standing by the fence looking wistfully down the street. The afternoon coach was in and she was idly watching to see who came in it, but not with her usual vim. The spectre of the shadow of death was hovering too near to Phoebe for Miranda to take much interest in things in general.

Three days after Phoebe's midnight walk Miranda had gone out to see her and bring her down to take tea with Mrs. Spafford. What was her dismay to find that she was refused admittance, and that too very shortly.

"Phoebe's sick abed!" snapped Emmeline. She had been tried beyond measure over all the extra work that was thrown on her hands by Phoebe's illness, and she had no time for buttered words. "No, she can't see you to-day nor next day. She's got a fever an' she don't know nobody. The doctor says she mus' be kep' quiet. No, I can't tell yeh how she got it. The land only knows! Ef she ever gits well mebbe she ken tell herself, but I doubt it. She'll uv forgot by that time. What she does know she fergets mostly. No, you can't

215

go an' take care of her. She's got folks 'nough to do that now, more'n she needs. There ain't a livin' thing to do but let her alone till she comes out of it. You don't suppose *you* c'd take care o' her, do yeh? *H'm!* Wal, I ain't got time to talk," and the door was shut in her face.

Miranda, however, was not to be turned aside thus easily. With real concern in her face she marched around the woodshed to the place under the little window of the kitchen chamber that she knew was Phoebe's room.

"Phoebe!" she called, softly; "Phoe-bee!"

And the sick girl tossing on her bed of fever called wildly, "Don't you hear that Phoebe-bird calling, mother! Oh, mother! It's calling me from the top of the barn. It says, 'Phoebe, I'm here! Don't be afraid!' " and the voice trailed off into incoherence again.

Granny McVane hobbled to the window, perplexed, for she too had heard the soft sound.

"Oh, is that you, Granny?" whispered Miranda. "Say, what's the matter with Phoebe? Is she bad?"

"Yes, real bad," whispered back Granny. "She don't know a soul, poor little thing. She thinks her mother's here with her. I don't know much about how it happened. There was an accident and the horse ran away. She was out in that awful storm the other night. She's calling and I must go back to her."

In much dismay Miranda had hurried back to the village. She besieged the doctor's house until he came home, and could get only gravity and shakings of the head. "She may pull through, she may—" the old doctor would say, doubtfully. "She's young and strong, and it might be—but there's been a great shock to the system, and she doesn't respond to my medicines. I can't tell."

Every day the story was the same, though David and Marcia had gone themselves; and though Miranda travelled the mile-and-a-half every afternoon after her work was done, out to the Deane farm, there had been no change. The fever raged on, nor stayed one whit in its course. The faithful heart of Miranda was as near to discouragement as it had ever come in its dauntless life.

And now this afternoon she had just returned from a particularly fruitless journey to the farm. She had been unable to get sight or sound of any one but Emmeline, who slammed the door in her face as usual after telling her she wished she would mind her own business and let folks alone that weren't troubling her, and Miranda felt as she trudged back to the village with tears in her homely eyes, as if she must cry out or do something. She had never quite come to a place before where her wits could not plan out some help for those she loved. Death was different. One could not outwit death.

Then, like a slowly dawning hope, she saw Nathaniel Graham coming up the street with his carpet-bag in his hand.

Nathaniel had come up for a day to tell his uncle and cousin all about this dear friend of his whom he so much desired to have made welcome for a week or two for his sake. He had been made junior partner in a law firm, the senior partner being an old friend of Judge Bristol's, and his work would be strenuous, else he would probably have planned to be at the old home all summer himself. As it was, he could hope for but a few days now and then when he could be spared.

Nathaniel came to a halt with his pleasant smile as he recognized Miranda.

"How do you do, Miss Miranda? Are all your folks well? Are Mr. and Mrs. Spafford at home? I must try to run over and see them before I go back. I'm only here on a brief visit, must return to-morrow. How is the place getting on? All the old friends just the same? Do you ever see Miss Deane? She's well, I hope."

Nathaniel was running through these sentences pleasantly, as one will who has been away from a town for a time, and

217

he did not note the replies carefully, as he thought he knew pretty well what they would be, having heard from home but a day or two before. He was just going on when something deep and different in Miranda's tone and clouded eyes made him pause and listen:

"No, she ain't well, Phoebe Deane ain't. She's way down sick, an' they don't nobody think she's goin' to get well, I'm sure o' that!" Then the unexpected happened. Two big tears welled up and rolled down the two dauntless, freckled cheeks. Nobody had ever seen Miranda Griscom cry before.

A sudden nameless fear gripped Nathaniel's heart. Phoebe Deane sick! Near to death! All at once the day seemed to have clouded over for him.

"Tell me, Miranda," he said, gently, "she is my friend, too, I think. I did not know—I had not heard. Has she been ill long? What was the cause?"

"'Bout two weeks," said Miranda, mopping her face with the corner of her clean apron, "an' I can't find out what made her sick, but it's my 'pinion she's bein' tormented to death by that long-legged blatherskite of a Hiram Green. He ain't nothin' but a big bully, fer he's really a coward at heart, an' what's more, folks 'll find it out some day ef I don't miss my guess. But he ken git up the low-downdest, pin-prickenist, soul-shakenest tormentin's that ever a saint hed to bear. An' ef Phoebe Deane ain't a saint I don't know who is 'cept my Mis' Spafford. Them two 's ez much alike 's two pease—sweet-pease, I mean, pink an' white ones in blow."

Nathaniel warmed to Miranda's eloquence and kindled to her poetry. He felt that here was something that must be investigated.

"I believe that man is a scoundrel!" said Nathaniel, earnestly. "Do you say he really dares to annoy Miss Deane?"

"Well, I rather guess you'd think so! She can't stir without he's at her side, tendin' like he b'longs there. She can't bear the sight o' him, an' he struts up to her at the church door like he owned her, an' ef 'twant fer me an Rose an'

Mis' Spafford she couldn't get red of 'im. She can't go to the post-office any more 'thout he hants the very road, though she's told him up 'n down she won't hev a thing to do 'ith him. I hev to go after her an' take her home when she comes to see us, fear he'll dog her steps, an' he's scared her most to death twice now, chasin' after her, once at night when she was comin' down to your house to bring some letter she'd found."

Nathaniel's face grew suddenly conscious, and a warm glow of indignation rolled over it. He set down his carpet-bag and came close to the fence to listen.

"Why, w'd you b'lieve it, thet feller found she liked to go to th' post-office fer a walk, and he jest follered her every time, an' when she quit goin' he hunted up other ways to trouble her. They tell a tale 'bout th' horse runnin' away an' her bein' out in a big storm the night she was took sick, but I b'lieve in my soul he's t' th' bottom of it, an' I'd like to see him get his come-uppance right now."

"Miranda, do you happen to know—I don't suppose you ever heard Miss Deane speak of receiving a letter from me."

Miranda's alert eyes were on his face.

"Long 'bout when?" she demanded, keenly.

"Why last December, I think it was. I wrote her a note and I never received any reply. I wondered if it might have got lost, or whether she did not like my writing it, as I am almost a stranger."

"No, sir-ree, she never got that letter! I know fer sure, 'cause I happened to speak to her 'bout hearin' Hiram Green askin' pertick'ler fer her mail in the post-office one day; and I found out he gets the Deanes' mail quite often an' carries it out to 'em; an' I tole her I thought she wouldn't like him meddlin' with her mail, an' she jest laughed an' said he couldn't do her any harm thet way, cause she never got a letter in her life 'cept one her mother wrote her 'fore she died. Thet was only a little while back, 'bout a month 'er so, 'way after January, fer the snow was most gone the day I tol' her.

She can't uv got your letter no how. I'd be willin' to bet a good fat doughnut thet thet rascally Hiram Green knows what come o' thet letter. My, but I'd like to prove it on him!"

"Oh, Miranda, he would scarcely dare to tamper with another person's mail. He's a well-informed man, and must know that's a crime. He could be put into prison for that. It must have got lost if you are sure she never received it."

"Could he?" said Miranda eagerly; "could he be put in prison? My! But I'd like to help get him lodged there fer a spell 'til he learned a little bit o' politeness toward th' angels thet walks the airth in mortal form. Dast! Hiram Green dast? He's got cheek enough to dast ennythin'. You don't know him. He wouldn't think enny one would find out! But say, I'll tell you what you ken do. You jest write that letter over again, ef you ken rem'mber 'bout what you wanted to say b'fore, an' I'll agree to git it to her first hand this time."

Nathaniel's face was alight with the eagerness of a boy. Somehow Miranda's childish proposal was pleasant to him. Her homely, honest face beamed at him expectantly, and he replied with earnestness:

"I'll do it, Miranda, I'll do it this very day, and trust it to your kindness to get it to her safely. Thank you for suggesting it."

Then suddenly a cloud came over the freckled face, and the gray eyes filled with tears again.

"But I mightin't ever git it to 'er, after all, yeh know. They say she's jest hangin' 'tween life 'n death to-day, an' t'night's the crisis."

A cloud seemed suddenly to have passed before the sun again, a chill almost imperceptible came in the air. What was that icy something gripping Nathaniel's heart? Why did all the forces of life and nature seem to hang upon the well-being of this young girl? He caught his breath.

"We must pray for her, Miranda, you and I," he said, gravely; "she once promised to pray for me."

"Did she?" said Miranda, looking up with solemn awe through her tears. "I'm real glad you tole me that. I'll try, but I ain't much on things like that. I could wallup Hiram Green a grea' deal better'n I could pray; but I s'pose that wouldn't do no good, so I'll do my best at the prayin'. Ef it's kind of botched up mebbe yours'll make up fer it. But say you better write that letter right off. I've heard tell there's things like thet'll help when crisises comes. I'm goin' t' make it a pint t' git up there t'night, spite o' that ole Mis' Deane, an' ef I see a chance I'll give it to her. I kind of think it might please her to have a letter t'git well fer."

"I'll do it, Miranda, I'll do it at once, and bring it around to you before dark. But you must be careful not to trouble her with it till she is able. You know it might make her worse to be bothered with any excitement like a letter from a stranger."

"I'll use me bes' jedgment," said Miranda, with happy pride. "I ain't runnin' no resks, so you needn't worry."

With a new interest in his face Nathaniel grasped his carpet-bag and hurried to his uncle's house. He found Janet ready with a joyful welcome, but he showed more anxiety to get to his room than to talk with her.

"I suppose it was dusty on the road to-day," she conceded, unwillingly, "but hurry back. I've a great deal to ask you, and to tell; and I want you all to myself before your friend comes."

But once in his room he forgot dust and sat down immediately to the great mahogany desk where paper and pens were just as he had left them when he went away. Janet had to call twice before he made his appearance, for he was deep in writing a letter.

> My dear Miss Deane, (he wrote.) They tell me you are lying very ill and I feel as if I must write a few words to tell you how anxious and sad I am about you. I want you to know that I am praying that you may get well.

I wrote you sometime ago asking if you were will-ing to correspond with me, but I have reason now to think you never received my letter, so I have ventured to write again. I know it may be sometime before you are able even to read this, but I am sending it by a trusty messenger and I am sure you will let me know my answer when you are better. It will be a great source of pleasure and profit to me if you will write to me sometimes.

Yours faithfully,
Nathaniel Graham

He folded and addressed it, sealing it with his crest, and then Janet called for the second time:

"Yes Janet, I'm coming now, really. I had to write a let-ter. I am sorry, but it couldn't wait."

"Oh, how poky! Always business, business!" cried Janet. "It is well your friend is coming to-night for it is plain to be seen we shall have no good of you. How is it that you have grown old and grave so soon, Nathaniel? I thought you would stay a boy a long time."

"Just wait until I send my letter, Janet, and I will be as young as you please for two whole days."

"Let Caesar take it for you, then. There is no need for you to go."

"I would rather take it myself, cousin," he said, and she knew by his look that he would have his way.

"Well, then, I will go with you," she pouted, and taking her sunshade from the hall table unfurled its rosy whiteness.

He was somewhat dismayed at this, but making the best of it smiled good-humoredly and together they went out into the summer street and walked beneath the long arch of maples newly dressed in green.

"But this is not the way to the post-office," she cried, when they had walked some distance.

"But this is the way for my letter," he said, pleasantly.

"Now, Janet, what have you to ask me so insistently?"

"About this Martin friend of yours. Is he nice? That is, will I like him? It isn't enough that *you* like him, for you like some very stupid people sometimes. I want to know if I will like him."

"And how should I be able to tell that, Janet? Of one thing I am sure, he will have to like you," and he surveyed his handsome cousin admiringly. "That's a very pretty sunshade you have. May I carry it for you?"

"Well, after that pleasant speech perhaps you may," she said, surrendering it. "About this young man, is it really true, Nathaniel, that he is a minister, and that he is to preach for Dr. MacFarlane while the doctor goes to visit his daughter? Father thought you had arranged for that. You see it is very important that I like him, because if I don't I simply cannot go to church and hear him preach. In fact I'm not sure but I shall stay away anyway. I should be so afraid he'd break down if I liked him, and if I didn't I should want to laugh. It will be so funny to see a minister at home every day, and know all his faults and his little peculiarities, and then see him get up and try to preach. I'm *sure* I should laugh."

"I am sure you would dare do nothing of the kind when Martin preaches."

"Oh, is he then so terribly grave and solemn? I shall not like him in the least."

"Wait until he comes, Janet. The evening coach will soon be in."

They had reached the Spafford house now, and Nathaniel's anxiety about delivering his letter was relieved by seeing Miranda hurry out to the flower-bed again with a manner as if the demand for fresh flowers had suddenly become greater than the supply. She was quite close to the fence as they came up, but she remained unconscious of their presence until Nathaniel spoke.

"Is that you, Miss Miranda?" he said, lifting his hat as though he had not seen her before that afternoon. "Will you kindly deliver this letter for me?"

He handed her the letter directly from his pocket, and Janet could not see the address. Miranda took it serenely.

"Yes, sir," she said, scrutinizing the address at a safe angle from Janet's vision, "I'll deliver it safe an' sure. Afternoon, Mis' Janet. Like a bunch o' pink columbine to stick in yer frock? Jes' matches them posies on the muslin delaine." And she snapped off a fine whirl of delicate pink columbine. Janet accepted it graciously and the two turned back home again.

"Now I can't see why Caesar couldn't have done that," grumbled Janet. "He's just as trustworthy as that funny red-haired girl."

"You would not have got your columbine," smiled Nathaniel, "and I'm sure it was just what you needed to complete the picture."

"Now for that pretty speech I'll say no more about it," granted Mistress Janet, well pleased.

And so they walked along the shaded street, where the sunlight was beginning to lie in long slant rays on the pavement and play strange yellow fancies with the smart new leaves of the maples. Nathaniel talked as he knew his cousin liked to have him do, and all the time she never knew that his heart had gone with the letter he had given to Miranda. Perhaps it was her interest in the stranger who was coming that kept her from missing something. Perhaps it was his light-hearted manner, so free from the perplexing problems that had filled his face with gravity on his recent visits. Perhaps it was just Janet's own happy heart, glad with the gladness of life and the summer weather, and the holiday guests.

Yet underneath Nathaniel's gay manner there ran two thoughts side by side—one, the fact that Miranda had said Phoebe had repulsed Hiram Green; the other, that she was lying at death's door; and all the time his strong heart was going out in a wild, hopeful pleading that her young life might yet be spared to joy. He felt that this mute pleading was her due, for had she not lifted her clear eyes and said, "Oh, I will," when he had asked her to pray for him? He must return it in full measure.

The evening coach was late, but it rolled in at last, bringing the eagerly-watched-for guest, bronzed from his months in the South. The dinner was served around a joyous board, the Judge beaming his pleasure upon the little company. The evening was prolonged far beyond the usual retiring hour, while laughter and talk floated on around him, and all the time Nathaniel was conscious of that other house but two miles away, where life and death were battling for a victim.

He went upstairs with Martin for another talk after the house was quiet, but at last they separated; and Nathaniel was free to sit by the window in his dark room looking out into the night now grown brilliant with the late rising moon, and keep tryst with one who was hovering on the brink of the other world.

21

"I'M a notion to go up an' stay there t'night!" announced
Miranda, as she cleared off the tea things. "This's the crisis,
an' they might need me fer sumthin'. Any how I'm a 'going'
ef you don't mind."

"Will they let you in?" asked Marcia.

"I shan't ask 'em," said Miranda, loftily. "There's more
ways 'n one o' gettin' in, an' ef I make up my mind to git
there you'll see I'll do it."

Marcia laughed.

"I suppose you will, Miranda. Well, go on. You may be
needed. Poor Phoebe! I wish there was something I could do
for her."

"Wal, thur is," said Miranda, with unexpected vim. "I've
took a contrac' thet I don't seem to make much headway on.
I'd like to hev you take a little try at it, an' see ef you can't
do better. I 'greed t' pray fer Phoebe Deane, but t' save my
life I can't think uv any more ways uv sayin' it thun jest to
ast, an' after I've done it oncet it don't seem quite p'lite to
keep at it, z' if I didn't b'lieve 'twas heard. The minister
preached awhile back 'bout the 'fectual fervent prayer uv a
righteous man 'vailin' much, but he didn't say nothin' 'bout

a red-headed woman. I reckon I ain't much good at prayin',
fer I'm all wore out with it, but ef you'd jest spell me a
while, an' lemme go see ef thur ain't sumpthin' to *do,* I think
it would be a sight more availin' than fer me to set still an'
jest pray; 'sides, ef you ain't better 'n most any righteous
man I ever see, I'll miss my guess."

Thus the responsibility was divided, and Marcia with a
smile upon her lips and a tear in her eye went away to pray,
while Miranda tied on her bonnet, tucked the letter safely in
her pocket after examining its seals and address most mi-
nutely, and went her way into the night.

She did not go to the front door, but stole around to the
wood-shed where with the help of a milking-stool which
stood there she mounted to the low roof. Strong of limb and
courageous she found the climb nothing. She crept softly
along the roof till she reached Phoebe's window, and
crouched to listen. The window was open but a little way,
though the night was warm and dry.

"Granny, Granny McVane," she called, softly, and Granny, startled from her evening drowsiness, stole over to the
window wondering. A candle was burning behind the water
pitcher and shed a weird and sickly light through the room.
Granny looked old and tired as she came to the window, and
it struck Miranda she had been crying.

"Fer the land sake! Is that you Mirandy?" she exclaimed in
horror. "Mercy! How'd you get there? Look out! You'll fall."

"Open the winder till I come in," whispered Miranda.

Granny opened the window cautiously.

"Be quick," she said, "I mustn't let the air get to the
bed."

"I should think air was jes' what she'd want this night,"
whispered Miranda, as she emerged into the room and
straightened her garments. "How's she seem? Any change?"

"I think she's failing, I surely do," moaned the old lady,
softly, the tears running down her cheeks in slow uneven
rivulets between the wrinkles. "I don't see how she can hold

out till morning anyhow. She's jest burnt up with fever, and sometimes she seems to be gasping for breath. But how'd you get up there? Weren't you scairt?"

"I jes' couldn't keep away a minute longer. The doctor said this was the crisis an' I hed to come. My Mrs. Spafford's home prayin' an' I come to see ef I couldn't help answer them prayers. You might need help to-night, an' I'm goin' to stay. Will any of her folks be in again to-night?"

"No, I reckon not. Emmeline's worn out. The baby's teething and hasn't given her a minute's let-up for two nights. She had his gums lanced to-day and she hopes to get a wink of sleep, for there's likely to be plenty doing to-morrow."

Miranda set her lips hard at this and turned to the bed, where Phoebe lay under heavy blankets and comfortables, a low moan, almost a gasp, escaping her parched lips now and then.

The fever seemed to have burnt a place for itself in the whiteness of her cheeks. Her beautiful hair had been cut short by Emmeline the second day because she could not be bothered combing it. It was as well, for it would not have withstood the fever, but to Miranda it seemed like a ruthless tampering with the sacred. Her wrath burned hot within her, even while she was considering what was to be done.

"My goodness alive," was her first word, "I should think she would hev a fever. It's hotter'n mustard in here. Why don't you open them winders wide? I should think you'd roast alive yerself. And land sakes! Look at the covers she's got piled on! Poor little thing!" Miranda reached out a swift hand and swept several layers off to the floor. A sigh of relief followed from Phoebe.

Miranda placed a firm cool hand on the burning forehead, and the sufferer seemed to take note of the touch eagerly.

"Oh, mercy me! Miranda, you mustn't take the covers off. She must be kept warm to try and break the fever. The doctor's orders were very strict. I wouldn't like to disobey him. It might be her death."

"Does he think she's any better?" questioned Miranda, fiercely.

"No." The old lady shook her head sadly, "he said this morning there wasn't a thread of hope, poor little thing. Her fever hasn't let up a mite."

"Well, ef he said that, then I'm goin' to hev my try. She can't do more 'n die, an' ef I was goin' to die I'd like to hev a cool comf'table place to do it in, wouldn't you, Granny, an' not a furnace? Let's give her a few minutes' peace 'fore she dies, any way. Come, you open them winders. Ef anythin' happens I won't tell, an' ef she's goin' to die any way I think it's wicked to make her suffer any longer."

"I don't know what they'll say to me," murmured the old lady, yielding to the dominant Miranda. "I don't think mebbe I ought to do it."

"Well, never mind what you think now, it's my try. Ef you didn't open 'em I would, fer I b'lieve in my heart she wants fresh air, an' I'm goin' to give it to her ef I hev to fight every livin' soul in this house, an' smash all the winder lights, so there! Now, that's better. It'll be somethin' like in here pretty soon. Where's a towel? Is this fresh water? Say, Granny, couldn't you slip down to the spring without wakin' anyone an' bring us a good cold drink? I'm dyin' fer a dipper o' water, I come up here so fast, and it'll taste good to Phoebe, I know."

"Oh, she mustn't have a drop o' water," exclaimed the old lady, in horror. "Fever patients don't get a mite of water."

"Fever fiddlesticks! You git that water, please, an' then you kin lay down on that couch over there an' take a nap while I set by her."

After much whispered persuasion and bullying Miranda succeeded in getting the old lady to slip downstairs and go for the water, though the spring-house was almost as far as the barn and Granny was not used to prowling around alone at night. While she was gone Miranda boldly dipped a towel in the water pitcher and washed the fevered brow and face.

The parched lips crept to the wetness eagerly, and Miranda began to feel assurance to the tips of her fingers. She calmly bathed the girl's hot face and hands, until the low moans became sounds of relief and content. Then quite unconscious that she was anticipating science she prepared to give her patient a sponge bath. In the midst of the performance she looked up to see Granny standing over her in horror.

"What are you doing, Mirandy Griscom? You'll kill her. The doctor said she mustn't have a drop of water touch her."

"I'm takin' the fever out uv her. Jes' feel her an' see," said Miranda, triumphantly. "Put yer lips on her forrid, thet's the way to tell. Ain't she coolin' off nice?"

"You're killing her, Miranda," said Granny, in a terrified tone, "and I've cared fer her so carefully all these weeks, and now to have her go like this! It's death coming that makes her cold."

"Death fiddlesticks!" said Miranda, wrathfully. "Well, ef 'tis, she'll die happy. Here, give me that water!" and she took the cup from the trembling hand of Granny and held it to Phoebe's dry lips. Eagerly the lips opened, and drank in the water, as Miranda raised her head on her strong young arm. Then the sick girl lay back with a long sigh of content, and fell asleep.

It was the first natural sleep she had had since the awful beginning of the fever. She did not toss nor moan, and Granny hovered doubtingly above her, watching and listening to see if she still breathed, wondering at the fading of the crimson flames upon the white cheeks, dismayed at the cooling of the brow, even troubled at the quiet sleep.

"I fear she'll slip away in this," she said at last, in a sepulchral whisper. "That was an awful daresome thing you did. I wouldn't like them to find it out on you. They might say you caused her death."

"But she ain't dead yet," said Miranda, triumphantly, "an' ef she slips away in this it's a sight pleasanter 'n the way she was when I crep' in. Say now, Granny, don't you think so, honest?"

"Oh, I don't know," sighed Granny, turning away sadly. "Mebbe I oughtn't to have let you."

"You couldn't a he'ped yerself, fer I'd come to do it, an' anyway, ef you'd made a fuss I'd hed to put you out on the roof er somethin' till I got down. Now, Granny, you're all tired out. You jes' go over an' lie down on thet couch an' I'll set by an' watch her a spell."

The conversation was carried on in close proximity to Granny's ear, for both nurses were anxious lest some of the sleeping household should hear. Granny knew she would be blamed for Miranda's presence in the sick room, and Miranda knew she would be ousted if discovery were made.

Granny settled down at last, with many protests, owned she was "jest the least mite tuckered out," and lay down for what she called a "cat-nap." Miranda, meantime, wide-eyed and sleepless, sat beside Phoebe and watched her every breath, for she felt more anxiety about what she had done than she cared to own to Granny. She had never had much experience in nursing, except in waiting upon Marcia, but her common sense told her that people were not so likely to get well as long as they were uncomfortable, therefore without much consideration she did for Phoebe what she would like to have had done for herself if she were ill. It seemed the right thing, and it seemed to be working, but supposing Granny were right, after all!

Then Miranda remembered the two who were praying. "H'm" she said to herself, as she sat watching the still face on the pillow, "I reckon that's their part. Mine's to do the best I know. Ef the prayers is good fer anything they ought to piece out whar' I fail. An' I guess they will, too, with them two at it."

After that she got the wet towel and went to work again, bathing the brow and hands whenever the heat seemed to be growing in them again. She was bound to bring that fever down. Now and then the sleeper would draw a long sigh as of contentment, and comfort, and Miranda felt that she had received her thanks. It was enough to know that she had given her friend a little comfort, if nothing else.

The hours throbbed on. The moon went down; the candle began to sputter, and Miranda lighted another. Granny slept and actually snored, weary with her long vigil. Miranda had to touch her occasionally to stop the loud noise lest some one should hear and come to see what it was. But the rest of the household were weary, too, for it was in the height of the summer's work now, and all slept soundly.

When the early dawn crept into the sky Miranda felt Phoebe's hands and head and found them cool and natural. She stooped and listened and her breathing came regularly like a tired child's. For just one instant she touched her lips to the white forehead and was rejoiced that the parched burning feeling was gone. There remained yet the awful weakness to fight, but at least the fever was gone. What had done it she did not care, but it was done.

She went gently to Granny and wakened her. The old lady started up with a frightened look, guilty that she had slept so long, but Miranda reassured her.

"It's all right. I'm glad you slep', fer you wan't needed, an' I guess you'll feel all the better fer it to-day. She's slep' real quiet all night long, ain't moaned once, an' jes' feel her. Ain't she feelin' all right? I b'lieve the fever's gone."

Granny went over and touched her face and hands wonderingly.

"She does feel better," she admitted, "but I don't know. It mayn't last. I've seen 'em rally toward the end," dubiously; "she'll be so powerful weak now, it'll be all we can do to hold her to earth."

"What's she ben eatin'?" enquired Miranda.

"She hasn't eaten anything of any account for some time back."

"Well, she can't live on jest air an' water ferever. Say,

Granny, I've got to be goin' soon, er I'll hev to hide in the closet all day fer sure, but 'spose you slip out to the barn now while I wait an' get a few drops o' new milk. Hank's out there milkin'. I heard him go down an' git his milk-pails an' stool 'fore I woke you up. We'll give her a spoonful o' warm milk. Mebbe that'll hearten her up."

"It might," said Granny, doubtfully. She took the cup and hurried away, Miranda taking the precaution to button the door after her lest Emmeline whom she could hear moving around in her room should take a notion to look in.

When Granny got back Miranda took the cup and putting a few drops of the sweet warm fluid in a spoon she touched it to Phoebe's lips. A slow sigh followed, and then Phoebe's eyes opened and she looked straight at Miranda and seemed to know her, for a flicker of a smile shone in her face.

"There, Phoebe, take this spoonful. You've ben sick, but it'll make you well," crooned Miranda, softly.

Phoebe obediently swallowed the few drops and Miranda dipped up a few more.

"It's all right, dear," she said softly. "I'll take care o' you. Jes' you drink this, an' get well, fer I've got somethin' real nice in my pocket fer you when ye're able. But you must take yer milk an' go to sleep."

Thus Miranda fed her two or three spoonfuls, then the white lids closed over the trusting eyes, and in a moment more she was sleeping again.

Miranda watched her a few minutes, and then cautiously stole away from the bed, to the astonished Granny who had been watching with a new respect for the domineering young nurse that had usurped her place.

"I guess she'll sleep most o' the day," Miranda whispered. "Ef she wakes up you jes' give her a spoonful o' fresh milk, er a sup o' water, an' tell her I'll be back bime-by. She'll understan' an' that'll keep her quiet. Tell her I said she mus' lie still an' get well. Don't you dast keep them winders shet up all day again, an' don't pile on the clo'es. She may need a light blanket ef she feels cool, but don't fer mercy's sake get her all het up again, er we might not be able to stop it off so easy next time. I'll be back's soon es it's dark. By-by. I' mus' go. I may get ketched es 'tis."

Miranda slid out the window and down the sloping roof, dropping over the eaves just in time to escape being seen by Emmeline, who opened the back door with a sharp click and came out to get a broom she had forgotten the night before.

The morning was almost come now, and the long grass was dripping with dew as Miranda swept through it.

"Reckon they'll think there's ben a fox er somethin' prowlin' round the house ef they see my tracks," she said to herself, as she hurried through the dewy fields and out to the road.

Victory was written upon her countenance as she sped along, victory tempered with hope. Perhaps she was not judge enough of illness, and it might be that her hopes were vain ones, and apparent signs deceitful, but come what might she would always be glad she had done what she had. That look in Phoebe's eyes before she fell asleep again was reward enough. It made her heart swell with triumph to think of it.

Two hours later she brought a platter of delicately poached eggs on toast to the breakfast table just as Marcia entered the room.

"Good-morning, Miranda. How did it go last night? You evidently got in and found something to do."

Miranda set down the platter and stood with hands on her hips and face shining with morning welcome.

"I tell you, Mrs. Marcia, them prayers was all right. They worked fine. When I got mixed and didn't know what was right to do I just remembered them an' cast off all 'sponsibility. Anyhow, she's sleepin' an' the fever's gone."

Marcia smiled.

"I shouldn't wonder if your part was really prayer, too," she said, dreamily. "We are not all heard for our much speaking."

It was a glorious day. The sun shone in a perfect heaven without a cloud to blur it. A soft south breeze kept the air from being too warm. Miranda sang all the morning as she went about her belated work.

After dinner Marcia insisted she should go and take a nap. She obediently lay down for half an hour straight and stiff on her bright neat patchwork quilt, scarcely relaxing a muscle lest she rumple the bed. She did not close her eyes, however, but lay joyously smiling at the bland white ceiling, and resting herself by gently crackling the letter in her pocket, and smiling to think how Phoebe would look when she showed it to her.

In exactly half an hour she arose, combed her hair neatly, donned her afternoon frock and her little black silk apron that was her pride on ordinary occasions, and descended to her usual post of observation with her knitting. Naps were not in her line and she was glad hers was over.

A little later the doctor's chaise drove up to the door, and Miranda went out to see what he wanted, a great fear clutching her heart. But she was reassured by the smile on his face, and the good will in the expressions of his wife and her sister, who were riding with him.

"Say, Mirandy, I don't know but I'll take you into partnership. Where'd you learn nursing? You did what I wouldn't have dared do, but it seemed to hit the mark. I'd given her up. I've seen her slipping away for a week past, but she's taken a turn for the better now, and I believe in my soul she's going to get well. If she does it'll be you that'll get the honor."

Miranda's eyes shone with happy tears.

"You don't say, doctor," she said. "Why, I was real scared when Granny told me you said she wasn't to hev a sup o' water, but it seemed like she must be so turrible hot—"

"Well, I wouldn't have dared try it myself, but I believe it did the business," said the doctor, heartily.

"Yes, you deserve great credit, Miranda," said the doctor's wife. "You do, indeed," echoed her sister, pleasantly.

"Granny ain't tole Mis' Deane I was there, hes she?" asked Miranda, to cover her embarrassment. She was not used to praise except from her own household.

"No, she hasn't told her yet, but I think I shall tell her myself by to-morrow if all goes well. Can you find time to run over to-night again? Granny might not stay wide awake all the time. She's fagged out, and I think it's a critical time."

"Oh, I'll be there!" said Miranda, gleefully. "You couldn't keep me away."

"How'll you get in? Same way you did last night?" asked the doctor laughing. "Say, that's a good joke! I've laughed and laughed ever since Granny told me, at the thought of you climbing in the window and the family all sleeping calmly. Good for you, Miranda. You're made of the right stuff. Well, good-by. I'll fix it up with Mrs. Deane to-morrow so you can go in by the door."

The doctor drove on, laughing, and his wife and sister bowing and smiling. Miranda, with high head of pride and heart full of joy, went in to get supper.

Supper was just cleared away when Nathaniel came over. He talked with David in the dusk of the front stoop a few minutes and then asked diffidently if Miranda was going up to see how Miss Deane was again soon.

David, because of his love for Marcia, half understood, and calling Miranda left the two together for a moment while he went to call Marcia, who was putting Rose to bed.

"She's better," said Miranda, entering without preamble into the subject nearest their hearts, "the doctor told me so this afternoon. But don't you stop prayin' yet, fer we don't want no half-way job, an' she's powerful weak. I kinder rely on them prayers to do a lot. I got Mrs. Spafford to spell me at mine while I went up to help nurse. She opened her eyes oncet last night when I was given' her some milk, an' I tole her I had somethin' nice fer her if she'd lie still an' go to sleep an' hurry up an' git well. She kinder seemed to understand, I most think. I've got the letter all safe, an' jest ez soon ez she gits the least mite better, able to talk, I'll give it to her."

"Thank you, Miss Miranda," said Nathaniel, "and won't you take this to her? It will be better than letters for her for a while until she gets well. You needn't bother her telling anything about it now. Just give it to her. It may help her a little. Then later, if you think best, you may tell her I sent it."

He held out a single tea-rose, half blown, with delicate petals of pale saffron.

Miranda took it with awe. It was not like anything that grew in the gardens she knew.

"It looks like her," she said, reverently.

"It makes me think of her as I first saw her," he answered, in a low voice. "She wore a frock like that."

"I know," said Miranda, understandingly, "I'll give it to her, and tell her all about it when she's better."

"Thank you," said Nathaniel. Then Marcia and David entered, and Miranda went away to wonder over the rose, and prepare for her night's vigil.

22

GRANNY greeted Miranda with a smile as she crept in at the window that night. Phoebe, too, opened her eyes in welcome, though she made no other sign that she was awake. Her face was like sunken marble now that the fever was gone from it, and her two great eyes shone from it like lights of another world. It startled Miranda as she came and looked at her. Then at once she preceived that Phoebe's eyes had sought the rose, and a smile was hovering about her lips.

"It was sent to you," she answered the questioning eyes, putting the rose close down to the white cheek. Phoebe really smiled then faintly.

"She better have some milk now," said Granny, anxiously. "She's been asleep so long an' I didn't disturb her."

"Yes, take some milk," whispered Miranda, gently, "an' I'll tell you all 'bout the rose when you're better."

The night crept on in quiet exultation on Miranda's part. While Phoebe slept Miranda and the rose kept vigil, and Granny sank into the first restful sleep she had had since she came to nurse Phoebe. The house was quiet. There was nothing for the watcher to do much of the time but to watch. Now and then she drew the coverlet up a little higher when a fresh breeze came through the window; or again gave a drink of water, or a spoonful of milk. The candle was shaded by the water pitcher, and the frail sweet rose looked spectral in the weird light. Miranda looked at the flower, and it looked back at her. As the hours slowly passed Miranda found her lips murmuring:

"Thanks be! Thanks be!"

Suddenly she drew herself up with a new thought.

"Land sakes! That's sounds like prayin'. Wonder ef 'tis. Anyhow it's thanks-givin', an' that's what I feel. Guess it's my turn to give thanks."

The next day the doctor had a talk with Albert Deane. He told him how Miranda had crept in at the window and cared for Phoebe; and how he believed it had been Phoebe's salvation. Albert was deeply affected. He readily agreed that it would be a fine thing for Phoebe if Miranda could be got to come and help Granny care for her, now that she seemed to be on the fair road to recovery.

It was all arranged in a few minutes and Emmeline was not told until just before Miranda arrived.

"It's very queer," she said, with her nose in the air, "that I wasn't consulted. I'm sure it's my business more'n yours to look after such things, Albert Deane. An' I wouldn't uv had that sassy creature in the house fer a good deal. Hank's sister would 'a' ben a sight better, an' could a' helped me between times with Phoebe's extry work. I'm sure its bad enough havin' sickness this way in the midst o' hayin' season, an' me with all them men to feed, an' not havin' Phoebe to help. I could 'a' sent fer my own sister, when it comes to that, an' 'twould 'a' ben a sight pleasanter."

But before there was time for a protest or apology from Albert there came a knock at the door, and without waiting for ceremony Miranda walked in.

"Ev'nin', Miss Deane," she said, unconcernedly. "Everything goin' well? I'll go right up, shall I?" Her smiling insolence struck Emmeline dumb for the moment.

"Well, I vow!" declared Emmeline. "Will yeh listen to the impedence. 'Will I go right up?' es ef she was the Queen o' Sheby er the doctor himself."

But Miranda was marching serenely upstairs and if she heard she paid no heed.

"She doesn't mean any harm, Emmeline!" pleaded Albert. "She's jest Phoebe's friend, so don't you mind. It'll relieve you a lot, and if you want Hank's sister to come over too I guess we can manage it."

Thus was Miranda domiciled in Phoebe's room for a short space, much to the comfort of Phoebe and the satisfaction of Miranda.

Emmeline was only half mollified when she came upstairs to look around and "give that Griscom girl a settin' down," as she expressed it. But she who attempted to "sit" on Miranda usually arose unexpectedly.

"Where'd that come from?" was Emmeline's first question, as she pointed at the unoffending rose.

"Mirandy brought it," said Granny, proud of her colleague. "H'm!" said Emmeline, with a sniff. "It ain't healthy to hev plants round in a bedroom I've heard. D'you raise that kind down to Spaffords?"

"We ain't got just to say a-plenty yet," said Miranda, cheerfully, "but we might hev sometime. Would yeh like a slip?"

"No, thank yeh," said Emmeline, dryly, "I never had time to waste good daylight fussin' over weeds. I s'pose Mis' Spafford don't do much else."

"Oh, 'casionally!" answered Miranda, undisturbed. "This spring she put up a hundred glasses o' blueberry jelly, made peach preserves, spiced pears, an' crab-apple jam, crocheted a white bed-spread fer the spare bed, an' three antimacassars fer her Aunt Hortense's best parlor chairs, did up the second story curtains, tucked a muslin slip fer Rose, sewed carpet rags enough fer a whole strip in Shorty Briscutt's new rag carpet, made a set o' shirts fer Mr. Spafford, knit nine pair o' stocking', spun the winter's yarn, cut out an' made Rose's flannel petticoats, an' went to missionary meetin', but o' course that ain't much, nothin' to what you'd do."

(Oh Miranda, Miranda! of the short prayers and the long tongue! telling all that off with a straight face to the sour-faced woman, Emmeline!)

"She must be a smart woman!" said Granny, much impressed.

"She is," said Miranda, glibly, "but here all the time I was fergettin' we'd ought not to talk. We'll bring that fever up. Is there anything special yeh wanted me to look after t'night, Mis' Deane? 'Cause ef there is jest don' hesitate to say so. I'm here to work an' not to play."

And before she knew it, Emmeline found herself disarmed and walking meekly down stairs without having said any of the things she had meant to say.

From that time forth Phoebe grew steadily better, though she came near to having a serious set-back the day Miranda went down to the village on an errand and Emmeline attempted to "clean up" in her absence, finishing the operation by pitching out the tea-rose into the yard below the window.

"I never see such a fuss," complained Emmeline to Miranda, who stood over Phoebe and felt her fluttering pulse, "all about a dead weed. I declare I can't understand folks gettin' 'tached to trash."

Emmeline was somewhat anxious at the upset state of the patient, who was yet too weak to talk much, but who had roused herself to protest vigorously as the rose was hurled through the window, and then could not keep back the disappointed tears.

But Miranda, mindful of the weak state of her patient, and wishing to mollify Emmeline as much as possible, tried to pour oil on the troubled waters.

"Never mind, Mis' Deane, no harm done. Phoebe jest wanted to keep them leaves fer her han'kerchers, they smell real nice. I'll pick 'em up, Phoebe. They won't be hurt a mite. They're right on the green grass."

Miranda stole down and picked up the leaves tenderly, washing them at the spring, and brought them back to Phoebe. Emmeline had gone off sniffing with her chin in the air.

"I was silly to cry," murmured Phoebe, trying feebly to dry her tears, "but I loved that sweet rose. I wanted to keep it just as it was in a box. You haven't told me about it yet, Miranda, how did she come to send it?"

"It ain't hurt a mite, Phoebe, only jest three leaves come off. I'll lay it together in a box fer yeh. Now lemme put my bonnet off, an' you lay quiet an' shet your eyes while I tell you 'bout that rose. First, though, you must take your milk.

"It wan't her at all that sent you that rose, Phoebe Deane. You s'picioned 'twas Mrs. Marcia, didn't you? But 'twan't 't all. It was a man—"

"Oh, Miranda!" The words came in a moan of pain from the bed, "Not—not—Miranda, you would never have brought it if Hiram Green—"

"Land sake, child, what's took yeh? 'Course not. Why ef that nimshi'd undertake to send yeh so much ez a blade o' grass I'd fling it in his mean little face. Don't you worry, dearie, you jest listen. 'Twas Nathaniel Graham sent you that rose. He said I wasn't to say nothin' 'bout it till you got better, an' then I could say 'twas from him ef I wanted to. I didn't say anythin' yet 'cause I hed more to tell, but I ain't sure you are strong 'nough to hear any more now. Better take a nap first."

"No, Miranda; do tell me now."

"Wal, I reckon I better. I've most busted wantin' to tell yeh sev'ral times. Say, did you ever get a letter from Nathaniel Graham, Phoebe?"

"Why no, of course not, Miranda. Why would I get a letter from him?"

"Wal, he said he wrote yeh one oncet, an' he ast me did I know ef you'd got it, an' I said No, I was sure you didn't, 'cause you said oncet you hadn't ever got a letter 'cept from your mother, an' so he said he'd write it over again fer yeh, an' I've hed it in my pocket fer a long time waitin' till I dared give it to yeh. So here 'tis, but I won't give it to yeh 'thout you promise to go right to sleep 'fore you read it fer you've hed more goin's on now than's good fer yeh."

Phoebe protested that she must read the letter first, but Miranda was inexorable, and would not even show it to her until she promised. So meekly Phoebe promised, and went to sleep with the precious missive clasped in her hands, the wonder of it helping her to get quiet.

She slept a long time, for the excitement about the rose had taken her strength. When she awoke, before she opened her eyes she felt the letter, pressing the seals with her fingers, to make sure she had not been dreaming. She almost feared to open her eyes lest it should not be true. A letter for her all her own! Somehow she almost dreaded to break the seal and have the first wonder of it over. She had not thought what it might contain.

Miranda had brought a little pail of chicken broth that Marcia had made for Phoebe, and she had some steaming in a china bowl when Phoebe at last opened her eyes. She made her eat it before she opened the letter, and Phoebe smiled and acquiesced.

She lay smiling and quiet a long time after reading the letter, trying to get used to the thought that Nathaniel had remembered her, and cared to write to her; cared to have her write to him, too; it was not merely passing kindness toward a stranger. He wanted to be friends, real friends. It was good to feel that one had friends.

Phoebe looked over at the alert figure of Miranda, sitting bolt upright, watching her charge with anxiety to see if the letter was all that it should be, and then she laughed a soft little ripple that sounded like a shadow of her former self.

"Oh, you dear, good Miranda! You don't know how nice it all is to have friends, and a real letter."

"Is it a good letter?" asked Miranda, wistfully.

"Read it," said Phoebe, handing it to her, smiling. "You

certainly have a right to read it after all you have done to get it here."

Miranda took it shyly, and went over by the window where the setting sun made it a little less embarrassing. She read it slowly and carefully and the look on her face when she returned it showed she was satisfied.

"I seen him the mornin' he went back to New York," she admitted, after a minute. "He said he'd look fer that answer soon ez you got better. You're goin' to write, ain't you?" anxiously. " 'Cause he seemed real set up about it."

"How soon may I answer it?" she answered.

"We'll see," said Miranda, briskly. "The first business is to get strong."

They spent happy days together, those two girls, with nothing to worry them; and as Phoebe began to get strong and could be propped up with pillows for a little while each day Miranda at length allowed her to write a few lines in reply to her letter, and this was the message that in a few days thereafter travelled to New York.

My Dear Mr. Graham:

It was very pleasant to receive your letter and to know that you thought of me and prayed that I might get well. I think your prayers are being answered.

It will be good to have a friend to write to me, and I shall be glad to correspond with you. I want to thank you for the beautiful rose. It helped me to get well. Its leaves are sweet yet.

I have been a long time writing this, for I am very weak and tired yet, and Miranda will not let me write any more now, but you will understand and excuse me, will you not?

Your friend,
Phoebe Deane

Miranda had to go home soon after that, for it was plain

Emmeline was wanting to get rid of her, and Marcia was to
have guests for a couple of weeks. 'Squire Schuyler and his
wife were coming to visit for the first time since little Rose's
birth, for it was a long journey for an old man to take, and
the 'Squire did not like to go away from home. Miranda felt
that she must go, much as she hated to leave Phoebe, and so
she bade her good-by, and Phoebe began to take care of herself.

She was able to walk around her room, and soon to go
downstairs, but somehow when she got down into the old
atmosphere something seemed to choke her, she felt weary
and wanted to creep back to bed again. So, much to
Emmeline's disgust, she did not progress as rapidly as she
ought to have done.

"You need to git some ambition," said Emmeline, in disgust, the first morning Phoebe came down to breakfast, and
sat back after one or two mouthfuls. There was fried ham
and eggs, and fried potatoes. Anybody ought to be glad to
get that, Emmeline thought.

But somehow they did not appeal to Phoebe, and she left
her plate almost untasted.

"I think ef you'd get some work and do somethin' mebbe
you'd get your strength again. I never see anybody hang
back like you do. There ain't any sense in it. What's the matter with yeh, anyway?"

"I don't know," said Phoebe, with an effort at cheerful-
ness. "I try, but somehow I feel so heavy and tired all the
time."

"She isn't strong yet, Emmeline," pleaded Albert, kindly.

"Wal, don't I know that?" snapped Emmeline. "But
how's she ever goin' to get strong ef she don't work it up?"

Such little pin-pricks were hard to bear when Phoebe felt
well, and now that her strength was but a breath she seemed
not to be able to bear them at all, and after a short effort
would creep back to her room and lie down.

Miranda discovered her all huddled in a little heap on her

bed late one afternoon when she came up to bring Phoebe her second letter, for Nathaniel had arranged that for the present he would send his correspondence to Phoebe through Miranda. Neither of them said aloud that it was because Hiram Green brought up the Deanes's mail so often, but both understood.

Miranda and the letter succeeded in cheering up Phoebe, but the ex-nurse felt that things were not going with her charge as prosperously as they should, and she took her trouble back to Marcia.

"Let's bring her down here, Miranda," proposed Marcia. "Father and mother are going home on Monday and it will be quiet and nice here. I think she might spend a month with us and get strong before she goes back and tries to work."

Miranda was delighted and took the first opportunity to convey the invitation to Phoebe, whose cheeks grew pink and eyes bright with anticipation. A whole month with Mrs. Spafford and Miranda! It was too good to be true.

It was Monday morning when they came for her with the big old chaise. Emmeline and Hank's sister were out hanging up clothes. Emmeline's mouth was full of clothespins, and her brow was dark, for Hank's sister talked much and worked slowly. Moreover, she made lumpy starch and could not be depended upon to keep the potatoes from burning if one went out to feed the chickens. It was hard to have trained up a good worker and then have her trail off in a thunder-storm and get sick and leave the work all on one's hands without ambition enough to get well. Emmeline was very ungracious to Marcia. She told Albert that she didn't see what business Mrs. Spafford had coming round to run their house. She thought Phoebe was better off at home, but Albert felt that Mrs. Spafford had been exceedingly kind.

So it was with little regret that Phoebe was carried away from her childhood's home, and into a sweet new world of loving kindness and joy, where the round cheeks and happiness of health might be coaxed back. Yet to Phoebe it was not an unalloyed bliss, for always there was the thought with her that by and by she must go back to the old life again, and she shuddered at the very thought of it, and could not bear to face it. It was like going to heaven for a little time and having to return to earth's trials again.

The spring had changed into the summer during Phoebe's illness and it was almost the middle of July when she began her beautiful visit at the Spaffords.

23

HIRAM Green had been exceedingly quiet since the night of the runaway.

The old plow-horse had kicked something loose about the chaise in his final lurch before he started to run, and it goaded his every step. He thought Hiram was striking him with a club. He thought the thunder was pursuing him; he thought the lightning was reaching for him as it darted through out the livid sky; and down the road he flew, mile after mile, not slowing up for curves or excrescences in the road, but taking a short cut at the turns, rearing and shying at every flash of lightning. The chaise came lurching after, like one tied to a whirlwind, and Hiram, clinging, cursing, lashing out madly with his whip, was finally forced to spend his time in holding on, thinking every minute would be his last.

As the horse saw his own gate at last, however, he gave a final leap into the air, and bounded across the ditch, regardless of what was behind him, perhaps hoping to rid himself of it. The chaise lurched into the air and Hiram was tossed lightly over the fence and landed in the cow pasture. Something snapped, and the horse entered his own dooryard free at last from the thing which had been pursuing him.

The rain had begun to come down in driving sheets now, and brought Hiram to his feet in spite of his dazed condition. He looked about him in the alternate dimness and vivid brightness, and perceived that he was close to the Deanes. A moment's reflection made it plain that he must get up some kind of a story, so he put on the best face that he could and went in.

"We've hed an axident," he explained, limping into the kitchen, where Emmeline was trying to get supper and keep the fretful baby quiet. "The blamed horse got scared at th' lightnin'. I seen what was goin' to happen an' I held him on his haunches fer a second while Phoebe jumped. She's back there a piece now, I reck'n, fer that blamed critter never stopped till he landed to home, an' he placed me in a awkword persition in the cow pasture, with the chaise all broke up. I guess Phoebe's all right, fer I looked back an' thought I saw her tryin' to wave her hand to me, but I 'spect we better go hunt her up soon 's this here storm lets up. She'll likely go in somewheres. We'd just got past old Mis' Duzenberry's."

That was all the explanation the Deanes had ever had of the adventure. Phoebe had been too ill to speak of it at first, and after she got well enough to come downstairs and Albert had questioned her at the table about it she had shuddered, and turned so white saying: "Please don't, Albert. I can't bear to think of it," that he had never asked her again.

During her illness Hiram had been politely concerned about her welfare, taking the precaution to visit the post office every day and inquire solicitously for any mail for her in a voice loud enough to be heard all over the room, and always being ready to tell just how she was when any one inquired. It never entered Albert's head that Hiram was not as anxious as he was during those days and nights when the fever held sway over the sweet young life. As for Emmeline, she made up her mind that where ignorance was bliss 'twas folly to be wise, and she kept her lips sealed, accepting Hiram's explanation, though all the time secretly she thought there might be some deeper reason for Phoebe's terrible appearance than just a runaway. She was relieved that Phoebe said nothing about it, if there had been trouble, and hoped it was forgotten.

The day after Phoebe went to the Spaffords to visit, Hiram came up to see Emmeline in the afternoon when he knew Albert was out in the hayfield.

"Say, do you still favor livin' down to the village?" he asked, seating himself without waiting for an invitation.

Emmeline looked up keenly, and wondered what was in the air.

"I hev said so," she remarked, tentatively, not willing to commit herself without further knowledge.

"Wal, you know that lot o' mine down there opposite the Seceder church? It has a big weepin' willer same 's in the church yard, an a couple o' plum-trees in bearin'. How'd you like to live on thet lot?"

"H'm!" said Emmeline, stolidly. "Much good 'twould do me to like it. Albert'll never buy that lot, Hiram Green, there ain't no use askin' him. You wasn't thinkin' of buildin' there yerself, was yeh?" Emmeline looked up sharply as this new thought entered her mind. Perhaps he wanted her to hold out the bait of a house in the village to Phoebe.

"Naw, I ain't goin' to build in no village at present, Mis' Deane," he remarked, dryly. "Too fur from work fer me, thank you. But I was thinkin' I'd heard you say you wanted to live in the village, an' I thought I'd make a bargain with you. Say, Emmeline, 'taint no use mincin' matters. I'm a' goin' to marry Phoebe Deane, an' I want you should help me to it. I'll make you this offer. It's a real generous one, too. The day I marry Phoebe Deane I'll give you a deed to that lot in the village. Now, what d'yeh say? Is't a bargain?"

"What to do?" questioned Emmeline. She would be caught in no trap. "I've done all I know now. I'd like my sister Mandy to come here to live, an' there ain't room fer her while Phoebe stays; but I don't see what I kin do, more'n what I've done a'ready. Wouldn't she make up to yeh none the day you come home from the barn raisin'?"

"Wal, I was gettin' on pretty well 'til that blamed horse took an' run," said Hiram, shifting his eyes from her piercing ones.

"Wal, I can't compel her to marry you," snapped Emmeline.

"You don't hev to," said Hiram. "I've got my plans laid, an' all you got to do is stand by me when the time comes. I ain't tellin' my plans jest yet, but you'll see what they be, an' all is, you remember my offer. Ef you want that village lot jest remember to stand by me."

He unfolded his length from the kitchen chair and went out. Emmeline said nothing. When he reached the door he turned back and said:

"I broke ground this mornin' fer a new house on the knoll. Me an' Phoebe'll be livin' there by this time next year."

"Well, I hope to goodness yeh will," responded Emmeline, heartily, "fer I've hed trouble 'nough a'ready with this business. I'll do what I ken, o' course, but do fer goodness' sake hurry up!"

The house on the knoll steadily progressed. Hiram came little to the Deane house during Phoebe's absence, but spent his time at the new building when his farm work did not demand his presence. He also came often to the village and hung around the post-office. He was determined that nothing should escape his vigilance in that direction. Seeing him there one day when the mail was being distributed Miranda took her place in the front ranks and asked in a clear cool voice:

"Anythin' fer Phoebe Deane? She's stayin' t' our house fer a spell now an' I'll take her mail to her."

Miranda well knew that the only mail Phoebe was likely to receive came addressed to herself, so she was more than surprised when the post-master with his spectacles on the end of his nose held up a letter whose address he carefully studied, and handed to her rather reluctantly. He would have liked a chance to study that letter more closely.

But nothing fazed Miranda. She took the letter as composedly as if there ought to be two or three more forthcoming, and marched off. Hiram Green, however, got down scowling from his seat on the counter and stalked over to the postmaster.

"I sh'd think you'd hev to be keerful who you give letters to," he remarked, in a low tone. "Phoebe Deane might not like thet harum-scarum girl bringin' her letters. Did you take notice ef that letter was from New York? She was expectin' quite a important letter from there."

The postmaster looked over his spectacles at Hiram patronizingly.

"I sh'd hope I know who to trust," he remarked, with dignity. "No, I didn't take notice. I hev too much to do to notice post-marks."

Hiram, however, was greatly shaken up by the sight of that letter in Miranda's triumphant hands, and betook himself to the hayloft to meditate. If he had known that the letter merely contained a clipping about the progress of missions in South Africa, which Ann Jane Bloodgood had sent thinking it might help Phoebe to recover from her illness, as she heard she was feeling "poorly" yet, and "hoped she would soon hear she was better!"

But Hiram had no thought but that the letter was from Nathaniel, therefore his reflections were bitter.

Two days afterward Hiram was one of a group about a New York agent who had come down to sell goods. He was telling the story of a mob, and his swaggering air and flashy clothes attracted Hiram greatly. He thought them far superior to any of Nathaniel Graham's, and determined to model himself after this pattern in future.

"Oh, we do things in great shape down in New York,"

he was saying. "When folks don't please, we *mob* 'em. If their opinions ain't what we like, we *mob* 'em. If they don't pay us what we ask, we *mob* 'em. Heard 'bout the mob down in Chatham Street last summer—er it might have been two years ago. A lot of niggers met to hear a darkey preacher in a little chapel down there. We got wind of it, an' we ordered 'em to leave, but they wouldn't budge 'cause they'd paid their rent, so we just *put* 'em out. There was a man named Tappan who lived down in Rose Street, an' he was there. He was an Abolitionist, an' we didn't like him. He'd had somethin' to do with this meetin', so we follered him home with hoots and threats, and give his house a good stoning. Did him good. Oh, we do things up in great shape in New York. Next night we went down to the Bowery Theatre. Manager there's English, you know, and he'd said some imperlite things about America, we thought, something about our right to own slaves, so we give him a dose. Oh, we're not afraid of anything down in New York."

Hiram was greatly fascinated by this representative New Yorker, and after the crowd had begun to disperse he went to the stranger and buttonholed him.

"Say, look a'here!" he began, holding a five-dollar bill invitingly near to the New Yorker's hand. "I know a feller you ought to mob. I could give yeh his name an' address real easy. He's prominent down there, an' I reckon 'twould be worth somethin' to you folks to know his name. Fact is, I've an interest in the matter myself, an' I'd like to see him come to justice, an' I'm willin' to subscribe this here bill to the cause ef you see your way clear to lookin' the matter up fer me."

"Why, certainly, certainly," said the stranger, grasping the bill affably, "I'll do anything I can for you. I'll hand this over to the treasurer of our side. In fact I'm the treasurer myself, and I thank you very much for your interest. Anything I can do I'm sure I'll be glad to. Can you tell me any more about this?"

Hiram tooled him off to a quiet corner and before the interview was ended he had entered into a secret plot against Nathaniel Graham, and had pledged himself to give the stranger not only one but four more five-dollar bills when the work should be complete, and Nathaniel Graham stand revealed to the world an Abolitionist, a man who should be suppressed. It was all arranged before the stranger left on the evening stage-coach that he would write Hiram what day a move would be made in the matter, and just how far he felt they could go.

Hiram went home chuckling and felt that revenge was sweet. He would get the better of Nathaniel Graham now, and Nathaniel would never know who struck the blow.

A few days afterward there came a letter from the stranger saying that all things were prospering, but it would be impossible to get up a thoroughly organized mob and do the work without a little more money, for their funds were low; and would it be possible for Hiram to forward the twenty dollars now instead of waiting?

After a sleepless night Hiram doled out the twenty dollars. The stranger wrote that the time had been arranged, and he would let him know all about it soon. They thought they had their man pinned down tight. The night Hiram received that letter he slept soundly.

Meantime the world had been moving in an orbit of beauty for Phoebe. She was tended and guarded like a little child. They made her feel that her presence was a joy to them all. Every member of the family down to Rose made it a point to brighten her stay with them. Rose brought her flowers from the garden, David brought the latest books and poems for her to read, Marcia was her constant loving companion, and Miranda cooked the daintiest dishes known to the culinary art for her tempting. The letters went back and forth to New York every day or two, for as Phoebe was growing better she was able to write longer epistles, and Nathaniel seemed always to have something to say that needed an immediate answer. Phoebe was growing less shy of him, and more and more opened her heart to his friendship like a flower turning to a newly-risen sun.

Janet Bristol had been away on a visit during Phoebe's illness, but while she was still with the Spaffords, Janet returned, and one afternoon came to return Mrs. Spafford's call.

Phoebe wore a thin white frock whose dainty frills showed modestly her white throat and arms now taking on something of their old roundness. She was sitting in the cool parlor with Marcia when the caller arrived. Her mother's locket was tied about her throat with a bit of velvet ribbon, and her hair, now coming out in soft curls, made a lovely fluffy halo of brown all about her face.

Janet watched her while she talked with Marcia, and wondered at the sweet grace of form and feature. Somehow her former prejudice against this girl melted strangely as Phoebe raised her beautiful eyes and smiled at her. Janet felt drawn to her against her will, yet she could not tell why she held back, only that Nathaniel had been so strangely stubborn about that letter. To be sure that was long past, and her mind was fully occupied just now with Nathaniel's theological friend, Martin Van Renssaeler. She was attempting to teach him the ways of the world, and draw him out of his gravity. He seemed to be a willing subject, if one might judge from the number of visits he made to the Bristol home during that summer.

Then, one bright, beautiful day, just a week before Phoebe's visit was to close, Nathaniel came up from New York.

He reached the village on the afternoon coach, and as it happened Hiram Green stood across the road from the tavern where the coach usually stopped, lounging outside the post office and waiting for the mail to be brought. He did not intend that any Miranda Griscom should stand in his way. Moreover, this night was the one that had been set for Nathaniel Graham's undoing, and there might be a letter for himself from his agent in New York. It filled Hiram with a kind of intoxication to be getting letters from New York.

He stood leaning against a post watching the coach as it rolled down the village street drawn by the four great horses, enveloped in a cloud of dust, and drew up at the tavern with a flourish. Then suddenly he noticed that there were passengers, two of them, and that one was Nathaniel himself.

Hiram felt weak in the knees. If a ghost had suddenly descended from the coach he could not have been more dismayed. Here he had put twenty-five good dollars into Nathaniel's discomfiture, only to have him appear in his own town smiling and serene as if nothing had been about to happen. It made Hiram just sick. He watched him and the other young man who had been his fellow passenger, as they walked down the street toward the Bristol house. He had sat down when the coach stopped, feeling inadequate to the work of holding himself upright in the midst of his unusual emotions. Now he got slowly up and went away toward his home, walking heavily, as if he had been stricken. With head bent down he studied the ground as he walked. He forgot the mail, forgot everything, save that he had put twenty-five dollars into a fruitless enterprise.

Midway between the post-office and his home he stopped and wheeled around with an exclamation of dismay:

"Gosh Ninety!"

Then after a pause he let forth a series of oaths. It was plain Hiram was stirred to the depths of his evil nature. He had just remembered that Phoebe was down in the village at the Spaffords and would be likely to see Nathaniel. His ugly face contracted in a spasm of anger, that gradually died into a settled expression of vengeance. The time had come, and he would wait no longer. If he had been more impulsive and less of a coward he would have shot his victim then and there, but such was not Hiram's way. Stealthily, with deadly surety he laid his plans; with the patience and the fatality that could only come from the father of lies himself.

Three whole days did Nathaniel stay in the village, and much of that time he spent at the Spafford house, walking and talking, and reading with Phoebe. Three whole days did Hiram spy upon him at every turn, with evil countenance and indifferent mien, lounging by the house, or happening in the way. He had written an angry letter to the man in New York, who later excused himself for not having performed his mission on account of Nathaniel's absence, but promising it should yet be done, and demanding more money.

Janet and Martin Van Renssaeler came down to the Spafford house the last evening, and made a merry party. Hiram hid himself among the lilac bushes at the side of the house, like the serpent of old, and watched the affair all the evening, his heart filled with all the evil that his nature could conceive.

Phoebe, in her simple white frock, with her lovely head crowned with the short curling hair, and her exquisite face agleam with the light and mirth that belong to youth, and which she was tasting for almost the first time, made a beautiful picture. So Miranda thought as she brought in the sugary seed-cakes, and great frosted pitcher of cool drink, made from raspberry and currant jelly, mixed with water from the spring. If Miranda could have known of the watcher outside, the evening might have ended in comedy, for she would certainly have emptied a panful of dishwater from the upper window straight into the lilac bushes. But Miranda's time had not yet come, and neither had Hiram's.

So Nathaniel and Phoebe sat by the open window and said a few last pleasant words, and looked a good-by into one another's eyes, the depth and meaning of which neither had as yet fathomed. They did not know that not two feet away was the evil face of the man who hated them both. He was so near that his viperous breath could almost have touched their cheeks, and his wicked heart, burning with the passionate fires of jealousy and hatred, gathered and devoured their glances as a raging fire will devour fuel. He watched them, and he gloated over them, as a monster will gloat over the victims he intends to destroy.

THE next morning on the early coach Nathaniel and Martin went away. Hiram was there to see that they were really gone, and to send word at once to New York.

That afternoon Phoebe went back to her brother's house, the light of health and happiness beginning to glow in her face. It was hard to go back, but Phoebe was happy in the thought that these friends were true, who would continue even in the midst of daily trials.

Everybody had urged her to stay longer, but Phoebe felt that she had already stayed longer that she should have done, and insisted that she must begin life again, that it was not right to lie idle.

The truth was, Phoebe had in mind a little plan which she wanted to think about and talk over with Albert. This stay with the Spaffords had brought to a climax a great longing she had had in her heart to go to school somewhere for a little while. She had a great thirst for knowledge, and she began to think that perhaps it might be possible to gratify it, for there was that money of hers lying idle in the bank. She might take some of it and go away for a year to a good school if Albert thought so, and she almost believed he would if only he could be persuaded before Emmeline heard of it.

Phoebe had felt her own deficiencies more and more by reason of her delightful correspondence with Nathaniel Graham. She wished to make herself more his equal, that she might really be able to write letters worthy of his perusal. She little dreamed of the trouble that was swiftly descending.

In modern war we sow our harbors and coasts thick with hidden mines ready to explode should the enemy venture within our borders. In much the same fashion that morning Hiram Green started out to lay his mines in readiness for the sweet young life that was unwarily drifting his way.

He had dressed himself soberly, as befitted the part he was to play. He harnessed his horse and chaise, and taking a wide berth of country in his circuit for the day, he drove first to the home of an old aunt of his to whom he had never been bound by many loving ties, yet who served his purpose, for she had a tongue that wagged well, and reached far.

After the greetings had been exchanged Hiram sat down with a funeral air in the big chair his relative had brought out of the parlor in honor of his coming, and prepared to bring forth his errand.

"Aunt Keziah," he began, in a voice which indicated momentous things to come, "I'm in deep trouble!"

"You don't say, Hiram! What's up now? Any of the children dead or sick?"

"No, I ain't afflicted in that manner this time," said Hiram. "It's somethin' deeper than that, deeper than sickness er death. It's fear o' disgrace."

"What! Hiram! You ain't ben stealin' er forgin' anybody's name, surely?" The old lady sat up as if she had been shot and fixed her eyes—little eyes like Hiram's, with the glitter of steel beads—on her downcast nephew's face.

"No, Aunt, I'm thankful to say I've been kep' from pussonel disgrace," murmured Hiram, piously, with a roll of his eyes indicating that his trust was in a power beyond his own.

"Well, what is it, then? Speak up quick. I'm too old to be kep' in hot water." The aunt spoke snappishly. Hiram perceived that he had made his impression.

"Well, you see it's this way, Aunt. You must uv heard I was takin' notice again."

"That was to be expected, Hiram, you so young an' with children to look after. I hope you picked out a good worker."

"Yes," admitted Hiram, with satisfaction, "she's a right smart worker, an' I thought she was 'bout as near perfect all through as you could find 'em, an' I kinder got my heart set on her. I've done everythin' she wanted that I knowed, even to buildin' a new house down on the knoll fer her, which wasn't necessary 't all, bein' as the old house is much better 'n the one she's ben brung up in. Yet I done it fer her, an' I ben courtin' her fer quite a spell back now; ben to see her every night reg'lar, an' home from meetin' an' singin'-school whenever she took the notion she wanted to go."

Hiram drew a long sigh, got out a big red and white cotton handkerchief and blew his nose resoundingly. The old lady eyed him suspiciously to gauge his emotion with exactness.

"Long 'but six er eight weeks ago" —Hiram's voice grew husky now—"she took sick. 'Twas this 'ere way. We was comin' home from a barn raisin' over to Woodbury's, an' it was gettin' near dark, an' she took a notion she wanted to pick some vi'lets long the roads. I seen a storm was comin' up, an' I argued with her agin it, but she would hev her way, an' so I let her out an' tole her to hurry up. She got out an' run back o' the kerridge a piece an' begun pickin' an' in a minute all on a sudden somethin' hit the horse's hind leg. I can't tell what it was, mebbe a stone er it might 'a' ben a stick, but I never took no thought at the time. I grabbed fer them reins, an' jest as the horse started to run there come a big clap o' thunder that scared the horse worse 'n ever. I hung on to them reins, an' lookin back I seen her standin' kind o' scared like an' white in the road a lookin' after me, an' I hollered back, 'You go to the Widder Duzenberry's till I come back fer yeh. It's goin' to rain.' Then I hed to tend to that horse, fer he was runnin' like the very old scratch. Well, 'course I got him stopped and turned him round an' went back, but there wasn't a sign of her anywhere to be seen. The Widder Duzenberry said she hedn't seen her sence we druv by fust. I went back fer her brother, an' we searched everywhere, but we couldn't find her no place, an' will you b'lieve it, we couldn't find a sign of her all night. But the next mornin' she come sailin' in lookin' white an' scared and fainted away, an' went right to bed real sick. We couldn't make it all out, an' I never said much 'bout it, 'cause I didn't 'spicion nothin' at the time, but it all looked kinder queer afterward. An' waht I'd like to know is, who threw that ar stone thet hit the horse? You see, it's all come out now thet she's been cuttin' round the country with a strange young man from New York, she's met him off in the woods an' round. They say they used 'ter meet not far from here— right down on the timber lot back o' your barn was one place they used to meet. There's a holler tree where they'd hide their letters. You 'member that big tree taller than the rest, a big white oak, 't is, that has a squirrel harbour in it? Well, that's the one. They used to meet there. And once she started off on some errand fer her sister-in-law in the coach, an' he es bold es life went 'long. Nobody knows whar they went, some sez Albany, some sez Schenectady, but anyhow she never come back till late the next day, an' no countin' fer where she'd been.

"Her sister-in-law is a nice respectable woman, and they all come of a good fambly. They'll feel turrible 'bout this, fer they've never 'spicioned her any more'n I done. She's got a sweet purty face like she was a saint—"

"Them is always the very kind that goes to the dogs," quoth Aunt Keziah, shaking her head and laying down her knitting.

"Well, Aunt Keziah," said Hiram, getting out his hand-kerchief again, "I come to ask your advice in this matter. What be I to do?"

"Do?" snapped Aunt Keziah. "Do, Hiram Green? Why be thankful you found out 'fore you got married. It's hard on you, 'course, but 'tain't near so hard es 'twould 'a' ben ef you'd 'a' found out after you was tied to 'er. An' you just havin' had such a hard time an' all with a sickly wife dyin'. I declare, Hiram Green, you suttin'ly hev been preserved!"

"But don't you think, mebbe, Aunt Keziah, I ought to stick to her? She's such a purty little thing, an' everybody's down on her now, an' she's begged me so hard not to give her up when she's in disgrace. She's promised she'll never hev nothin' more to do with these other fellers—"

There were actually some hypocritical tears being squeezed out of Hiram's little pig-eyes and rolling down in stinted quantities upon the ample kerchief. It would not do to wipe them away when they were so hard to manufacture, so Hiram waited till they were almost evaporated and then mopped his eyes vigorously.

"Well, Hiram Green, are you that soft-hearted? I declare to goodness, but you do need advice! Don't you trust in no sech promises. They ain't wuth the breath they're spoken in. Jest you hev nothin' more to do with the hussy. Thank goodness there's plenty more good workers in the world—healthy ones, too that won't up 'n die on ye jest in harvest."

"Well, Aunt Keziah!"—Hiram arose and cleared his throat as if a funeral ceremony had just been concluded—"I thank yeh fer yer good advice. I may see my way clear to foller it. Jest now I'm in doubt. I wanted to know what you thought, an' then I'll consider the matter. It ain't as though I hedn't been goin' with her pretty steady fer a year back. Yeh see what I'll do'll likely tell on how it goes with her from now on."

"Well, don't you go to be sentimental like, Hiram. That wouldn't set on you at your time o' life. Jest you stand by your rights an' be rid of her. It's what your ma would 'a' said ef she was alive. Now you remember what I say. Don't you be soft-hearted."

"I'll remember, Aunt," said Hiram, dutifully, and went out to his chaise.

He took his slow and doleful way winding up the road, and as soon as he was out of sight beyond the turn the alert old lady put on her sunbonnet and slipped up to her cousin's house half a mile away. She was out of breath with the tremendous news she had to tell, and marvelling all the way that Hiram had forgotten to tell her not to speak of it. Of course he intended to do so, but then of course he wouldn't object to having Lucy Drake know. Lucy was his own cousin once removed, and it was a family affair in a way.

Hiram's next visit was at the Widow Duzenberry's.

Now the Widow Duzenberry had often thought that her good daughter would make a wise choice for Hiram Green, and could rule well over the wild little Greens and be an ornament to the house and farm of Green. Therefore it seemed a special dispensation of Providence that Susanna had that afternoon donned her best sprigged chintz and done her hair up with her grandmother's high-backed comb. She looked proudly over at her daughter as Hiram sat down in the chair that Susanna had primly placed for him near her mother.

When the few preliminary remarks were concluded, and the atmosphere had become somewhat breathless with the excitement of wondering what he had come for, Hiram cleared his throat ominously and began:

"Mrs. Duzenberry," he said, and his countenance took on a deep sadness, "I called to-day on a very sad errand." The audience was attentive in the extreme. "I want to ask, did you take notice of me an' Phoebe Deane a ridin' by, the day of Woodbury's barn raisin'?"

"Wal, yes," admitted old Mrs. Duzenberry, reluctantly. "Now 't you mention it, I b'lieve I did see you drivin' by, fer there was black clouds comin' up an' I says to Susanna, says I, 'Susanna, we mebbe ought to bring in that web o' cloth that's out to bleach. It mebbe might blow away.' "

"Well, I thought p'raps you did, Mis' Duzenberry, an' I want to ask, did you take notice of how we was sittin' clost to one 'nother, she with her head restin' on my shoulder like? I hate to speak of it, but Mis' Duzenberry, wouldn't you 'a' thought Phoebe Deane was real fond o' me?"

Mother Duzenberry's face darkened. What had the man come for?

"I certain should," she answered, severely; "I don't approve of sech doin's in open road."

"Well, Mis' Duzenberry, mebbe 'twas a little too sightly a place, but what I wanted to know from you, Mis' Duzenberry, was this. You saw what you saw. Now, won't you tell me when a man has gone that fur, in your 'pinion is there anything thet would justify him in turnin' back?"

"There might be," said the old lady, somewhat mollified.

"Well, what, fur instance?"

"Wal, he might 'a' found he thought more o' some one else," and her eyes wandered toward her daughter, who was modestly looking out of the window.

"Anything else?" Hiram's voice had the husky note now as if he were deeply affected.

"Wal, I might think of somethin' else, gimme time."

"What ef he found out she wasn't all he thought she was?"

Mother Duzenberry's face brightened.

" 'Course that might 'fect him some," she admitted.

"I see you don't understand me," sighed Hiram. "I take it you ain't heard the bad news 'bout Phoebe Deane."

"She ain't dead, is she? I heard she was better," said Susanna, turning her sharp thin profile toward Hiram.

"No, my good friend," sighed Hiram, "It's worse'n death. It certainly is fer that poor girl. She's to be greatly pitied, however much she may have erred."

The two women were leaning forward now, eager for the news.

"I came to you in my trouble," said Hiram, mopping his face vigorously, "hopin' you would sympathize with me in my extremity, an' help me to jedge what to do. I wouldn't like to do the girl no wrong, but still, considerin' all that's come out the last two days—Say, Mis' Duzenberry, you didn't see no man hangin' round here that day little before we druv by, did you? No stranger, ner nuthin'?"

"Why, yes, ma," said Susanna, excitedly. "There was a wagon come by a goin' toward the village and there was two men, an' one of 'em jumped out an' took somethin' from the other, looked like a bundle er sumthin', an' he walked off towards the woods. He had butternut-colored trousers."

"That's him," said Hiram, frowning, "they say he always wore them trousers when anybody's seen him with her. You know the day they went off in the stage to Albany he was dressed that 'a' way!"

"Did they go off in the stage together in broad daylight? That's scandalous!" exclaimed the mother.

"You know most o' their goin's on happened over near Fundy Road. Aunt Keziah knows all 'bout it. Poor ole lady. She's all broke up. She always set a good store by me, her only livin' nephew. She'll be wantin' me to give up havin' anythin' more to do with Phoebe now, since all this is come out 'bout her goin's on, but I can't rightly make up my mind whether it's right fer me to desert her er not in her time o' trouble."

"I should think you was fully justified," said Mrs. Duzenberry, heartily. "There's other deservin' girls, an' it's puttin' a premium on badness to 'ncourage it that way."

"Good afternoon, Mis' Duzenberry." Hiram rose sadly. "I'm much 'bliged to yeh fer yer advice. I ain't sure yet what I shall do. 'Course I'll be 'bliged to yeh ef you'll jest keep people from talkin' much as yeh ken. I knowed you knowed the fac's an' I thought 'twould be best to come straight to you. Good afternoon, Miss Susanna. Perhaps we may meet again under pleasanter circumstances."

"Land alive!" exclaimed Susanna, as they watched him drive sadly away. "Don't he look broke up! Poor feller!"

"Serves him right fer makin' up to a little pink-cheeked critter like that," said the mother. "Say, Susanna, I ain't sure but you better put on yer bonnet an' run up to Keziah Dart's house an' find out 'bout this. We've got to be real keerful not to get mixed up in it, nohow, but I should like to know jest what she's done. Ef Keziah ain't home run on to Page's. They'll mebbe know. He said they'd ben seen round there. But speak real cautious. It won't do to tell everything you know. I'll mebbe jest step over to the toll-gate. They'll be wantin' to know what Hiram Green was here fer. It won't be no harm to mention he was callin' on you. It might take their 'tention off'n him, so's they wouldn't speak 'bout him goin' so much with Phoebe. My! Ain't it a pity! But that's what comes o' havin' good looks. You know I allus told you so, Susanna."

Susanna tossed her head, drew her sunbonnet down over her plain face and went off, while her mother fastened the door and went up to the toll-gate.

Hiram's method as he pursued his course the rest of the afternoon was to call ostensibly on some other business, and then speak of the gossip as a matter of which every one knew, and refer to those on whom he had called before as being able to give more information concerning facts than he could. He did not ask any more advice, but in one case where he was asked what he was going to do about it he shook his head dubiously and went away without replying.

Most of his calls were in the country, but before he went home he stopped at the home of the village dressmaker. His excuse for going there was that his oldest girl needed a frock for Sunday, and he thought the old woman who kept house for him had enough to do without making it. He asked when she could come, and said he would let her know if that day would be convenient. Just as he was leaving he told her that as she was going everywhere to other people's houses he supposed she would soon hear the terrible stories that were going round about Phoebe Deane, but he wished that if she heard anything about his breaking off with Phoebe she would just say that he intended not to do anything rashly, but would think it over and do what was right.

The keen-eyed newsmonger asked enough questions to have the facts well in hand, and looked after Hiram's tall, lanky form with admiration. "I tell you," she said to herself, "it ain't every man would hev the courage to say that! He's a good man! Poor little Phoebe Deane. What a pity! Now her life's ruined, fer of course he'll never marry her."

Then Hiram Green, having wisely scattered his calumnies against the innocent, betook himself virtuously to his home, and left his thistle seed to take root and spring up.

Phoebe Deane, meantime, settled down in her own little kitchen chamber beside her candle and prepared to write a letter to Nathaniel Graham, as she had promised him she would do that very night, and in it she told him her plans of going away to school.

25

THE tongues which Hiram had set wagging were all experts and before many days had passed the fields of gossip were green with springing slander and disgrace for the fair name of Phoebe Deane.

All unconsciously she moved above it, making happy plans, and singing her sweet song of hope. She did not mind work, for it was pleasant to feel strong again. She even hummed a sweet tune that she had heard Marcia play. Emmeline was puzzled to understand it all.

But the thing that puzzled Emmeline most of all was that Hiram Green had not been near the house since the day he had the talk with her about the village lot, and had boasted that he was going to marry Phoebe before another year.

Steadily every day Hiram's new house was growing. Emmeline could see it from her window, and she wondered if perhaps he was preparing to break his promise and court another girl instead of Phoebe, or was this a part of his plan to stay away until the house was done? It troubled Emmeline every day. Neither could she understand how Phoebe could be happy and settle down so cheerfully, having driven her one suitable lover away.

Phoebe had ventured to discuss the plan of her going away with Albert, who seemed rather disappointed to have her go, but was nevertheless willing, and said that he thought such a plan would have pleased her mother. He broached the subject to Emmeline, and thereupon brought down upon the family a storm of rage. Emmeline scoffed at the idea. She said that Phoebe was already spoiled for anything in life, and that if she used up her money getting more spoiling she couldn't see how in the world she expected to support herself; for *she* wouldn't be a party to Phoebe's living any longer on them if she spent her money on more schooling. Then Emmeline put on her bonnet and ran across the field to Hiram's farm, where she found him at the knoll superintending the putting up of a great stone chimney.

"Say, look-a-here, Hiram Green," she began, excitedly, getting him off a little way from the workmen, "what do you mean by sech actions? Hev you give up Phoebe Deane, er haven't yeh? 'Cause ef yeh ain't yeh better be tendin' to business. She's got it int' her fool head now to go off to school, an' she'll do it, too. I ken see Albert's jest soft enough to let 'er."

Hiram smiled a peculiar smile.

"Don't you worry, Emmeline. I know what I'm 'bout, an' you'll git your corner lot yit. Phoebe Deane won't go off to no boardin'-school, not yit awhile, 'er I'll miss my guess. Jest you leave it to me!"

"Oh, very well!" said Emmeline, going off in a huff. She returned by a roundabout route to her home, where she proceeded to make life miserable for Phoebe and Albert in spite of all that they could do.

Then one morning, lo! the little town was agog with the gossip about Phoebe Deane, and it had grown into enormous proportions, for as it travelled from the circle of country round about into the town it condensed into more tangible form, and the number of people who had seen Phoebe Deane with strange young men at the edge of dark, or in lonely places, grew with each repetition. Everybody seemed to know it and be talking about it except Phoebe herself and her own family and friends. Somehow no one had quite dared to mention it before any of them yet, it was too new and startling.

Sunday morning the Deanes went to church, and there were strange turnings away from them, and much whispering, nodding, and nudging as they passed. It had not been expected that Phoebe would appear in church. It was considered brazen in her to do so. It was evidently all and more true.

Hiram Green came to church but he did not look toward the Deanes' pew. He sat at the back with pious manner and drooping countenance, and after church made his melancholy way out without stopping to talk, or attempting to get near Phoebe. This was observed significantly; also the fact that Mrs. Spafford walked down the aisle in friendly converse with Phoebe Deane as if nothing had happened. Evidently she had not heard yet. Somebody ought to tell her. They discussed the matter in groups on the way home.

Old Mrs. Baldwin and her daughter Belinda were much worried about it. They went so far as to call to the doctor and his wife who were passing their house that afternoon on the way to see a sick patient.

"Doctor," said Mrs. Baldwin, coming out to the sidewalk as the doctor drew up to speak with her, "I ain't a going to bother you a minute but I just wanted to ask if you knew much about this story that's been going round about Phoebe Deane. It seems as though some one ought to tell Mrs. Spafford. She's been real kind to the girl, and she don't seem to have heard it. I don't know her so well, or I would, but somebody ought to do it. I didn't know but you or your wife would undertake to do it. They walked down the aisle together after church this morning, and it seemed too bad. David Spafford wouldn't like to have his wife so conspicuous, I know. Belinda says he was out of town yesterday, so I s'pose he hasn't heard about it yet, but I think something ought to be done."

"Yes, it's a very sad story," chirped the doctor's wife. "I just heard it myself this morning. The doctor didn't want to believe it, but I tell him it comes very straight."

"Oh, yes, it's straight," said Mrs. Baldwin, with an ominous shake of her head and a righteous roll of her eyes. "It's all too straight. I had it from a friend who had it from Hiram Green's aunt's cousin. She said Hiram was just bowed with grief over it, and they were going to have a real hard time to keep him from marrying her in spite of it."

The doctor frowned. He was fond of Phoebe. He felt that they all had better mind their own business and let Phoebe alone.

"I would be quite willing to speak to Miss Hortense or Miss Amelia Spafford," said the doctor's wife. "I'm intimate with them, you know, and they could do as they thought best about telling their niece."

"That's a good idea," said Mrs. Baldwin. "That quite relieves my mind. I was real worried over that sweet little Mrs. Spafford, and she with that pretty little Rose to bring up. They wouldn't of course want a scandal to come anywhere near them. They better look out for that Griscom girl. She comes from poor stock. I said long ago she'd never be any good, and she's been with that Phoebe Deane off an' on a good bit."

"Oh, I think that was all kindness," said the doctor's wife. "Mrs. Spafford was very kind during Phoebe Deane's illness. The doctor knew all about that."

"Yes, I s'pose the doctor knows all 'bout things. That's the reason I called you, and on Sunday too; but I thought it was a work of necessity and mercy. Well, good afternoon, Doctor, I won't keep you any longer."

"There's that pretty Miss Bristol ought to be told, too, ma," reminded Belinda.

"That's so, Belinda," said the doctor's wife. "I'll take it

upon myself to warn her, too. So sad, isn't it? Well, good-by," and the doctor's chaise drove on. The doctor was inclined to prevent his wife from taking part in the scandal business, but his wife had her own plans which she did not reveal. She shut her thin lips and generally did as she pleased.

The very next day she took her way down the shaded street and called upon the aunts of the house of Spafford, and before she left she had drooped her eyes and told in sepulchral whispers of the disgrace that had befallen the young protégée of their niece, Mrs. David Spafford.

Aunt Amelia and Aunt Hortense lifted their hands in righteous horror and thanked the doctor's wife for the information, saying they were sure Marcia knew nothing of it, and of course they would tell her at once and she would henceforth have nothing further to do with the Deanes.

Then the doctor's wife went on her mission to Janet Bristol.

Janet Bristol was properly scandalized, and charmingly grateful to the doctor's wife. She said of course Phoebe was nothing to her, but she had thought her rather pretty, and interesting. She was obviously bored with the rest of the good woman's call, and when it was over she betook herself to her writing desk where she scribbled off a letter to her cousin Nathaniel concerning a party she wished to give and for which she wanted him and his friend Martin Van Rensselaer to come up. At the close she added a hasty postcript.

"The doctor's wife has just called. She tells me I must beware of your paragon, Miss Deane, as there is a terribly scandalous story going around about her and a young man. I didn't pay much attention to the horrid details of it, I never like to get my mind filled with such things, but it is bad enough, and of course I shall have nothing further to do with her. I wonder Mrs. Spafford did not have the discernment to see she was not all right. I suspected it from the first you know, and you see I was right. My intuitions are usually right. I am glad I have not had much to do with her."

Now it happened that Rose was not well that Sunday and Miranda had stayed at home with her, else she would surely have discovered the state of things, and revealed it to Marcia. And it happened also that Marcia started off with David on a long ride early Monday morning, therefore when Aunt Hortense came down on her direful errand Marcia was not there, and Miranda, seeing her coming, escaped with Rose through the back door for a walk in the woods. So another day passed without the scandal reaching either Miranda or Marcia.

It was on Monday morning that the storm broke upon poor Phoebe's defenceless head.

A neighbor had come over from the next farm a quarter of a mile away to borrow a cup of hop yeast. It was a queer time to borrow yeast, at an hour in the week when every well-regulated family was doing its washing, but that was the neighbor's professed errand. She lingered a moment by the door with the yeast cup in her hand and talked to Emmeline.

Phoebe was in the yard hanging up clothes, and singing. The little bird was sitting on the weather-vane and calling merrily: "Phoe-bee! Phoe-bee!"

"Are yeh goin' to let her stay here now?" the visitor asked in a whisper fraught with meaning, and nodded her head toward the girl in the yard.

"Stay?" said Emmeline, looking up aggressively. "Why shouldn't she? Ain't she been here ever since her mother died? I s'pose she'll stay till she gets married."

Emmeline was not fond of this neighbor, and therefore did not care to reveal her family secrets to her. She lived in a red house with windows both ways and knew all that went on for miles about.

"Guess she won't run much chance of that now," said the neighbor, with a disagreeable laugh. She was prepared to be sociable if Emmeline opened her heart, but she knew how to scratch back when she was slapped.

"Well, I sh'd like to know what you mean, Mis' Prinn. I'm sure I don't know why our Phoebe shouldn't marry es likely es any other girl, an' more so'n some what ain't got good looks."

(Mrs. Prinn's daughter was not spoken of generally as a beauty.)

"Good looks don't count fer much when they ain't got good morals."

"Indeed! Mis' Prinn. You do talk kind of mysterious. Did you mean to insinuate that our Phoebe didn't have good morals?"

"I didn't mean to insinuate anything, Mis' Deane. It's all over town the way she's been goin' on, an' I don't see how you can pertend to hide it any longer. Everybody knows it, an' b'lieves it."

"I'd certainly like to know what you mean," demanded Emmeline, facing the woman angrily. "I brung that girl up, an' I guess I know what good morals is. Phoebe may have her weak points, but she's all right morally."

"Fac's is fac's, Mis' Deane," said the neighbor, with a relish.

"I deny that there is any fac's to the contrary," screamed Emmeline, now thoroughly excited into championing the girl whom she hated. The family honor was at stake. The Deanes had never done anything dishonorable or disgraceful.

"I s'pose you don't deny that she spent the night out all night the time o' the storm, do yeh? How d' ye explain that?"

"I should like to know what that hes to do with morals."

The neighbor proceeded to explain with a story so plausible that Emmeline grew livid with rage.

"Well, 'pon my word, you've got a lot to do runnin' round with sech lies as them. Wher 'd you get all that, I'd like to know?"

"It all come straight enough, an' everybody knows it, ef you are stone blind. Folks has seen her round in lonely

places with a strange feller. They do say he kissed her right
in plain sight of the road near the woods one day. An' you
know yerself she went off and stayed all night. She was seen
in the stage-coach 'long with a strange man. There's
witnesses! You can't deny it. What I want to know, is, what
are you goin' to do 'bout it? 'Cause ef you keep her here after that I can't let my dotter come here anymore. When girls
is talked about like that decent girls can't hev nothin' to do
with 'em. You think you know a hull lot 'bout that girl out
there, singin' songs in this brazen way with the hull town
talkin' 'bout her, but she's deceived you, that's what she's
done; an' I thought I'd be good enough neighbor to tell you,
ef you didn't know a'ready. But es you don't seem to take it
as 'twas meant, in kindness, I'd best be goin'."

"You'd best had," screamed Emmeline, "an' be sure you
keep your precious dotter to hum. Hum's the place fer
delikit little creatures like that. You might find *she* was
deceivin' *you* ef you looked sharp enough."

Then Emmeline turned and faced the wondering Phoebe,
who had heard the loud voices and slipped in through the
wood-shed to escape being drawn into the altercation. She
had no idea what it all was about. She had been engaged
with her own happy thoughts.

"I'd like to know what all this scandal's about, Phoebe
Deane. Jest set down there and explain. What kind of goin's
on hev you hed, that all the town's talkin' 'bout you? Mis'
Prinn comes an' says she can't let her dotter come over here
any more ef you stay here. I don't know that it's much loss,
fer she never come to 'mount to much, but I can't hev folks
talkin' that way. No decent girl ought to have her name
kicked around in that style. I may not hev hed a great
ejacation like you think you've got to have, but I knowed
enough to keep my name off folks' tongues, an' it seems you
don't. Now I'd like to know what young man or men you've
been kitin' round with. Answer me that? They say you've
been seen in the woods alone, and walkin' at night with a

strange man, an' goin' off in the stagecoach. Now what in the world does it all mean?"

Phoebe, turning deathly white, with a sudden return of her recent weakness, sank upon a kitchen chair, her arms full of dried clothes, and essayed to understand the angry woman who stormed back and forth across her kitchen, livid with rage, pouring out a perfect torrent of wrath and incriminations.

When there came a moment's interval Phoebe would try to answer her, but Emmeline, roused beyond control, would not listen. She stormed and raged at Phoebe, calling her names, and telling her what a trial she had always been, until suddenly Phoebe's new found strength gave away entirely and she dropped back in a faint against the wall, and would have fallen if Albert had not come in just then unperceived, and caught her. He carried her upstairs tenderly and laid her on her bed. In a moment she opened her sad eyes again and looked up at him.

"What's the matter, Phoebe?" he asked, tenderly. "Been working too hard?" But Phoebe could only answer by a rush of tears.

Albert, troubled as a man always is by woman's tears, stumbled downstairs to Emmeline to find out, and was met by an overwhelming story.

"Who says all that 'bout my sister?" he demanded, in a cool voice, and rising with a dignity that sat strangely upon his kindly figure. "She ain't your sister," hissed Emmeline. "She ain't any but a half relation to you, an' it's time you told her so an' turned her out of the house. She'll be a disgrace to you an' your decent wife an' children. I can't have my Alma brought up in a house with a girl that's disgraced herself like that."

"You keep still, Emmeline," said Albert gravely. "You don't rightly know what you're saying. You've got excited. I'll attend to this matter. What I want to know is, Who said this about my sister? I'll go get Hiram Green to help me, and we'll face the scoundrel, whoever it is, and make him take it back before the whole town."

"What ef it's true?" mocked Emmeline.

"It isn't true. It couldn't be true. You know it couldn't, Emmeline."

"I'm not so sure o' that," raged his wife. "Wait till you hear all," and she proceeded to recount what Mrs. Prinn had told her.

"I am ashamed of you, Emmeline, that you'll think of such a thing for a minute, no matter who told you. Don't say another word about it. I'm going out to find Hiram."

"Ain't you noticed that Hiram ain't ben comin' here lately?" Emmeline's voice was anything but pleasant. Albert looked at her in astonishment.

"Well, what o' that? He's a good man, and he's fond o' Phoebe. He'll be sure to go with me and defend her."

Albert went out and she saw him hurrying down the road toward Hiram's.

Hiram, like an old spider, was waiting for him in the barn. He had been expecting him for two days, not thinking it would take so long for the news to spread into the home of the victim. He looked gloomy and non-committal as Albert came up, and greeted him with half-averted eyes.

"I've come to get your help," said Albert, with expectant good will. "Hiram, hev you heard all this fool talk about Phoebe? I can't really believe folks would say that about her, but Emmeline's got it in her head everybody knows it."

"Yes, I heard it," admitted Hiram, reaching out for a straw to chew. "I spent one hull day last week goin' round tryin' to stop it, but 'twant no use. I couldn't even find out who started it. You never ken, them things. But the wust of it is, it's all true."

"What!"

"Yes," said Hiram, dismally, " 'tis. I'm sorry t' say it to you, what's ben my friend, 'bout her I hoped to marry some day, but I seen some things myself. I seen thet day they talk 'bout in the edge o' the woods, an' I seen her cut an' run when she heard my wagon comin', an' when she looked up an' see it was me she was deadly pale. That was the fust I knowed she wasn't true to me."

Hiram closed his lying lips and looked off sorrowfully at the hills in the distance.

"Hiram, you must be mistaken. There is some explanation."

"All right, Albert, glad you ken think so. Wish't I could. It mos' breaks my heart thinkin' 'bout her. I'm all bound up in havin' her. I'd take her now with all her disgrace an' run the resk o' keepin' her straight ef she'd promise to behave herself. She's mighty young, an' it does seem too bad. But yeh see, Albert, I seen her myself with my own eyes in the stage-coach along with the same man what kissed her in the woods, an' yeh know yerself she didn't come back till next night."

With a groan Albert sank down on a box near by and covered his face with his hands. He had been well brought up and disgrace like this was something he had never dreamed of. His agony amazed the ice-hearted Hiram, and he almost quailed before the sight of such sorrow in a man, sorrow that he himself had made. It embarrassed him. He turned away to hide his contempt.

"It comes mighty hard on me to see you suffer thet way, Albert, an' not to be able to help you," he whined after a minute. "I'll tell you what I'll do. I'll marry her anyway. I'll marry her an' save her reputation. Nobody'll dast say anythin' 'bout my wife, an' ef I marry her that'll be es much es to say all this ain't so, an' mebbe it'll die down."

Albert looked up with manly tears in his eyes.

"That's real good of you, Hiram. I'll take it as mighty kind of you if you think there isn't any other way to stop it. It seems hard on you, though."

"I ain't thinkin' o' myself," swelled Hiram. "I'm thinkin' o' the girl, an' I don't see no other way. When things is true, you know, there ain't no way o' denyin' them, 'specially when folks hes seen so many things. But just oncet get her good an' respectably married an' it'll all blow over an' be forgot."

They talked a long time, and Hiram embellished the stories that had been told by many a new incident out of his fertile brain, until Albert was thoroughly convinced that the only way to save Phoebe's reputation was for her to be married at once to Hiram.

Albert went home at last, and entered the kitchen with a chastened air. Emmeline eyed him keenly. Phoebe had not come downstairs and his wife had all the work to do again. She was not enjoying the state of things.

Albert sat down and looked at the floor.

"Hiram has been very kind," he said, slowly, "most kind. He has offered to marry Phoebe at once and stop all this talk."

A light of understanding began to dawn in Emmeline's eyes.

"H'm!" she said. Then, after a thoughtful pause. "But I guess Miss Phoebe Deane'll hev a word to say 'bout that. She don't like him a bit."

"Poor child!" moaned Albert. "She'll have to take him, whether she likes him or not. Poor little girl. I blame myself I didn't look after her better. Her mother was a real lady and so good to me when I was home. I promised her I'd keep Phoebe safe. She was such a good woman, it would break her heart to have Phoebe go like this."

"H'm! I don't reckon she was no better than other folks, only she set up to be!" sniffed Emmeline. "Anyhow this is just what might 'a' ben expected from the headstrong way that girl went on. I see now why she was set on goin' off to school. She knowed this was a' comin' an' she wanted to slip an' run 'fore it got out. But she got caught. Sinners generally does." Emmeline wrung out her dishcloth with satisfaction.

"I'll go up now and talk with Phoebe," said Albert, rising sadly as if he had not heard his wife.

"I'm sure I wish you joy of your errand. Ef she ac's to you

es she does to me you'll come flyin' down faster'n you went up."

But Albert was tapping at Phoebe's door before Emmeline had finished her sentence.

26

"PHOEBE," said Albert, gently sitting down beside the bed where she lay wide-eyed, in white-faced misery, trying to comprehend what this new calamity might mean, "I'm mighty sorry for you, little girl. I wish you had come to me with things more. I might 'a' helped you better if I hadn't been so stupid. But I've found a way out of it all for you. I've found a good man that's willing to marry you and give you the protection of his name and home, and we'll just have you married right away quietly here at home, and that'll stop all the talk."

Phoebe turned a look of mingled horror and helplessness on her brother. He did not comprehend it, and thought she was grasping for a thread of hope.

"Yes, Phoebe, Hiram Green is willing to marry you right off in spite of everything, and we've fixed it up to have the wedding right away, to-morrow. That'll give you time to straighten out your things, and Hiram to get the minister—"

But Albert stopped suddenly as Phoebe uttered a piercing scream of fear and started up as if she would fly from the room.

Albert caught her and tried to soothe her.

"What's the matter now, little girl? Don't look like that. It'll all come out right. Is it because you don't like Hiram enough? But child, you'll get to like him more as you know him better. Then you'll be so grateful to think what he saved you from. And besides, Phoebe, there isn't any other way. We couldn't stand the disgrace. What would your mother think? She was always so particular about how you should be brought up. And to have you turn out disgraced would break her heart. Phoebe, don't you see there isn't any other way?"

"Albert, I would rather die than marry that wicked man. He is a bad man. I *know* he is bad. He has been trying to make me marry him for a long time, and now he is just taking advantage of this terrible story. Albert, you know these stories are not true. You don't believe them, Albert, do you?"

She looked at him with piteous pleading in her beautiful eyes, and he had to turn his own eyes away to hide their wavering. He could not see how this sweet girl could have gone wrong, and yet—there was the evidence!

"You do," said Phoebe. "Albert, you do! You believe all this awful story about me! I never thought you would believe it. But Albert, listen! I will never marry Hiram Green! You may kill me or send me away, or anything you like, but you cannot make me marry him!"

Albert turned his eyes away from the pitiful figure of the pleading girl and set his lips firmly.

"I'm sorry Phoebe, but it's got to be done," he said, sorrowfully. "I can't have this talk go on. I'll give you a little more time to get used to it, but you can't have much, for this story has got to be stopped. We'll say a week. One week from to-day you'll have to marry Hiram Green, or I'll be forced to turn you out of my house. And you know what that means. I couldn't allow any respectable person to harbor you. You've disgraced us all. But if you marry Hiram it'll be all right presently. Marriage covers up gossip. Why, Phoebe, think of my little girl Alma. If this goes on everybody'll point their fingers at her and say her auntie was a bad girl and brought dishonor on the family, and Alma'll grow up without any friends. I've got to look out for my little girl as well as you, Phoebe, and you must believe me, I'm doing the very best for you I know."

Phoebe sat down weakly on the edge of her bed and stared wildly at him. She could not believe that Albert would talk to her so. She could not think of anything to say in answer. She could only stare blankly at him as if he were a terrible apparition.

Albert thought she was quieting down and going to be reasonable, and with a few kind words he backed out of the room. Phoebe dropped back upon her pillow in a frenzy of horror and grief. Wild plans of running away rushed through her brain, which was after all utterly futile, because her limbs seemed suddenly to have grown too feeble to carry her. Her brain refused to think, or to take in any facts except the great horror of scandal that had risen about her and was threatening to overwhelm her.

Emmeline declined to take any dinner up to her. She said if Phoebe wanted anything to eat she might come down and get it, she wasn't going to wait on a girl like that any longer. Albert fixed a nice plate of dinner and carried it up, but Phoebe lay motionless with open eyes turned toward the wall and refused to speak. He put the plate on a chair beside her and went sadly down again. Phoebe wondered how long it would take one to die, and why God had not let her die when she had the fever. What had there been to live for, anyway? One short bright month of happiness!

The memory of it gripped her heart anew with shame and horror. What would they say, all those kind friends? Mrs. Spafford and her husband, Miranda, and Nathaniel Graham? Would they believe it, too? Of course they would, if her own household turned against her. She was defenceless in a desolate world. She would never more have friends and smiles and comfort. She could not go away to school now, for what good would an education be to her with such a disgrace clinging to her name and following her wherever she went? It would be of no use to run away. She might better stay here and die. They could not marry her to Hiram Green if she was dead. Could one die in a week by just lying still?

So the horror in her brain raged over and over, each time bringing some new phase of grief. And now it was a question if her friends would desert her; and now it was the haughty expression on Janet Bristol's face that day she carried the letter to Nathaniel; and now it was the leer on Hiram's face as he put his arm about her on that terrible drive; and now it was the thought that she would have no more of Nathaniel's long, delightful letters.

All day long she lay in this state, and when the darkness fell a half delirious sleep came upon her, which carried the fears and thoughts of the day into its unresting slumber. The morning broke into the sorrow of yesterday, and Phoebe, weak and sick, arose with one thought in her mind; that she must write at once to Nathaniel Graham and tell him all. She must not be a disgrace to him.

With trembling hands, and eyes filled with tears, she wrote:

> Dear Mr. Graham:
> I am writing to you for the last time. A terrible thing has happened. Some one has been telling awful stories about me and I am in disgrace. I want you to know that these things are not true. I do not even know how they started, for there has never been any foundation for them. But everybody believes them, and I will not disgrace you by writing to you any more. You will probably be told the worst that is said, and perhaps you will believe them as others do. I shall not blame you if you do, for it seems as if even God believed them. I do not know how to prove my innocence, nor what the end of this is to be. I only know

that it is not right to keep you in ignorance of my shame, and to let you write any longer to one whose name is held in dishonor. I thank you for all the beautiful times you have put into my life, and I must say good-by forever.

Gratefully,
Phoebe Deane

The letter was blistered with tears before it was finished. She addressed it and hid it in her frock, for she began to wonder how it would get to the mail. Probably Miranda would never come near her again, and she could not be seen in the village. She dared not ask any one else to mail the letter lest it would never reach its destination.

She spent the rest of the day in quietly putting to rights her little belongings, unpacking and gathering together things she would like to have destroyed if anything should happen to her. She felt weak and dizzy, and the food that Albert continued to bring her seemed nauseous. She could not bring herself to taste a mouthful. It was so useless to eat. One only ate to live, and living had been finished for her, it appeared. It was not that she had resolved to make away with herself by starvation. She was too right-minded for that. She was simply stunned by the calamity that had befallen her, and was waiting for the outcome.

Sometimes as she stood at the window looking out across the fields which had been familiar to her since her childhood she had a feeling that she was going away from them all soon. She wondered if it meant that she was going to die. She wondered if her mother felt so before she died. Then she wondered why she did not run away; but always when she thought that, something seemed holding her back, for how could she run far when she could not keep up about her room but a few minutes at a time for dizziness and faintness! And how could she run fast enough to run away from shame? It could not be done. Whenever in her dreams she started to run away she always stumbled and fell and then seemed suddenly struck blind and unable to move further; and all the village came crowding about her and mocking her like a great company of cawing crows met around a poor dead thing.

Late Tuesday afternoon Miranda came out to see her. Emmeline opened the door and her countenance grew black when she recognized the visitor.

"Now, you ken just turn right around and march home," she commanded. "We don't want no folks around. Phoebe Deane's in turrible disgrace, an' you've hed your part in it ef I don't miss my guess. No, you ain't goin' to see her. She's up in her room, and ben shut up there ever since she heard how folks hes found out 'bout her capers. You an' yer Mis' Spafford can keep yer pryin' meddlin' fingers out o' this an' let Phoebe Deane alone from now on. We don't want to see yeh any more. Yer spoilin' an pettin' has only hastened the disgrace."

The door slammed in Miranda's indignant face and Emmeline went back to work.

"She needs a good shakin'," remarked Miranda, indignantly to herself, "but it might tire me, an' besides I've got other fish to fry."

Undaunted she marched to the back shed and mounted to Phoebe's window, entering as if it had been always the common mode of ingress.

"Wal, fer the land, Phoebe Deane, what's ben a happenin' now?" she asked, mildly, surveying Phoebe, who lay white and weak upon her bed, with her untasted dinner beside her.

"Oh, don't you know all about it, Miranda?" Phoebe began to sob.

"No, I don't know a thing. I ben shet up in the house cookin' fer two men Mr. David brung home last night, and they et an' et till I thought there wouldn't be nothin' left fer the family. They was railroad men er somethin'. No, I guess 'twas bankin' men. I fergit what. But they could eat if they did wear their best clothes every day. But say, ef I was you, I wouldn't talk very loud fer the lady down stairs wasn't real glad to see me this time, an' she might invite me to leave rather suddint ef she 'spicioned I was up here."

But Phoebe did not laugh as Miranda had hoped. She only looked at her guest with hungry, hopeless eyes, and it was a long time before Miranda could find out the whole miserable story.

"And Miranda, I've written Mr. Graham a note telling him about it. Of course I couldn't disgrace him by continuing to write any longer, so I've said good-by to him. Will you do me one last kindness? Will you mail it for me?" Phoebe's whisper was tragic. It brought tears to Miranda's well-fortified eyes.

" 'Course I'll mail it fer yeh, child, ef yeh want me to, but 'tain't the last kindness I'll do fer yeh by a long run. Shucks! D'you think I'm goin' to give in this easy an' see you sucked under? Not by a jugful. Now look-a-here, child; ef the hull fool world goes against yeh, I ain't a goin' ner my Mrs. Marcia ain't, neither, I'm plumb sure o' that. But *ef* she did I'd stick *anyhow,* so there! Cross my heart ef I don't! *Now.* D'yeh b'lieve me? An' I'll find a way out o' this somehow. I ain't thought it out yet, but don't you worry. You set up 'n' eat that there piece o' bread an' butter. Never mind ef yeh don't feel like it, you eat it fer me. I can't do nothin' ef yeh don't keep yer strength up. Now you do your part an' we'll get out o' this pickle es good es we did out o' the other one. I ain't goin' to hev all my nursin' wasted. Will yeh be good?"

Phoebe promised meekly. She could not smile. She could only press Miranda's hand, while great tears welled through the long lashes on her cheeks.

"So that old serpent thinks he's got you fast, does he? Well, he'll find hisself mistaken yet, ef I don't miss my guess. The game ain't all played out by a long shot. Marry you next week, will he? Well, we'll see! I may dance at your

weddin' yet, but there won't be no Hiram Green as bridegroom. I'd marry him myself 'fore I'd let him hev you, you
poor little white dove." And Miranda pressed a great impulsive kiss upon Phoebe's white lips and stole out of the window.

As she hurried along down the road the waving grain in
the fields on either side reminded her of whispered gossip.
She seemed to see a harvest of scandal ripening all about the
poor stricken girl whom she loved, and in her ignorant and
original phraseology she murmured to herself the thought of
the words of old, "Lo, an enemy hath done this." Miranda
felt that she knew pretty well who the enemy was.

27

"I hev a notion I'd like to go to New York," said Miranda, bouncing in on Marcia.

"Well," said Marcia, "I think you would enjoy the trip sometime. We might keep a lookout for somebody going who would be company. Or perhaps Mr. Spafford will be going again soon and he would have time to look after you."

"'Fraid I can't wait that long," said Miranda. "I've took a great notion I'd like to have a balzarine frock, an' ef I'm goin' to hev it I'd best get it straight off an' git more good out of it. I look at it this way. I ain't goin' to be young but once, an' time's gettin' on. Ef you don't get balzarine frocks when you're young you most likely won't git 'em 't all, 'cause you'll think 'tain't wuth while. I've got a good bit of money laid by, an' ef you've no 'bjections, an' think you ken spare me fer a couple o' days I think I'd like to go down to New York an' git it. I don't need no lookin' after, so you needn't worry 'bout that. Nobody steals me, an' es long es I got a tongue I ken ast my way 'round New York es well es I can 'round Fundy er any other place."

"Why, of course I can spare you, Miranda, and I suppose you'd be perfectly safe, only I thought you'd enjoy it more if you had good company. When did you think you'd like to go?"

"Well, I've been plannin' it all out comin' up the street. I've baked, an' washed, an' the sweepin' ain't much to do. Ef you don't mind I think I'll go to-morrer mornin'."

"What in the world makes you want to go in such a hurry?"

"Oh, I've just took the notion," said Miranda, smiling. "Mebbe I'll tell yeh when I get back. I shan't be gone more'n a year."

Marcia was a little worried at this sudden turn of affairs. It was not like Miranda to hide things from her. Yet she had such confidence in her that she finally settled down to the thought that it was only a whim and perhaps a good night's sleep would overcome it. But the next morning she found the table fully set for breakfast, and the meal prepared and keeping warm. Beside her plate a scrawled note lay:

> Mrs. Marcia, deer. I'll liklie be bak tomorer nite er next, but donte worrie. I got biznes to tend to an I'll tel you bout it wen I get home.
>
> yours til deth,
> respectfuly,
> Miranda Griscom
>
> P.S. you mite praye ef your a mind. Tak keer uf Feby ef I dont git bak.

Before Marcia could get time to run up and see Phoebe, for she somehow felt that Miranda's sudden departure to New York had to do with her visit to Phoebe the day before, Miss Hortense arrived, with her most commandatory air.

"Marcia, I came on a very especial errand," she began primly. "I was down on Monday, but you were away." There was reproach in the tone.

"Yes, I went with David," responded Marcia, brightly, but Miss Hortense would brook no interruption.

"It's of no consequence now. I would have come yesterday, but we had company all day, the Pattersons from above Schenectady. I couldn't leave very well. But I hurried down this morning. It's about that Deane girl, Marcia. I suppose you haven't heard the dreadful reports that are going around. It really is disgraceful in a decent town. I'm only glad she got out of your house before it became town talk. It all shows what ingratitude there is in human nature, to think she should repay your kindness by allowing herself to be talked about in this shameful way."

Marcia exclaimed in dismay, but Miss Hortense went straight on to the precise and bitter end, giving every detail in the scandal that had come to her ears, details at which even Hiram Green would have opened his eyes wide in surprise, and would never have believed that they grew out of his own story.

Marcia listened in rising indignation.

"I am sorry that any such dreadful story is abroad, Aunt Hortense," she answered, earnestly, "but really, if you knew the girl, you would understand how impossible it is for this to be true. She is as sweet and pure and innocent as my little Rose."

"I should be sorry to have David's child compared to that miserable girl, Marcia," said Miss Hortense, severely, rising as she spoke, "and I am sure that after my warning if you do not shut that wretched creature forever out of your acquaintance I shall feel it my duty to appeal to David, and tell him the whole story, though I should dislike to have to mention anything so indelicate before him. David is very particular about the character of women. He was brought up to be; and Amelia and I both agree that he must be told."

"I shall tell him myself, of course, and he will see if anything can be done to stop this ridiculous gossip," said Marcia, indignantly. "David is as fond of Phoebe as I am."

"You will find David will look on it in a very different way, my dear. You are young and a woman. You do not know the evil world. David is a man. Men know. Good-by, my dear. I have warned you!" And Aunt Hortense went pensively down the street, having done her duty.

Marcia put her bonnet on, took little Rose, and walked straight out to Albert Deane's house, but when she reached it there was denied admission. Alma opened the door, but did not ask the caller in. In a moment she came back from consulting her mother and said: "Ma says Aunt Phoebe's up in her room an' don't wish to see no one."

The door was shut unceremoniously by the stolid little girl, who was embarrassed before the beautiful, smiling Rose in her dainty attire. Marcia turned away, dismayed, hurt, at the reception she had received and walked slowly homeward.

"Wasn't that a funny little girl," said Rose. "She wasn't very polite, was she, mother?"

Then Marcia went home to wait until she could consult with David.

When Nathaniel received his Cousin Janet's letter his anger rose to white heat. Every throb of his heart told him that the stories about Phoebe were false. Like Miranda, he felt at once that an enemy had done this, and he felt like searching out the enemy at once and throttling him into repentance. He read the postscript through twice and then sat for a few minutes in deep thought, his face shaded by his hand. The office work went on about him, but his thoughts were far away in a sunlit autumn wood. After a little he got up suddenly and going into the inner office where he could be alone, sat down quickly, and wrote:

My Dear Phoebe:
    (He had never called her that before, it was always "Miss Deane.")
    I have loved you for a long time, ever since that afternoon that I found you among the autumn leaves in the woods. I have been trying to wait to tell you until I could be sure you loved me, but now I can wait no

longer. I am lonely without you. I want you to be here with me. I love you, darling, and will love you forever, and guard you tenderly, if you will give me the right. Will you forgive this abrupt letter, and write immediately, giving me the right to come up and tell you all the rest?

> Yours in faithful love,
> Nathaniel Graham

After he had sent it off enclosed to Miranda, he scribbled another, to Janet.

Dear Janet, (it read) wherever did you get those ridiculous stories about Phoebe Deane? They are as false as they are foolish. Everybody that knows her at all knows they could not be true. I insist that you deny them whenever you have the opportunity, and for my sake that you go and call upon her. I may as well tell you that I am going to marry her if she will have me, and I want you, Janet, to be like a sister to her, as you have always been to me. Any breath against her name I shall consider as against mine also, so please, Janet, stand up for her for my sake.

> Your loving cousin,
> Nathaniel

After these two letters had been despatched Nathaniel put in the best day's work he had ever done.

Miranda had reached Albany in time to catch the evening boat down the Hudson. She was more tired than she had ever been in all the years of her hard-working life. The bouncing of the stage-coach, the constant change of scenery and fellow passengers, the breathlessness of going into a strange region, had worn upon her nerves. She had not let a single thing pass unnoticed and the result was that even her iron nerves had reached their limit at last. Besides, she was more worried about Phoebe Deane than she had ever been about anything in her life. The ethereal look of the girl as she bade her good-by the night before had gone to her heart. She half feared Phoebe might fall asleep and never waken while she was gone on her desperate errand of mercy.

"Land sake alive," she murmured to herself, as she crept into her bunk in the tiny stateroom and lay down without putting off any of her garments save her bonnet and cape. "Land sake alive! I feel as ef I'd ben threshin'. No, I feel as ef I'd ben *threshed!*" she corrected. "I didn't know I hed so many bones."

Nevertheless she slept little, having too much to attend to. She wakened at every stop in the night, and she heard all the bells and calls of the crew. Half the time she thought the boat was sinking and wondered if she would be able to swim when she struck the water. Anyhow she meant to try. She had heard it "came natural" to some people.

When morning broke over the heights above the river she watched them grow into splendor and majesty, and long before the city was in sight she was on deck sniffing the air like a veteran war-horse. Her eyes were dilated with excitement, and she made a curious and noticeable figure as she gripped her small bag of modest belongings, and sat strained up and ready for her first experience of city life. She felt a passing regret that she could not pause to take in more of this wonderful trip, but she promised herself to come that way again some day, and hurried over the gang-plank with the others when the boat finally landed.

Tucked safely away in her pocket was Phoebe's letter to Nathaniel and safe in her memory was its address. Every passenger with whom she had talked upon the voyage—and she had entered into conversation with all except a man who reminded her of Hiram Green—had given her detailed directions how to get to that address, and the directions had all been different. Some had told her to walk one way and take a cab, some another way. Some had suggested that she take a cab at the wharf. She did none of these things. She gripped her bag firmly and marched past all the officials, through the buildings, out into the street. There she stood a moment bewildered by the noise and confusion, a marked figure even in that hurrying throng of busy people. Small boys and drivers immediately beset her. She looked each over carefully and then calmly walked straight ahead. So far New York did not look very promising to her, but she meant to get into a quieter place before she made any inquiries.

At last after she had walked several blocks and was beginning to feel that there was no quiet place, and no end to the confusion, she met a benevolent old gentleman walking with a sweet-faced girl who looked as she imagined little Rose would look in a few years. These she hailed and demanded directions, and ended by being put into a Broadway coach under the care of the driver, who was to put her out at her destination.

Nathaniel was in the inner office attending to some special business when the office boy tapped at the door.

"There's a queer client out here," he whispered. "We told her you were busy and could not be bothered, but she says she has come a long distance and must see you at once. Shall I tell her to come again?"

Nathaniel glanced through the door, and there, close behind the careful office boy, stood the wily Miranda. She had run no risks of not seeing Nathaniel. She had followed the boy, strictly against orders.

Her homely face was aglow with the light of her mission, but in spite of freckles and red hair, and the dishevelled state of her appearance, Nathaniel put out an eager hand to welcome her. His first thought was that she had brought an answer to his letter to Phoebe, and his heart leaped up in sudden eagerness. Then at once he knew that it was too soon for that, for he had only sent his own letter in the evening mail.

"Come right in, Miranda," he said, eagerly, "I'm glad to

see you. Are you all alone?" Then something in her face caused a twinge of apprehension.

"Is every one all well?"

Miranda sat down and waited until the door was shut. Then she broke forth.

"No, everythin' ain't all well. Everythin' 's all wrong. Phoebe Deane's in turrible trouble, an' she's wrote a letter sayin' good-by to you, an' ast me to mail it. I said I would, an' I brung it along. I reckon it didn't make no diff'rence whether it travelled in my pocket er in the mailbag, so it got here."

She held out the letter, and Nathaniel's hand shook as he took it. Miranda noticed that he looked pale.

"What has happened, Miranda?" He asked, as he tore open the letter, hardly knowing what he feared.

"Oh, it's that ole snake-in-th'-grass," said Miranda; "I'd be willin' to stake my life on that. No knowin' how he done it, but it's done. There's plenty to help in a business like gossip, when it comes to that. There's ben awful lies told about her, and she's bein' crushed by it. Wal, I hed to come down to New York to get me a new balzarine frock an' I jest thought I'd drop in an' tell yeh the news. Yeh don't know of a good store where I won't get cheated, do yeh?" she asked, making a pretense of rising.

"Sit down, Miranda," commanded Nathaniel. "You're not going away to leave me like this. You must tell me all about it. Miranda, you know, don't you, that Phoebe is my dear friend. You know that I must hear all about it."

"Well, ain't she told you in the letter? I reckon you'll go back on her like her own folks hev done, won't you? An' let that scoundrel git her next week like he's planned."

"What do you mean, Miranda? Tell me at once all about it. You know Phoebe Deane is very dear to me."

Miranda's eyes shone, but she meant to have things in black and white.

"How dear?" she asked, looking up in a business-like

way. "Be you goin' to b'lieve what they all say 'bout her, an' let them folks go on talkin', til she's all wilted down an' dead? 'Cause ef you be, you don't get a single word out o' me. No, sir!"

"Listen, Miranda. Yesterday I wrote to Phoebe asking her to marry me!"

Satisfaction began to dawn upon the face of the self-appointed envoy extraordinary.

"Well, that ain't no sign you'd do it again to-day," said Miranda, dryly. "You didn't know nothin' 'bout her bein' in trouble then."

"Yesterday morning, Miranda, I received a letter from my cousin telling me all about it, and I sat down at once and asked Phoebe to marry me."

"You sure you didn't do it out o' pity?" asked Miranda, lifting sharp eyes to search his face. "I shouldn't want to hev nobody marry her out o' pity, the way Hiram Green's going to do, the old nimshi!"

"Miranda, I love her with all my heart, and I will never believe a word against her. I shall make it the object of my life to protect her and make her happy if she will give me the precious treasure of her love in return. Now are you satisfied, you cruel girl, and will you tell me the whole story? For the little I heard from my cousin has only filled me with apprehension."

Then the freckles beamed out and were lost in smiles as Miranda reached a strong hand and grasped Nathaniel's firm white one with a hearty shake.

"You're the right stuff. I knowed you was. That's why I come. I didn't darst tell Mis' Spafford what was up, 'cause she wouldn't 'a' let me come, an' she'd 'a' tried to work it out in some other way. But I hed it all figgered out, an' there wasn't time for any fiddlin' business. It hed to be don t' woncet ef 'twas to be did 't all, so I told her I wanted a pleasure trip an' a new balzarine, an' I come. Now I'm goin' to tell you all 'bout it, an' then ef there's time fer the balzarine 'fore the evenin' boat starts I'll get it, otherwise it'll hev to git the go-by this time, fer I've got to git right back to Phoebe Deane. She looked jest awful 'fore I left, an' there's no tellin' what they'll do to her while I'm gone."

Nathaniel, with loving apprehension in his eyes, listened to the story, told in Miranda's inimitable style, his face darkening with anger over the mention of Hiram's part.

"The scoundrel!" he murmured, clenching his fingers as if he could hardly refrain from going after him and giving him what he deserved.

"He's all that," said Miranda, "an' a heap more. He's made that poor stupid Albert Deane think all these things is true, an' he's come whinin' 'round with his 'sorry this' an' 'sorry that,' an' offered to marry Phoebe Deane to save her reputation. Es ef he was fit fer that angel to wipe her feet on! Oh, I'd like to see him strung up, I would. There's only one man I ever heard tell of that was so mean, and he lived here in New York. His name was Temple, Harry Temple. Ef you ever come acrost him just give him a dig fer my sake. He an' Hiram Green ought to be tied up in a bag together an' sent off the earth to stay. One o' them big, hot-lookin' stars would be a fine place, I often think at night. Albert, he's awful taken back by disgrace, an' he's told Phoebe she hez to git married in jest a week, er he'll hev to turn her out o' the house. Monday mornin' 's the time set fer the marriage, an' Albert 'lows he won't wait 'nother day. He's promised his wife he'll keep to that."

Nathaniel's face grew stern as he listened, and asked questions. At last he said:

"Miranda, do you think Phoebe Deane cares for me? Will she be willing to marry me?"

"Wal, I sh'd think, ef I know anythin' 't all 'bout Phoebe Deane, she'd give her two eyes to, but she'll be turrible set 'gainst marryin' you with her in disgrace. She'll think it'll bring shame on you."

"Bless her dear heart," murmured Nathaniel, "I suppose

she will," and he touched her letter tenderly as if it had been a living thing. Miranda's eyes glistened with jubilation, but she said nothing.

"But we will persuade her out of that," added Nathaniel, with a light of joy in his eyes.

"If you are quite sure it will make her happy," he added, looking at Miranda keenly. "I wouldn't want to have her marry me just to get out of trouble. There might be other ways of helping her, though this way is best."

"Well, I guess you needn't worry 'bout love. She'll love you all right, er my name ain't M'randy!"

"Well, then, we will just have a substitute bridegroom. I wonder if we'll have trouble with Hiram. I suppose very likely we will, but I guess we can manage that. Let me see. This is Thursday. I can arrange my business by tomorrow night so that I can leave it for a few days. If you can stay over till then I will take you to my landlady, who is very kind and will make your stay pleasant. Then we can go back together and plan the arrangements. You'll have to help me, you know, for you are the only medium of communication."

"No, I can't stay a minute longer 'n t'night," said Miranda, rising in a panic and glancing out the window at the sun as if she feared it were already too late to catch the boat; "I've got to get back to Phoebe Deane. She won't eat, an' she's just fadin' away. There might not be any bride by time you got there. 'Sides, she can't git your letter till I get back no how. I'll hev to go home on the boat to-night, an' you come to-morrow. You see, ef there's goin' to be a weddin' I'd like real well to git my balzarine made 'n time to wear to it. That'll give me plenty time, with Mis' Spafford to he'p cut 't out. Do you s'pose there's time fer me to go to a store? It took a long time to git up here from the river."

Nathaniel arose.

"You have plenty of time, and if you'll wait ten minutes I will go with you. We can get some dinner, and go to the store, and we can arrange things on the way."

Miranda settled down in the great office chair and watched Nathaniel's white fingers as they wrote on the legal paper. When it was finished and folded he took another piece of paper and wrote:

My Darling:

I have just received your letter, and I am coming to you as quickly as I can arrange my business to get away. Miranda will bring you this and will tell you all I have said. I will be there in time for the wedding morning, and if you will have me instead of Hiram Green I shall face the whole world by your side, and tell them they are liars. Then I will bring you back with me to stay with me always. My heart is longing to see you and comfort you, but I must not write any more for I have a great deal to do before I go. Only this I must say, if you do not feel you love me, and do not want to marry me, I will help you some other way to get free from this trouble, and to have it all explained before the world. There is just one thing I am resolved upon, and that is that you shall be guarded and loved by me, whether you will marry me or not. You are too precious to suffer.

Yours with more love than you can ever fathom,
Nathaniel

He sealed, addressed it, and handed it to Miranda, who took it with a gleam of satisfaction in her honest eyes. She was almost willing to run home without her balzarine now that she had that letter. She did not know what he had written, of course, but she knew it was the right thing and would bring the light of hope again to Phoebe's eyes.

Then they went out into the bustling, strange streets of the city.

Miranda was too excited to eat much, though Nathaniel took her to his own boarding-place and tried to make her feel at home. She kept asking if it wasn't almost time for the boat to leave, until he had to explain to her just how much time there was, and how quickly they could get to the wharf.

They went to a store, and Miranda did not take long to pick out her frock. It seemed as if the very one she had always longed for most lay draped upon the counter, and with quick decision she bought it. It had great stripes of soft colors in palm-leaf pattern, blended into harmony in oriental manner, in the exquisite fabric. It seemed to her almost too fine to go with red hair, but she bought it with joyous abandon. The touch of rich blue and orange and crimson with the darker greens and browns stood out against the delicate whiteness of the background and delighted her eye. She bought a dainty ruffled muslin shoulder cape to wear with it, and a great shovel bonnet with a white veil tossed hilariously back from its cumbersome shirred depths. Then Nathaniel added a parasol with a pearl handle that would unhinge and fold up, and Miranda climbed into the coach and rode off to the evening boat feeling that she had had the greatest day of her life. She looked about her on the interesting sights of the city, with a kind of pity that they had to stay there and not go with her to the wedding.

28

MIRANDA reached home on the afternoon coach and bounced into the house with a face full of importance.

"Wal, I'm glad to git back. Did you find the blueberry pies? I put 'em out the pantry winder to cool, an' fergot 'em. I thought of 'em when I was on the boat, but 'twas mos' too late to come back then, so I kep' on.

"Here's my balzarine. Do yeh like it?" and she tossed the bundle into Marcia's lap. "I'm goin' right at it when I git the work done in the mornin' fer I want to hev it t' wear at Phoebe Deane's weddin'. Did yeh know she was goin' to marry Nathaniel Graham? Say, where's that Rose? I'm most starved fer a sight o' her little sweet face. Yer lookin' real good yerself. All's well?"

Marcia listened smilingly to Miranda's torrent of words, and gradually drew the whole story from her handmaid, laughing heartily over the various episodes of Miranda's journey and gravely tender over what Nathaniel had said. Then Miranda heard about Marcia's call on Phoebe, and how she had written Phoebe a letter asking what she could do to help her, and inviting her to come at once to them, but had received no answer.

GRACE LIVINGSTON HILL

"An' yeh won't, neither," said Miranda, decidedly. "She'll never git no letter, I'm sure o' that. Ef that old skunk of a Hiram Green don't git it fust, Mis' Deane 'll ferret it out an' keep it from her. She's the meanest thing in the shape of a woman I've seen yit, an' I've hed some experience."

Then Miranda rapidly sketched her plan of procedure, and Marcia added some suggestions. Together they prepared the supper, with the single object of getting Miranda off to Phoebe as soon as the darkness should come.

It was quite dark and Phoebe was lying in a still white heap upon her bed when Miranda stole softly in. By her side lay a long white package she had taken from her little trunk in the closet, and on it was pinned a note. "Dear Miranda, if I die, please take this, from Phoebe."

She had not lighted her candle, and she had not eaten a mouthful all day. The terrible faintness and weakness were becoming constant now. She could only lie on her bed and wait. She could not even think any more. The enemies all about her with their terrible darts had pierced her soul, and her life seemed ebbing away. She felt it going, and did not have the desire to stop it. It was good to be at rest.

Miranda stole in softly, and began to move quietly about the room, finding the candle and softly striking the flint and tinder. Phoebe became gradually conscious of her presence, as out of the midst of a misty dream. Then Miranda came and looked down tenderly into her face.

"Raise yer head up, you poor little thing, an' drink this," whispered Miranda, putting a bottle of strong cordial to her lips, that she had taken the precaution to bring with her. "I've got two o' the nicest letters fer yeh that ever was writ, an' another one from my Mrs. Marcia, an' ef yeh don't git some color into them cheeks, an' some brightness into them eyes now, my name ain't Mirandy."

Miranda handed out the letters one at a time, in their order.

She brought the candle, and Phoebe with her trembling

hands opened the first, recognizing the handwriting, and then sat up and read with bated breath.

"Oh, Miranda," she said, looking up with a faint color in her cheeks, "he has asked me to marry him. Wouldn't it be beautiful! But he didn't know when he wrote it—" and the brown head went down as if it were stricken like a lily before a fierce blast.

"Shucks!" said Miranda, dabbing away the mistiness from her eyes. "Yes, he did know, too. His cousin wrote him. Here, you read the other one."

Again Phoebe sat up and read, while Miranda held the candle and tried not to seem to look over her shoulder at the words she could feel in her soul if she could not see with her eyes.

"Oh, it can't be true!" said Phoebe, with face aglow with something that almost seemed the light of another world. "And I mustn't let him, of course. It wouldn't be right for him to have a wife like this—"

"Shucks!" said Miranda again. "Yes, 'tis true, too, and right an' all the rest, an' you've got to set up and get spry, fer there's a sight to do, an' I can't stay much longer. That weddin' 's comin' off on Monday mornin'—time set fer it. 'Tain't good luck to put off weddin's an' this one 's goin' to go through all right."

"Mr. Nathaniel, he's goin' to bring his cousin an' the Jedge, an' my Mr. David an' Mrs. Marcia's comin' wether they're ast er not, 'cause they knew 'twant no use fer um to wait fer an invite from that sister-in-law of yourn, so they're comin' anyway. Mr. Nathaniel said as how you weren't to worry. He'll git here Saturday night sure, an' ef there was any other 'rangement you'd like to make he was ready, an' you could send your word by me, but he 'greed with me 'twould make less talk ef the weddin' come off at your home where 'twas to be in the furst place, an' then you could go right away from here an' never come back no more. Say, hev ye got anythin' thet's fit to wear? 'Cause ef yeh ain't I'll let yeh have my new balzarine to wear. I'll hev it all done by Sat'day night. Mrs. Marcia's goin' to help me."

Between tears and smiles Phoebe came to herself. Miranda fed her with some strong broth which she had brought along and which she managed to heat after laboriously holding the pail over the candle flame. Then together in the dim candle-light the two girls opened the great white box that lay on the floor beside the bed.

"It's my wedding dress, Miranda. Mother made it for me long ago, before she died, and put it in my trunk to keep for me. It was marked, 'For my little girl when she is going to be married.'

"I opened it and found the letter on the top, for I thought I was going to die, and I wanted to read mother's last letter, but I did not take the frock out because I thought I would never wear it, and it made me feel so bad that I left it in its wrappings. I thought if I died I would like to have you have it, because it is the most precious thing I have and you have done more for me than anybody else ever did, but mother."

Miranda gulped a sudden unexpected sob at this tribute, and it was some time before she could recover her equanimity though she said "Shucks!" several times.

They took the white bridal garment out of its wrappings and Phoebe tried it on, there in the dimness of the room. It was thin white book-muslin, all daintily embroidered about the neck and sleeves by the dead mother's hand. It fell in soft sheer folds about the white-faced girl, and made her look as if she were just going to take her flight to another world.

In another paper was the veil of fine thread lace, simple and beautiful, and a pair of white gloves which had been the mother's, both yellow with age, and breathing a perfume of lavender. A pair of dainty little white slippers lay in the bottom of the box, wrapped in tissue paper also. Miranda's eyes shone.

"Now you look like the right kind of a bride," she said, standing back and surveying her charge. "That's better 'n all the balzarines in New York."

"You shall wear the balzarine and stand up with me, Miranda," whispered Phoebe, smiling.

"No, sir! We ain't goin't to hev this here weddin' spoiled by no red hair an' freckles, even if 't has got a balzarine. Janet Bristol's got to stan' up. She'll make a picter fer folks to talk 'bout. Mr. Nathaniel said he'd manage his cousin all right, an' 'twould quiet the talk down if his folks took sides along of you. No, sir, I ain't goin' to do no standin' in this show. I'm goin' to set, an' take it all in. Come now, you get into bed, an' I'll blow out the light an' go home. I reckon I'll be back to-morrer night to take any messages you want took. They'll be plenty o' chance fer you to rest 'fore Monday. Don't say nothin' to yer folks. Let 'em go on with their plans, an' then kinder s'prise 'em."

The next morning Phoebe arose and feeling much refreshed dressed herself carefully and went downstairs. She had a quiet, grave look upon her face, but in her eyes there was a strange light which she could not keep back. Emmeline looked up in surprise when Phoebe came and took hold with the work. She began to say something slighting, but the look in Phoebe's face somehow stopped her. It was a look of joyful exaltation; and Emmeline, firmly believing that the girl was justly talked about, could not understand, and thought it hypocrisy.

Albert came in in a few minutes, and looked relieved.

"Well, Phoebe, I'm glad you've made up your mind to act sensibly, and come downstairs. It wasn't right to fight against what had to be and everyone of us knew was for the best," he said.

Phoebe did not answer. In spite of the help that was coming to her it hurt her that Albert believed the slander against her, and the tears came into her eyes as he spoke. Emmeline saw them and spoke up in a sermonizing tone:

"It's right she should feel her shame and repent, Albert. Don't go an' soft-soap it over es ef she hadn't done nothin' to feel sorry fer."

Then Phoebe spoke.

"I have done nothing to feel sorry for, Emmeline. I have not sinned. I am only sorry that you have been willing to believe all this against me."

Then she went quietly on with her work, and said no more, though Emmeline's speech was unsealed and she gave Phoebe much good advice during the course of the day.

The next morning near church time Emmeline told Phoebe that Hiram was coming over to see her that morning, and she might open the front parlor to receive him.

"I don't wish to see Hiram, Emmeline," she answered, calmly. "I have nothing whatever to say to him."

"Well, upon my word, Phoebe Deane," said Emmeline, getting red in the face with indignation over the girl. "Goin' to git married to-morrow mornin' an' not wantin' to see Hiram Green! I should think you'd want to talk over 'rangements."

"Yes, I am going to be married to-morrow morning," said Phoebe, with a triumphant ring to her voice, "but I do not want to see Hiram Green. I have no arrangements to talk over with him. My arrangements are all made."

Phoebe went away to her room and remained there the rest of the day.

Nathaniel had arrived. She knew that by special messenger coming and going over the wood-shed roof. There had been sweet messages of cheer, and he had promised to come for her in the morning. Everything was arranged. She could possess her soul in peace and quietness and wait. Her enemies would soon be put to flight. Nathaniel had promised her that, and although she could not see in the least how, she trusted him perfectly.

She had sent her love to him, and the locket with her mother's picture. It was all she had to give her lover, and he understood. It was the one she had worn the first time he ever saw her.

The balzarine frock was finished. The last hook was set in place before supper Saturday night, and Marcia had pronounced it very becoming. It was finished in spite of the fact that Miranda had made several secret excursions into the region of Hiram Green's house and farm. She had made discoveries which she told to no one, but over which she chuckled when quite alone in the kitchen at work. On her first trip she had seen him go out to his milking, and had passed close to the house, where his window was open. She had glanced in, and there on the sill her sharp eyes had discovered the bit of red seal with the lion's head upon it. She had carried too many letters with that seal not to know it at once, and she gleefully seized it and carried it to Nathaniel. She had evidence at last which would give her power over the enemy.

She also discovered that Hiram Green attended to his milking himself, and that he had a habit—if one might judge from two mornings as samples—of going to the spring-house himself with the milk and placing the pans on the great stone shelf. This she had seen by judicious hiding behind shrubbery, and trees, and spring-house itself, and spying upon him. Birds and squirrels tell no tales, and the dewy grass soon dried off and left no trace of her footsteps. During one of these excursions she had examined the fastening of the spring-house most carefully, and knew the possibilities of button, hasp, staple, and peg.

The Spaffords and Miranda went to church as usual, and so did the Bristols. The advent of Nathaniel and his friend Mr. Van Rensselaer in the Bristol pew diverted attention from the empty seat behind them, for this morning the Deanes were conspicuous by their absence.

The day passed quietly. Miranda made her usual visit in the early evening. Phoebe had asked her to stay with her, but Miranda said she had some things to do, and departed sooner than usual. The night settled into stillness and Phoebe slept in joyous assurance that it was her last night in the room where she had seen so much sorrow.

In the morning she went down to breakfast as usual. She

did not eat much, to be sure, but drank some milk, and then washed the breakfast dishes as calmly as if she expected to keep on washing them all the rest of her life in this same kitchen.

"Hiram'll be over 'bout half past nine, I reckon," said Albert. He had been instructed by Emmeline to say this. "The minister won't come till ten. If you need to talk to Hiram you'll have plenty of time between. You better be all ready."

"I shall not need to talk to Hiram," said Phoebe, as she hung up the dish towels. There was that in her voice as she said it that made Albert look after her wonderingly.

"She's the queerest girl I ever see!" grumbled Emmeline. "One would think by her looks that she expected a chariot of fire to come down a' take her straight up to heaven, like 'Lijah. It's kind of dreadful the way she ac's! 'F I was Hiram I'd be 'fraid to marry her."

Miranda arrived over the shed roof soon after Phoebe went upstairs. She wore her old calico, and if one who knew had observed closely, he would have said it was a calico that Miranda never used any more, for it was very old. Her hair was combed with precision and on her head was an elaborate New York bonnet with a white barège veil, but her balzarine was in a bundle under her arm. It was not calculated for roof travel. It was well for their plans that the shed roof was back and well hidden from the kitchen door, else Miranda might have been discovered.

"There! Emmeline can hev that fer a floor cloth," said Miranda, as she flung her old calico in the corner. "I don't calc'late to return fer it." She fastened her balzarine with satisfaction, adjusted her muslin shoulder cape, her bonnet, and mantilla, the latter a gift from Mrs. Spafford, laid her new sunshade on a chair, and pronounced herself ready.

"Has Hiram Green come yet?" asked Phoebe, anxiously. She was dreading a scene with Hiram.

"Wal, no, not 'zactly," said Miranda. "An what's more, I don't think he will. Fact is I've got him fixed fer a spell, but

I ain't goin' to say nothin' more 'bout it at present, 'cept that
he's detained by bus'ness elsewhar. It's best you shouldn't know
nothin' bout it ef there's questions ast, but you don't need to
worry. 'Less sompin' quite unusual happens he ain't likely to
turn up till after the ceremony. Now, what's to do to you
yet? Them hooks all fastened? My, but you do look han'some!"

"Oh, Miranda, you haven't done anything dreadful, have
you?"

"No, I ain't," laughed Miranda. "You'd jest split your
sides laughin' ef you could see him 'bout now. But there!
Don't say 'nother word. I hear voices. The Bristols hev
come, an' the minister, too. I reckon your sister-in-law'll hev
her hands full slammin' the door in all them faces."

Phoebe, aghast, pulled the curtain aside and peered out.

There in the yard were several carriages, and more driving in the gate. She could hear a great many voices all at
once. She saw Mrs. Duzenberry and Susanna getting out of
their chaise, and Lemuel Skinner and his wife Hannah, and
she thought she heard the village dressmaker's voice high
above all, sharp and rasping, the way it always was when she
said: "That seam needs pressin'. It does hike up a mite, but
it'll be all right when it's pressed."

Phoebe retreated in dismay from the window.

"Oh, Miranda! How did all those people get down there!
Emmeline will be so angry. She is in her room dressing yet.
It doesn't seem as if I dared go down."

"Fer the land sake, how should I know? I s'pose Providence sent 'em, fer they can't say a single word after the ceremony's over. Their mouths'll be all nicely stopped. Don't
you worry."

Miranda answered innocently, but for one instant as she
looked at Phoebe's frightened face her guilty heart misgave
her. Perhaps she had gone a step too far. For it was Miranda
who had slipped here and there after church on Sunday and
whispered a brief invitation to those who had gossiped the
hardest, wording it in such a way that they all thought it was

a personal invitation from Phoebe. In every case she had added, "Don't say nothin' till after it's over," and each thinking himself especially favored had arrived in conscious pride, and as they passed Hiram Green's new house they had remarked to themselves what a fine man he was for sticking to Phoebe in spite of all the talk.

But Miranda never told her part in this, and Emmeline never got done wondering who invited all those people.

Miranda's momentary confusion was covered by a gentle tap on the door, and Phoebe in a flutter rushed to hide her friend:

"I'm afraid it's Emmeline," she whispered. "She may not let you go down."

"Like to see her keep me up," said Miranda, boldly. "My folks hes come. I ain't 'fraid now," and she boldly swept the trembling bride out of the way and threw the door open.

Janet Bristol in a silken gown of palest pink entered and walked straight up to Phoebe.

"You dear little thing!" she exclaimed. "How sweet you look. That frock is beautiful and the veil makes you perfect. Nathaniel asked me to bring you this and make you wear it. It was his mother's."

She fastened a rope of pearls around Phoebe's neck and kissed her as a sister might have done.

Miranda stood back and gazed with satisfaction on the scene. All was as it should be. She saw nothing further to be desired. Her compunctions were gone.

"Nathaniel is waiting for you at the foot of the stairs," whispered Janet. "He has his mother's ring for you. He wanted me to tell you. Come, they are ready. You must go ahead."

Down the stairs went the trembling bride, followed by her bridesmaid. Miranda grasped her precious parasol and tiptoed on behind.

Nathaniel stood at the foot of the stairs, waiting for her. Emmeline, with a red and angry face, was waiting on her most unexpected guests and had no time to notice what was going on about her. The original wedding guests, consisting of a row of little Greens and the old housekeeper, were submerged in the Sunday gowns of the new arrivals.

"Where's Hiram?" whispered Albert, in Emmeline's ear, just as she was giving Hiram's Aunt Keziah Dart a seat at the best end of the room.

"Goodness! Ain't he come yet? I s'posed he was upstairs talkin' to Phoebe. I heard voices."

She wheeled around and there stood the wedding party.

Nathaniel, tall and handsome, with his shy, pale bride upon his arm; Janet, sparkling in her pink gown and enjoying the discomfiture of guests and hostess alike, and smiling over at Martin Van Rensselaer, who stood supporting the bridegroom on the other side; it bewildered Emmeline.

The little assemblage reached out into the front door yard, and peeped curiously in at the doors and windows as if loth to lose the choice scene that was passing. The old minister was talking now and a hush fell over the company.

Anger and amazement held Emmeline still as the ceremony progressed.

"Dearly beloved, we are gathered together—" said the minister, and Emmeline looked around for Hiram. Surely the ceremony was not beginning without him! And who was that girl in white under the veil? Not Phoebe! It could not be Phoebe Deane, who but a few short minutes before had been hanging up her dish towels. Where did she get that veil and frock? What had happened? How did all these people get here? Had Phoebe invited them? And why did not somebody stop it?

"Let him speak now, or forever after hold his peace," came the words, and Emmeline gave a great gasp and thought of the corner lot opposite the Seceder church.

It was then that Emmeline became conscious of Miranda in her balzarine and New York bonnet, the very impersonation of mischief, standing in the doorway just behind the bride and watching the scene with a face of triumph.

An impulse came to her to charge across the room upon the offending girl and put her out. Here surely was one who had no right in her house and knew it, too. Then all at once she caught the eye of Judge Bristol fixed sternly upon her face, and she became aware of her own countenance and restrained her feelings. For after all it was no mean thing to be allied to the house of Bristol, and to know that the cloud of dishonor which had threatened them was lifted forever. She looked at Judge Bristol's fine face and heavy white hair, and began to swell with conscious pride.

The last "I will" was spoken, the benediction was pronounced, and the hush that followed was broken by Nathaniel's voice.

"I want to say a few words," he said, "about a terrible mistake that has been made by the people of this village regarding my wife's character. I have made a most thorough investigation of the matter during the last two days and I find that the whole thing originated in an infamous lie told with intention to harm one who is entirely innocent. I simply wish to say that whoever has spoken against my wife will have to answer to me for his words in a court of justice, and if any of you who are my friends wish to question any of her past actions be kind enough to come directly to me and they will be fully explained, for there is not a thing in her past that will not bear the searching light of purity and truth."

As soon as he had ceased speaking David and Marcia stepped up with congratulations.

There was a little stir among the guests; the guilty ones melted away faster than they had gathered, each one anxious to get out without being noticed.

The Bristol coach, drawn by two white horses, with coachman and footman in livery, drew up before the door, Nathaniel handed Phoebe in and they were driven away in triumph, the guests that they passed shrinking out of sight into their vehicles as far as possible.

Albert and Emmeline looked into each other's dazed faces; then turned to the old housekeeper, and the row of little Greens, their faces abnormally shining from unusual contact with soap and water, and asked in concert:

"But where is Hiram?"

Miranda, as she rode guilelessly in the carryall with Mrs. Spafford, answered the same question from that lady, with:

"Whar d' you s'pose? I shet him in the spring-house airly this mornin'!"

Then David Spafford laid down upon his knee the reins of the old gray horse, and laughed, loud and long; could not stop laughing; and all day long it kept breaking out, as he remembered Miranda's innocent look, and thought of Hiram Green, wrathful and helpless, shut in his own spring-house while his wedding went on without him.

There was a wedding breakfast elaborate and gay at Judge Bristol's, presided over by Janet, who seemed as happy as though she had planned the match herself, and whose smiling wishes were carried out immediately by Martin Van Rensselaer.

There was one more duty for Nathaniel to perform before he took his bride away to a happier home. He must find and face Hiram Green.

So, leaving Phoebe in the care of Mrs. Spafford and his cousin Janet, and himself accompanied by his uncle, Martin Van Rensselaer, and Lemuel Skinner in the capacity of village constable, he got into the family carryall and drove out to Hiram's farm.

Now Nathaniel had not been idle during the Sabbath which intervened between his coming back to the village and his marriage. Aside from the time he spent at the morning church service, he had been doing a Sabbath day's work which he felt would stand well to his account.

He had carefully questioned several of the best known gossips in the village with regard to the story about Phoebe. He had asked keen questions that gave him a plain clue to the whole diabolical plot.

His first act had been to mount his fast horse, and ride out to Ann Jane Bloodgood's, where he had a full account of Phoebe's visit together with a number of missionary items which would have met with more of his attention at another time. Possessed of several valuable facts he had gone pretty straight to most of the houses which Hiram had visited on the first afternoon when he scattered the seed of scandal, and facing the embarrassed scandal-mongers, Nathaniel had made them tell just who had been the first to speak to them of this. In every case after a careful sifting down each owned that Hiram himself had told them the first word. If Nathaniel had not been a lawyer, and keen at his calling, he might not have been able so well and so quickly to have followed the story to its source, as he did. Possibly his former encounter with Hiram Green, and his knowledge of many of his acts, helped in unravelling the mystery.

The old housekeeper and the little Greens had not been at home long when the carryall drew up in front of the door, and the four men got out.

"I ben everywhar but to the spring-house," said the housekeeper, shaking her head dolefully, "an' I can't find trace of him nowhar. 'Tain't likely he'd be in the spring-house, fer the door is shet an' fastened. I ken see the button from the buttery winder. It's the way I allus tell when he's comin' in to breakfast. It's my 'pinion he's clared out 'cause he don't want to marry that gal, that's what I think."

"When did you last see Mr. Green?" questioned the Judge, sternly.

"Why, I seen him take the milk pails an' go down towards the barn to milk, an' I ain't seen him sence. I thought 'twar queer he didn't come eat his breafast, but he's kinder oncertain thet way, so I hurried up an' got off to he'p Mis' Deane."

"Have the cows been milked?" The Judge's voice ignored the old woman's elaborate explanations.

"The hired man, he says so. I ain't ben down to look myself."

"Where are the milk pails?"

"Well, now, I ain't thought to look."

"What does he usually do with the milk? He surely has not taken that with him. Did he bring it in? That ought to give us a clue."

"He most gen'rally takes it straight to the spring-house—" began the old woman.

"Let us go to the spring-house," said Nathaniel.

"I don't see what business 'tis o' yourn," complained the old woman, but they were already on the way, so after a moment's hesitation she threw her apron around her shoulders and went after them. The row of little Greens followed, a curious and perplexed little procession, ready for any scene of interest that might be about to open before them, even though it involved their unloving father.

It was Lemuel Skinner, with his cherry lips pursed importantly, who stepped forward by virtue of his office, turned the wooden button, drew out the peg, pulled off the hasp, and threw the heavy door open.

Out stumbled Hiram Green, half blinded by the light, and rubbing his eyes.

"Mr. Green, we have called to see you on a matter of importance," began Lemuel apologetically, quite as if it were the custom to meet householders on the threshold of their spring-houses.

"Sorry I can't wait to hear it," swaggered Hiram, blinking, and trying to make out who these men were. "I got 'n engagement. Fact is, I'm goin' to be married, an' I'm late a'ready. I'll hev to be excused, Lem!"

"It's quite unnecessary, Mr. Green," said Lemuel, putting out a detaining hand excitedly; "quite unnecessary, I assure you. The wedding is all over. You're not expected any more."

Hiram stood back and surveyed Lemuel with contempt.

"Gosh Ninety!" he sneered. "How could that be when I wasn't thar? I guess you didn't know I was goin' to marry Phoebe Deane. I'm right sure there wouldn't no one else marry her."

Nathaniel stepped forward, his face white with indignation.

"You are speaking of my wife, Mr. Green," he said, and his voice was enough to arrest the attention of even the self-complacency of a Hiram Green. "Let me never hear you speak of her in that way again. She did not at any moment in her life intend to marry you. You know that well, though you have tried to weave a web of falsehood about her that would put her in your power. The whole thing is known to me from beginning to end, and I do not intend to let it pass lightly. My wife's good name is everything to me; though it seems you were willing to marry one whom you had yourself defamed.

"I have come here this morning, Mr. Green, to give you your choice between going to jail or going with me at once and taking back all the falsehoods you have told about my wife."

Hiram, in sudden comprehension and fear, glanced around the group, took in the fact of the presence of Judge Bristol; remembered Nathaniel's threat of the year before about bringing him up before his uncle, remembered that Lemuel Skinner was constable; and was filled with consternation.

With the instinct of a coward and a bully he made a sudden lunge forward towards Nathaniel, his fists clenched, and his whole face expressing the fury of a wild animal brought to bay.

"You lie!" he hissed.

But the next instant he lay sprawling at Nathaniel's feet, with Lemuel bustling over him like an excited old hen.

It was Martin Van Rensselaer who had tripped him up just in time.

"Now, gentlemen, gentlemen, don't let's get excited," cackled Lemuel, laying an ineffective hand on the prostrate Hiram.

"Step aside, Mr. Skinner," said Nathaniel, towering over Hiram; "let me settle this matter first. Now, sir you may take your choice. Will you go to jail and await your trial for slander or will you come with us to the people before whom you scattered this outrageous scandal, and take it all back?"

"You've made a big mistake," blustered Hiram. "I never told no stories 'bout Phoebe Deane. It's somebody else 's done it 'ef 'tain't true—I was goin' to marry her to save her reputation."

"How did you think that would save her reputation?" questioned Judge Bristol, and somehow his voice made cold chills creep down Hiram's spine.

"Why, I—I was goin' to deny everythin' after we was married."

"Your stories don't hang very well together," remarked the Judge dryly.

"You will be obliged to deny them now," said Nathaniel, wrathfully. "Take your choice at once. I'm not sure after all but the best way would be to house you in jail without further delay. It is almost a crime to let such a low-lived scoundrel as you walk at large. No one's reputation will be safe in the hands of a villain like you. Take your choice at once. I will give you two minutes to decide."

Nathaniel took out his watch.

There was silence over the meadow behind the springhouse, but a little bird from a tree up the road called: "Phoe-bee! Phoe-be!" insistently, and a strange tender light came into Nathaniel's eyes.

"The time is up," said Nathaniel.

"What do you want me to do?" asked the captive, sullenly.

"I want you to go with me to every house that you visited the day you started this mischief and take it all back. Tell them it was untrue, and that you got it up out of whole cloth for your own evil purposes."

"But I can't tell a lie," said Hiram, piously.

"Can't you? Well, it will not be necessary. Come, which will you choose? Do you prefer to go to jail?"

"Gentlemen, I'm in your hands," whined the coward. "Remember I have little children."

"You should have remembered that yourself, and not brought shame upon them and other innocent beings." It was the Judge who spoke these words, like a sentence in court.

"Where hev I got to go?"

Nathaniel named over the places.

Hiram looked black, and swallowed his mortification.

"Well, I s'pose I've got to go. I'm sure I don't want to lose my good name by goin' to jail."

They set him upon his feet, and the little posse moved slowly up the slope to the house and thence to the carryall.

After they were seated in the carryall, Hiram in the back seat with Lemuel and Martin on either side of him, Nathaniel turned to Hiram.

"Now, Mr. Green, we are going first to your aunt's house, and then around to the other places in order. You are to make the following statement and nothing else. You are to say: 'I have come to take back the lies which I told about Miss Phoebe Deane, and to tell you that they are none of them true. I originated them for my own purposes.'"

Hiram's face darkened. He looked as if he would like to kill Nathaniel. He reached out a long arm again as if he would strike him but Lemuel clutched him convulsively, while Martin threw his whole weight upon the other side and he subsided.

"You can have from now until we reach the jail to think about it, Mr. Green. If you prefer to go to jail instead you will not be hindered. Mr. Skinner is here to arrest you on my charge if you will not comply with these conditions."

Sullen and silent sat Hiram. He did not raise his eyes to see the curious passers-by as he rode through town.

They looked at Nathaniel and the Judge, driving with solemn mien as if on some portentous errand; they noted the stranger and the constable on either side of the lowering Hiram; and they drew their own conclusions, for the news of the wedding had spread like wild-fire through the village.

Then they stood and watched the carryall out of sight, and even followed it to see if it stopped at the jail.

As they drew near the jail Nathaniel turned around once more to Hiram:

"Shall we stop and let you out here, or are you willing to comply with the conditions?"

Hiram raised his eyelashes and gave a sideways glance at the locality, then lowered them quickly as he encountered the impudent gaze of a small boy and muttered:

"Drive on."

Hiram went through the distasteful ordeal sullenly. He repeated the words which Nathaniel insisted upon, after one or two vain attempts to modify them in his own favor, which only made it worse for him in the eyes of his listeners.

" 'Pon my word," said Aunt Keziah Dart in a mortified tone. " 'F I'd uv told fibs like that I'd 'a' stuck to 'em, an' never giv in, no matter what. I'm 'shamed to own I'm kin to sech a sneak, Hiram Green. Wan't there gals 'nough 'round the country 'thout all that to do?"

At the Duzenberrys Susanna rendered Hiram the sympathy of silently weeping in the background, while the Widow Duzenberry stood coldly in the foreground acting as if the whole performance were a personal affront. She closed the interview by calling after Hiram from her front door.

"I'm sorry to see yeh in trouble, Mister Green. Remember you'll always find a friend here," and Hiram brightened up some. Nevertheless, there was very little of his old conceit left when he had gone over the whole ground and was finally set free to go his way to his own home.

Then Nathaniel and Phoebe hastened away in the family coach towards Albany to begin their long life journey together.

Later that afternoon Hank Williams coming up from the village brought with him a letter for Hiram Green which he stopped to leave, hoping to find out from Hiram what had happened during the afternoon. The old housekeeper took

the letter saying, "Hiram wan't well," and Hank went on-
ward crestfallen.

A few minutes later Hiram tore open his letter. It read:

Mistur Grene,
    You hev ben fond out. We want no mor lyres an
crimnles in our toun. We hev fond the seels off'n
Phebe Denes leter in yor poseshun an we hev uther
good evedens thet you open unitd stats male we will
giv yo 1 wek to sel ot an lev toun EF yo ever sho yer
hed agin hear or in Noo York you wil be tard an
fethured an punisht cordin to law.
                                   yors fer reveng
                                   A Feller Tounsman

That night while his household slept Hiram Green went
forth from his home to parts unknown, leaving his little children to the tender mercies of Aunt Keziah Dart or whoever
might be touched with a feeling of pity for them.

And Miranda, who, without the counsel or knowledge of
anyone, had written the remarkable epistle which sent him
out, lay down serenely and slept the sleep of the just.

And that same night the moon shone brightly over the
Hudson River, like a path of silver for the two who sat long
on deck, talking of how they loved Miranda, with laughter
that was nigh to tears.

About the Author

Grace Livingston Hill is well-known as one of the most prolific writers of romantic fiction. Her personal life was fraught with joys and sorrows not unlike those experienced by many of her fictional heroines.

Born in Wellsville, New York, Grace nearly died during the first hours of life. But her loving parents and friends turned to God in prayer. She survived miraculously, thus her thankful father named her Grace.

Grace was always close to her father, a Presbyterian minister, and her mother, a published writer. It was from them that she learned the art of storytelling. When Grace was twelve, a close aunt surprised her with a hardbound, illustrated copy of one of Grace's stories. This was the beginning of Grace's journey into being a published author.

In 1892 Grace married Fred Hill, a young minister, and they soon had two lovely young daughters. Then came 1901, a difficult year for Grace—the year when, within months of each other, both her father and husband died. Suddenly Grace had to find a new place to live (her home was owned by the church where her husband had been pastor). It was a struggle for Grace to raise her young daughters alone, but through everything she kept writing. In 1902 she produced *The Angel of His Presence, The Story of a Whim,* and *An Unwilling Guest.* In 1903 her two books *According to the Pattern* and *Because of Stephen* were published.

It wasn't long before Grace was a well-known author, but she wanted to go beyond just entertaining her readers. She soon included the message of God's salvation through Jesus Christ in each of her books. For Grace, the most important thing she did was not write books but share the message of salvation, a message she felt God wanted her to share through the abilities he had given her.

In all, Grace Livingston Hill wrote more than one hundred books, all of which have sold thousands of copies and have touched the lives of readers around the world with their message of "enduring love" and the true way to lasting happiness: a relationship with God through his Son, Jesus Christ.

In an interview shortly before her death, Grace's devotion to her Lord still shone clear. She commented that whatever she had accomplished had been God's doing. She was only his servant, one who had tried to follow his teaching in all her thoughts and writing.